DRAKONIA  BOOK TWO

BORN OF THE LESSER MOON

DAP DAHLSTROM

Gardland Books

Dedicated to Gary Dahlstrom

DapDahlstrom.com

Published by Gardland Books

Printed in USA

Book design, cover design and map by Dap Dahlstrom

ISBN: 979-8-9872044-3-6 (Ebook)

ISBN: 979-8-9872044-4-3 (Paperback)

First Edition

Apakoh Ice Shelf

Temple of the
Ice Queen

Inkuiuk
Tundra

NORTHERN
CONTINENT

Yaglin Kareth

KARSIK RANGE

The Thousand Isles

Kjarik Point

Malgrin's Isle

The Lonely Isle

EASTERSEA

Gozlin

Kren

Kara

Giorin

Suz

Bay Isle

Two Moon
Bay

Keln

Palace of the
Drakyn Queens

Bay Towne

KRAIDA

Cara
Bay

Flying River

HARTBONE RANGE

Forest

Tia Cara

Valley of the Legions

Dmisi

Dageki Lands

DRAKONIA
(CHARTED LANDS)

Forest

Volcano Lands

Krasa Ktel

Cygnan
Lake

RUNNING RIVER

WESTERSEA

Great
Waste

Escarpment

DRAKYN'S TEETH RANGE

River Cyn

The
Maze

Ancient
Keeps

Mistra

Kyndri

Giyi

Lysi City

Southern
Isles

CHAPTER ONE

Nothing but Time

A different kind of storm is brewing.

Oppressive, bunny-shaped clouds hop along the bleeding sky, overshadowing the cowering leporine residents of the Swordsong Plain. Below, the mottled slate grasses lurch in place, resembling their namesake blades more than the ballet-limber leaves that once cavorted here on the sweet breeze, before the disruption. The spurious pasture is humming a dirge, a death march performed by an army of one-armed soldiers. The troops are condemned to this tortured field of battle for eternity, which now amounts to approximately two months.

One contail doesn't cower from this spectacle, but instead stands tall to meet his fate. Bolstered by too-many-drinks bravado and awash in transmograffically-induced psychosis, he watches helplessly as chartreuse lightning spews from the clouds. Two human figures step from a massive stone cube a second after it first exists.

The contail hops away unsteadily through the disquieting pseudo-flora, waving a human fist with a stiff middle finger that he pulls from his ass with aplomb. He titters and hiccups expansively, drunk on his latest creation, Uncle Pica's rabbit piss ale.

His giggles grow to guffaws, as the unimaginable weight of the cube crushes his burrow, collapsing his ingeniously designed layout beneath it. At least, this month's does and kits are safe, having escaped his eccentricities to abscond with his rival, a physically superior but mentally deficient buck, who couldn't imagine this calamitous event, or anything, for that matter.

The contail's escape from this catastrophe is no accident. Along with the confusion, pain and depression that accompanied his inadvertent transformation at the hands of a reckless transmo-grifer-in-training, he's been gifted with unusually accurate foresight. He's been aware that the cube would appear at this moment, to this location, for weeks. He could have moved, dug another masterpiece of domestic bliss, but why? He knows he'll live only until tomorrow morning anyway, when he'll, thankfully, succumb to cardiac arrest moments before being torn apart by a hungry and unusually vicious gyrofalcon.

That one likes to play with her food, but then, they all do.

Sure, he could run and hide, but that won't change a thing. Trapped by his fate, the more he struggles to avoid it, the more certain his destiny will stomp on his head and crush him like a bug.

His fuzzy tail jerks spasmodically, and his endearing brown eyes bulge. He heaves a weighty sigh and wraps his aching head with both front paws.

Anxiety. Fear. Foreboding.

As a small-brained prey animal, he's ill-equipped to deal with this newfound awareness. It's no fun being an omniscient bunny in the later days of the world.

The two humans step forward confidently, ignoring the contail, and gaze about them as if they've done this trick many times before, which they have. The broad-shouldered blond man slaps his hat on his leg, bringing rise to a cloud of dust that, the contail senses, did not originate in this century.

He speaks, as the contail knows he will. "That gardamn leijong bastart and his fruckin' prophesy. He lied to us!"

The lithe woman at his side shakes back her long, silver hair and speaks softly. The contail finds her voice melodic and soothing.

"Not exactly, Trey. He said 'progeny,' not child. Now that I think about it, he never once said that *our daughter* would be the one."

"Oh, great, so we're cursed to search through eternity to find this one descendant of ours, this 'chosen one,' who may or may not exist, in this or some future age, while in the meantime, whenever we leave the cubes, you're one step closer to death. Not to mention that with every generation, the number of our descendants grows exponentially."

The woman is silent, gazing out across the peculiar plain, but not appearing to see it. Trey eyes her with concern. "Are you feeling ill again?"

"No, I'm fine. It's just that everything about the later days is so disturbing; as if we're standing on a precipice, about to tumble over the edge." She breathes deeply, as if fishing for an answer from the breeze.

Trey looks up at the oddly colored sky and whistles.

"Wow, is that sky cracked? And what's that leaking out? It looks like blood."

"It very well may be, but that's not important. We landed far from when and where I intended, into the later days of the later days. Even my placement of the cube is unpredictable now. But we were lucky. I think we've stumbled onto the right place and time. The drakyn's eye has reappeared. It wasn't destroyed after all."

Her eyes light up and the contail is amazed by their silver luminosity, the intensity and determination they broadcast.

"Where is it? Can you tell?" asks Trey. The contail detects a tiny spark of reluctant hope in his tone.

"Not far from here, below the southern coastal mountains. The Drakyn's Teeth, I think they still call them."

Trey's look reflects his doubt. "Are you sure it'll lead us to this descendant?"

"It will always be drawn to her, and her to it. We just have to hope that this time, she's the one we're looking for."

"You've said before that this era is chaotic, that using transmogrifee is dangerous and unpredictable. Don't you have trouble even seeing the future here?"

Wren frowns. "Yes, it's just not as clear anymore, as if my lens on the future has grown cloudy. Entropy has at last brought the world to the tipping point. We're far into the age when transmogrifee has been relearned. Its overuse now threatens Drakonia with something even worse than what we faced in our time. But this is what we've been looking for, I can feel it. Both the stone and our descendant are here, if we can get to them in time."

"Time," he scoffs. "We have nothing *but* time."

She looks at him, fear and uncertainty flashing in her eyes. "Not anymore. I'm afraid that my time outside the cubes is limited, plus, time itself is running out. We've got to act fast. Armageddon rushes at us, while we stand here discussing it." She pulls away from him brusquely, as if to leave.

He touches her shoulder gently. Concern darkens his usually sunny features.

She takes a calming breath, straightening her shoulders and speaking with certainty, though her voice breaks at the end. "Let's get this over with so we can go home and watch our daughter grow up."

After an uncomfortable silence, when her eyes glisten, she turns to him and speaks with a theatrical sweep of her arm. "Are you ready to don the mantle of the omnipotent Lord of Dreams?"

Trey frowns, then counters with his signature, 'heavily put-upon' sigh. "If I must, but you're sure it'll work?"

"It works every time, my love. You're a natural."

"I hope you're right. I'll do it, but only if you become that ridiculous giantess that you're so fond of."

"I think I'd better take on a disguise. I'm afraid our descendant and I look so much alike that it would be a shock to see us together. Plus, it will allow us to help her develop her talent and convince her that the sacrifice is necessary."

"Good. It sounds like this could work—finally. I'm getting tired of our little quest. With all this time-hopping, I'm starting to feel like a living coo-coo clock, and someone keeps resetting me to midnight. Coo-coo, coo-coo," he sings as he flaps his arms, reminding the contail of the lowland grouse males who strut absurdly before their inexplicably reluctant girlfriends.

Wren snorts and laughs at Trey's antics, then turns back to the cube. Taking his hand in hers, they step inside together and fade away.

The contail pulls up abruptly from his half-hearted escape, as the perplexing humans disappear, having taken no notice of him or his plight. The hulking stone edifice pops out of existence a second later, as abruptly as it arrived, leaving him alone to cry over the unfairness of his abbreviated mortality. What sounds to the contail like a vegetative version of *Dead Soldier Waltz* erupts from the moaning grasses around him.

The contail weeps and rails at his bitter destiny. He cries to himself, as he has many times before, proving that his omniscience has a few cracks, "What in the frucking world is a coo-coo clock?"

Chapter Two

Eye of the Psy

Nikki gazed out through the distorting crystal wall, her thoughts far from the approaching storm.

What difference does it make who leads the Mistrans, when none of them have enough control left to light an emerock lantern without blowing up the entire aerie?

Fruck!

Why had they chosen her?

The answer bit at her like a mountain lizard whose jaws won't release until its victim dies of the unbearable pain.

"Because I'm young, weak and expendable."

Her words echoed in the empty space. She gazed back at the silent kelpfibre loom. Silent now because its weaver was undoubtedly deep in the caverns beneath the aerie, safe from the storm and far from the fool who now stood here berating herself for her gullibility.

"Master Artisan and leader of all fruckin' Mistra. Bahh!"

Nikki threw her hands down in disgust, only to encounter something soft and furry beneath her touch. A deep, melodious purr filled the room, and the crystal walls reflected a warm orange glow.

"Moonchaser! What're you doing here? You should be below with the others."

The big feline responded by nuzzling her hand. Nearly as tall as a small pony, the grella rubbed against her leg affectionately, almost toppling her over in his enthusiasm. Nikki laughed.

"OK, stay. I think you're immune to the effects of the psy storm anyway. What is it about your kind? You have no transmograffic talent of your own, yet you seem to be resistant to its effects, like no creatures I've ever seen. It was a challenge just to give you some speech."

Moonchaser responded by plopping down at her feet and licking his fur with graceful arcs of his muscled neck.

Nikki returned her gaze to the swirling maelstrom outside. In the dark, the psy storm could almost be considered lovely, with sparkling lights aglow with tints of pink and electric blue. But she knew what deadly fate awaited anyone foolish enough to be drawn into those lights. The psy daemons wanted only one thing, for her to suffer as they suffered. These remnants of transmogrifee battles roamed the world unchecked, wreaking madness and death wherever they touched living things.

The lights played about the surface of the water far below her. She saw a dark shape on the surface, struggling among the lights. Could there be a boti out there? Everyone knew the sea was too wild to sail upon. Convinced she was imagining what she saw, she turned from the sights below her.

Was she putting her and Moonchaser in danger by staying in this exposed chamber? Nikki turned to leave, until she realized that it was already too late. The swirling mass had crept into the space around her. The air crackled and hissed. She smelled rotting meat. Minuscule lightning bolts reached down from equally tiny clouds, illuminating distorted faces that glared at her with visceral loathing.

"You," grated a voice that popped and ground like a separating joint. "You who live and walk and breathe. This we cannot tolerate. You must be like us." The thing cackled and wheezed at once, its face a nauseating blur, as if it had lost its original form and searched for it frantically.

Nikki tried to run but tripped over her own feet with an uncharacteristic lack of grace. The world dissolved beneath her and became another. Her face hit the mud with a squelch. Raucous laughter made her ears burn. She rose indignantly, wiping mud from her eyes, and almost fell again. The world tilted around her, but it was not hers. This one consisted of low hills covered in leaden mud and pathetic tufts of dead and dying grasses, not the high stone and clear crystal of Mistra that she had always known. And it was cold, bitterly cold. Moonchaser was gone. Mistra was gone.

Another bizarre laugh, followed by a jeering taunt. "Can't even find her feet, Karklyn. What sort of champion have you dug up from the cesspits this time to entertain us?"

Champion? She looked down at her numb fingers and saw a huge sword grasped there. She barely had time to lift it in quavering hands when she caught a blur of motion to her right. Karklyn—if that was its name—had not even given her a chance to get her bearings before attacking. Nikki's many hours of training with Tbrin took over and she parried the blow, but just barely in time. Her already cold-deadened hands shuddered and buzzed from the impact as the two weapons met with a screech of protesting metal. She would have dropped the sword, had not shock and cold held her muscles in a deathly grasp. Above her loomed the most bizarre creature she had ever seen or imagined. Vaguely reptilian in appearance, as many native creatures of Drakonia were, its giant head sported double rows of needle-sharp predator's teeth. She gagged at the stench of rotting meat emanating from the strands of tissue and gobs of flesh stuck within them. Around the huge head a broad cartilaginous cape of cardinal red waved and rustled, dancing around as the creature moved. Its slate gray torso and abbreviated front limbs would have seemed amusingly pudgy if her sense of humor hadn't been burned away by the sight of it. In contrast, its rear limbs were huge and stout, ending in giant claws that bit fiercely at the ground with every step. Stone-hard muscles bunched and swelled as it moved. Its mincing prance gave the impression that it was about to leap from the ground and take flight at any moment, even though this drakyn bore no wings.

Nikki knew this was the creature legends called a drakyn, not from ever having seen one in the flesh, but from the descriptions and drawings in one of her favorite primers, *Chronicles of the Drakyn War*. It was said the book was over eight-hundred years old, but she couldn't believe anything could be that ancient, even though the leather cover was in tatters and pages seemed to be missing. She only hoped she would have a chance to read from that ancient tome again. Right now, the odds did not appear to lean in her favor.

The line of watchers jeered at Karklyn's breech of challenge protocols, and she saw that they were even more ghastly and bizarre in appearance than her opponent. Some had human torsos and drakyn heads. Others had wings or multiple flailing limbs or two donkey heads that brayed at each other. In horror, she ogled them a moment too long and Karklyn attacked again, hefting his sword high over his head with his tiny, but surprisingly strong, front limbs, poised to bring a death blow down on her head. Knowing it was too late to step back, she went in the only safe direction left to her, under. She dove between the creature's legs just as his sword stuck in the muck behind her head with a loud "plonk." As she fell, her right leg caught on a hidden root in the mud, and she heard a sickening crunch as the bone snapped. The pain took a second to reach her, and in that moment, she found an eternity to think. What could she do now? She couldn't fight with a broken leg and there was no time to heal it properly. She would have to deliver a deadly blow before this monster had another chance to attack. Knowing it was her last breath if she failed, helped to further slow time.

With infinite care, she grasped the sword in two hands and chose what looked like a vulnerable spot. She thrust upward with all her remaining strength and will, screaming as the underbelly of the beast split open, covering her in its warm green-brown blood and sticky viscera. The intestines plopped into the mud beside her, and Nikki marveled at the lovely wisp of steam that rose from the pile. Then reality came back to her, and she realized with a jolt that she wasn't done. She recalled the words of the legendary Wren Weatherspring in *Chronicles of the Drakyn War.*

Remember that the drakyn possess amazing regenerative skills. To be sure of killing one, you must remove the head or heart. Even then it is possible for a talented transmogrifer to bring one back to life with just a drop of its blood. Indeed, I witnessed this myself when—

Nikki lost track of the entire quote as the pain grew, coming down like an avalanche on her will to continue this fight.

Just lie down and die. Let it all be over, her tortured body counseled. But she couldn't listen. With strength she didn't know she possessed, she pulled herself up on one leg beside the thrashing, squalling creature. She lifted the sword as high as her quaking arms could raise it, and let it fall, hoping it would be enough. Nikki had done her share of butchering the massive lunkerfish that sometimes had the ill fortune of finding their way into the nets of the fishwives and knew that the spine comprised the most difficult bones to sever. To lop off your enemy's head in the throes of battle was as likely as the Drakonian sun was to rise in the North instead of the South; that is, not possible with the weapons that most fighters possessed. Yet her sword cut through the creature's neck as if it were as soft as a ripe bangusfish belly. She stared in awe as the drakyn's head paused, then slowly gathered speed and rolled unevenly downhill, seeming to wink at her with every horrible revolution. The watchers hissed and clapped—when opposing hands were present—their grudging approval. She'd won this challenge.

For a second, she glowed in the heat of hubris. Then she collapsed. Pure agony lit a searing fire to her thoughts, until her pain threshold mercifully let her fade, to fall softly into the welcome and welcoming arms of darkness.

She woke to sunlight washing the walls and floor of the chamber. She was siting where she had been with Moonchaser when the storm began. The big cat nuzzled her neck and seemed none the worse for his experience. She felt a dull ache in her limbs and her head hurt, but at least she'd survived.

She heard a voice and slowly looked up to find Akriast looking down at her with an almost sweet expression on her ancient, gnarled face.

"I'm so pleased to find you alive, little one."

Was she really?

"Kobel the weaver was found unharmed in one of the lower caves. Apparently, she'd gone down to the halls of the Brennen to visit her talentless daughter Cheslia before the storm and just forgot to tell me. You know how old folks are, always forgetting to mention these little things." Akriast chuckled, an insincere sound that Nikki didn't believe for a second.

"How unfortunate for you," Akriast continued. "But you seem to have weathered the storm well, dear, except of course for your leg. Now I wonder how that could have happened in a psy storm? The psy daemons aren't supposed to be able to cause physical harm."

Nikki looked up at her with a dazed expression. "My leg?"

She let her gaze fall slowly, just then becoming aware of the terrible throbbing that rose from her leg.

She realized in horror that her right leg had been badly broken, the pale bone exposed. It had been hastily and improperly healed, with mud, leaves of grayish grass and clumps of dirt, twigs and pine needles protruding from the wound.

She felt the trickle of blood on her thigh and remembered the nightmare that had carried her far from home. Her clothing, her arms and legs were all coated with rusty mud of a color and slimy, clinging tenacity like nothing she'd ever experienced in Mistra.

She stared at her shaking hands and willed the horrible dream to end, but it would not. It was only beginning.

CHAPTER THREE

The Empty Hand

Nikki drove the point of her dueling sword deep into her opponent's chest. She followed through with a probing thought, from her back and shoulder muscles to her arm, into her hand and through the length of the blade to the point of entrance, through the skin and upper tissues past a rib, through the heart and into the upper left chamber, where the splayed tip had ripped a gaping hole. A good hit.

She removed the blade, expecting the man to collapse immediately, but improbably, he raised one finger to the hole in his chest to stop the oozing blood. The blood flow ceased, and the hole faded away. With a malignant smile, he launched a new attack.

Nikki fought on, knowing that she was exhausted and starting to make small errors. Sweat dripped from the tip of her nose and her leather fighting gear chafed her skin, impossibly weighing twice what it had when she'd put it on. Her long silver-blonde hair rippled down the length of her spine in rhythm to her rapid movements. Though she was fully recovered from the physical effects of the psy storm, the psychological ones still lingered. She hadn't been sleeping well.

"You move quickly for one so large," she groused between ragged breaths. Her opponent's only response was to step up the level of his attack. Nikki was beginning to lose her concentration. Her arms and legs burned with exhaustion. She began to doubt that she could beat this opponent.

He came at her now with three quicker-than-the-eye steps, followed by a deep thrust. She parried artfully, just avoiding the razor tip of his blade. Just as she did it, she knew it was a mistake. Her opponent anticipated her move and bettered it with a riposte to her undefended left side. Before she could respond, the point of his weapon had buried itself deep in her left shoulder. Nikki fell back, reeling in pain and shock.

As she fell, a deep, resonant voice cried, "Hold!" Her opponent stopped in mid-motion; the tip of his weapon poised under her chin. Grabbing her shoulder in pain, she rolled out from under the deadly point. She managed to half-kneel on the cold stone. Her shoulder burned in agonizing pain. Her vision blurred.

Her opponent began to shrink in upon himself, until a small greenish lizard lay before them on the stone floor, hissing indignantly.

Then Tbrin was standing over her, and the pain faded to bearable. She glanced at her shoulder, but there wasn't even a mark where the weapon had entered her skin. Her now tiny opponent turned to escape, but Tbrin gathered him up gently, almost affectionately.

"Thanks," she grumbled, not knowing whether to be angry with Tbrin for pushing her too hard or ashamed of her own poor performance. Tbrin helped her to her feet with one hand and placed the little creature in a large, gilded cage with the other.

"Why do you put Kamie in a birdcage? He doesn't have wings."

"Shouldn't we all have aspirations?" replied Tbrin wryly.

Kamie looked up at them with huge rotating eyes, eyes too big and bright for his minuscule body. His skin was almost painfully beautiful to watch, as patches of primary colors vied against each other in constant flux. He stood on stout little hind legs, but his smaller front limbs sported featherless quills, mere stubs that would take great imagination to be seen as wings.

"He's an odd choice for a familiar, isn't he? Wouldn't be much use to you in a transmogrifee battle, it seems to me."

"His species is important. The kamilon lizard may be the progenitor of all transmogrifers on Drakonia."

Nikki sighed, fearing that Tbrin would launch into one of his tedious natural history lessons. Instead, he turned away without another word to face a table littered with the odd paraphernalia of his esoteric research. She stared at his back and wondered if she would ever really understand him.

She flexed her sore shoulder and grunted in derision at her failure in the sword practice. If she had learned anything from Tbrin, it was that the quickest way to lose any fight was to allow the possibility of defeat to enter your thoughts. If he pushed her, it was only because a master transmogrifer had two choices in Mistra, excel or succumb, and to succumb was not merely to fail but to die. These exercises ingrained her reflexes and increased her reaction time, if nothing else, and she could ill-afford to be slow.

"You're distracted today," Tbrin said. "You can't learn unless I have your full concentration. Let's try again tomorrow. Perhaps we'll do hand-to-hand in the energy redirection style. Isn't that your favorite?"

Nothing sounded good to her right now. It all seemed like a useless waste of time. She still didn't know why she continued these lessons, practicing ancient skills no longer used by anyone in Mistra except for her and Tbrin. Her own duties were mostly ceremonial anyway. Still, the feeling nagged at her that battle skills were abilities she would one day need. Plus, she preferred pastimes that demanded a combination of physical skill and mental acuity to anything the other talented did to waste their time.

Ball gowns and gossip, she thought with derision.

Then she mentally chastised herself, realizing how much she sounded like her long-dead mother. No one had ever been good enough for their mother, not her talentless brother Benna for sure. But Nikki was the talented one, so she had not escaped the constant haranguing to be better, faster, smarter than she was at any given moment. Nikki had grown up competitive and by and large hated by her peers. Nikki didn't really care, or so she told herself. It wasn't that she disliked people, she just didn't understand them. The never-ending bickering, deceit and manipulation seemed to her just a waste of time.

She could be brutally honest at times, she told herself, but the truth was that it was pretty much the only way she could be. She tried to empathize with others. She had learned to fake emotions she didn't understand with surprising skill. A skill that had vaulted her to the highest position in Mistra.

Now, if she could just survive long enough to enjoy it. She snorted at her gallows humor and replaced her sword to its scabbard with a flourish of finality and frustration.

She watched Tbrin as he worked at his table. Nikki saw the tension in his back, a back still broad and unbent. His hair retained its red shade, though streaks of gray were beginning to creep in. The look of age resided more in his face, or perhaps in his eyes, though Nikki couldn't remember him looking much different than he did now.

Her thoughts turned again to her visions in the storm. "I just don't understand how it happened," she said quietly. "A psy storm can't cause physical damage, unless I really was sent into the past—or the future. And I'm sure I saw a boti out there, in the middle of the storm, but I checked, and none are missing. What's going on? My dreams have been so strange. I sense a looming danger, as if..." Her voice trailed off into a shaky whisper.

Tbrin turned to her, and there was anger in his gray eyes for a second, then they calmed and he said in a controlled voice, "Keep it together, girl. You could have caused the damage to yourself. The mind is the greatest power, especially for the talented. The youngest apprentice knows that. Have you learned nothing? How long has it been since you almost died from your own foolishness?"

"Holy fletshit! Are you still bringing that up? I was only six." It was Nikki's turn to be angry. Did he really expect her to believe that she had broken her own leg during the storm? But the reference to her childhood accident really galled her.

"Why do you constantly remind me?" she blurted. "It was ages ago. I'm no longer a silly child, I'm the Master Artisan of all Mistra. Didn't anyone teach you that it can be dangerous to offend the powerful?"

As soon as she said it, she knew she'd gone too far. Even though Tbrin had always refused any leadership position in Mistra, she had seen glimpses of his real transmogrifee talent and knew that it was considerable. It was just that whenever he brought up the incident from her childhood, Nikki felt the panic swell in her like water rising over her head and the anger rose with it. She thought of the prank that had killed her. It was a child's game, to steal the breath away. It was one of the first tricks they had learned, even though it was forbidden, or perhaps because it *was* forbidden. Nikki and her schoolmates had hidden in a passageway to play. It was the simplest transmogrifee to counteract, but she'd panicked when her friends took the breath from her. They ran away laughing, unaware that she was dying, surrounded by air that she couldn't inhale. Tbrin had found her there, still and unbreathing, and returned her to the living. After that, he'd taken her in, teaching her to control the fear that would soon have meant her death in the competitive world of the talented. Still, it haunted her, caused her to doubt that she had what it took to be what she pretended to be.

"I remind you because someday I might not be here to help you," he replied gruffly. "There is another possible impetus for your vision."

Tbrin hesitated. "Perhaps you've felt it, but chaos is increasing. Transmogrifee is becoming undependable. Reality itself seems to be losing its grip on the world. If we don't find an answer to the increasing disruptions soon, entropy could tear our world apart."

The old man's hands rummaged among the minerals and pigments on his table. Reaching for something, he spilled a vial, tipping the odious contents onto a pile of dried fishtails that came to life and began to flop wildly, tipping more vials in their convulsive dance across the table and onto the floor. Tbrin swore, groping at the mess ineffectually. Among the strange trappings of his art, he grasped desperately at one of his precious primers, lifting it like a baby he was saving from a fire. It was then that Nikki noticed how his hands shook. She wondered if it was his own end he feared. The thought of losing him suddenly hurt her, as a cold sword point never could.

Now embarrassed by her outburst, she said, "You're in better shape than I am, old man. You'll probably outlive me. Besides, I still have a lot to learn. I need to keep you around for a bit longer."

Tbrin grunted in amused agreement but said in a grave tone, "It's not my own death I fear." He paused. When he spoke again, his voice was gentle. "You've done well, better than any apprentice I've ever had. But time is running out. All the time I've wasted. If I'd only known sooner—but events have moved so quickly. You might have to leave Mistra soon. I've seen it coming. You need to listen. Before our ability to use transmogrifee weakens beyond the point of salvation, you'll need to find a new drakyn's eye and stabilize genetic matter."

What the fruck was genetic matter?

Nikki didn't understand Tbrin's strange ramblings any better now than she had as a child. Was he hiding something from her, and if so, why? To protect her, or him? They should be equals now, two old friends discussing matters of great import. But no, Tbrin would always be the crazy sensei. All the fletshit about the end of the world was driving her crazy, too. Correction, crazier.

Didn't he realize that what she didn't know could kill her? She needed real transmograffic and battle skills, not vague warnings.

Nikki thought about the possibility of leaving Mistra. It had been a shared fantasy for her and her brother Benna, to travel the world on some soul-expanding adventure. But that had only been a childish fantasy, hadn't it? She had responsibilities now. Nothing she could imagine could force her to leave Mistra.

But nightmares involving the flatlands—and worse—haunted her.

"Tbrin, have you ever been down to the plains, or beyond?"

"It was so long ago," he began. "I'd almost forgotten what it was like. I have a few of the old primers left to remind me. They speak of endless desert, choking volcanic dust and earthquake fissures, carnivorous hordes, sandstorms that cut skin like razors and acid rivers that fry the flesh from your bones." When she stared at him in horror, he chuckled. "Perhaps it wasn't quite that bad. I could be exaggerating—just a little."

He grinned mischievously, then his look grew serious. "What I tell you must go no farther than this chamber. There are ways to take the power of Mistra with you when you go. It's forbidden of course, and we only resort to it in these direst of circumstances."

Everyone knew that it was unsafe to leave Mistra, especially for the talented, whose power depended on proximity to the drakyn's eye, the stone that amplified and sustained their transmograffic talent. Nikki knew that Tbrin had lived his whole life in the aerie, but lately, he'd been saying ridiculous things, talking of great deeds and the transmogrifee wars with the authority of one who had been there, eight centuries ago.

And there were the rumors. Some said that Tbrin had secretly used lifeforce to continue his consciousness from generation to generation.

Using lifeforce was akin to murder. The dying took the consciousness of a newborn, robbing that person of his life and his future. It was a dangerous thing to attempt. To be found out meant immediate death for him and all those related to him. Families watched their own very carefully. Once, he might succeed unnoticed, but could he have done it for centuries?

"There's so much more I need to know," she began tentatively.

Tbrin looked at her sadly.

"You want to know about the beasts, the drakyn," he said. It was a statement. "They're extinct of course."

"But how did Wren Weatherspring have the power to finally eliminate them, if, as you've said, they were almost impossible to kill? I think that part of the *Chronicles* has been lost. It doesn't say *how* she beat them."

Tbrin had a distant look in his eyes as he responded. "In many ways, they killed themselves. We wouldn't have had a chance without their demented sense of honor and ceremony. They insisted on facing us on our terms, often in our form. Defeating an enemy, using only as much strength as the other possessed, gave them great honor in battle. Outright murder was forbidden. Only a drakyn totally lacking in honor would do such a thing, especially in front of witnesses," he added with a wry snort.

Tbrin's eyes suddenly widened in fear, as if he saw some ghastly possibility. "Could it be?" he asked himself quietly. "Could he have survived, after all?"

"What? Who?" asked Nikki. She was bewildered yet fascinated.

But Tbrin continued as if he hadn't heard her question. "Of course, they cheated at this game whenever they could get away with it, and just like humans, some were more treacherous than others. They could play their sick battle-games and win because their regenerative skills were incredible. I think it was almost an innate talent for them, ingrained from generations of conflict. The only way to kill them was to remove the head or heart. Lacking either, they'll be unable to regenerate by themselves. But beware, you could chop him into countless pieces, and he will still hold on to some primitive living matter that can be reconstituted. Another drakyn could reconstruct him."

"Why do you say, 'he?'" asked Nikki, "I thought the real warriors were the females."

"That's why they're so hard to kill. Semli will be cunning, crueler than you can imagine. You must match his strength, his total lack of compassion, or you won't have a chance."

A long, uncomfortable silence followed. Nikki watched his eyes regain their focus until he realized what he'd said.

"But that's all ancient, arcane knowledge you'll probably never need," he ended lamely.

He let out a sigh and pulled out a misshapen gray lump from the detritus of his workspace.

"What's that?"

"This will protect your power when you travel to the flatlands. You must always keep it with you. Never, NEVER lose it! Understand?"

She stared at the ugly lump of grit that he held out. Had Tbrin finally lost his mind completely?

"Don't look at me like that, girl. It's not what it appears. I put a glamor on it. It's a fragment of the drakyn's eye."

"What? You can't take that from the council chamber! Are you mad?"

Tbrin went on, ignoring her objections. "Without it, your power will wane the farther you get from Mistra, until you're nothing but a feeble flatlander, with no talent, no hope of surviving what's to come."

He grabbed her sword and, with a flourish, brought the two together. There was an explosion of blue light and the air sparked with electricity. When he pulled his hand away, the hilt of her plain sword was adorned with a beautiful green jewel. At its center glowed a tiny drakyn's eye, just like the one in the aerie stone, only smaller.

"Here," he said, handing her a plain, silver coin on a chain. "This is what I call the empty hand illusion. If the sword is lost or taken, the drakyn's eye material will transfer inconspicuously to this coin. It appears worthless, so it's unlikely to be taken. Your enemies will think they have procured something valuable from you in the sword, but they will only grasp the empty hand. Keep the medallion with you and wear it always."

Perhaps she had underestimated the old fool. If this sword and talisman could augment her power, she might be better prepared for the danger they both foresaw. Tentatively, she reached for both objects. When she touched the hilt of the sword, she shivered, as the unnatural chill of the drakyn's eye stone raced from her fingertips to her heart like an arrow of dread.

CHAPTER FOUR

Kakuni Unbound

When the sailfish screamed, Chendri knew they were all going to die. She wiped water from her eyes. She could just make out Dreyk in the stern. Rain and seawater whipped the captain's blond braid around his face. The emergency sails flailed about in tatters around him, revealing, then hiding his imposing form. The broken jackline lashed the deck with more rage than a slaver's strap. The crew, ignoring their duties, cowered from the onslaught of the psy daemons as the phantasms dipped and bit and snarled about them. Chendri knew that hope was fading. So far, the madness had spared Kakuni, but it was only a matter of time. The sailfish screamed again, and Chendri realized that the daemons were starting to affect the sailfish as well.

As if reading her mind, Dreyk shouted, "Chendri, cut the sailfish loose!" She could see, even through the squall, that his rough, weatherworn features were grim, his jaw clenched.

"But we need her!" she retorted uncertainly. Her voice was consumed by the wind, and she doubted that he heard her.

Kakuni screamed again. The cry of primeval pain bit deep into her heart. There was something so wrong about all of this. Sailfish did not scream in anguish; they sang gentle songs to ease the knots away. They hummed lilting tunes of the beauty in the sea and sky and the pure joy of living. But all that was gone now.

Lady Chaos and her ugly sister Bad Luck have tipped their bloody claws into our lives and now all is lost.

Dreyk grasped the rail until his veins stood out like the ridges of Mount Hespius back home. He slapped the rail with one hand, holding on for dear life with the other. He shouted, "The daemons are driving her mad. She must dive. Set her free, Chendri. Now!"

Chendri turned, growling even as she stumbled to obey his command. She knew he was right, but freeing the sailfish meant they couldn't escape the storm. Despite her foreboding, she grasped the stays with shaking hands and pulled the levers that undid the tethers of the sailfish harness. She struggled to the other side and did the same. She watched helplessly as the great beast fell away into the depths, her heart descending with the massive sea creature. They were doomed. No one could escape a psy storm at sea if the sailfish was not able to tow them away from the danger. With the sailfish gone and the emergency rigging in tatters, they would be dead in the water, easy prey for the psy daemons who drove living beings mad.

Turning, she came face to face with the hulking mass of the sailmaster, Krin. His face was a wild mask of terror, his eyes wide and as pale as those of a deep sea lunkerfish.

"Get away. Must get away," he rumbled.

"Get yourself together, Krin. There's no place to go. We just have to weather this—"

Without warning, Krin threw himself on top of her and pulled them both over the side.

Chendri screamed but doubted that anyone could hear her. The shock of the cold water as they hit drove the breath from her lungs. She had just escaped from Krin's thrashing limbs when something grabbed her ankle and pulled her down with unbelievable force. At first, she could do nothing but imitate a rag doll, unable to reach her ankle to find out what beast had her in its grasp. Finally, she gathered the strength to reach down. She felt what held her and hope escaped with the last of her breath. She was tangled in the sailfish harness. Kakuni would not stop until she reached the safe depths of the ocean floor. She knew she would be drowned long before that. She struggled to free herself, until her arms and her heart no longer had the strength to resist.

As she sank, a strange thought came to her.

Just like Dreyk to lead them so far from the shipping lanes, into this gardamn wild and unpredictable southern sea. Just like him to abandon her again, even though he had promised to never leave her. She should have told him that she was with child, but what difference would it make? They were all dead anyway.

CHAPTER FIVE

In the Land of Daemons

Nikki returned to her sleeping rooms, but her petulant mood hadn't improved. Reaching for her cloak, she bumped the sculpture she'd been working on, an abstract affair consisting of soaring wings and crystal limbs. It wobbled, then steadied itself on the pedestal. Suddenly, its delicate, hopeful tone disgusted her, and she gave it a shove. In slow motion, she watched it fall until it crashed to the floor, breaking into a million pieces with a bright, brittle sound. She waved an arm and the pieces gathered themselves like a swarming nest of transparent ants. When the mass had clumped together, it reverted to its original shape, a gray, malformed lump of clay.

The fragile dreams of a child, she thought bitterly.

As she was turning to leave, something caught the edge of her vision in the high window.

"Moonchaser, come down from there! Grellas can't fly, in case you forgot."

She rushed to the window with outstretched arms, forgetting that his weight would probably crush her if he jumped into her arms. The huge cat ignored her, trying to appear graceful as he twisted on his narrow perch. He made a pretense of watching the sea far below. One paw slipped, but he caught himself with his tail. Nikki worried that she wouldn't be able to overcome the grella's natural resistance to transmogrifee before he hit the ocean far below.

"Turn me into a blat or a wipperill as I fall," purred the big cat. "I know you can do it. I see you do it to yourself all the time. Though I would rather eat one than be one," he added slyly.

Realizing that logic wouldn't work, she resorted to reverse psychology. "I wouldn't waste transmogrifee on a pest like you," she said. "Besides, I'm going to see the stranger now, so I won't be around to save you."

"You saw him yesterday. Will he look so different today?"

"I think you're jealous!"

At this, the huge feline leapt down from the window with fluid grace, landing soundlessly at her feet. His enormous opal eyes gazed into hers searchingly until she had to turn away. Perhaps she had done too good a job of enhancing his natural cunning and intelligence. She'd needed a nighttime guardian she could trust, but along the way he'd become dear to her, despite her teasing.

"I knew that would get you down," she said. "Avoid trouble for a while, please. I don't need any more surprises today—and stay away from Cressida. You know she's terrified of you."

Ignoring her, he growled, "Don't think I'm stupid. You will learn nothing from this man. These distant lands you dream of are not so interesting once you must survive there, believe me. It's good here. Plenty of fish. Leave this stranger who floats up like a dead kelterfish alone. Let him find his own way home."

"Where would you be if I had no interest in strangers? When I found you on the lower steps, you were starving."

"Resting my stomach, it's a grella way. Humans do not understand."

"I can't believe that you would ever go willingly without your dinner. Besides, this is not a dead fish. He's a traveler who could tell us about what's out there. Aren't you the least bit curious about how he got here, and from where?"

"No. When is dinner, by the way?"

Nikki didn't bother with an answer. The big cat knew better than anyone when the dinner hour was near, and he wasn't timid about reminding Cressida, the poor cook, who completely misunderstood his intentions. She consistently misinterpreted his growling speech for a threat.

Now the cat's attention was diverted by a tiny flying insect, a neon green wipperill, which he pawed at tentatively, then lunged at with surprising speed, his great jaws snapping shut with a resounding clap where the insect had been a second before. Nikki could only laugh as so small an adversary thwarted the huge cat. For all the enhancements she had given him, he was still a playful kitten at heart. Now he was chasing his elusive prey down the corridor with all his energy. The mass of flailing paws, orange fur, and gyrating tail disappeared into another room down the hall, followed by a truncated scream and the sound of breaking ceramics.

Nikki moaned and hurried from the room. All she needed now was another session trying to calm Cressida and assure the cook that the big cat wasn't trying to make a meal of her. She headed for her back door, an escape route that she'd installed when she first took over the quarters of the master transmogrifer. She didn't want to go the way of her predecessor, disappearing in the night, never to be seen again. An accident, they'd said, and Andris had become so clumsy in his old age, although he had only been a few years older than Nikki was now.

Perhaps just clumsy enough to be caught by a deadly transmogrifee, she thought with dark humor.

At the door, she adjusted her cloak. Her pale arms and long silver-blonde hair stood out brightly from its crimson folds, framing a youthful face with intense gray eyes that gleamed with intelligence and curiosity. Her robe took flight behind her as she stepped forward, billowing in the sudden wind that was always present on this high walkway. She stepped forward, though no stone was visible beneath her feet.

Nikki looked down at the sheer cliffs that dropped away beneath her. Perhaps she had many fears, but heights wasn't one of them. She reveled in the wild joy of the wind, balanced high above the world by her will alone.

Today, she was anxious to get down to the lower levels, and she hurried across the invisible walkway to the hidden door at the far end. At a motion of her hand, the door opened onto an ordinary set of stone stairs. She took the steps two at a time, almost flying. She was grateful that her route to the healing hall would take her through the quarters of the brennen. She enjoyed her time in the lower halls among the fishwives with their gossip, the fishermen, netsmen, and gaffers who punctuated their work with ribald stories and drinking tales. They were her friends, while the talented ones she'd grown up with, she regarded with careful respect at best. She'd learned early the ugly truth; in Mistra, it could be deadly to develop lasting relationships and power at the same time.

She soon came out in the main hall below. Though the walls were still semi-transparent, the depth of crystal did strange things to the light, as if it became confused by the many curves it must make to penetrate here. Patches of color and texture played on the floor and walls, the distorted shadows of those moving on upper levels. Even her own shadow behaved differently here, taking on the shape of a soft, muted dancer, circling her as she moved.

Nikki felt cold eyes on her neck and turned to find herself facing the sculpture that was rumored to be as old as Mistra itself. A carved figure rested inside a huge block of crystal. It was a tall figure of a long-dead monster, the drakyn. The mighty beast bore the drakyn's winged form, it's powerful body and massive legs defined by rippling muscles in minute detail. Huge jaws sported double rows of carnivorous teeth and a fringe of blood-red cartilage framed the massive reptilian head. Its jeweled eyes seemed to follow her every movement with a mocking gaze. As always, she had to stop to return the imagined challenge.

Crystal inside crystal, the sculpture had a life of its own, seeming to move with the shadows, translucent energy always in flux. Though she knew it was only a work of art, she couldn't help thinking of it with a combination of dread and fascination. No one knew the artist, but the work was ancient. Some said it had been done by Kodo himself to commemorate their victory over the drakyn, while others said it was the work of dozens of artists and had taken generations to complete. Whatever the truth, that reality was now lost in the past, while the image remained, its locked transmogrifee so strong that it could not be mutated or augmented in even the slightest way, by even the strongest transmogrifer.

Why was the drakyn dignified in this way, instead of Wren Weatherspring? she wondered as she had many times before. Perhaps they had wanted to honor the losers? That seemed unlikely to her. The drakyn had been bitter, merciless enemies, so why recognize them at all?

She turned and walked away from the figure. She could feel its eyes on her as she moved, and she imagined she heard the rustle of wings. At the end of the hall, she turned back sharply, but of course the drakyn hadn't moved. It stared down on her with an expression of mockery, or so she thought, and her reaction made her feel foolish.

Nikki derided herself for letting her imagination run rampant. She left the corridor, stepping through a large arching doorway. The cavern grew as she walked until she stood in a huge open area. A cool breeze carried the scent of seawater and rotting fish. The ceiling was barely visible above, lost in clouds of moisture. Condensed drops occasionally splattered around her, and one cold drop hit her squarely on the top of the head, running down her scalp. She shook it off with a shiver as she walked, and soon she reached the shores of a gigantic underground lake.

At one end, were the openings where the seawater entered at high-sea. Above one opening, a walkway led to the outer cliffs. The tide was at ebb and only gentle waters lapped at the white gravel shore before her. At the other end were the aqueducts that routed water to the other levels, with the station where the master waterman would sit at highsea, separating the salt from the flow that became the aerie's drinking water. Hirrin was absent now, and she was thankful for that. Though she always enjoyed their conversations, she sometimes found it hard to escape him. She couldn't blame him for wanting to talk. He probably had the most boring job in all Mistra.

She stepped carefully out onto the white gravel beach and took a deep, rich breath of the humid air. It carried the scent of kelp and fish and other, indefinable scents. Redolent with varied life in all stages of decay and rebirth, all in perfect balance, a symphony of smells that only nature could perform. She loved these aromas, though she knew that not everyone shared her sentiment.

Though she was alone on this side of the lake, she could make out figures on the distant shore, workers at long tables, sorting and cleaning the sea plants and fish that formed the main staples of Mistra. Behind them were the drying racks, where the purest flowcrystal directed light and heat from above onto the rows of kelp and kelterfish. At the sight of this familiar activity, she felt isolated and friendless. She longed to cast off her ceremonial robes and don the simple green tunic of the brennen, to join the workers at their tables until her fingers too were stained and dry, and her heart full of the joy of a simple day's work finally completed. But it wasn't to be today—or any day. She would grow tired and careless under the weight of pomp and facade, until one day she too would have an official accident, as had her predecessor.

Drawing her eyes reluctantly from the far shore, she stepped to the edge, as if she intended to walk across. Her hands danced and her robe billowed out behind her as she gathered herself. The robe's colors mutated swiftly, coalescing from opal to shimmering magenta to deep cobalt and into a combination of all colors, a swirl of something becoming. She let her fears go, let her thoughts wander into that state of fertile stillness that only the artist understands. In her mind, she created a work of art, of imagination, and then she arranged the particles of her own existence into this dream shape. Though she'd done it a thousand times before, still, it filled her with wild exhilaration. Without preamble, she leapt, an acrobatic step that took her far out over the still water. The colors in her robe separated into a thousand ruby streamers that whistled in the air as she fell back down toward the water. But, before her body touched the surface, the woman completely disappeared, replaced by a winged shape that caught the air at the last second, rising from the surface with a triumphant cry.

On a raft far out on the water, Bennakia Theisborne, the apprentice kelp tender, woke from his dreaming to the silken rustle of wings overhead. The bird was almost out of sight before he could scramble to his feet. His hasty motion set the raft rocking, waking his companion, who wasn't at all pleased.

"What is it now, Benna? Can't a man get a moment's peace?"

"Kyla, wake up!" cried Benna. "It was Nikki, I think, or another of the talented, in the shape of a greatbird. If only I had the talent," he ended wistfully.

But Kyla was likely concerned with things other than Benna's lack of transmograffic ability. He was old, his usefulness waning. Mistra was an isolated society in a harsh environment, where resources were limited. They didn't have the luxury of supporting unproductive members in their old age.

"Best get back to work, boy. We don't have all day to get this load in. No more nappin' on the job."

Benna knew better than to argue that it had been Kyla's idea to nap, so he rose and began to help the older man pull the hooked longpole onto the raft with its dripping load of kelp. As he worked, Benna couldn't keep his eyes from straying to the far shore. That night his dreams would be filled with the bittersweet joy of flying.

Nikki stepped down onto the gravel at the lake's far edge with a wry chuckle. Kyla would probably work poor Benna to death for the rest of the day. She felt a sudden pang of pity for her younger brother, who had never exhibited the slightest sign of the talent that the other highborn seemed to possess. But she knew pity would do him no good, and she quickly erased the thought. He'd compensated for his lack of transmogrifee with other abilities. Perhaps someday, such practical skills might be needed.

Her gown settled gently around her as her human shape returned. She set off for the cavern's remote wall. She reached an isolated door and was soon descending another set of stairs.

Here a stronger scent assailed her. Fish, dried kelp, sweat, and smoke mingled to create the overwhelming miasma that was the hallmark of the brennen. Of course, the brennen took no notice of these smells, having been steeped in them every day of their lives for generations. Nikki welcomed these odors and only wished she could stay longer, but her route led to the eastern overlook on the aerie's far side.

She quickly altered her form just enough to pass inconspicuously. Her features became a little rougher and her skin turned a deep gold.

She pulled her cloak close and rubbed vigorously, saying a few mumbled words, until she wore the simple green tunic and trousers of a brennen fishwife. She made her way through the busy hall, trying to avoid notice, although most of the brennen saw through her disguise. It was all but impossible to hide the glowing aura of a high artisan, but they showed their respect for the talented by acquiescing to their whims and fancies. Besides, all knew what could happen to those who offended the highborn.

As she walked, she worked her way east until the light increased around her, and she knew she was almost to the healer's hall. Although she was at a lower level than her chambers on the west side, she was on the highest levels of the cliffs' eastern side, where light entered through many terraced levels. She arrived at a curtained door bearing the healer's embroidered emblem, a kestrel with a glowing heart. She pulled the curtain aside, shielding her eyes from the light, for the entire eastern wall of this room was the purest flowcrystal, as transparent as the air itself. Before her was a lush, indoor garden, well-tended but informal in its design. A warm breeze flowed from high ventilation windows, bringing the scent of flowers and greenery.

She passed some of the healer's patients, lounging in the spongy grass or strolling through the indoor garden. Auras always seemed to glow gently here, like a plant in spring growth. No one remained ill for long in the healer's hall. The healer started them on the road, then it was a simple matter for them to heal themselves. For a transmogrifer, to correct a thought was to correct the body as well.

At last, she came to the far wall of crystal and looked out. It was a clear day, and she could see a great distance, almost, she imagined, to the escarpment that marked the beginning of the habitable lands beyond. Puffs of volcanic clouds dotted the horizon, marking the beginning of the volcano lands far to the northeast. Directly below her was the pockmarked and twisted ground called the Great Waste.

Sometimes she could imagine the terrible transmogrifee battles that had caused such destruction, but such thoughts always left her unsettled, and she tried to avoid them.

The Great Waste was followed by a high desert region that covered most of the southern tip of the land, effectively isolating them from the gentler lands that were rumored to exist to the north. It was said that strange creatures lived in it, if life could exist in that sparse, arid land. But forbidding as it appeared, she never missed an opportunity to stand here and look down, sometimes for hours. She regretted that she couldn't stay longer now, but there were other matters of interest in the hall today.

She pulled away from the view and made her way through the green rooms until she came to a central area, where the foliage was especially dense and fragrant. A springy path led through gigantic blush-colored blossoms and fuzzy, round-leafed plants large enough to carry small pools of condensed moisture in their gaping mouths.

The path opened into a high walled room whose only furniture was a long, low bench, handcrafted of bentwood and woven pelngrass. Here the stranger sat, with the healer Kia beside him. Not wanting to intrude on their conversation, Nikki waited unseen in the shadows. The animated quality of their conversation surprised her. Only yesterday, the man had been wracked by fevered dreams, his speech all but unintelligible.

The healer was doing her work. The man's aura was strong, if fluctuating, and his voice was clear, though many of his words were of an unfamiliar vernacular. Kia listened to him intently, answering in a tone that was itself a healing force. Nikki knew that Kia's voice was working on many levels, healing the body and spirit with its gentle song. She didn't envy the healer her art, which brought her so close to the suffering of her patients. Though Nikki had apprenticed with the healer in her training, the experience had only drained her, while Kia seemed to grow even stronger from the energy she gave away. She had a special gift.

As Nikki watched, the man's face grew more animated, his aura flaring, his hands rising with his voice. She didn't have to hear all his words to understand. In the gray-blue depths of his eyes, she saw anger, frustration, and fear, but there was also strength, and control.

This was not a man who had escaped suffering in his life, emotional or physical. His face was scarred and weathered. His skin must once have been pale, but it was ruddy now from exposure to the elements, and there were crow's feet around his eyes. His nose was perhaps too hawkish for his face to be considered handsome, but his expression spoke of intelligence and humor. His hair was a wild shock of yellow, a color Nikki had never seen occurring naturally, and she wondered if he augmented or dyed it, but she didn't think this was a man who cared what others thought of his appearance. It flowed back from his high forehead like a bright flame, untamed but in perfect balance, like the mane of a wild cat. His movements gave the impression of great energy flowing beneath the surface. In his own element, she thought that he was probably a forceful man who would make decisions and stand by them, a man who many would follow.

She edged closer, not wanting to interrupt, but needing to hear more of the conversation if she could. The man was questioning Kia in an impatient tone.

"A crenda, don't you understand? A ship. It sails the sea."

Kia looked bewildered for a second, running her fingers through her short dark hair in frustration.

"Oh, you mean sargasso," she said. "But surely no man could ride on that?"

"Beckle save us, don't you people have boats?"

"Boti, yes, the two-man rafts we use in the kelp beds to carry—"

"Yes, that's it, but larger, with a sailfish in harness. My crenda, *Windsinger*, carried my crew and me across the Westersea until we were driven off course by that storm—what's wrong?"

Kia's eyes had grown huge, her astonishment for a second overriding her training. "You couldn't have come here across the sea!"

"We're sailors, fishermen, and traders. What else would we do?"

"Everyone knows that the sea is unnavigable," said Kia, almost as if she were speaking to a child. "The Sea of Obrion would swallow you before you could get a kelp-length from the rocks. Even at ebb tide, it's wild and untamable. Our transmogrifees are simply lost in its immensity. You must have stronger talent than we possess."

At these words, the stranger looked at her with suspicion and something bordering on panic. He rose, reaching to his side as if to pull a weapon, but no sword or scabbard had been found on him.

"The virtuous don't practice the evil arts," he said heatedly. "And of all the things I've been called in my life, I don't count liar among them."

Seeing him rise from his seat in confusion and anger, Kia remembered herself. When she spoke, her words again held the soothing tone that stilled even the air. As she spoke, the man visibly relaxed.

"Please don't misunderstand me," she said softly. "Much of our culture is so different from yours, but there is no evil here in the healing hall, believe me. Please sit and continue."

The man sat, but a note of suspicion remained in his voice.

"As I told you before, we were driven off course by an immense thunderstorm system and became lost in this wild sea. And then, to add insult to injury, the psy storm hit. The sailfish went wild, and we had to set her free. The currents and wind drove our ship into the rocks. When the crenda broke up, I somehow survived. I swam with all my strength, as if I was being drawn by some force, but I lost consciousness. In a dream, I remember arms pulling me from some kind of netting. Then I awoke here."

Suddenly Nikki's curiosity took over, and she stepped out of her hiding place. She touched Kia softly on the shoulder, and they exchanged a glance. The healer rose.

"I must see to my other duties," Kia explained, "but I leave you in a competent healer's hands. Nikkitheis TyaBorne, Master Artisan of Mistra."

With a last glance at the two, Kia left Nikki alone with the newcomer, who appraised her suspiciously. She settled herself on the bench and took a deep breath, trying to free her mind of tension so as not to pass it on to him.

"I'm very sorry that you were a victim of the storm," she began. "We had no idea that there were men on the oceans. If I'd known in time, I might have created some transmogrifee to save your boti—"

"Are you all shifters and daemons?" He pulled away from her and was studying her carefully as if he feared she might suddenly turn into a bird and fly away.

She smiled soothingly and used the calming speech.

"I'm sorry, I don't understand your words."

"Shapers, shifters, daemons."

"Daemons are only real in children's tales," said Nikki. "We practice the arts of creation, as we have since the elder times. Our legends state that, centuries ago, the great warrior Wren Weatherspring defeated the beasts, drakyn they were called. We now live in their ancient keep, though it has changed much from the dank drakyn's lair it must once have been. Please believe that we are not daemons, but ordinary folk who mean you no harm."

He looked at her quizzically, and visibly relaxed. Was he beginning to trust her?

"I believe you, though I'm not really sure why." After a moment of silence, he asked, "And no others of my crew were pulled in?"

"No, I'm sorry. You were fortunate, becoming entangled in our nets during the storm. That's how they found you, dangling from the cliff's edge. No one else was found." This she knew he'd been told before. Nikki watched as he seemed to deflate, as if the loss finally hit him with its full force. She studied her hands, trying to come up with something consoling to say. She heard a dry chuckle. Looking up sharply, she saw his lips twist into a bitter grin.

"So, my doom in Kraida is my salvation in this strange land."

"Your doom?"

"I'm what people call *kiva*. Many like me don't survive. It's a sensitivity to the storms and any transmogrifee that occurs near me. It must have drawn me in here." He paused, and Nikki could see him struggle with his memories, but his eyes brightened. "At home, I was one of the lucky ones. I managed to escape my fate at sea. The psy storms are less frequent there, at least the northern seas where I usually sail. It's been a bearable existence so far, but I never thought I'd long for the sight of Two Moon Bay as I do now." They sat in silence for a moment as the man remembered his lost friends and home.

"Where did you say you're from?" asked Nikki.

"I'm from Bay Towne, in Kraida," he said. "Though it seems unlikely that I'll ever see it again," he added quietly. "It must be far to the north of this strange land, across thousands of miles of unknown territory." He paused, then said, "My only way home is probably by sea. Could I see where I was pulled from the water—if it is allowed."

"Of course," replied Nikki. "But Kia may not want you to leave so soon. You were almost drowned and have been in fever for days."

"Is this place my prison, then?" he asked in a deceptively calm voice.

"Of course not!" Seeing his expression, she decided. He had too active a spirit to stay long in the healer's hall, and she wanted to gain his trust.

"You look strong enough to me. It's not far down to the harvest hall."

The harvest hall was one of the oldest parts of the aerie and had remained largely unchanged for generations. The walls here were opaque stone, the primitive rock of the mountains themselves, and while the rest of the aerie was not cave-like at all, but bright and airy, this place seemed solid and ancient. Torches at intervals along the wall provided dancing golden light. The air was pungent with the scent of sea creatures and plants in all stages of decay, and the floor glittered with fish scales. They were alone in the hall, and their words echoed in the cavern. They stood looking up at the rough archway that filled much of the far wall. Brilliant blue sky illuminated the large open archway, though little of its light seemed to penetrate the dark interior. The distant cries of sea birds and the crash of waves from far below were barely audible. From the hall floor where they stood, they could see rough walkways that led up over the opening, accompanied by rope railings mounted in the stone. At the top hung a system of nets and gaff hooks. As a fisherman himself, Dreyk seemed to gather all this in and grasp its purpose quickly.

"The tide rises this high?"

"Yes, at highsea. But the tides can be unpredictable. We often have little warning. You would be in great danger if you were to come here alone. The power of the drakyn's eye provides me with some awareness of Obrion's mood."

"If the drakyn are gone, how is it that you have one of their eyes?"

She chuckled. "It's not an actual eye, of course. No one really knows what it is or where it came from. There are stories, but I believe it's just an odd stone with unusual properties. It affects everything around it, as if it's a source of transmograffic power. A skilled artisan can do great works of creation with it. It amplifies talent."

"But how does it work? Does it speak to you?"

"No, not really. At least not in any kind of spoken language. It's more like a silent music that only the talented can hear and shape into power."

"And you are one of these talented ones, even though you wish sometimes that you were not."

Nikki turned to him sharply, expecting to find criticism in his eyes, but their clear depths held only compassion.

"Yes," she said. "Am I so transparent?"

"I told you, I'm kiva. It's my misfortune to be more receptive than any person needs to be. It's made life interesting, at least. I thought that traveling would spare me, but it just seems to lead me from one disaster to another."

Again, a tone of bitterness and resignation colored his words, and she had to wonder what misfortunes had befallen him.

"When you have fully recovered, perhaps you will share some of your adventures with us."

It seemed that he was about to refuse when he looked at her, and his expression softened.

"Unlike the others I've met here, you seem to have a real interest in the outside world. Have you been far from this colony?"

"Farther than anyone," she replied excitedly. "My brother Benna and I have explored the peaks, and I've been down to the six-hundredth step, all the way to the marm caves."

A low chuckle started in his throat, but he seemed to think better of it when he saw her earnest expression. His tone was somber when he replied.

"There are many places less pleasant than this in the world. Your people are lucky to be so isolated. I've felt no earthquake tremors, smelled no volcanic smoke since I've been here. And even though this strange power surrounds us, I feel no ill effects. I couldn't believe it at first. I thought it was the fever, but I haven't felt so free of care in years."

He took a deep breath of the sea air. The breeze pulled his bright hair back from his face, and his eyes sparkled, reflecting the cerulean blue of the sky. Nikki thought that he did look much better. She didn't have the heart to tell him that she and the healer were the ones protecting him, and that without her help, he might indeed feel transmogrifee being performed around him.

"Kia's healing power is legendary. Perhaps that's what you feel."

"Perhaps," he replied with a half-hearted nod.

He studied her curiously, and she could tell that there was a question he hesitated to ask.

"What is it?"

"It's just—I've always wondered about this shaping or transmogrifee, as you call it. What is it, really? Where does it come from? Why are some born with it and others not?"

She hesitated, wondering how much she should tell him. "It's hard to explain something that's just a part of you, like a bird trying to explain to a snail how it feels to fly."

"So now I'm a snail, am I?"

She laughed, knowing that he was teasing her. "We don't know why only some are born with the talent. Transmogrifee is an innate skill that can be amplified with study and practice. We can see into the workings of an object, how it's put together, the tiniest elements that make up all things. Once you can see these tiny particles, it's a relatively simple matter to rearrange them, change, or augment them. It takes vision and imagination, and knowledge. It's an art form and science in one. But it can be very dangerous, and great care is needed not to disrupt the natural order beyond the tipping point."

"This tipping point, that's what can happen during transmogrifee battles, correct?"

"Yes. Some of the horrible byproducts of these battles linger, like what you saw in the psy storm that brought you here."

She noticed that his attention had strayed from their conversation, his gaze far out in the distant sky.

"Would you like to go up to the nets so we can see down to the ocean?" She thought it would do him good. His eyes turned a warmer blue at her words.

"Yes, I'd like to get my bearings. Were it night, the stars could tell me our general position."

Nikki laughed as she took his hand and led him up the stone steps.

"You are amazed at our talents, yet you speak to the stars?"

"It's not quite the kind of speaking that you imagine," he replied with a gentle laugh.

The steps now took all their attention as they climbed, and they were forced to cling to the clammy rope railing to avoid a fall on the slime and scales that covered every surface.

At the top, they turned from the arch, down a narrow corridor that had been unseen from below. Dreyk hesitated in the dark, but Nikki pulled him forward, eager to feel the warmth of the sun and the caress of the sea wind on her face. The tunnel made a sharp turn outward, then sea and sky erupted before them. They were on a small protruding platform of rock. Only a narrow ledge prevented a fall to the sea far below.

For a long moment, they stood in silence, as their eyes adjusted to the light. The sea roiled beneath them, attacking the cliffs with savage fury. Tiny dots wheeled over the surface, the brave sea birds who fished these turbulent waters. From above, sounds drifted down to them, the aerie banners flapping in the wind, delicate chimes, distant laughter. Dreyk leaned forward and glanced up to see the aerie of crystal ascending to dizzying heights, dressed in every imaginable color and texture. In front of them, the cloudless sky stretched uninterrupted to the horizon, and the wild ocean followed it, disappearing into the distant haze.

Nikki broke the silence. "This is one of my favorite spots. I come here often."

"I can see why. It's quite a view."

He stepped close to the edge and gazed down at the rocks and crashing waves.

"The sea here is truly unpassable," he said quietly. "I think I'll have to become a sea bird or a drakyn to escape this place. I see now why Kia reacted as she did to the idea of sailing the oceans."

"This is lowsea. It's quite calm now. But wait until tonight. I think the fishwives will be busy cleaning kelterfish tomorrow."

Dreyk swayed beside her, and she quickly pulled him from the edge.

"Let's sit," she said. "I fear I've been self-indulgent to let you do too much too soon."

"No, I'm fine. I was just thinking of Chendri, my...first mate." She wondered why he had paused. Did this first mate mean more to him than he wanted to say? "But it doesn't look like I'll ever get back there to tell her family how she was lost. I haven't seen a stick of wood in this place to build another crenda, even if I could sail from this treacherous place."

"Try not to think about that now. We'll get you home, I promise."

Her voice held such conviction that he looked at her in surprise.

"Do you divine the future as well?"

"No, of course not, but sometimes I sense things, or dream them, and often the dreams come true. I can't see details, but I know how it will feel, the colors, and smells. I know it sounds crazy."

"No, I can relate to that. I do the same thing. But my dreams of late have been filled with strange sights, looming fear, a horrible beast larger and stronger than anything I could ever best. I guess I should've heeded the warnings; the dreams must have been warning me of the impending shipwreck."

Nikki was silent, thinking of her own experience in the psy storm and the dreams that had haunted her since.

CHAPTER SIX

A Nightmare Recalled

Akriast the elder paused for a wheezing breath and to rally her flagging courage on the high steps of the aerie of Mistra. Above her loomed her destination, the Chamber of the Stars. It was a place seldom used even in the best of weather, but no one else would brave it now when wild Obrion raged. She would have the time she needed.

The rain lashed her face as the sea wind buffeted her frail body. An especially strong gust caught in her cloak, threatening to send her withered form gliding like a winged mountain squirrel far out over the crystal spires. She flattened herself against the steps, clinging tenuously as the sea wind dragged at her cloak. Her long nails scrabbled at the wet rock as she slid perilously close to the edge. She swore at them both, the beast-sea Obrion and the anonymous shaper of these steps.

"Too smooth, too smooth! What whelp transmogered these? Beauty and craft above all else but an old woman can't stand on them in the vile wind. *Bachich tey, garach ni!*"

The wind stilled, as if cowed by her curses in the ancient tongue. She scrambled up the last few steps as quickly as her aged bones would carry her, lest the sea wind change his mind. She paused on the landing and looked toward the horizon, squinting in the face of the setting sun as it slid between the rain clouds toward the distant ocean. Far below her, the waters of the sea glittered in the golden light with benign loveliness.

Deceiver, she thought.

She knew the beast for what he was, a perpetrator of death and ruin, who could rise from ebb tide six-hundred steps below to a wild fury in minutes when both moons were full, battering even the upper halls with killing force. Despite the break in the clouds, she could see the dark mass of another kind of storm as it lumbered toward the coastline.

"Perfect!" she purred.

She looked around and snorted in derision at the gaudy raiment of the aerie below her. Mistra was putting on its last show of the day, a brilliant explosion of color as the rich horizontal rays of evening light hit the banners, parapets, spires, and embellishments that spiraled crazily from top to bottom. Sunset here was not so much an event as a performance, an architectural color play enacted by all the dead artisans of Mistra living on in their works. It cascaded down the mountain, every piece of flowcrystal, croma silver and mercura coming to life in this last brilliant moment of the sun.

Akriast gazed across at the highest pinnacles of the aerie. She would have been surprised to see the look of awe on her own craggy features. Mistra was palace and city in one, the uppermost halls being the domain of its most powerful citizens. The highest living chambers, formed of the clearest crystal, were reserved for the Master Artisan, and here the centuries of occupants had performed some of their greatest feats of design, so that now the entire top of the aerie was a thing of delicate, translucent beauty. Even Akriast was not immune to its effects. Below the Master Artisan's chambers were the living quarters of the elite of the aerie, the council members who ruled the arts and political life of everyone in Mistra. Here Akriast's eyes narrowed, and she quickly let her gaze fall to the next levels. Below this, the distinction between palace and teeming city became blurred, as the upper levels gave way to the halls of the artisans, shopkeepers and recorders. Finally came the lowest levels, the most in danger from the ferocious and unpredictable tides. Here were the homes of the brennen, the simple kelptenders, fishermen and unskilled workers who were the backbone of Mistran society. Her gaze softened, as if remembering a long-lost joy, but the look quickly turned cold. Forcing her gaze upward again she resumed her climb.

Akriast was now venturing out into the uninhabited peaks to the side of the aerie. Her destination, the Chamber of the Stars, was little more than a finger of glass jutting out from the ragged peaks to her right. The chamber itself leaned far out into the sky. What had started as a geological oddity had been refined by Mistran stonemasters into a crystal room that afforded an uninterrupted view of both the ocean below and the stars above.

"A place of great power," she mumbled. "It will be remembered for ages to come as the place where it all began, and the storytellers will say, 'There in the Chamber of the Stars did the great transmogrifer Akriast come into her power at last.'"

She chuckled, bringing on a fit of wheezing. With effort she stilled her coughing and straightened her back.

To either side she felt the brooding presence of the watchers, the sharp twin peaks of Shelat and Ibor, great fangs in the sheer coastal range that Mistrans called The Drakyn's Teeth. For eight hundred years, these stark mountains had waited for the return of their true masters, and she had waited with them, plotting in the dark for the revenge that still burned in her like magma.

Now the time was right. She believed that she had found the answer at last.

What a fool you've been. All that time spent trying to *break* the binding, when she could have circumvented it instead. It was so simple she hadn't seen it. Until now. Perhaps in a way it was better that the answer had come so slowly. The time was ripe. She had plotted the course of the moons, Bekel and Meika, and read the old primers over and over. She now believed that soon, there would be a great upheaval in the balance. Death and chaos would result, and the new Master Artisan was weak and malleable. Akriast would gain the position of power and dignity that she deserved. But she needed allies. The generations of waiting had taken their toll—even on her. The past seemed no more than an ancient rumor now. So long had she lived with the weak, that perhaps her spirit had grown feeble as well. She must use all her remaining strength and talent now, before it was gone forever.

"Jelebron, quintecha barachni!" She spat the archaic words in the language of the old ones, that language that lived now in her mind alone, but she heard the quaver in her voice. Could she recall a great empire with only a memory? The doublemoons said it could be done. She had to try or die a powerless old hag, eaten alive by her own bile.

Turning her back on the wind, she slipped into the Chamber. When she entered the high room, she was reminded again why it unsettled her. The crystal here was so pure that it was like stepping onto a floor of open sky. Below her, the ragged mountains fell away and only the ocean, in turbulent miniature, stirred below. It was humiliating now to be so fearful of heights, when she could still recall flying, diving from great heights only to pull up within inches of the surf. All that so long ago. Perhaps she had been an old woman too long and had lost her nerve.

"You might as well get on with it, old hag," she mumbled. "You know you can't live forever." She cackled at her own bad humor, and this seemed to give her strength. She relaxed, jostling her mis-matched clothing back into position where the wind and the climb had twisted them.

With determination, she stepped to the center of the room. Pulling a small berry from one of her many bags, she tossed it into the air where it hung, softly spinning in place. At her quiet word, the berry grew into a soft, glowing orb of light, illuminating the chamber with a cool, blue glow. The room it revealed was empty, but for Akriast herself, and the wind that whistled through the open doorway and out a small ventilation window, high up in the crystal wall. Nervously, she attempted to smooth the wrinkles from her tunic, then fingered the small, brightly dyed bags that hung between her sagging breasts and at her waist. A shaking hand run through her wild gray hair revealed brows of the brightest turquoise. It was out of fashion to wear her mother's prime in this way, but she was proud of the fact that she had risen from the lower levels to her position of power in the colony in a mere lifetime and might rise higher than any imagined before all was done.

She held her hands out in front of her to still their shaking. A crystal table rose from the floor at her bidding, forming on its surface a phantasmagoria of strange objects; vials, bottles, boxes, decanters, jars, bags and pouches of every imaginable color and design. Some flickered as if lost between shapes, and some were broken, their glittering contents dancing in the swirling air like a tiny galaxy of stars at play.

Through this strange collection she searched with trembling fingers. Many containers she tossed aside until she found a small azure blue jar that brought a crooked smile to her leathery face. It had no seam or lid. In the glass of its surface, strange figures were carved. Serpentine fish with jagged wings whirled in a frozen dance across its surface. As she stared, the figures began to glow a dull red. She raised the jar to her face. Her bony hands caressed, and her voice cajoled, singing softly.

Suddenly she tossed the jar into the air as if it had burned her hand, but it fell spinning to her palm. She touched it with the very tip of one long, ragged fingernail, cutting into it as if it were clay on a pottery wheel. It formed a lid that popped into the air and clattered to the table. A sickly green glow erupted from inside. Its fluorescence reflected in her dark eyes and illuminated her intent features as she peered deeply into it. Akriast stuck a craggy, shaking finger into the jar and pulled it out covered with golden, sun-glinted flakes that flashed like the eyes of a lightning eel. With a self-satisfied grunt, she tossed the contents of the jar high into the air, so that sparkles cascaded onto the table and floor. Not all the glittering fragments came to rest. A few hung in the air above the table, revealing a squat, vaguely human shape that appeared to have been present all along, invisible, waiting to be revealed.

Working frantically, Akriast pulled dried pigments and herbs from the bags at her waist and throat, pressing them into the shape as if she were applying clay to a sculpture. Her humming continued its gentle beckoning, calling to all things lost and forgotten. Objects rose from the table and floated close. Even the walls strained inward, drawn by the irresistible power of her transmogery.

Intensely she worked at her creation, giving it depth and form, until a recognizable shape began to appear. Her frail stick fingers and sharp elbows jabbed at the air as she worked. After a time, her voice wavered. Her breathing became labored and ragged. Finally, she stopped, letting her hands fall heavily to her sides and breathing harshly.

On the table before her sat a woman. Her head was bowed, her knees pulled tight to her chest. Akriast ran a finger lovingly down the figure's back, and the spine arched beneath her touch, but the form flickered. Akriast let out her breath in a labored gasp. This work had been harder than she had imagined, and she was now struggling to hold the image. She forced herself to concentrate only on the human form she wished to create—but another, stronger image that slithered, there in the back of her awareness, threatened to overwhelm them both.

At last, her willpower won out and the image solidified. Firm hands freed themselves from the mass of the body and fluttered aimlessly, groping at a face that was still a disturbing blur. Akriast gently pulled the hands away. With the flourish of an artist applying the last stroke to a masterwork, she traced her fingers along the brow of the blank face. When she drew her hand away the face sported ruby eyebrows and eyes as emerald green as the sea at the height of sunseason.

Finally, Akriast pulled back, dizzy and weak from her exertions. The figure on the table gathered itself to step down. It was a human woman, fully animate now, moving as if in a trance. Suddenly the figure lifted its arms as if it might try to fly. It opened its mouth, and the room was filled with a shattering cry. The cry grew in volume, then descended the scale, growing into a roar. Lightning flashed outside and the sky answered with a stone-shuddering boom. The woman's body wavered, then began trading shapes with something hideous, too large for the tiny space. Akriast cried out in terror and fell back, scurrying for the door with her remaining strength. Behind her, the creature screamed again, this time in pain, as the great shape tried to fill a soldi rock room far too small to accommodate it. The cry was cut off and the room fell abruptly into a waiting quiet, broken only by the sound outside of the rain tapping insistent fingers on the stone and wind moaning in the spires. The air crackled and a bitter, suffocating smell permeated the air.

The light globe flickered, then went out completely. After a few seconds, the light returned to reveal an empty room. Akriast sobbed in exhaustion and defeat, finally gathering the energy to rise. She had reached the door when something caught her eye.

In the corner huddled a naked human shape with eyes that captured Akriast in a wild gaze. The figure stood on shaking legs and lurched toward Akriast, grabbing her by the shoulders. The woman's voice was hoarse, as if it hadn't been used in a very long time.

"I know you, but—where have I been? Was I sleeping? I am so forgetful. What is my name?"

Akriast scanned the woman's face intently as if searching for something, then let out a girlish giggle that grew into a fierce, triumphant laugh that echoed in the small chamber.

"You are my mistress, Queen Jelebron, the greatest drakyn warrior queen this world has ever known. You've been dead these long seasons. I drew you from memory using an ancient transmogrifee formula. I couldn't bring you back in your true shape, though I tried every incantation that I knew to break the binding that prevents drakyn from being recalled. Finally, I realized that if I could recall you as your chosen human avatar, you might in time be able to return to your original shape. I'm ashamed to say that it took me eight-hundred years to figure it out."

"Eight-hundred years! And the mountains still stand? How can I live so long after my time?"

"It's taken longer than I expected, but patience will ensure our victory. The Master Artisan is weak, and the council of Mistra grows complacent."

"Victory over whom?"

"Your memory will return, and I hope your ability to transform with it. Until then you must remain hidden. I'll help you. Lean on me."

The woman called Jelebron let out a weak chuckle. "You shake as badly as I do, old woman," she said.

Akriast looked at Jelebron slyly for a second, then chuckled. "I am no more what I seem than you are, but all this will be clear to you in time. When we regain our strength, we will recall others, as I have summoned you. We need followers who are willing to do the unpleasant work."

"Then there is unpleasant work, as you call it, for us to do. Why does that fill me with such excitement?" For the first time, life flickered in Jelebron's cool green eyes.

Akriast chuckled again, the delicate tinkle of a young girl's laughter. In this lilting tone she crooned, "Because you are drakyn, my friend. Killing is in your blood."

Jelebron paused again. Finally, she asked, "Why did you not bring forth the other?"

"The other?"

"My son. I sense him near, or at least most of him. In the ocean."

"You mean Kodo?"

"No, not that traitor," hissed Jelebron, "Semli, the other. Now I remember. When the witch Weatherspring destroyed him, there was a creek. I think that some of his genetric material, perhaps just a dusting of it, survived and made its way to the sea. I thought him weak, but that one has shown quite a talent for survival."

"We will collect him, as soon as you are well enough."

With renewed strength Akriast supported the other woman and they stumbled forward. As they passed by the window, Jelebron's eyes were drawn upward to the open sky. Her body trembled, her mouth opened and closed mutely as if she were searching for words, or thoughts.

Finally, she croaked: "The air is filled with energy. A strange storm is approaching."

"Yes," agreed Akriast. "And we must use it to our advantage! Nikkitheis Tyaborne rules as Master Artisan, but she is weak and a fool. There is peace, but together we will change that. Come quickly now, before you're seen."

Jelebron clung for a moment to the windowsill, her fingers tight and pale on the stone. The wind had stilled. On the horizon, the future hung, deadly silent and foreboding. A great beast of destiny, it crouched, gathering itself to spring on its unwary prey.

CHAPTER SEVEN

An Accidental Victory

T he next day, Nikki took Dreyk to the harvest hall again, to help him set his worries aside, at least for a while.

They sat peacefully together, enjoying the view and feeling no need to fill the beauty of this place with superfluous words. Nikki liked that about her new friend. He was easy to be with.

She'd brought a picnic of sorts; a smooth spiregrape white wine, dried herrins, high mountain wrenberries, together with sweet kelpcakes and the green cheese called blatgruyere that was a Mistran delicacy.

Dreyk exclaimed, "Green cheese? Now I know you're trying to torture me."

"Just try it, please," begged Nikki. "I'm sure you'll love it."

"OK, but I need to know how it's made, first."

"Oh, that's easy. It sits in a cave over winter. Nothing to it."

"Ah, and pray tell, what is this cheese made from?"

"Well, there's raw marm milk."

"And?"

"And that's it. It's a simple white mold cheese that is aged in the blat caves of lower Mistra. There's an organic rind that forms on the surface of each brick. Some washing of the rind is involved, but not being a master cheesemaker, I can't give you all the details."

Nikki felt it unnecessary to mention what sort of organic material was deposited by the thousands of flying lizards who roosted upside down over the cheese.

Dreyk finally tried a bite of the cheese, after a glass or two of the dry mountain wine and said, "Not bad, not bad at all."

Slowly Nikki became aware that his attention was focused on something far out to sea.

"What do you see?" she asked.

"I'm not sure, a greatbird perhaps, or a thais, flying erratically, but very fast. I've never seen one fly like that."

Nikki watched the horizon, but at first, she could distinguish nothing from the speckled haze. Dreyk must have very good vision. Finally, a tiny black fleck separated itself from the background. It flew in a ragged line toward them, and as its image grew, so did her misgiving, until an unreasoning fear gripped her. She rose on shaking legs and retreated from the edge, her eyes dark and wide with fear. She spoke in a harsh whisper.

"It can't be! They're all gone!"

"Who—what?" Dreyk had risen and was watching her curiously.

"The ancient beasts, the drakyn, but they're only legends now. They haven't existed on this shore for generations. But this all seems so familiar—as if I've been here before."

"In dreams?"

"Yes."

For a second, their eyes locked, and she saw the horrible truth reflected in his eyes.

"You've had such dreams also?" she asked.

"Yes, and they didn't end well."

A distant cry interrupted their thoughts. It echoed across the water, filling all who heard with dread.

"No bird utters such a cry," said Dreyk. "If you truly are people of transmogrifee, now would be a good time to start practicing some!"

"I have no transmogrifee to counter something like this, and there's no time to get everyone out of here."

"But you said that your people defeated the drakyn."

"That was centuries ago, and the actual *way* they were defeated has been lost. We're not strong enough to fight such a monster!"

"We must find weapons!"

He disappeared down the tunnel toward the main hall. She knew she had to stop him, or he would surely be killed. Despite her fear, she was moved by his willingness to sacrifice himself for strangers, and that was exactly what he would be doing if he tried to fight a drakyn with human weapons alone.

Seeing his courage, she was moved to act. She knew she had to do something, but what? She stood immobile for another second, frozen by uncertainty as the speck grew larger, its rasping screams rising above the crash of the waves. She gathered her thoughts and centered herself as best she could. It would take all her strength just to face this thing. Where was Tbrin? Surely, he would come to her aid. But there was no time to wait for him. Already, the air was filled with a sickening stench. Gauging from the speed with which it approached, she feared she wouldn't have time to do what she planned. She tore her eyes from the sky and followed Dreyk back down into the harvest hall, concentrating upon a new shape even as she ran.

The highsea alarm had been sounded, and a few bewildered brennen were gathered on the floor. To this hapless group, Dreyk was shouting and waving his arms. The others stared at him as if he'd lost his senses. They finally appeared to understand him, and one handed him a long-handled pole with a large, barbed hook lashed to its tip. Dreyk hefted this in his hands, testing its balance, before he turned to face the archway.

He was walking forward tentatively when Nikki reached him, pushing him back roughly.

"Don't be a fool!" she screamed. "This is not some kelterfish that you can snag with that tiny hook. Get back. I need room."

His look was one of surprise that quickly changed to terror.

"Your face," he murmured. "It's changing—"

"I've got to concentrate." she yelled at him. "Get behind me—all of you!"

With that, she pushed him again, this time with so much force that he was thrown back into the group of watchers, knocking some of them over with him. Most of them were stumbling over themselves anyway in their hurry to escape. She allowed herself a deep-throated chuckle at their pitiful display, before she turned her full attention on the new shape she was weaving. It was as if an old nightmare was waking in her, bringing with it ancient rage that burned out of control. She was becoming lost in it, consumed by the overwhelming need to protect her keep and oust the usurper. The cries of her enemy were now deafeningly close.

Without warning, the cavern was darkened, as a huge form swallowed the light. The drakyn filled the archway, its claws pawing at the rock as it crumbled beneath its weight. The sound of falling rock faded down the mountainside.

For a second, she thought the creature might lose its grip and fall, but the mighty claws simply buried themselves into the rock as easily as if it they were biting into rotting flesh. Leathery wings flapped at the air, sending gusts of putrid wind toward them. The stench was alien and nauseating, the smell of death that had been denied far past its time. The drakyn opened its mouth, blowing steam through ragged rows of blood-stained teeth. When it shook its huge, bony head, ribbons of cartilage wrapped and unwrapped themselves around its long neck. Its huge, sack-like body was almost comically stuffed into the confined space.

The drakyn stepped forward to face Nikki, who now sported an equally gruesome visage. The drakyn's speech came out as a grating whine, painful to human ears.

"You make a pathetic drakyn," it screeched. "But I see through your flimsy guise. I know you, Nikkitheis Tyaborne, and in this form or another, I will eviscerate you. Tonight, I'll feast on the vermin who have stolen my keep. Like rats, you'll run from the nest, and I'll eat you one by one, vile *hifn*."

The creature spat out the word in the ancient tongue of the drakyn, more a hiss than a word, and somehow Nikki understood from ancient memory that he'd used the drakyn word for the ultimate blasphemy, human.

The creature was larger and more frightening than any nightmare, and she feared that it was right; the form she had taken might not be enough to defeat it, although it had taken all her strength to fill it. She knew instinctively that the true shape of the drakyn was much smaller, though larger than a human. There was no time to create a more accurate transmogrifee, and she didn't think it would matter. Her opponent might have spent days on his creation, perhaps incorporating other living and non-living flesh to create this monstrosity.

Nikki tried to match the other drakyn's size. She could feel her own essence being stretched as tight as a drumskin. She feared that the shell she had created would be quickly deflated by those slashing claws, each tipped with odious brown stains. But she knew that to succumb to her fear now would mean death for them all. She used the last of her energy to take the transmogrifee one step further, from the deceptive arts into the art of being. Wild and unreasoning ecstasy filled her as the essence of the beast grew inside her. Now she truly was a drakyn, a creature as deep and dark as the space between life and death, and just as dangerous.

She turned to the little creatures behind her to tell them to run, but all that came out was a wheezing, rumbling hiss. She saw the horror of what she'd become on their faces. Those few who remained, now scattered, all but one, who scurried from the shadows, dragging a tiny shaft that appeared far too heavy for it to wield alone.

Nikki forgot the humans and put her whole soul into the thing she'd become, calling up the darkest, deepest parts of herself. She was no longer Nikki. She was queen of the keep and she would defend it with her life. She pulled a deep breath into powerful new lungs and turned to face her rival.

The other drakyn took a step into the cavern, ducking its massive head to fit into the now cramped quarters. Its tail came forward from where it had been hanging over the edge and writhed in dizzy circles before her. At its tip was a vile snake's head with dripping yellow fangs and burning amber eyes. These eyes fixed on her with hypnotic intensity. The snake's head lunged at her before she could even imagine a defense. Burying its fangs deep into her shoulder, it began to suck her lifeblood away.

Nowhere in her dreams had she seen this ghastly aberration. She screamed a drakyn's primeval screech of fear and agony. The tiny human part of her that remained, probably saved her life. It reasoned calmly that, though the snake's jaws had clamped down with such a vise-like grip that it was unlikely to be torn out without ripping half her side with it, there might still be a chance, if only the blood loss didn't kill her before she had time to do what she intended. Already, she felt her heart labor as the blood was being sucked from her body. But instead of fighting it, she let her body slump forward, closing her eyes. The sound of claws grating on stone told her that the drakyn was drawing up to make the final kill. She forced herself to wait until she felt his foul breath on her skin. At the last possible second, she pulled herself up and lunged with all her remaining strength, biting deep into the other drakyn's neck. When the snake's head loosened its grip just enough, she ripped it from her shoulder with a foreclaw, flinging it with so much force that it hit the far wall with a wet smack. The other drakyn let out a cry that shook the very rock, but the hideous tail lay limp and bleeding where it fell.

Brown blood spurted from the wound in her shoulder, but she had no time to staunch it. Instead, she tightened her grip on the pulsating neck of her enemy.

What followed was a bloody blur of flailing limbs and wings as the beasts lost all control in their hunger for blood. They rolled together on the stone floor while the whole mountain shivered with their thrashing.

With her teeth still deeply embedded in the other drakyn's neck, Nikki felt claws ripping at her abdomen, and a sticky fluid, that she realized must be her own blood, tickled her skin. She knew she couldn't hold on much longer. If she didn't bleed to death herself, she might drown on the other drakyn's blood, that now filled her throat with an agony of liquid fire.

With the last of her strength, she forced the monster back. They lay locked together at the cliff's edge. She felt the rock crumbling beneath them, and a surge of victory filled her. She would plunge them both to their deaths, and her keep would be safe.

She was dimly aware of a tiny form beside them. The pitiful little human was still there, digging at her opponent with that tiny, barbed hook in a futile attempt to break its scaly skin. One of their struggling claws caught it, perhaps without even intending to, and the little creature was thrown back against the wall where it lay very still.

Something about this rankled her, though she couldn't remember why it should, and she pulled her fangs from the other drakyn to let out a deafening scream of rage. As she did so, a huge section of the floor gave way, and her opponent flapped his wings in a feeble and desperate attempt to keep his balance. She grabbed one of his flailing wings in her powerful jaws and heard a popping noise as bone, cartilage, and socket separated, then the shredded wing was ripped from her jaws, and her enemy fell from sight. She attempted to follow the progress of his fall, but dizziness overtook her, and she too fell into darkness, to remember no more as a drakyn that day.

CHAPTER EIGHT

Master's New Pet

D reyk woke with fire in his head, the nightmare still clinging to him like some hideous beast he couldn't shake. He tried to lift his head, but the fire only flared stronger. He reached over to grasp the edge of his cot on *Windsinger*, but someone had stuffed it with seagrass, instead of the soft fleece he'd bought in the bazaar at Tia Cara. He tore at it in frustration, calling to Chendri, but there was no answer.

Then he remembered. The crenda was gone, destroyed. And that was only the beginning of the nightmare. He was being held in a den of daemons who could alter their shapes at will. They were twisting his mind, torturing him with visions of horribly grotesque monsters. He opened his eyes to face them and demand a quick and merciful death, but when he did, he saw only the lovely face of Kia the healer, her brows furrowed with worry.

"You've slept long," she said simply.

He tried to ask for water, but the words wouldn't form themselves. She appeared to understand anyway and helped him raise his head to the cup she offered. The water was sweet and helped to ease the fire in his head.

"I had a horrible dream. A witch transmogered into this wretched beast and..." he began, and the words took all his strength. He lay back in the soft grass bed and slept again.

When he woke, his head was clearer. He realized that he was in the healer's hall. He felt dry and empty, as if some terror had been stolen from him, and perversely, he wanted it back. He looked around for Kia, but she was nowhere in sight. He glimpsed a movement behind him and turned to find himself face to face with the biggest grella he'd ever seen. Though he'd seen the huge felines from a distance, he'd always given them a wide birth. He'd never been this close to one. It was an impressive sight.

"I hope you're not hungry," he whispered, not expecting a reply. As far as he knew, grellas had no developed speech. To his amazement, the grella replied in an odd growling tone. After a moment, Dreyk realized that he could understand some of the words.

"I've just eaten, thank you," said the cat. "Besides, I've found male human flesh to be tough and tasteless."

"How fortunate for me," he replied, swallowing hard. "I'm Dreyk."

"I know. You're my master's new pet. Perhaps you can wake her."

Dreyk wasn't excited about being referred to as a pet, but he also wasn't about to offend the grella in any way, at least until he was sure the cat really had no taste for human flesh, male or otherwise.

"I don't know. I guess I can try," he replied. "Where is she?"

"This way."

The grella headed off faster than Dreyk could follow, so he lifted himself from his bed painfully and, when he had his balance, headed in the general direction the cat had taken. He came to an open glade with giant blue leaves overhanging an organic doorway. Here the cat sat waiting patiently. As soon as Moonchaser saw Dreyk, he disappeared into the doorway. Dreyk followed, ducking his head under the fragrant leaves as he entered the room. Before him, the only occupant lay in an unnaturally still sleep.

The grella sat back on his haunches beside the prone form and stood still as a stone lion himself. Before him, lay a frail woman with pale hair fanned out around a pallid face, making her appear small and vulnerable. Bloodstained fingers rested motionless on her chest. Purple bruises covered her exposed skin, while bandages wrapped everything else.

He wondered what disaster had befallen this poor woman, and his heart filled with compassion. She looked too young to have such pain. As he watched her, something in her face triggered his ailing memory. Round lips, a little too full for the face, lovely almond eyes and an adventurous spirit with little experience to back it up, a great strength hidden until it had been called for. Then he remembered it all. She wasn't a beast, as he had dreamed. She was just a fighter who had worked a great transmogrifee to defeat a monster. Gazing at her quiescent form, he knew that he could never completely fear or hate her for what she could do. It changed something in him, something that had lived in terror of the unknown, now awakened to the fact that, in this case at least, the unknown was not something he should be afraid of.

He sank down beside her, his limbs shaking and his head pounding with the effort it had taken to get this far. He lifted one of her limp hands with infinite care.

"Nikki. You created a greater force than I could ever have dreamed possible, to protect us."

The woman stirred in her sleep but didn't wake.

He mumbled as if to himself, "You must have defeated the drakyn. We're safe. You can wake up now."

The woman stirred again, and pain twisted her face. He regretted disturbing her sleep for a second, but then her eyes opened and locked onto his as if he were her anchor to the waking world. She spoke in a hoarse whisper.

"Yes, we did it. The beast is gone, at least for now."

"So, it takes a fisherman to wake you when the most talented healers have exhausted all their wiles trying," said Kia, who had stepped up quietly behind them. She knelt and hugged Nikki carefully but with emotion. Tears filled her eyes.

"I'm so glad you're back with us. You slept so long, I despaired of your ever waking. I used all my craft and some things I shouldn't know, and still you slept."

"How long?" whispered Nikki.

"Nearly four days."

"What? I must get up."

Kia held her down and spoke soothingly.

"The drakyn is gone. He fell into the ocean, dead. You've got to rest a little longer. There's nothing to fear now."

"No," rasped Nikki. "A nightmare can't be drowned. Drakyn can only be killed by removing heart or head, and sometimes that isn't even enough. He'll be back, and we aren't ready."

"You're still lost in dreams, Nikki. Rest and think no more of daemons. You're safe here."

"Yes—for now," said Nikki, as she drifted back toward sleep. "I'll just have a little rest, then I'll..."

When she was breathing deeply, Dreyk turned to Kia.

"Will she be alright?" he asked quietly.

"Yes, now she should rest in natural sleep, not the artificial state on the edge of death that she had occupied. But you look exhausted too. Let me help you back to bed."

"I think it's hunger, more than fatigue. I believe I could even stomach that atrocious kelp mush you make here. I'm that famished."

Kia took another look at Nikki, who was now sleeping peacefully, and turned to Dreyk with mischief in her eyes.

"Then perhaps you'd like my delicacy, fish-eye stew."

Dreyk responded with an exaggerated groan, realizing that, in his present state of hunger, even fish-eye stew sounded good.

As they left the room, the grella padded softly at their heels, licking his chops.

Dreyk swirled the gratefully anonymous contents of his soup bowl with absent-minded intensity. At this hour, the meal hall was almost empty, except for a few stragglers like him. He spent most of his time here now, or in the nearby healing chamber. While Nikki was recovering well, she was still unable to leave Kia's care, and he hesitated to do much exploring alone. Though he hadn't yet been affected by any transmogrifee, he could feel it now, the prickling on his skin that told him it was near. He wished more than ever to escape this place, but where would he go, and how?

In the days since his own recovery, he'd made no friends here. The barriers between talented and artless appeared insurmountable, and the subtle feeling that he might be in danger if he revealed that he was totally bereft of transmograffic talent kept him from opening up to anyone. Then there was the problem of vernacular and basic point-of-view: How did you explain sailing to someone who couldn't even imagine it, or boatbuilding to someone who would never need to use his hands to fashion anything?

The soup sloshed over onto the table, and he looked up nervously. He noticed a young man watching him from down the table. He was probably still in his teens, and a wild mass of sandy brown hair framed a pixie-like face with an upturned nose. His mischievous expression made Dreyk think of the trickster, the mythical creature of Kraida legend who tied your shoelaces together when you weren't looking and made bread fall to the floor, butter side down. He was slight, but with well-muscled shoulders and strong hands. He fidgeted in his seat, as if about to burst with barely controlled energy. He scooted down the bench to sit across from Dreyk. His sparkling brown eyes returned Dreyk's gaze with a knowing look.

"I have no aura," blurted the boy. "That's what you see, or rather what you don't see."

"Forgive me if I was staring," replied Dreyk. "I'm afraid I can't detect auras. To be quite honest, it was your hands I was noticing; they're callused. I was beginning to think that no one actually *worked* here."

The boy laughed. "Oh, the brennen work, believe me, but the youngest highborn knows a transmogrifee of protection or healing to prevent this." He gestured at his calloused hands. "Those are abilities I will never have. I'm totally lacking in transmograffic talent."

The boy said these words in a matter-of-fact tone, but Dreyk had to wonder. How difficult must it have been to grow up deaf and blind to transmogrifee, in a place where transmograffic acts were woven into every aspect of daily life? Already he could relate to this boy.

"I had sort of the opposite problem in my homeland. In Kraida, transmogrifee is forbidden, but it's still practiced in alleys, behind closed doors. Whenever the slightest creation is worked, I can feel it. It eventually made me an unwilling outcast in my own land."

"As am I, or at least soon to be. My name is Benna. I'm Nikki's brother."

Dreyk was silent for a minute. So far, he'd met no one he felt he could trust. Was this boy different? Deciding that eventually, he would have to trust someone, he said, "I see the resemblance now, but let me ask, if I can be blunt, how have you survived here? I've overheard talk of even the talented who lost favor or power and were never seen again. I wondered if I might not suffer the same fate soon. I didn't realize how much Nikki was protecting me until now."

Benna rubbed his face and replied, "It's unlikely that any harm will befall you, since Nikki has shown an interest in you. No one is willing to test her, even while she's still weak. She has a great talent, always has. She's protected me as much as she could since our parents died, but it hasn't been easy for her, watching my back and hers at the same time. But I think I've found a solution," he said with a wink.

Benna was silent for a second, as if making up his mind on some point, then he leaned forward, speaking softly for Dreyk's ears alone. "I heard you asking Klev the cook about the six-hundred steps."

"Yes, but his answers were not encouraging. It sounds like a treacherous route, and it could take days to reach the arid plains below, with no way to get fresh supplies or water along the way. It seems a miracle that your people ever found this place, though I suppose a transmogrifer could simply sprout wings and fly—"

"Exactly what I had in mind," interrupted Benna.

"But you said you could work no transmogrifee."

"I can't, but when one organ is damaged, others compensate. I've spent my whole life learning to use these." He held up his scarred hands. "At first, I worked on a raft sturdy enough to survive the tides of Obrion, but lately, I've given up on that idea. The storms are just too dangerous. But I have the answer now. She will be our lady of rescue! If you want, I'll take you up to the peaks to see her, but we've got to hurry. The sun is near setting."

Dreyk was intrigued, but also a little leery of the boy's eccentric energy. The fear that he might be dealing with the village lunatic followed close behind him as he chased Benna through the maze of tunnels. The way grew progressively darker, but the boy didn't once slacken his pace, and Dreyk found himself lagging behind. At last, Benna stopped, and Dreyk came up beside him, breathing hard.

"Stay close," said Benna. "We're in the older parts now. The walls get quite opaque before we reach the top. I suspect that this was once the drakyn's back door, but no one uses it now." Soon, the way grew too dark to navigate safely, and Benna pulled up abruptly. Kneeling, he pulled a crystal jar, half-filled with a clear fluid that appeared to be water, from his pack. He unscrewed the lid, grasping it by a handle in the form of a golden snake. He dumped a handful of foul-smelling green powder into the jar. Dreyk jumped as light exploded inside, illuminating the tunnel walls with a sickly green glow. Dreyk wore a suspicious expression as he bent over the glowing orb.

"Either you lied about having talent, or you've discovered a new kind of lantern."

"Oh, there's no transmogrifee in this. I discovered it when I was a kid. I needed something to see with in these old tunnels. The powder is ground from emerock. It burns on contact with water, no talent required."

"How strange, but perhaps I could use this at sea. It appears to burn cleaner and brighter than marm oil, if you can get used to that sickly green color. That is, if I ever sail again," he added softly.

They went on. Gradually the light increased, until the lantern was no longer needed. Turning a corner, they came abruptly out on top of the mountain, the light momentarily blinding them. Benna set his lantern near the entrance and hurried forward.

When he stepped out, Dreyk swayed with vertigo. The two peaks that Benna pointed out as Shelat and Ibor stood to either side, so close it seemed he could touch them. To the east, the sky was a hazy blue curtain over the desert. Around them, boulders baked in the sunseason heat. No plants, no signs of life, not even lichen or insects, were evident.

They worked their way over this rock maze until they neared the cliff's edge. Here, the rock gave way to a shale platform. The cliff was so steep and precipitous that they couldn't see the mountainside below them. Dreyk peered tentatively over the edge, not knowing how secure the ledge might be. He wasn't overly fond of heights, and the thought of falling from here made him dizzy. He searched for the horizon to steady himself, but it was lost in the distant haze, which led him to realize just how far from home he really was.

He turned from the disquieting view to the strange object that Benna was pointing out to him with pride. At first, it was hard to distinguish anything amid the glittering rubble of a thousand seemingly random elements. It was adorned with brightly colored sheer fabrics, flickering gold and croma ropes and hoops, and flapping, papery sheets of unknown material in every imaginable color and shape.

Dreyk must have stared at Benna in stark disbelief because the boy's nervous energy only increased.

"Well, I need to clean up a bit," murmured the boy as he started to pull loose objects away from a larger shape. To Dreyk's amazement, an almost recognizable craft was revealed. Three approximately chair-sized baskets hung from a framework that supported a large, diaphanous wing.

Dreyk assumed that the third had been designed for Moonchaser. Would the big cat agree to such a flight?

"I've been working like a madman to finish this before the seasonal winds come," continued Benna. "These ropes are to hold it down: the evening updraft can be quite wicked up here in the warm season."

Dreyk said nothing, thinking, *like a madman?*

"What do you think?" continued Benna, "I named her *Hawkwind*. I know she lacks some precise steering capabilities, but after all, we only need to reach the desert floor."

"It's the speed with which we would reach it that worries me," said Dreyk at last.

"Oh, she'll fly. I know it!"

"What does Nikki think of this plan?"

Benna studied his feet.

"You haven't told her about it yet, have you?"

"You don't understand!" blurted Benna. "When you grow up with talent as she did, you don't have any choice. You've got to be the best, or someone will eliminate you as a threat. And even when you get to the top, it usually doesn't last very long." Benna became uncharacteristically still. At last, he said, "No Master Artisan has ever died of old age. We must leave Mistra soon."

"How long do you think she has?"

"There's a council meeting in a few days. There've been rumors—"

"You hope to convince her to leave before she is eliminated by her enemies."

"Yes, that's a little blunt, but I'm really worried. I haven't been able to convince her of the danger, even though leaving is all we've dreamed of for years. She's afraid to make a leap into the unknown, and she uses her responsibilities here as an excuse. I fear that we've already waited too long, and when the attack comes, there will be little warning. She's still weak from the fight with the drakyn. Moonchaser guards her, but even with his help, she won't be able to combat them, especially if several of the highborn move against her together. But Moonchaser and I have conspired. If she's injured, he'll come to get me. If her power is depleted in the battle, she'll be unable to work a change, and it'll be up to Hawkwind and me to get us out of here. No one suspects me because I have no talent. We'll be gone long before the arrogant fools realize what's happened. And there's another thing I've got to consider." Here Benna hesitated, as if not wanting to give reality to his thoughts. "If Nikki doesn't survive, I'll be alone. Many would see me as an easily eliminated nuisance."

"You really have thought this thing through, haven't you?" Dreyk looked at the boy with new respect. "Perhaps you're right."

Dreyk stood in thought for a long moment, gazing absently, first at the distant horizon, then at the makeshift glider. He spoke, as if to no one in particular, "The moons be with us, but I can't see another way."

Then he turned to face Benna. "Can you rig this beast to carry another?"

CHAPTER NINE

The Amoeba Memoirs

S emli was not feeling himself. Although it's difficult to kill a drakyn, it takes energy to heal wounds, and in his fight with Nikki and the ensuing fall, his energy stores had been seriously depleted. She'd caused much damage with her claws and teeth, and without the use of his wings, he'd hit the ocean with full force, crushing most of his internal organs. Fortunately, he'd had the presence of mind to begin the change before he even hit the water. The extent of his wounds made it necessary to choose a primitive life form, one that could heal itself more readily than a complex organism, self-amputating the useless parts and cloning new ones. As amoeba, he could alter his shape by extending and retracting his pseudopods, using far less energy than larger organisms needed to survive.

He'd done it by instinct, and that had saved his life. He'd existed so long in that microbial purgatory that his parts returned there by instinct, even though his semi-consciousness screamed "no" as he did it. But there was a slight hitch to his emergency plan; he had no brain. Without a brain, unaided, he would have no way of returning to a sapient form. As he had for the last eight-hundred years, he bobbed on the turbulent waters as a simple-celled amorphous mass of protoplasm. He was unseeing and unseen, except for a curious kelterfish, who nibbled on a trailing bit of unpalatable flesh and spat it out.

He found the entrance to the Marm cave by chance, as the current pulled him through the narrow channel and up into the quiet pool. It was an accident that saved his life. It was often said that Semli was lucky, but it was more than that; he appeared to have a disregard for life that always gave him an edge. He thought that the one who cares least about winning would win again and again. This is what he believed, at any rate, and at least this one time, it proved true.

Akriast found him there, and at first, she didn't even recognize him, thinking that it was her hopes that gave life to a pale mass floating just beneath the surface of the water. But she detected a delicate aura there, albeit the strange cool tint of an organism living without thought. She stepped into the water and waded out to it, pulling it back with her to the shallows, where she maneuvered it gently into her lap, feeling for life.

Yes, there was a primitive heart forming, and some healing had already begun. The damaged wing had been discarded, and here and there, the heat of life's activity glowed as cells cloned themselves into the needed mass and shape.

Akriast carefully laid the creature back into the water and stepped ashore to reach for her herbs and pigments. She mixed up a healing poultice of lizardweed and hynia, applying this to the gaping yellow wounds. Here and there, she sprinkled mugwort and azure pigment for growth, with a few quiet words of encouragement. Semli's aura gained some color, and a rudimentary brain stem grew under her coaxing touch.

In time, Semli's more complex drakyn shape began to emerge, but Akriast was almost embarrassed for him. What warrior had such deformed, withered limbs and mottled skin? There was something terribly wrong with Semli. No wonder he never wore his true shape, and his mother would not be seen with him in that form. Yes, an embarrassment to drakynkind, he was, but there was no doubt that

Semli was good at what he did, and for that alone he was worth keeping around. She imagined him in the human shape he had most often donned, that of a young prince, long of limb and dark-haired, with the unconscious grace and charisma that had brought all the young court hopefuls to his chamber at the palace of the queens, all those years ago.

Semli, as a human being, lay naked on the rocky pool's edge. As the water dried on his skin, he shuddered with the cold, and the primordial half-memory of what he had been. If he ever had the patience to write his memoirs, he'd have to leave out the last eight-hundred years, plus a few other moments not worth remembering, like his death at the hands of Wren Weatherspring.

Akriast gave him her cloak, laying it over him and adjusting it with a maternal tuck.

Stuttering with the cold, he rasped, "I sh-should th-thank you for pulling me from th-that hell, not once, but twice. I owe you for that."

"You'll get a chance to repay us, young one."

"Is mother upset with my failure?"

"She knows that these things happen. Shen is occupied now solidifying our political position, an odious task, but it must be done. Tonight, she will confront Nikki at the council meeting."

"I'm sure that mother will have much to say about my inadequacies now." Semli's deep voice was barely audible as he hung his head.

"On the contrary, I blame myself," soothed Akriast. "Nikki is proving more of a threat than I thought possible. You needed to arrive from the outside, diverting suspicion from us, but it gave her time to prepare. She put up quite a fight and has a nasty predilection for survival. I should've known better than to send you out to such a battle. I'd forgotten that your strength has always been in treachery and deceit. Open warfare does not become you. A claw in the back is more your style."

Semli responded well to her flattery. Warmth and color returned to his skin. "Well, it did seem so blatantly melodramatic," he whined. "I felt a posturing fool, all that fletshit about eating the rats as they ran from the nest, and who knew she could take drakyn form?"

"I think that the girl has hidden talents," Akriast mused. "But I have a plan to eliminate her before she gets any stronger, without risk to any of us," she added, seeing his expression turn hopeful.

"Then I can rest," sighed the prince, leaning back.

"Unfortunately, no," said Akriast. "We may need you again. I said, 'if all goes as planned.' There's a slim chance she could survive, in which case she will undoubtedly try to escape Mistra. If that happens, it'll be your job to follow and eliminate her, far from informing eyes. She must disappear without a trace. Do it any way you choose, poison, paid assassin, knife in an alley or death by overweening desire. I don't care how, just get her out of our way.

"And there is another thing that might pique your interest."

Semli's eyes took on an intense focus. "What?"

"Wren and Trey are here. It's your chance to get revenge for the hell she condemned you to for the last eight centuries."

"That's more like it," said Semli in a stronger voice. As he pulled himself up to a sitting position, the robe fell away, revealing his broad, muscular chest, dark nipples, and trim torso. With one firm hand he lazily scratched the scar on his neck where it itched from the rapid healing.

"I think I'm going to enjoy this," he crooned, and his face lit up with moon-white teeth and a broad, almost unbearably charming smile.

CHAPTER TEN

Out of my Depth

Nikki confronted Tbrin on her way to the council meeting. Since her recovery, Tbrin had been noticeably absent, causing Nikki's anger and suspicion to grow to explosive proportions. He saw her coming and stopped in the hall, his expression one of resignation.

"I know that drakyn was no illusion, Tbrin. Somehow, it was the real thing, wasn't it? You knew," she hurried on, her anger erupting. "You knew all along that the drakyn would return, and you told me nothing. For all I know, you brought the beast yourself!"

"No, I didn't! This isn't the place for this discussion, Nikki. I'm sorry for what happened, but you must believe that I had nothing to do with it. I was occupied with the other. It was my duty to prevent this, a duty that I have failed utterly. For some time, I've known that my own powers were dwindling. In fact, this waning of talent has begun to affect the entire aerie. Don't you feel it? After so long, I thought the danger was over, but I was wrong. Somehow, she's found a way to recall these abominations, and now we must fight them."

"Them? How many are there?"

"I think there are as yet only two, though the moons know that two of those monsters is enough to destroy an entire world."

Tbrin looked around nervously, then continued in a hushed voice. "I should've told you everything from the beginning, but I didn't want to involve you in this if I didn't have to. I thought I could handle it myself. Now I need your help. But I can't say more here. Meet me at the dreaming pool after the council meeting."

Tbrin turned away before she could ask him more. As she watched his cloaked form disappear down the hall, she wondered if she should trust him, and if she had a choice.

Nikki was alone in the council chamber. She settled into the Master Artisan's chair with her usual reluctance. It was such a pretentious affair, all crystal, gems, and magna-gold. It would have made the largest Mistran look small and vulnerable. She could imagine how ridiculous and fragile she must look in it now. Her eyes traveled around the massive stone walls of the council hall, each section etched in twenty-foot-high relief with the deeds of each Master Artisan, to the blank wall that awaited her great works, for her triumphs. She wondered what the record would show, or even if she would rank a spot at all. Perhaps she would just be conveniently forgotten as an embarrassment to the highborn.

She had defeated the drakyn once, but that would be little help if he nursed his wounds in the mountains, only to return stronger and even more vengeful. The drakyns' capacity for violence was legendary, as was their skill at transmogrifee. Cunning, cruelty, deceit, and torture, these had been the high arts of drakynkind. And now there were two of them loose in the world, with only her uncertain talents and the questionable loyalty of Tbrin to defend against them. It was an ancient vow, made by the first warrior-artisans at the end of the drakyn wars, but it was her sworn duty to defend Mistra against the drakyn. With the aid of the drakyn's eye, the Master Artisan was said to be invincible, but the actual methods used to defeat the drakyn were lost. Who

would ever have thought that the legends would become reality again
after so long?

She leaned back in the massive chair, and it seemed that the weight
of the stifling air would overwhelm her. Reminding herself for the
hundredth time that she had never wanted this position, she let out
a deep sigh. She knew that there were others more fit. Crea or Nashi
would have been better choices for Master Artisan. Both were great
artists in their own right, but perhaps with a strength that she lacked.
Only of late had she begun to understand the politics of her position.
Her talent was in diplomacy and arbitration. She had been chosen to
appease the Golden Sect, who preached peace and art above all else.
And she knew why she had accepted the position of Master Artisan.
As a potential to the throne, she would have been a threat to anyone
who was chosen. Without the drakyn's eye to enhance her power, she
would be an easy target. At the time, it had been an obvious choice
between life and death. Now it didn't look quite as simple. In fact, it
had begun to look like no choice at all.

She stepped down from the throne, struggling in irritation with
her gilt ceremonial gown on the steps. At the bottom, she leaned her
forehead against the clear stone of the crystal tank that circled the hall.
Inside it, captive fishes swam with determination. On and on they
swam, day after day, forever moving in a circle and never finding escape. In this never-ending spectacle, they lived out their lives, unaware
that they were less than free or that there was more to life than what
they could see. Was she not the same?

"I feel like you, out of my depth and on display for everyone's
amusement," she whispered into the tank.

Whose idea had it been to create this tank? she wondered. Probably
Cressdan. He always found a way to humiliate others in the name of
art and beauty. Was he her enemy, or only one of them? She really
didn't think him capable of bringing forth such a dangerous creature

as a drakyn. It would have taken a great deal of skill and years of preparation. He just didn't have the depth of deviousness that was required. And Tbrin had said, "she." *Who then?*

She pushed herself away from the tank as she felt the first of the council members coming. Still far down the hall, two of them were approaching. She pushed her hearing to encompass them, touching gently so that neither would be aware of her eavesdropping. They were speaking in hushed tones, no louder than the brush of their marmskin robes on the slick, cold stone of the hall.

One was Gril, always early to council and feast hall, always with the longest speech and the least to say, a big man who had always reminded Nikki of a giant pufferfish: full of air but having little substance. With him was Kinsa, a stocky redhead who alone seemed never to tire of Gril's ramblings. They were lovers, but Nikki thought it less a matter of affection than political expediency. They must have thought they were well out of her range, for they were whispering openly of her demise.

"She'll never make it past moonfall," whispered Gril. "If the council doesn't replace her, then an assassin will take her by morning."

"The attack from this vile creature has left her weak and vulnerable, and no one knows for sure that she killed it. The golden sect will no longer have the strength of the past. They will not protect her when a challenger steps forward. Akriast has been seen of late in the tower of stars, and she has been visibly absent from chamber meetings. So unlike her, the old busybody."

She felt rather than heard the harumph of disbelief from the other man.

"Akriast? What power could she have left to challenge the Master Artisan? She's nothing but a burned-out old bag of bones and spite!"

At these words, Nikki drew back, not needing to hear more.

She told herself that no one was strong enough to challenge her, at least not while she still controlled the drakyn's eye. However, there remained the problem of who had recalled the drakyn. She assumed it had been an act of transmogrifee. Long dead species did not just reappear out of the air. And if there were two of these vile creatures now, where were they hiding? Why hadn't they attacked again?

Her mind was frantically going over the possibilities, when Gril and Kinsa entered the hall. She pulled herself out of her reverie to offer them the formal greeting. Then there were other arrivals, and she went through the motions of her office in a daze.

She became aware that the last calling bell had been rung. She took her place at the head of the room and raised her arms; the signal that discussion—or challenge—could begin, but the challenge was only brought after the death or abdication of the Master Artisan. It had only rarely been used while a Master Artisan still held power.

To her chagrin, Akriast stepped forward confidently. Pulling from her tunic the red banner of challenge, she waved it high above her head. Akriast had to wait for the shouts of astonishment to die down before she could speak. Was that a look of victory in her eyes?

"Friends, it is our misfortune to be the warders of our aerie now, during these trying times," spoke Akriast. "Before us lies great upheaval and change. It will be our responsibility to ensure the continued survival and prosperity of our people. If the drakyn can now return from ancient times to attack us, none will be safe."

She looked toward Nikki. "It is far from my desire to speak ill of Nikkitheis TyaBorne, who has held the chair with such grace and wielded the drakyn's eye so ably. If you recall, it was I who nominated her. But times have changed, and a stronger hand is now needed."

"Who would you recommend, Akriast, a doddering old woman like yourself, perhaps?" That from Gril, who had never tried to hide his dislike for Akriast. Nikki knew that Gril was a secret member of a militaristic faction who counseled raiding parties to find gentler, more productive places to live. They always seemed to fail to mention that such lands would undoubtedly already have residents who would want to keep their lands, and lives, for themselves. Nikki believed that there had to be a balance, a way they could live in peace. And because the drakyn's eye made it possible for them to live quite comfortably in Mistra, the sect had never been taken seriously.

Before Akriast could respond to Gril's attack, Cressdan stepped forward. He was a tall, imposing man whose size gave weight to his words. When he spoke, it was in the slow, dry manner that characterized his speech.

"Let us be blunt and waste no time. None now will challenge Mistress TyaBorne. She is young and extraordinarily strong in talent. Akriast, you are old and frail. Alone, you would not stand a chance against her, even if her defeat of the drakyn has weakened her. Which, I will remind you, she accomplished unaided. It is in all our best interests to retain her. Perhaps she lacks the bloodthirsty militarism that certain sects still advocate, but there are none now living who could out-transmoger her. Were she threatened, her attackers might find more than one who would stand with her."

Nikki was touched and surprised by his loyalty, even if it was based more than a little in his own keenly developed sense of self-preservation. Akriast and Cressdan had been enemies for years. Cressdan knew well that any council that Akriast controlled would not be a healthy place for him.

But Akriast appeared undaunted by his scathing words. Instead, she stepped to one of the curtained anterooms to the side of the hall, pulling the fabric aside with a flourish.

"None now living, you say, Cressdan. But perhaps you will change your tone. I have not been idle, letting the horrors of our past creep up on us unawares. The portents have been clear for centu–years," she corrected herself. "I have recalled one who will aid us, a great warrior-artisan of earlier times, who fought the drakyn with her mighty skills and knew them well. She will lead us now."

As Jelebron stepped out, a tense quiet gripped the hall. Nikki noticed that nothing had been spared to effect. The woman stood tall, imperious, and regal in a flowing mantle, collared with the finest marmskin and studded with tiny twinkling stars. Her auburn hair glowed with inner fire, obviously enhanced, and her emerald eyes flashed a challenge that caused many in the room to drop their eyes in fear. Under her crimson cape, she wore a war harness of an unfamiliar dark gray leather, and at her waist hung a brilliant sword of croma, in an intricately woven scabbard of leather. In horror, Nikki became suddenly aware of the texture, color and smell of the leather she wore. To all appearances, the queen wore the tanned hide of a human being. Nikki looked around, but all she saw on the faces of the group was awe.

Did no one else see her for what she was?

Jelebron gazed at the council members with an expression that made each one question themselves. When she spoke, Nikki felt a strange prickling on her skin and knew that the woman was using a coercion transmogrifee. To Nikki's surprise, all the faces in the room turned toward Jelebron with rapt expressions. Nikki wondered how she could be the only one to see through this woman.

"The drakyn that Nikki fought in the harvest hall was not killed," began Jelebron with a dramatic flourish. "He will return to kill us all if we are not prepared. In my time, I fought these beasts, the mighty drakyn. I know how to defend against them and how to defeat them. I offer my services now as Master Warrior to help Mistra prepare. Young Nikki will, of course, retain her position in an honorary capacity." She added this as an aside, as if it were a trivial matter.

Cressdan wasted no time, and Nikki was amazed at how quickly he and the council were capitulating. "This does change things," he began tentatively. "Though a committee surely should be formed to

address the admitted use of an illegal transmogrifee to recall the dead."
He glanced darkly at Akriast as he spoke. "And the position of Master
Warrior hasn't been filled in generations. As we are all well aware, it was
long ago replaced by the Master Artisan, who rules with this council's
aid and consent. For myself, I will acquiesce to the talent and power of
Queen Jelebron, and I would like to be the first to offer my loyalty to
her."

A murmur of consent rippled through the room.

"Wait!" yelled Nikki. "You don't even know this woman. Can't you
see that she's using her talent to sway your opinions? I still wield the
drakyn's eye. It can't be controlled by two at once, and its power can't
be taken from me while I still live and control it, both of which I intend
to do for some time. This isn't the time to panic. We are at war with
no one."

Was that a look of admiration or surprise on Akriast's face? It was
Jelebron who spoke.

"Yet war is coming, and we need to prepare for it now before it's
too late. I know how to fight, gather resources, plan attack. Of these
things, you know nothing. Besides, I think you will find that the eye
no longer will be the crutch you have made it. Look!"

With that, the queen strode forward, and Nikki thought she was
heading for her throne, but she swept by it, up the stairs to the hidden
alcove behind the throne. She brought down the wall that hid it from
view with a flash of her hand, and the eye appeared. A terrified gasp
rose from the group. Normally the drakyn's eye should have been
invisible, hidden in the disturbing reality shifts that made it impossible
for all but the most powerful even to approach it. It sat in an eerie glow
on a pedestal intricately carved in the shape of a great upturned claw.
In its bed of stone, the eye glowed with a pale light. Patterns played
across its marbled surface in a constant, unsettling dance, but as they
watched, the light appeared to fade.

More cries rose from the room as Jelebron did the forbidden, lifting the eye from its pedestal with her bare hands. Ignoring the protests, she raised it high over her head, turning it so everyone could see. To Nikki's horror, there appeared a wide crack in the surface of the stone, and out of the crack oozed a green haze.

"The eye is failing," she proclaimed loudly. "Its power soon will be lost forever. We must find a way to survive without it. We can't remain forever in this isolated keep. There are ripe lands below, fresh for the picking, colonies of the weak and the heedless. We must use our superior strength and abilities, to fight for a better land to live in, and eventually, for the rule of all Drakonia."

Akriast stepped forward quickly, sensing that Jelebron was trying to take the council too far, too soon.

"But we have time for all this," crooned Akriast in a soothing tone. "We must first work on our defenses, should the drakyn return, and form a plan for our immediate survival without the power enhancement of the eye."

Nikki stood in silent shock as she saw the source of her power and talent ebbing away. She felt vaguely sick and disoriented. How could so much have happened without her knowledge? Had her talent been fading? She had thought her recent weakness resulted from her fight with the drakyn, but now she had to face the fact that it was more than just a temporary setback. Why hadn't she seen this coming?

Akriast and Jelebron had drawn the highborn around them, and they were deep in discussion. The outcome of which was the only thing that was clear to Nikki. She had already been dethroned. How long did she have before they eliminated her? Quickly, she enveloped herself in a simple deception that would make her absence unnoticed and left the chamber.

Suddenly Jelebron appeared before her in the hallway. Nikki looked back, but the woman was also in the room behind her. Was this a projection? The tall, imposing woman looked down at her with a dismissive expression that said that Nikki was nothing more than an annoying bug to be squashed at will.

"Tbrin protects you, but the old bastart won't live forever, and then you'll be mine." The woman pushed Nikki back against the cold stone of the hall with a knurled hand, and Nikki felt trapped, her breath caught in her throat. Jelebron rubbed Nikki's breast in a casual manner. Nikki could see desire catch fire in the other woman's eyes. She felt sudden revulsion and fear. So close, the smell of the woman was overwhelming. Then Nikki realized that the smell was familiar to her.

"You're drakyn!" she gasped. Jelebron laughed, but there was a tension in the sound.

"So observant, little one. I see that the hiding doesn't work as well on you, but no one else knows, and they won't, until it's too late. Go ahead and tell them. They'll only think you're crazy." Jelebron laughed again, grabbing for her, and Nikki panicked. Pulling herself from the other woman's grasp, she sprinted down the hall, feeling like a child. Jelebron's laughter followed her, goading her on. Taking a deep breath, she forced herself to slow her pace and control her fear, but try as she might, she couldn't escape the dread that now haunted her every step.

CHAPTER ELEVEN

The Lord of Dreams

T housands of tiny boti foundered in the water and crowded against the shores of the dreaming pool. The wide, cupped leaves of the acrida trees would float on in desultory persistence until the dry winter winds blew the pool away and battered the fragile leaf boats into brittle organic dust.

Nikki sat in a stone chair at the water's edge, hugging her shoulder where it ached from her recent injury. Kia said that she was healing well, but they both knew it was a lie. Some wounds were deeper than they appeared, and some would not heal in a lifetime. She knew that the memory of the shape she had been forced to take to defeat the drakyn, and what she had pulled from her soul to do it, would stay with her until she, like the acrida leaves, became dust and flew with the heedless wind.

Often now she had the same dream, chasing slow, bleating herds of hoofed animals, a species that she had never seen in real life. She hunted them from the air, feeling the rush of the wind and a hunger unquenchable, hearing the crack of their spines as her claws hit them, tasting their milky-sweet blood.

She needed no help deciphering this dream. It spoke of her frustration and anger, but most of all her fear. If she were right about Jelebron, they were all in grave danger. But she could convince no one. Even Kia insisted that the drakyn she fought had been an illusion created by a rival. She rubbed her shoulder where it burned. That illusion had possessed one hell of a bite, she thought bitterly.

And how quickly her allies had turned on her. The promises Jelebron made seemed so transparent to her. Had humankind defeated the drakyn, only to take their place as beasts of avarice and war? She could not believe that Akriast and Jelebron could fool the entire council, but she could find no one now who would back her against them. She was alone.

She looked around, as the wind whistled through the steep peaks. Tbrin had not been here when she arrived. Soon it would be dark, and the bridge of sighs was not something that even she wanted to navigate in the dark. Nikki had to face the fact that he wasn't coming, and her doubts returned. Had he been lying? Was he in on the plot himself? Part of her just couldn't believe that he would betray her, while another part told her bitterly that it was the most likely explanation. What had he told her, really? It had all been hints and vague warnings. Now there were things she had to know, and he wasn't here. She had only one option left.

She lifted the leaf boti to her lips, downing its bitter liquor in one quick draught before she could weaken and change her mind. There were other acrida trees in the mountains, but only here in this soil did their leaves produce the drug. Some did not return from the dreaming pool, and most did not return the same. She saw no other choice now. She needed help, information. She needed a miracle. She returned the fragile boti reverently to the surface of the pool and sat back, waiting for the visions to begin.

Nikki tried to concentrate on her questions and then on nothing. She tried pacing and sitting utterly still, breathing deeply and hardly breathing at all, but none of it seemed to make any difference. Time passed, and she saw nothing. In frustration, she railed at the perverse Saint Murphy rule that the more you wanted a thing, the less likely you were to get it. When she gave up trying, the sky turned to purple, then pink. The world rocked. She was nauseous and dizzy. After a time, she noticed a large box on the far horizon. From it strode a human form, distant and bright, hanging in the sky like an early star. The tiny figure approached with purposeful strides, his white robes billowing out as if in the wind, even though the air now was unusually still.

Suddenly, he appeared just across the pool from her, so close that she could see the glow of the brightest stars behind his clear eyes. A speckled galaxy glinted from the sword at his waist, and across the ebony length of his belt strode the moons, Beckle and Meika, as if they were crossing the deep sky at night. His hair was shaped of wind, untamable and bright. Like his face, it became what she wanted it to be, but she could never completely see it, or accurately recall it later. He was the Lord of Dreams and she had come to ask him for the answers to her deepest need.

She began to speak, but he interrupted her with a flash of his capable hands. He didn't speak, yet his ideas were clear in her mind. He didn't seem to see her so much as see through her, to her fears and needs. He looked at her, and for a moment, it was all clear, what she must do and why. Knowledge filled her mind with painful speed and clarity, but it was too much for her to grasp so soon, and she fell back in the chair, screaming with the torment of it, begging him to stop.

The image cleared for a second, and she found herself looking into a chamber of the healing hall, where a woman labored in childbirth. Kia kneeled at the woman's side, her gentle, strong hands aiding in the birth. At once, Nikki realized that something was wrong. The woman doubled up in terrible pain as the baby came forth. She gasped, the scream fading into a garbled wail, then silence. The woman was dead. Kia reached down for the baby, then pulled back in terror. Something lay there, something not human, yet terribly familiar to Nikki from her nightmares. The distorted baby cried out, but no breath followed, and soon it followed its mother into darkness.

Nikki found herself feeling thankful that neither the child nor the mother had lived.

As quickly as the vision came, it was gone. The image of the Lord of Dreams faded into a haze that melted upward into the sky. His absence made her suddenly ill. She leaned over the edge of the chair and emptied her stomach. She sat back, shaken and weak. Sweat glistened on her forehead as she pushed her hair back with numb fingers. She tried to feel her fingertips, but they were gone, stolen, like her position of power. Uncertainty returned to her, and she could not remember what he'd said, what had been so clear a moment ago.

With a burst of light, his image returned. He held his sword high over her head and brought it down with all the force of his muscled arms. Being a sword of vision alone, it passed through her without harm, but she felt the ice of his disapproval in her veins. "You will undertake this journey, as I have commanded. Our future depends upon you."

Then in a flash of blue lightning, he was gone, leaving her utterly alone.

She lay back in the chair, exhausted. Her hand felt something in the sand at her side. Before her was a scroll of some thick papyrus, fortunately not made of human skin. When she opened it with shaking hands, it revealed an intricate drawing. It was a map, though of a place totally unfamiliar to her. At the bottom, in an archaic script was penned, *Kodo's Keep.*

Nikki's confusion was only increased as the memory of what the Lord of Dreams had said came back to her in fragments. What he asked of her was impossible. Was she to abandon her people now, when they needed her most? It was just impossible. Yet, if her visions of the drakyn were true, how would she stop them without a great power?

She stood on quavering legs and looked around her. She felt suddenly that the weight of what he asked was just too much for her. She just wanting to lie down and sleep forever. Behind her, she heard a resounding crack, as the chair of dreaming split in two, the huge stone falling neatly into halves on the ground. She felt dizziness overtaking her, but despite it she laughed.

"Well, that settles it then. Say no more, I'll go." With that, she fell, collapsing gently into the dry moss at the pool's edge.

As dusk was creeping in, Dreyk and Benna found her by the pool. A delicate rain was falling, dotting the water with competing silver rings that flickered in the light of the rising moons. She woke when Benna shook her gently, and she smiled up into his worried face. Moonchaser paced nearby, searching the horizon as if looking for the culprit who had harmed his mistress.

"You always seem to know when I need you, little brother. I think you've been holding out on me, and, in fact, have more talent than I do."

"It's no transmogrifee, Nikki," replied Benna in a serious tone. "We've been looking for you everywhere. Moonchaser led us here."

As they helped her to her feet, Benna took one curious glance at her map. No one said a word about the cloven chair, and Nikki was grateful that she wasn't asked to explain.

"Let us help you back to your room," said Dreyk, concern evident in his tone. "Cressida will make you some sunweed tea. You shouldn't push yourself like this. Recovery takes time."

"There's no more time left," she murmured, but said no more as they helped her down the steep way to her chambers.

The sunweed tea tasted good, and it warmed her through. The fireplace at the end of the room, with its burning kelp root, warmed their faces as they sat at a long low table in its glow. When she felt stronger and could feel her fingers again, she gave Benna a searching glance.

"I saw you looking at that map. I think you have something to say."

Benna studied his cup, his face warming to a guilty red. "There's no way to keep secrets from you, Nikki. Yes, it did seem familiar, what little I glanced of it. I was afraid that if I brought it up, you would insist on an expedition right now, and you need rest."

Seeing her resolute expression, he sighed and pulled the scroll from his pack. He laid it on the table, carefully smoothing the wrinkles from its yellowed surface.

"I've made some maps myself, but it's taken me years. I had no idea that anyone else knew of these tunnels," said Benna. "But I'm pretty sure there is no chamber here where it says, 'Kodo's Keep' in your drawing."

"This is a map of the halls of Mistra?" asked Dreyk, leaning forward to examine it.

"No, not exactly," replied Benna. "These are the oldest tunnels, unchanged since the time of the drakyn and long out of use. Exploring them is difficult, even with the emerock lantern."

"You probably wouldn't believe me if I explained," said Nikki. "But trust me, I must find this chamber. It may contain some weapon or transmograffic formula that I could use to restore order to Mistra."

"But we have a plan," began Benna, his face desperate. "You're in great danger. We must leave now, while we can."

"We've been over this many times before, Benna. I can't leave yet, not now." Her eyes were distant and hazy as she recalled her meeting with the Lord of Dreams. Now, it seemed more like a silly dream than reality. But she couldn't deny that he had counseled the same thing; leave Mistra now. Was she just being arrogant, unable to face the fact that she had failed, and now must run from everything and everyone that had made up her life so far? And run to what end? Where would they go? What could be gained in the wilderness below? Perhaps something in that chamber would give her the answers she needed, or a reason to stay.

"We must find this room tonight," she said.

"No!" cried Dreyk. "Let us search while you stay here. If we find anything, we can bring it back—"

"How would you know what to look for?" she retorted. "Neither of you have as much talent as a kelterfish!"

Seeing their hurt expressions, she immediately regretted her outburst. "Forgive me," she said gently. "I understand that you both have my welfare in mind, but to hesitate now could mean death for us all. I really do feel stronger. The acrida wine always brings with it a period of deep sleep. I feel rested now. I know what to do."

Benna and Dreyk shared a brief look of exasperation and worry, but it was obvious that they couldn't hold her back if she insisted on going.

"All right," sighed Dreyk. "But we'll take it slow, and you tell us if you feel even the slightest fatigue."

"Yes, of course, I will," she lied smoothly.

The tunnels grew increasingly dark as they walked, and Benna used his lantern to save Nikki having to work even the slightest light transmogrifee. At first, Nikki railed at his blatant over-protectiveness, but had to admit to herself that he might be right; she might need every bit of energy she possessed for the tasks ahead. She was more fatigued than she had admitted.

Though the map led them far back into the mountain, the tunnel progressed at a gentle rate of decline, and Nikki was grateful. Already her legs shook, and her shoulder ached. She wasn't sure she could have made it back up on their return along a steeper route in her exhausted state.

Benna pulled up short in the narrow tunnel, and all three of them collided. Once they had disentangled themselves, Benna pulled out the map. "We must be near the eastern overlook," he said. "Somewhere under the healer's hall, I would guess. But this is where the map goes awry. It shows a tunnel here, leading to this Kodo's Keep, but there's no tunnel here and nothing to show that there ever was."

Nikki came up beside him, grabbing the map in frustration. "There must be a tunnel. Are you sure we're in the right place?"

"I'm sure. This is it."

"But look," said Nikki with growing excitement. "Isn't the map logical? Why is this tunnel indicated here if it doesn't connect to this one on the other side?"

"I just assumed that they stopped excavating or changed their minds, but you may be right." He held up the lantern with one hand and touched the wall with the other, feeling for any crack or obviously newer stonework. "Do you think there once was a tunnel, and they filled it in?" he asked.

"No," said Nikki, with a faraway expression that gave her eyes a glassy glow in the eerie lantern light, "I think it's still here."

"What do you mean?" asked Dreyk. He put his hand to the wall tentatively, but the stone remained cold and hard and very real.

Nikki said, "Have you heard of a time lock? It will open only for those who can take themselves into a moment, a specific moment in the past. That knowledge is one of the things the Lord of Dreams gave me." Nikki's eyes lost their focus. As she spoke, she pulled an herb from her waist pouch, crushing it in her hand. The air was filled with a dry, ancient smell.

"Nikki, don't!" yelled Benna, reaching for her, but he was too slow. She was gone, vanished before their eyes, as if she had never been there.

Dreyk and Benna stood in the dark, narrow hall, waiting for Nikki to return from the dusky past, or if the corridor were a trap, they would wait in vain until they had to face the fact that she was gone forever.

Nikki followed a soft light down the tunnel. She came to a door hung with a brightly beaded, woven seagrass curtain. From inside, the shadow of a song reached her ears, sung by a clear male voice. Entering, Nikki looked across the room to the source of the light. It took her some time to adjust to the fact that, in Mistra, it was nighttime, but here in the tunnel was daylight. A large stone window opened out over the plains far below. Benna had been right; this room must be directly below the healer's hall; it shared the same view. Below the window, a man sat at a weaving loom; his ebony hair glinting in the sunshine that must reach him here for only a short time each day. The man sat unmoving, as if locked in the moment he reached up to the loom. The tune he hummed found Nikki from a great distance. The man's lips didn't move. The air was still, too still. Nikki spoke a word, twirling her hand in the air to invoke the transmogrifee taught her by the Lord of Dreams. She felt the power of what held the man and knew she could never break it. But her urge to make the pattern right, to bring this painting to life, gave her the strength to enter the time lock that held the man in thrall. As the air seemed to thaw, he spoke without turning his head. His hands continued their motion across the loom as if they'd never been still.

"Trey—I think your people call him the Lord of Dreams—said you might be coming. Long have I ached for real companionship. He comes to me in dreams too, but it's just not the same as the real thing. He can't be close to me, you know. That might destroy us both. No need pushing our luck, eh?"

The man turned to her, and Nikki was amazed by his dress. It was that of a soldier, in a once-resplendent crimson and gold uniform, now worn and dusty from wear. The medals, ribbons and gold-fringed epaulettes told her he was a high-ranking member of some army, but where and when? There were no armies in Mistra. The man was lithe, yet muscular, with olive skin and ink-black hair, except for an odd streak of gold that appeared to be his natural, not transmogered shade. His face was handsome, but severe, with a prominent nose and arching ebony brows. On his face was an expression that spoke of sorrow, of hard decisions made, and a life lived completely, on the face of a young soldier who bore it all with bravery and intelligence. It was a remarkable face, that Nikki would never forget.

"You're Kodo, of the map?" asked Nikki.

"Yes, I'm Kodo. I have much to tell you about us, about the drakyn and the war, and what we need to do now."

Nikki looked at the man in puzzlement, watching his long, deft fingers as he worked the loom. Frowning, she said, "In my time, there is no war, so it must be long after yours. I was given a map to find this place by the Lord of Dreams. Though it felt like no more than a drug-induced vision, the map is real, isn't it? I mean, I'm here, aren't I?"

The man laughed. "I can't get used to what you call Trey—the Lord of Dreams—but I guess it fits."

Nikki felt suddenly dizzy. "I need a weapon, or a great transmograffic formula. There are usurpers in the aerie. The drakyn have returned, even as the drakyn's eye is fading. I will need an army to defeat them."

The man left his loom, hurrying to Nikki's side.

"Here, sit please, you look exhausted. Let me explain. In our time, the death and misery of the transmograffic wars threatened to cast our world into Armageddon, but Wren spent her life and considerable talent to end it, as did I. But what she did only postponed the end, until now it seems we've reached this ultimate crisis. The warp and weft of destiny have brought us around to this same perplexity again, and you're caught in it with us. Warp and weft, get it? With the loom?"

Nikki's expression didn't change.

Kodo sat Nikki down at the loom, as it was the only chair in the room. Nikki sank into it heavily, rubbing her eyes. She didn't understand a thing this man said. Was he related to Tbrin? It could be the time difference between them; Kodo was from a lost world. Nikki became aware that Kodo was still speaking.

"That's why you need to find the isle with the great tree. In your time, it will bloom with the fruits of power, producing stones like the one your people possess."

Nikki looked up in confusion. "What tree? Do you mean it's the source of the drakyn's eye?"

"Yes. Legends say that ancient sailors saw the tree rise from the ocean while fishing in the Northsea. When I was a young soldier, I thought it was just another sailor's drinking tale, but later I learned that it was the truth.

"When the whole thing with Wren happened, I just ran out of time. I'd been gathering information about the location of the tree. I had to weave what I knew about its location from memory, from the information I had gathered, hoping that I could someday find a hero who could locate the isle for me, since I am bound to the aerie. I see now that the task has fallen to you. A new drakyn's eye will give you the power to bind the drakyn again, or at least control them."

Now Nikki looked at the tapestry closely. It showed the Drakyn's Teeth range, the home of Mistra's aerie, at the southern tip of a great continent. Above this landmass was another continent, close to the high pole. Between the two continents was a bewildering maze of hundreds of islands and atolls, some so small they were only dots on the map. An arrow led from one tiny isle to a large circle, which contained an enlarged inset illustration of an isle with a huge tree at its center. The tree dwarfed the isle, pendulous branches stretching far out over the ocean. On every branch hung many fruits, strangely colored, patterned like marble, but glowing, as if each created its own light.

Nikki was beginning to understand. If the fruit of this strange tree was her drakyn's eye, then perhaps there was hope. If she could find a tree covered with these eyes, she would have power beyond any force on Drakonia. She realized that it was a lot of "ifs."

"This tree is the source of a transmograffic power greater than any in the world," said Kodo. "Greater even than what the drakyn possess. It's silly, isn't it, thinking all this time that the drakyn's eyes have anything to do with the drakyn? Perhaps early humans saw how the drakyn wielded the power of the eyes. But humans have never taken the time to truly understand the drakyn. Drakyn is a human word from an ancient fable brought with them from the gardlands. The drakyn are much like humans in many ways—and in other ways so alien that other species may never grasp their intricacies. It's ironic, isn't it, that our legends say that the gods dropped human beings to this inhospitable world as punishment to humans for their sins, and the drakyn believe that men were dropped from the sky to punish them—for growing weak and careless in battle."

"I'm afraid it is I who have been weak and careless," mused Nikki. "But perhaps with this knowledge, I'll be able to rectify some of my mistakes."

Was this what the Lord of Dreams had sent her to discover? It was still muddled in her mind. She spoke her disarrayed thoughts aloud.

"How can I leave Mistra to search for this tree? It could take so long to find, that there might be nothing left of Mistra to save when I get back. Perhaps it's insane to try."

"Perhaps," said Kodo, "but no more insane than the war and all the horrors that travel with it. If I have gained anything from it, it's only that we must do more than we think we're capable of to end it. I can see how worried she is. Sometimes she sees the future and the dangers there. I can't be sure how she will act, so you and all the Mistrans must be protected, even from Wren Weatherspring.

"Your eye is dying; in time, it may just fade as if it had never been. After that happens, I can't guarantee what will happen to the Mistrans. You must find a new one. You must use all your strength, and maybe more."

"But I have no strength!" Nikki blurted. "If you only knew how foolish I've been!"

"It takes a great will and talent to enter this time that binds me. The Lord of Dreams may have aided you in finding this place, but you came through on your own. You defeated a drakyn warrior on your own. You have power untried, hidden in you. I see it in your hands and your eyes. He chose well. He has waited all this time for you to be born."

"I find that unlikely. I'm not the greatest of my time, let alone of all time."

"Yet he chose you—"

"Fine," interrupted Nikki. "But you may be right, at least about this tree. With a new drakyn's eye, I might have the power to defeat these monsters once and for all. I don't think I can find it alone, but perhaps I'll find help along the way. The alternative is to do nothing and watch the beasts take over."

Nikki turned to leave the room, but a gentle hand held her back. "Take the tapestry," said Kodo. "I can create another. I have the time." He laughed at his own poor joke as he pulled the weaving from the frame.

"You have been very kind to someone you don't even know," Nikki said.

"But I do know you. You are so much like the young girl Wren once was."

Nikki turned away. She would have liked to spend more time with Kodo, but she knew that time was running out. She accepted the gift and turned to leave without a backward glance. She didn't want to look back to see the strange sight of a soldier working at a loom, in that room where the sun burned bright in the nighttime. Often afterward she thought of Kodo sitting like that, caught in time.

"Wait!" called Kodo. "I almost forgot the needle."

When Nikki looked back, Kodo was frantically pulling the thread from a simple sewing needle.

"Your needle!" Nikki exclaimed. "Why?"

"It will point the way."

Nikki was beginning to have doubts about the sanity of this man, but she took the needle, anyway, hoping that her doubt wasn't as clearly written on her face as it was in her thoughts.

Dreyk and Benna sat with their backs to the tunnel wall, both contemplating very dark futures and pondering their next move, when Nikki reappeared before them in the same spot from where she'd vanished.

Their gasps of surprise turned to sighs of relief when they saw her standing before them, unharmed. Before either could get out a question, she rushed ahead of them back the way they'd come. They hurried to catch up.

"We've got a lot to do," she said brusquely. "We need to be ready to leave by first sun tomorrow."

"What changed your mind so quickly?" gasped Benna. "Where have you been? What are you carrying?"

Not trusting herself to explain something that she didn't fully understand herself, she said simply, "It's a rug."

"Let's hope it's a magic rug," muttered Dreyk darkly.

"Let's just hope," was her reply. But they didn't hear her, because she was already far ahead of them, almost flying down the tunnel, moving with the resolution of one who has finally found a direction.

CHAPTER TWELVE

The Devotion of a Dead Grella

I t took a long time for Nikki to find sleep. After all her preparations to leave, there were still so many things she hadn't had time to do, so many regrets and good-byes that would have to go unsaid for the sake of secrecy and speed.

Tbrin had not been in his chamber, and she didn't have the time to search for him now. She wasn't sure she wanted to confront him anyway. If he were part of the plot against her, how would she react? She asked herself again and again if she could fight him if she had to. Perhaps it was just better to leave and never know.

She was thankful that they wouldn't have to use Benna's contraption to glide to the plains. After seeing it, she had to agree with Dreyk; they would surely reach the ground, but not necessarily intact. Any winged shape she could transmoger into would get them down from the heights more reliably. Benna worried her sometimes with his wild ideas, but now that they had finally agreed to leave Mistra, he at least seemed content, probably because he didn't foresee or understand the hardships they would face. Nikki felt so old when she was around him, even though she was only a couple of years older than Benna. Where had her youthful exuberance gone? She only hoped she could spare him growing up as quickly as she had been forced to do. She sighed and stretched, trying to loosen the knots in her shoulders.

"Face tomorrow when it arrives," she scolded herself.

Moonchaser snored noisily at her feet, oblivious to the pack he wore in preparation for their early-morning exodus.

Nikki lay on top of her covers, adjusting her pikeleather fighting gear. The cold croma of her sword touched her thigh, sending a shiver through her, even though the night was warm. She moved it and settled into a more comfortable position, again. Somewhere in her mental inventory of the necessary transmograffic herbs, minerals and pigments she'd packed, sleep did come, but then it seemed to last only a second.

She woke with a start, but the room was silent. It must have been well past midnight. The two moons, Bekel and Meika were both high overhead, casting competing strands of milky light across the floor. Then she heard it, a scratching sound, the patter of tiny feet.

"Rats!" she muttered aloud. "Remind me to do a rodent purging tomorrow." But she was only half-awake, forgetting that she would be gone by morning. Moonchaser snorted loudly in his sleep, as if in answer, then all was quiet again.

She fell back asleep, this time more soundly, and began to dream.

The room with thought lightning, the by-product that some artisans produced after a day of transmogrifee. Flashes of swirling colors vied with the moonlight as they whirled about her bed.

At some point, the dreams turned nightmarish, the colors ugly. Muddy tones and dark values trudged across the walls in a grotesque march of hideous night terrors. One of the shapes separated itself from the dream, stepping forward into the room, fully formed. A putrid stench dirtied the air, as the tall, shadow-thin creature stepped close, leaning over her with a necrotic claw held high, poised to strike. Moonchaser woke with a snarl and leapt at the apparition, but Nikki was already awake, forming a transmogrifee that hurled the beast to the wall. Moonchaser clawed at the empty air, landing on all fours. He stood between it and his mistress, preparing to leap again, but when the abomination hit the wall with a splat, it merely separated, and now instead of one attacker, there were three.

The trio stood together, each taller than a man, each with its own terrible stench, each with a hundred strange appendages that had one obvious purpose; to kill.

Nikki knew that the transmogrifee she had hurled at it was the most powerful she could call up. The things should be gone, but they looked more solid than before. Nikki guessed that there was some powerful shaper behind this, probably more than one, perhaps many working in concert, and that meant there was little hope of victory for her and Moonchaser.

"We should have left today, while we still had the chance," she muttered to herself. In answer, the three abominations spoke as one: "You should have left Mistra while you had the chance, but you were ever the fool, moondaughter." Then the creatures laughed. It was the sound of breaking bones and tearing flesh. Nikki shuddered, but she knew she had to control her fear, if they were going to survive. Had she heard something familiar in their speech? Who was it who always called her moondaughter? If she knew the names of her attackers, she might be able to use a transmogrifee to recall their true forms. Then the long practices with the sword wouldn't have been in vain; she knew of no one who could defeat her in physical battle, without some transmograffic assistance. The arts of warfare had long been forgotten in Mistra. It might give her the edge she needed, if she had the skill to break down this evil masquerade.

Her attackers gave her no more time to think, as all three moved forward, taking on clearer shapes. One sprouted an organic spear from its arm, bright and sharp as the hardest croma. It began slicing the air before it with quicker-than-the eye movements, and Nikki thought she could feel the air slipping into neat wedges between them.

The second beast was forming itself into a huge bowl, and to Nikki's horror, a bubbling ooze overflowed onto the floor, turning the stone to gelatin where it dripped.

The third creature grew a featureless head, sprouting hundreds of tentacular whips that now bit at the air with sharp-fanged, buzzing mouths that snapped at them voraciously. It advanced.

Nikki grabbed Moonchaser at the collar, even as he gathered himself to leap. "No! You're no use to me dead. Remember our practices. Be still, but call up the beast within. Gather your strength and lend it to me."

The cat growled, but stood stone-still, gathering his raging instincts into a tight ball as she had taught him.

In the seconds that she had left, Nikki searched beneath her attackers' facade, looking for the flaw that would reveal their identities. If she could recognize their auras, she might gain the information she needed to defeat them. She knew every Mistran, at least everyone with the strength to challenge her.

But their auras were disguised. All she could detect was a dull gray radiance, no more than would come from a piece of kelp, or an insect. It wasn't enough.

She called up a transmogrifee to give herself time. A clear bubble formed around her and Moonchaser. She rushed out the words as quickly as she could, reenforcing them with a warding motion of her hands. There was no time to do more, and she hoped it would hold.

Moonchaser roared. Beyond the bubble, her attackers quivered like heat dreams, wavering and flickering in and out of view. Nikki wondered why they responded to the big cat in this way but had no idea how she could use it to her advantage.

In the next instant, they popped out of view, and the air was filled with something deadly, a haze that absorbed the air and her bubble with it, surrounding them with a heavy, creeping miasma of dread.

"Don't breathe!" she screamed at Moonchaser, then almost inhaled herself. Their time had run out. Her mind groped for an answer. She hadn't survived years of danger and fear as a transmogrifer to give up now. If these were simple projections from another room of the aerie, they shouldn't have such strength. Were their auras also projected? Who were these three who faced her? She had to know.

Her lungs burned. The overwhelming desire to draw a breath distracted her as she tried to concentrate. She began to feel faint, but she clung to consciousness because it was her life. To let go now would mean a quick death for both. This knowledge gave her strength, and she channeled the primitive survival drive into one great spurt of transmograffic energy. She must use it well, as it would be her last chance.

To her transmogrifee, she added the raging feline force that Moonchaser provided. As his energy entered her, she felt suddenly, vividly alive. The wild blood pounded in her veins, obliterating all thought but the predatory thought; to rip the masks from her attackers like ripping the hide from a fleeing herdbeast, to shred their power and leave them naked and defenseless, then to kill without thought or remorse.

At first, the beasts were able to resist her, but they hadn't counted on her adding the predatory instincts of Moonchaser to her transmogrifee. The haze dissipated, leaving the figures as they had been, but quivering as if in great fear. Claws and poison tentacles dropped away. They dwindled, growing smaller and smaller, far too small to be human.

At last, three tiny shapes revealed themselves. They were shaking with fear, backed up against the wall as far as they could. Their fur was singed in places, and their noses twitched uncontrollably.

"Rats!" Nikki gasped. "I have been challenged by rats."

They squeaked as one, "Please don't let the cat eat us!" and then one said, "We didn't want to do this. They changed us, made us practice these horrible, violent acts. We didn't want to know these things. We want to be the way we were, with thought only for eating and multiplying."

Despite her exhaustion, Nikki felt compassion for these pathetic creatures. She said a word and tossed a pigment into the air from her pouches. The rats scurried off, simple rodents again.

Nikki let out a ragged sigh. Now totally exhausted, she slumped down, leaning back against her bed and closing her eyes. Her head throbbed with a thunderous pain. She felt that empty feeling of creative exhaustion and the thought of working any transmogrifee made her feel ill.

Moonchaser drowsed beside her as if in a waking dream, too tired to move. He would need time to recover from the energy drain she had imposed on him. She laid her hand on his fur, enjoying the warm, soft feel of it under her fingertips, enjoying the clean strength of his spirit.

"Good friend," she whispered, "you are the last person I want to harm, even at the risk of my own life."

"My mistress forgets," purred the cat. "Moonchaser owes you much. I was not even a person until you gave me speech and reason."

"Does that give me the right to use you up as I need? It seems you're another of my failures. I made a friend instead of a tool, and now you're far too precious to lose."

"Nikki is precious too. My loyalty is yours."

"And of what use to me is the devotion of a dead grella?" she snapped, but he always saw through her words to her underlying fears.

"You worry of another attack," he growled.

"Yes," she replied with a sigh. "If it happens before we can escape, we may be unable to recover the strength to defend ourselves. I fear we have more than a couple enemies now. Our hope lies in the possibility that they are unaware of our plans and are marshaling their forces for another attack. They may think they have time to finish us off. When they return, they will find that their victims have flown the aerie, literally. But we'd better go now. It's almost light. I only hope I have the strength left to create a winged creature for the flight to the plains. You may get your chance to be a bird, after all, my friend." Moonchaser's only response was a low, worried growl.

Nikki got to her feet too quickly and had to clutch at Moonchaser's fur to steady herself, until the dizziness passed. She felt more drained than she should be. Usually, she recovered quickly from an act of transmogrifee.

"We'll take my secret way," she said. "I know it's not your favorite route, but it'll get us out to the peaks quickly for our rendezvous with Benna and Dreyk. I hope they're early."

They slipped out of her chamber and onto her invisible walkway. Before she turned to go, Nikki glanced back for one last look at the world she had known and might never see again. She felt little remorse, but many regrets.

Turned from the room, she stepped out quickly, before she could lose her nerve. The wind fought her. It whined and whistled in the peaks around them. Moonchaser hurried ahead of her, eager to find solid ground. Then without warning, the world disappeared, and she was falling into a swirling abyss.

In her panic, all Nikki could think of was how quickly her attackers had learned. She searched for Moonchaser, but his essence was gone, out of her reach. They must have figured out what she was doing, using the cat to augment her power, now that the eye was weakening, and they had found the quickest way to separate them. She feared he would be killed, but she had little time to mourn, as it appeared that her own death was also looming. She struggled against the binding that held her, throwing all her energy into resistance, but it held her firm, and she was falling. It seemed that the invisible walkway had been dispelled while the hold had been put on her. She would be prevented from taking another form and would fall to her death on the sharp rocks below. She struggled with all her remaining strength, not to escape, now, but to give herself some kind of protection from the fall. There was no time for anything more, and in her weakened state she doubted that she could do even that. Her only choice was to do the unthinkable, to use some of her own lifeforce to combat the transmogrifee. In the face of death, the chance of becoming a psychic cripple seemed a small risk to take. She would have to worry about the consequences later, if she survived.

She pulled up the energy of her life itself, and she could feel the tearing, the rending of spirit, but it was too late to think of the damage. She put it into a transmogrifee that would offer some resistance against the fall, a thin shell of cushioning only. Her last irrational thought was that she hoped she could find a nice, soft spot to land.

Of course, that wasn't the case. She hit the steep rock with crushing force and began to slide. On impact, she felt intense pain in her shoulder and the burn of the rock on her skin as she slid, then the pain darkened her vision, and she lost consciousness.

When she woke, the pain was no less, but she had stopped falling and was wedged into a narrow crevasse. She turned her head experimentally, and gravel broke away beneath her, echoing down the mountain, until the sound was lost in the distance below. She might fall again at any second. Even if she had the strength left to move, how would she make it up this steep cliff face? All her transmograffic energy was drained. She felt hollow and cold.

"So, this is what death feels like," she whispered to herself, and the effort made her wince with pain.

The moons washed pale light onto her face. They were setting, and soon the sun would begin to warm the sky. She thought of Benna and Dreyk. If they still lived, she hoped that they hadn't waited for her, that they were far away from Mistra, beginning the new life that she would now never know. She closed her eyes and wished them the wisdom to run, and run fast from this dangerous place. She mentally disconnected her senses. There was no need for pain now. With a sigh, she let go of her fear and, commending her spirit to the Lord of Dreams, she slid into the murky waters of death.

Unknown to Nikki, Moonchaser had almost reached the far wall when the walkway collapsed beneath him. When he started his fall, his instincts took over, and with a prodigious leap, he managed to lodge his claws into the bottom of the door. His presence activated the door, but this gave him little advantage, as he clung by a tenuous claw-hold to the slick stone, unable to pull himself upward to safety. Here he clung for a long moment, waiting for some further attack, but all their attention must have been directed at Nikki. He could no longer feel her presence behind him. He was filled with unreasoning rage for a moment, then, as if he heard the calming words of his mistress, he forced his mind into their practiced channels. *Think first, act quickly, triumph over your enemies.*

First, he must get himself out of this vulnerable position before the attackers turned their attention to him. He couldn't get up, so his only course was to go down. He could barely turn his head and could see nothing directly below him. He closed his eyes and invoked his hunter eyes, a dream vision of places seen before. He saw it in his memory, a tiny ledge—there—just to the left and four man-heights below. Without giving himself time to fear, he let himself drop, reaching out at the last moment to grab at the narrow ledge. Even with his feline strength and agility, it was a close thing. He barely managed to hold on and regain his balance. From there, it was a relatively simple matter to work his way around the pinnacle and up onto the flat ridge. When he reached a place of safety, he paused to catch his breath and search the scene below for Nikki. He hadn't heard her fall, and it was some time before he located her body. She was far below him, apparently wedged in a narrow crack of the sheer cliff. He could see no movement, and he frantically meowed for her. He lacked the ability that she possessed to actively seek out the aura of another. All he could do was make himself available to her and hope that she would respond to his howls. He had to face the fact that she might be badly hurt or unconscious and unable to extricate herself. He didn't even consider the possibility that she might be dead.

The rising sun burst over the mountains, making his eyes water in the sudden light. This triggered a memory, and he turned from the cliff and ran with all his speed across the rocky ridge.

Dreyk and Benna were trying to avoid each other's gaze for fear one might bring up the possibility that Nikki wasn't coming after all. Benna fidgeted with the ropes that held Hawkwind to the ground, while Dreyk pretended again to rearrange his pack.

Dreyk was first to see the big cat as he approached at great speed. His first reaction was to draw his knife in defense, a natural reaction of any plains dweller who has seen the hunting grellas in action. As the cat drew closer, he recognized Moonchaser, but his relief was short-lived. Something must have gone terribly wrong for him to be here alone.

The cat gave them no time for questions. He paused only long enough to howl, "Come quickly, bring rope!" and he was gone again, racing back the way he'd come.

After only a moment of hesitation, they both moved at once, exploding into action as the tension of waiting was at last broken. Neither suggested that they were risking their lives by staying a moment longer, when their plans had obviously gone badly awry.

Benna gathered up a length of the gossamer rope, tearing it heedlessly from the miscellany he had collected. Dreyk sheathed his knife, and they both followed the quickly disappearing cat. Even moving at top speed across the rocky terrain, they soon lost sight of Moonchaser, but the cat bounded back to them, saying nothing, while the swishing of his tail said clearly, "Slow, you are too slow!"

After what seemed like a lifetime, they reached the edge of the cliff and looked down. The sun had now cleared the mountains, and Nikki could be seen clearly below them. She made no sound in response to their calls.

"What can we do?" cried Benna. "No one could climb down there. It's too steep."

Instead of answering, Dreyk looked around them. He found a weather-worn snag and pushed and pulled at it, testing its strength.

"This should do," he said, as he pulled the rope from Benna's hands, tying one end firmly to the snag and the other around his waist. At a point about halfway along its length, he looped it through Moonchaser's harness and tied it tightly. Approaching the edge, he called down to Nikki that he was coming down, but she didn't move or respond. He looked again at the rope, testing it with a sharp tug.

"Let's just hope this rope is stronger than it looks," he said with a tight grin. Benna could see how his hands shook.

"Be prepared to pull. I won't be able to get back up without your help."

"You're going down to get her? I thought you were afraid of heights. You never told me you could *climb mountains!*"

"It's not exactly a practiced skill, but I've seen it done."

Fortunately, his last words were lost against the rock as they lowered him carefully over the edge. Benna was worried enough about his sister, and Dreyk had become a friend that he didn't want to lose either. He peered over the edge with a deepening frown. Dreyk struggled awkwardly down the almost vertical incline. By the time he reached Nikki, his hands and knees were raw and scraped.

He barely had room for a foothold on the narrow ledge as he reached down to look at her. He spoke her name quietly, but there was no response. He felt her neck for a pulse, and at first, he feared that she might be dead, but after a moment, he felt a weak heartbeat. It was erratic and slow, but an undeniable sign that she still lived. How long she would live if he tried to move her, he didn't know. He realized that time might be short, and none of them might survive if he didn't move her quickly. Also, the narrow ledge didn't look like it would stand up to their combined weight. He reached under her as gently as he could and pulled her to him, balancing her over his shoulder as best he could. She was deeply unconscious, not even uttering a sound as he lifted her.

He called up to Benna to start pulling. Moonchaser strained his thickly muscled legs, trying to bury his claws into the stone itself to keep his footing as he pulled.

It was the most difficult thing that Dreyk had ever done. By the time he reached the top, he wasn't sure his muscles would hold out for another second. When at last he was able to lay Nikki down on level ground, he rolled over in exhaustion, breathing hard. His arms and legs tingled, and his fingers refused to unclench themselves.

Benna untied the ropes and looked at Nikki's wounds, tearing his own shirt in strips to bind her leg where it was still bleeding. Dreyk stood on shaking legs.

"We need to move, now!" he said. "Another attack may come at any time."

He lifted Nikki gently, and they started back. He didn't want to think about their next move, but he knew that their options were quickly diminishing. Without Nikki's help, they would have to rely on Benna's glider. He wasn't looking forward to that, but staying was now a more certain death.

At the eastern cliff's edge, he laid Nikki down and helped Benna with the ropes, as if by silent consent, they had agreed that this was the only way. Moonchaser hung back from the edge.

Dreyk turned to the big cat. "I'll have to tie you in, my friend, if you want to go with us. There's no life for you here now."

"Grellas do not fly," replied the cat. "I will find another way down." Moonchaser paced in obvious agitation.

Dreyk said, "You might never find us in all that." He waved his arm over the vast desert below. "Besides, Nikki is going to need you."

"Of what use to her is the devotion of a dead grella?" quoted the big cat.

"Come on, Moonchaser. Benna says this thing is perfectly safe."

"I will find you."

"Suit yourself," replied Dreyk. "I hope you make it. What am I saying! I hope we make it." He turned to Benna, who held the ropes in a white-knuckled grip.

Benna said in a matter-of-fact tone, "Get in and hold Nikki. I'll loosen the ropes and get it to the edge, then I'll jump in."

When they were set, Dreyk waved his arm to signal that he was ready. "There's no use waiting any longer. Either we fly, or we sink. We're in your hands, Captain."

The wind picked up, as if on cue, and the glider started to lift on its own. Dreyk yelled something like, "Here we go–ow..." His words were swallowed by the wind.

Benna jumped in, and suddenly they were aloft. After a second, they began to dip over the edge. Dreyk felt a heavy thud above him, and the glider started to swing wildly. He looked up to find a terrified grella face staring down at him from the overhanging wing. The cat had decided to jump at the last moment, landing on top of the glider just as it was clearing the edge. It might have worked, if he'd managed to land in the exact middle of the craft, but his weight was slightly to the left of center, causing the entire craft to dip sharply to the left. On top of that, Moonchaser was digging his claws into the wing material in a desperate attempt to keep his footing, and the wing was starting to tear. Dreyk found himself facing the cliff wall as the glider swung around. He screamed instructions to Benna, who was too busy trying to steer the unwieldy craft to listen, even if he could have heard above the wind.

Benna did manage to turn the glider just in time, and they faced the open air again, the desert still far below them. A gust caught them, and their speed picked up. The wind whistled even louder, whipping stray pieces of fabric to a frenzied cacophony of slapping and swishing sounds. Then suddenly the ground was very near, speeding by far too quickly. Dreyk thought he saw two winged shadows on the ground where there should have been only one, but he had no time to consider it further. Benna pulled up frantically on his rope-steering mechanism. It snapped in half in his hand. The ground disappeared, and they were facing toward the sky, then the underside of the glider was catching on the low shrubs of the desert, clipping them off or tearing them from their roots as it went. Views of the ground and the sky alternated in a dizzying dance as the glider rolled and flipped, shredding itself on the prickly foliage. Dreyk lost all sense of direction. All he could do was close his eyes and hold on.

He lay for some time before realizing that the wind had stopped, and the world had ceased its spinning.

With Nikki still clutched in his arms, he crawled out from the wreckage. He laid her down gently on solid ground and felt for a pulse.

It was there, but weak. He was grateful that she had at least survived the flight. He left her and started to search for Benna. He found him in a tangle of glider parts, scratched and bruised, but otherwise not seriously hurt.

They could find no sign of Moonchaser, though Benna thought he'd seen him jump just before impact. Finally, the big cat materialized out of the desert, limping toward them back along the route of their descent, which was clearly marked by the torn foliage and strewn glider remnants. Brightly colored silken shreds and sparkling streamers decorating the desert in the morning light, Dreyk thought, as if for a party.

Dreyk sat down heavily in the dirt, gathering handfuls of sand to his lips to kiss. He glanced up at the imposing peaks above them, where they'd been standing moments before, and felt suddenly giddy.

"Yes, let's have a party," he chuckled. "What a party!" Then he started to laugh hysterically and couldn't stop.

Tbrin watched the shadow of the glider come to rest far below him on the desert floor. He too had seen the shadows of two sets of wings in the morning light, and he alone knew what they meant. He had been too busy trying to control Jelebron to make his meeting with Nikki, but perhaps it had worked out for the best.

He turned from the edge. There was no time to worry about them now. Nikki would have to fight Semli alone—but he had taught her well, and she had the skill, whether she knew it or not. He started back across the rocky peaks, unaware of the weariness that showed in every step he took. At least the two drakyn were separated. He might have a better chance now, if he had to face Jelebron alone.

No, he told himself. *You wouldn't have a chance.*

He realized, with a bitter smile, that the best he could do now was to stay in the shadows, biding his time and hoping that the moon-daughter returned with the new drakyn's eye before it was too late. He wasn't without some power, but he would have to work in secret, fighting the silent battle his sect had been waging for eight hundred years. He told himself it was the only way, but when he reached his chambers, he couldn't sleep, despite his exhaustion. He paced in the sunlight, fingering the hilt of his ancient dueling sword with the gentle caress of a lover.

"Greshna, how I wish you could be here to see it when I remove their heads!"

He stopped in his tracks, and a dark smile lit his face. "But perhaps you can. If only I can learn the steps that Akriast used to recall the dead."

Chapter Thirteen

Born of Darkness

Nikki dreamed, but she wasn't the hero of her own life. She was some defenseless, thoughtless creature, a mouse or a vole, or maybe a cringing contail. She was lost on an endless plain, unable to run, unable to reach cover. At her cheek, the air fluttered with the touch of soundless predator's wings. She couldn't hear them, or see them, but she knew they were there, and her fear gave them life. They filled every inch of the sky, swooping down closer to her prone form with every moment that passed. She lay as if dead, frozen in her own sweat and urine, her scraggly fur matted and crusted with sand.

She thought, *Am I this scurrying rodent, whose only purpose is to live and die in fear of becoming an owl pellet? Am I to be the owl's regurgitated remains? Is that my legacy?* She waited for an answer she didn't expect, until a giant wolf arrived, striding into the dream with a purposeful air.

He stretched his powerful neck, howling at the sky with the voice of a hurricane, until all the owl wings were gone, and only the double moons gazed down on them with blurry eyes.

He said to her, "I am the hero of your life," then he swallowed her whole. She struggled, but it only made her sink deeper into his gullet. She screamed, but her screams rose from his throat, not hers, and mixed with his laughter.

"Now you have a purpose," he proclaimed loudly. "You're mine, no longer food for the owl."

She knew she could never escape him, so she tried to escape from the dream. She tried telling herself to wake. She tried imagining how she would wake, in a soft bed of white cloud just after sunrise, with a warm breeze kissing her face. But it didn't happen.

Instead, she felt only numb, the numbness slowly replaced with throbbing pain that grew as she approached the light. She withstood the pain as long as she could, before she withdrew, sinking into that deep, black pool that lies at the ultimate bottom of every soul. Draining hope, remorse and pain from her spirit, the clinging fluid enveloped her, pulling her down. It filled every hollow of her body and mind with dark forgetfulness, and in this liquid death, she slept.

CHAPTER FOURTEEN

Zoobilet, Shoobilet

The sun was sliding landward, and the temperature was dropping quickly. They cared for Nikki as best they could, checking for broken bones, finding none, and redoing her bandages. Dreyk became increasingly concerned when she didn't wake. He could find no head injury that would account for her unconsciousness. All they could do was to keep her warm and huddle beside her in the growing dark, too exhausted and worried to make conversation.

They had salvaged what they could from the wreckage of Hawk-wind, recycling the wings into a rough lean-to that would shade Nikki from the sun and wind. They had brought enough water for several days at most, and not much more food. Dreyk couldn't blame Benna for not planning well. He would have had no clear idea of what they would face, and Benna had probably intended to rely on Nikki's powers and Moonchaser's hunting abilities, and although the cat was basically unharmed, his left front paw was badly strained. Dreyk had wrapped it tightly with some pink gossamer fabric he had salvaged from the wreck. It would probably heal fine, but in the meantime, he wasn't going to be doing a lot of hunting. The cat was spending most of his time at Nikki's feet, his stillness communicating his worry more than anything else he might have done.

Dreyk berated himself for not being more observant on the way down. Which way was the nearest water, the nearest habitation? He should have been able to identify these things from the air. Then he laughed at himself, remembering the brief, wild ride of the great ship Hawkwind. They were lucky to be alive at all, and they would just have to take it one disaster at a time.

After a dry dinner of kelpmeal biscuits and ferky, Dreyk had stepped out to view the sunset. He found that he liked this arid, flat land. Its monotonous spaces reminded him of the ocean, and like the ocean, he was beginning to find that it held more mysteries than a casual glance might reveal.

Sturdy plants dotted the sandy ground in abstract patterns, knee high to the horizon. He had seen them in other lands. They were the sten; squat, radiant bushes, with brownish purple at their bases and dusty gray tops, reaching for the sun and infrequent rains. Everywhere were the sounds of tiny birds, scurrying rodents, and once, a brightly colored lizard darted in front of him, flicking its tongue at him before disappearing into the brush.

Although they had felt a few distant tremors during the day, re-minding him that he was back on familiar, if unpredictable soil, the ground was now still. The stillness brought a sense of peace, and Dreyk found himself relaxing despite his concerns. How could any danger approach unseen or unheard across such an expanse? The sky here was huge. From horizon to horizon it stretched, like a great bowl inverted on the land. Inside it, sounds echoed across from distant, gentle rises; the trilling of birds, a kestrel calling to his mate, the howl of a grella, or the whinny of a wild sagehorse. All these sounds combined to shape a delicate music that would tint his dreams with wonder, and hope.

Dreyk woke to the sound of hooves on dusty soil, reverberating with the jangle of bells, and for a second, he dreamed that he was back in

Bay Towne at the Festival of the Moons, but the sounds were wrong, and where was his mask?

Coming fully awake, he jumped up from his makeshift bed, scanning the horizon for a sign of attack.

Approaching them was the strangest beast he'd ever seen. It was huge in the trunk, yet with four spindly legs teetering along gamely beneath its massive weight. The creature wore a garish conglomeration of veils, beads and bells in unimaginable color combinations. It had two heads of hair, one orange and spiky, the other a huge unruly black mane.

The smell reached them before the creature did, the acrid scent of garo, a pungent snuff used in the northern isles, mixed with the unmistakable odor of sagehorse sweat, as well as other strange aromatics that Dreyk didn't recognize.

Benna and Moonchaser had both risen and were standing, Dreyk noted with irony, behind him. He glanced down to the knife at his belt. It had been a gift from Nikki, and so far, it had been useful for little things, like cutting rope, digging for roots and cleaning his nails, but now it looked pitifully small and useless. He only hoped that this would be a friendly beast, seeking directions, and that they would not be tested so early in their journey.

To their amazement, the beast strode up to them and split into two parts, the top half separating itself from the bottom with great difficulty, accompanied by much unintelligible but obvious profanity. It must have been a painful procedure for all concerned.

Now they were confronted by not just one beast, but two. The one with the orange mane and long face looked sadly relieved, stretched his swayed back, and wheezed loudly. The motion made his many bells clamor, and he looked at them, Dreyk thought, with an expression of silent apology.

The other creature approached them in a ponderous, bow-legged gate. It was huge, towering over them by a good half-man height. The girth of this behemoth almost rivaled its height, though the exact shape was hidden beneath many layers of various cloaks, veils, sashes, necklaces, ribbons and bells. Among the paraphernalia of its garb, Dreyk noticed a huge sword in a mercura and leather scabbard. The creature sported a brightly painted face, sienna and orange and vermilion stripes running from the wide nose into a huge head of curly black locks. Filled with tiny strings of beads, bells and streaming veils, this hair flowed behind the creature like a flooded river of swirling color and sound.

Dreyk couldn't be sure. Was it snarling, or smiling at them? At least it hadn't yet reached for the massive sword. Or was it merely going to sit on them to kill them? Nothing was clarified when the creature began to speak. If it was the common speech, it was no dialect he had ever heard.

"Y am Hyla Sdyzy Dkym, mercynyry to the transmogryffic master, mystress Freya Westry," it said. The sound was melodic, half song, half spoken word. The language sounded vaguely like the common speech, but appeared to have some strange vowels, spoken at different pitches.

"Did you say Westry?" asked Dreyk, in a leery tone.

"Please to forgive me, no? I be reverting to my native way of speaking, you see, after long days on the trail. This language of yours, so dull, yes, and yet too complicated. Why these monotonous sounds when a change of tone can say all?

"I am Hyla Sduzi Dkim, mercenary, bound to the mistress Westry. Warrior daughter of the Dynyky clan, I am proud to be. I seek one named Dreyk. That he would have with him a woman, the mistress said, and a boy, and a pet grella. That description, you lot seem to fit, yes?"

Dreyk stared at her in amazement, trying to gather his senses while she waited patiently with hands on hips. Her donkey contentedly munched on what dry vegetation he could find.

Finally, he blurted, "Yes, I'm Dreyk, but I can't believe that Westry sent you. How could she know I would be here on the plains, or who would be with me?"

"What you like to, you may believe, no? Far-seeing eyes, the mistress has, and her far-reaching hands am I. The herbs I have that will wake your mistress, and the words of the waking I've memorized. No great healer myself, I am, but my best will likely do for now, yes?"

"Our mistress?" asked Benna in confusion.

"Only one possible mistress is here that can I see, unless you boys are not as you appear," barked Hyla in an exasperated voice. "Now, out of my way, so I can work, yes?" With that she swept past them brusquely, kneeling at Nikki's side with great effort, much groaning and more profanity.

Behind her, the donkey brayed loudly, and Hyla turned to Dreyk and Benna, speaking with barely controlled impatience.

"He reminds me, ah. Yet to introduce you have I. Greet well Pollux, my companion and faithful mount."

"Is your donkey really named Pollux?" asked Benna.

The donkey brayed something that sounded like "Nonk-let."

"I studied that in my pre-history class. Isn't Pollux a twin in gardlander mythology? Where's the other donkey, then? And where's your donkey's missing ear?" snickered Benna.

The donkey again brayed "Nonk-let, nonk-let, Noo-bley, noo-bley."

"Zoobilet, Shoobilet!" exclaimed the giantess, frowning at the animal. "My difficult companion, you must excuse." The giantess glared at her mount as if willing him to shut up. "I'm afraid his airs of grandiosity, which his humble form does not merit, his former owner may have given him. Actually, a donklet is he, the unfortunate progeny of a gardlander donkey and a drakonian zoobilet, he is. The missing ear, I'm afraid, is a story for another time, yes?"

"How unusual," mused Benna. "But I think I like him anyway. I'll remember to refer to you as a donklet from now on, little guy." Benna reached forward to scratch the donklet's topknot, to which the animal responded by nodding his head vigorously.

"OK," replied the giantess. "On with it, shall we be?"

The donklet stepped forward and stared down at the prone form on the ground. Suddenly, he burst forth with a loud series of brays. His long tongue stood out as he bellowed, "Wren-hee, wren-hee, wren-hee!"

"He sure has an odd bray, doesn't he," observed Dreyk.

"Ignore him, please" said the giantess gruffly. "A little out of his head from the heat, I fear he is."

Already Dreyk could see that this was going to be an interesting association.

The giantess wasted no time. As soon as she finished a brief perusal of Nikki, her manner changed abruptly. She hurried, but with a purposeful briskness that seemed incongruous in one so large. With orders to the others to gather wood for a fire, she pulled items from her packs. The roots and herbs looked tiny in her huge hands.

Soon they had a healthy blaze going and Hyla asked for water for her pots. Dreyk was hesitant at first, since their own water supplies were low, but when she told him that the North Fork of the River Cyn was only a day's walk north, he was greatly relieved. He was content, at least for now, to let this woman take control, but he watched her every movement carefully, still not entirely sure that he trusted her.

When the water began to boil, the giantess added the herbs and other ingredients, crushing them in her huge hand and dropping them into the water with a mumbled word.

Soon the air was filled with the scent of flowers, of a bright spring day, of waking to the sun after a cleansing rain. In their minds, birds sang, the air sparkled, and the desert came to vibrant life before their senses.

Dreyk and Benna watched, their eyes brimming with hope.

"What I can, I will do," said the giantess. "But far along the journey she is, and may not want to be listening to us. Up to her now, yes?"

The giantess began a mumbled chant that changed to melodic song in her strong, clear voice.

All that Benna and Dreyk could do was sit and watch, filled with an almost painfully heightened awareness, as the giantess sang a gently beckoning song to the only one among them who seemed not to hear.

Nikki was back on the plain, running on and on through tall spiky bushes. She tried to escape from the maze, but everywhere it was the same; bright light, the dusty scent of sage and pollen, the twittering of brush birds and the squeaking of rodents, the intolerably loud pounding of their tiny heartbeats, and the heat of the sand beneath her feet. All these things so glaring and bright, so unlike the silence of the night, that cool forgetfulness that was her only desire.

She could feel the wolf—there—just behind her. She could hear his footfalls and smell his deadly breath. He terrified her. The wolf would never let her return to the light, even if she wanted to.

Then she heard a voice, a gentle voice like that of her mother, long lost in her distant memory. The sound awakened something in her that no transmogrifee could conjure, the memory of her mother on the last day of her life.

Nikki had been little more than a baby, but she remembered the sounds of the words, and later, when she knew more of language, she was able to give them meaning.

Her mother had a special voice. When she sang to Nikki, the tune enveloped her, softly caressing her ears like the finest fabric, but on this day the song turned slow and sad. It faltered, stopping entirely for long moments. Then her mother spoke in the strong, clear voice from before the illness, before the bed.

"My talented little one," she said. "I see the pattern of your life. It won't be easy. Sometimes it will seem like more than you can bear, but you must be strong. Take care of your brother and take care of yourself. Most of all take care of yourself, because in the end you'll be the only one who can. And remember that I loved you both with my life."

They were the last words she heard her mother speak, and later that day when this strong woman died, Nikki remembered that her mother's face hadn't looked peaceful or resigned. Her face had been tight, her fists clenched, as if she'd fought all the way.

Then Nikki was drowning. Panic rose in her throat, and she thrashed wildly for the light, but some dark fluid held her down. She screamed for help and fought the cloying blackness that filled her lungs. She felt arms reaching for her, grabbing at her and pulling her upward, into the light.

She took a gasping breath of the clean, bright desert air and opened her eyes.

Chapter Fifteen

Your Enemies are Everyone

Her forest had arrived, and it drew her in like a sweetbear to honey. The scent of fir and hemlock, the sound of a creek's nearby tittering, the exertion of the chase, the ecstasy of the kill, the taste of fresh wild heart blood on her tongue, it all called to her like nothing the desert, or even the rest of the world, could offer.

Within her forest, there were deer and elkin and contails to be hunted. In its creeks floated trout, eels and crawfish and water lilens that tasted like spring, no matter the season. There were herbs and berries and shrooms in fall, if the forest that arrived happened to be a fall forest. Sometimes the forest would only exist for the morning, sometimes it stayed for weeks. Char reveled in every moment.

Her favorites, of course, were the ghosts of the wood, the wily, the powerful, the wise and loyal elkin. She ran with them now. She ran for joy. Her giant heart thundered to the rhythm of her agile hooves. Her nimble-strong legs pumped as they churned up chunks of moss, flying leaves and other detritus of the forest floor. Her lungs filled and emptied great volumes of the dawn. Feral senses carried her accurately and swiftly over logs and under fallen limbs, along a trail that only she could navigate. As always, she led her elkin family behind her, their well-being in her mighty care. She was their leader, their matriarch. She had never led them wrong, except for this one time, when the sweet abandonment of care had blinded her to the danger.

When the arrow bit, shame overwhelmed the pain. How could she, the master shaper of this wood, forget the paramount rule of her kind? Pierced by the exultant cries of the hunters as they searched for her body, she crawled from them in terror, leaving a clear, sticky fluid trail behind her like a giant forest slug. As she struggled into the thornbrush to die, the words of her mother wouldn't let her rest. They haunted her in the prickly, blood-splattered sunrise that aimed to be her last.

"Always be aware, my wild heart, because your enemies are everyone."

CHAPTER SIXTEEN

To Catch a Lizard

N ikki woke to find herself surrounded by friendly faces. Moon-chaser licked her chin. She raised a slow hand to his fur, caressing it as if she just now remembered how good it felt to touch and be touched. Benna and Dreyk looked down at her with comically intense expressions of concern. She sensed, more than saw, the desert around her, and she lay very still for the moment, enjoying the scents on the dry air, the noises of busy creatures, and the rustling of brittle bushes in the breeze. The desert!

"We made it!" she croaked.

"Yes, it appears that we survived," said Dreyk dryly. "I wouldn't have bet on it, judging by our initial takeoff. You slept through the ride, but we're not offering to go up and do it again, so don't ask."

"Don't worry, I won't." She grinned, then yipped involuntarily as she tried to rise and sharp pains shot through her shoulder and leg. She saw the bandages on her leg, the dried blood.

"How long was I out?" Then she saw the giantess leaning over her, and her jaw dropped.

"Good morning to you, mistress," said Hyla calmly. "Since yesterday morning you have slept, if what these two tell me be true."

"A whole day—who are you?" asked Nikki, interrupting herself.

"Hyla is my name, but worry not about that now. To get up and start moving, I think would be the best thing for you. It is the wound coddled that cripples, as knows every warrior worth her sword."

Nikki noticed the singsong quality of the woman's speech, as if the giantess were trying to prevent herself from breaking into song.

"So soon?" exclaimed Dreyk. "She was badly hurt!"

The giantess said, "Her shoulder is bruised and evidence of an earlier injury, there is, but the hurt was mostly to the spirit, I am thinking. The result of over-extension in transmogrifee, my mistress would say. Though no transmogrifer am I myself, what battle can demand of the soul, this I have seen."

Dreyk almost opened his mouth to question her. He couldn't imagine this ponderous creature fighting, but not knowing how far she could be pushed, he let it go. She seemed to read his thoughts anyway, giving him a black look before she continued.

"Trust me, mistress, some gentle exercise will bring you to a better state, and a good meal wouldn't hurt either, yes? An accomplished chef am I also." This last she said directly to Dreyk, as if daring him to gainsay her. He wisely said nothing.

Nikki had to admit that the giantess was an excellent cook. Maybe it was the spices she used, exotic tastes that turned even bland groundroot into a culinary delight. Perhaps it was only the fact that Nikki hadn't eaten in days.

Nikki asked for the recipe and the giantess was thrilled to share. She pulled out a rough-looking accumulation of pages that might generously be called a book. Rifling through the stained and torn pages, she came up with one with green splatters all over it. As fragile as it appeared, it withstood the cavalier way that Hyla treated it as she offered it to Nikki. The recipe read:

Fried Spitting Lizard and Prickle-Tongue Cactus

First, catch a vegetarian Spitting Lizard. You'll know it from its unpalatable fly-eating cousin by its pebbly skin. Smooth-skinned lizards may also be poisonous, so pay careful attention. Find a tall Prickle-Tongue Cactus that looks large enough to be home to a lizard. Cut a small hole at chest height and another at the bottom. Drive out the lizard by inserting a stick in the top hole, or if this fails, drop a few hot coals into the opening. This is sure to make the lizard pop out. Kill it before it spits, or you'll regret it.

Skin, clean and dress the lizard meat. Be sure to remove the spit glands, or your dinner will taste like vomit.

Fry in hot lard with strips of the cactus.

Season with spicebug powder and the juice of one large contail bladder.

Saute until the lizard meat turns green.

Dress with Drakynfruit flowers and enjoy.

Nikki decided against sharing the ingredients with the others.

Even Dreyk had seconds, though he was noticeably silent during the meal. He didn't seem overly happy to have the giantess with them, even though it was obvious that they needed her. Nikki still didn't quite believe her explanation for arriving here, just when they needed her, and Dreyk hadn't been much help. When Nikki asked what he thought of Hyla, his reply was a simple, "Never trust a shaper."

The exercise had helped, once she was able to loosen her sore muscles. Her body was in much better shape than she would have expected, but her emotions were another thing. She didn't know what to think.

She felt disjointed, distant from her fears—and her hopes. What hopes now?

Nikki realized that dinner was over. Hyla was out in the brush, cleaning her precious pots with sand, while Dreyk, Benna, and Moonchaser sat with Nikki by the fire. A waiting quiet had settled over their faces. She felt like all eyes were on her. Were they waiting for her to tell them what they should do next?

For an instant, the panic of her dreams rose in her again, but she forced it down. Should she continue this search for the drakyn's eye, even though the chances were very slim that they would succeed?

She said with as much certainty as she could muster: "Even if I could continue this journey north, the way I am—"

She paused, not sure what to say next. The eyes that gazed at her seemed so much more mature, so much more in charge than she could ever be. Why were they looking to her like that?

"Anyway, if I can somehow find this isle that is supposed to contain this tree—what I'm trying to say is it's going to be a dangerous and possibly futile journey, and I don't expect any of you to go with me." She looked directly at Benna. "Now that you're free of the dangers of Mistra, there's no reason that you can't have a life of your own."

Benna said nothing, but turned to stare intently at the horizon, as if the sky would answer his questions, if only he could look hard enough.

As Benna avoided her gaze, Nikki could well imagine the turmoil of his thoughts. In their time together in Mistra, Benna had riddled Dreyk with questions about his sea voyages. Benna might make a good sailor, and it would give him a chance at a new life, away from the dangers of Mistra, but he was obviously torn by his loyalty to her. He would never allow her to make such a dangerous journey alone. Hopefully, they would have plenty of time before a final decision had to be made; plenty of time to convince him that she no longer needed him. She only hoped that she could lie well enough.

It was Dreyk who spoke first. "I must go north anyway. Tia Cara and Bay Towne lie almost at the top of the continent, and at either port I may be able to get another ship. Besides, it could only be to my advantage to travel with a master transmogrifer..."

Dreyk trailed off into silence, seeing Nikki's expression harden. The silence built up between them to a palpable level. Even Moonchaser sat up, the fur on his neck bristling.

"Did I say something wrong?" Dreyk asked at last.

Nikki let out a heavy sigh. "No, of course not. It's me. I forget that you can't see auras. I expended all my talent, and then some, in that last battle. It's gone."

Benna blurted, "But it will come back, won't it? If you rest?"

"No," said Nikki, her voice firm and emotionless, "no, it's gone forever. I'm no longer a transmogrifer."

At these words, they sat gaping at her in disbelief.

Benna began haltingly, "It's not so bad once you get used to it—that is at least for me—but then I was born without it and—"

It was the giantess who interrupted him, stepping up just in time to prevent him from digging himself into an even deeper hole. She dropped a prodigious load of scrap wood by the fire, wiped her hands on her flowing robes, and sat down with a thud. The ground trembled for a second, then stilled.

She spoke, as if to the fire, "In yourself have faith, mistress. Much more than we see now will time reveal, of that I have no doubt. Now sleep must you all. The camp will I guard, no? The North Fork of the River Cyn we should try to reach by tomorrow eve, and a long day it will be. Ride Pollux, you will mistress, and the rest of us will walk."

Then she settled back, crossing her arms in a way that said, "There, everything is settled," and Nikki couldn't help but appreciate her taking control. She only hoped that decisions would come as easily to her when the time came for her to finally take charge of her own destiny again.

CHAPTER SEVENTEEN

The Pop-up Forest

Moonchaser saw it first, or rather, he smelled it. They were at a rise in the desert floor, with a wide gully before them. They'd set up camp on this promontory, planning to make their way down to the barely discernable creek at its bottom, the same creek that the giantess proclaimed with relief to be the North Fork of the River Cyn. Nikki thought it too large a name for such a trickle of a waterway.

After a dinner of cactus flower and lizard legs fried in lard, they had all settled down to an uneventful evening, though Hyla kept watch, as she explained, just in case trouble found them. At dawn, it did.

Nikki woke to a growl in her ear. Turning her head, she saw the profile of the elegant feline. Moonchaser sat beside her with his nose in the air and his hackles raised, staring out over the canyon. Something was different, but at first Nikki couldn't define it. Then she realized that the air had changed. The breeze was damp and carried the scent of something green and fresh.

She stood up and stretched, peering over the edge to the ravine below. What had been empty the day before except for more desert and a meandering streamlet was now a lush forest of fir and hemlock, with the thirstier alders and cottonwoods indicating where the creek flowed. At first, Nikki thought she must be hallucinating. Then she saw the faces of the others and knew they were seeing the same thing.

"It's a forest," exclaimed Benna. "What's a forest doing here? Was that here last night? I swear—"

"No, it wasn't," said Hyla, matter-of-factly. "Go around, we had better be doing. Some transmogrifee gone wrong, is my guess. Not safe is it to enter such an anomaly. Disappear it could, just as easily as arriving, and disappear with it you would."

Apparently, Moonchaser hadn't been listening. Before Nikki could stop him, he loped down towards the forest. Nikki called, but the cat had already disappeared into the brush at the forest's edge.

Nikki followed, and the essence of the wood enveloped her like a welcoming dream. It was a vision filled with dappled sunlight caressing her skin, the susurrations of thousands of branches singing as one, and the earth and plant smells that filled her with longing for a simpler time, a slower time. The forest called to her deepest need for a moving, breathing peace, for being one of many and herself at the same time. She ran on and on, following the cat as he went deeper into the trees. She was vaguely aware of the others as they hurried to keep up, with Hyla at the rear. Nikki was so enveloped in the magic of the wood that she felt no foreboding, only an all-enveloping joy.

Abruptly, she pulled up, as she saw Moonchaser had stopped near a thicket of thornbrush. He was tugging at something beneath the tangled vines.

"What is it, boy? What did you find?"

To Nikki's horror, Moonchaser had a human foot in his mouth, and was pulling it from the brambles.

"No, no, what is that? Leave it!" Nikki screamed.

Moonchaser let go his prize and looked back at her beseechingly.

"Help, please. Can't let this be. The beast woman is dying. Needs our help."

The beast woman?

But Nikki didn't have time to think. She too tugged on the foot and was amazed as she dragged a woman from beneath the branches. The others had caught up to them, panting.

"What is it?" asked Benna.

Before them lay a bloody female form, long dark hair streaming. Her leather clothing was soiled with what appeared to be oil and sweat and other odious stains, one of them being fresh blood. The shaft of an arrow stuck out from her side.

Dreyk said, "Ugh, what's that smell?"

Ignoring him, Nikki leaned down and touched two fingers to the throat of the unconscious woman.

"I think she's alive, but just barely. Help me get her out from these brambles."

Together, they carefully pulled the woman away from the clinging vines, trying not to cause her even more damage. Her long black hair was tangled and filled with twigs and filth. A face that could have been lovely was smeared with leaves and dirt. Beneath the grime, her features were delicate and refined. There was something familiar about her face, but for the moment Nikki couldn't place it.

Nikki guessed that the smell was coming from her clothes; a grimy vest with more area taken up by stains than leather, an oversized shirt that might once have been white, but was now a darker shade of grime. Her leather pants and bare feet were covered in mud and blood. Her fingernails carried a collection of dirt that appeared to be ingrained, rather than recently acquired. The arrow protruding from her side was the brightest thing about her, its canary yellow fletching obscenely cheerful amid the horror it had caused.

Hyla pushed forward with the donklet Pollux beside her. Pushing the others aside, she spent a few minutes over the woman, applying her herbs and unintelligible incantations. Finally, she reached down, firmly pulling the arrow from the woman's side. The others gasped.

"OK it is, OK it is," explained the giantess. "Not near any important organs was the point."

"All *my* organs are important," muttered Benna.

Hyla stitched and wrapped the wound in what looked like some of her many veils. Then she gazed up at the others urgently.

"Here, help me. Up on Pollux let's put her. Careful!"

Together they placed their still-unconscious guest onto the back of the donklet, and Hyla, holding her charge up gently in the saddle, began to lead them forward, deeper into the wood.

"Wait," said Nikki, "I thought you said not to go into the forest. Now you're leading us *deeper* into it?"

"Well, mistress, in it now, are we not? Getting some water and making our way across this oddity our priority must be, if we can, no?"

"If we can?" muttered Benna. "Ahh, things are finally looking up."

CHAPTER EIGHTEEN

Wolf Storm

D reyk seemed to have developed more respect for Hyla in their time together. He hadn't questioned one of her decisions in hours.

She was proving her skill as a guide, and Nikki doubted that many could keep pace with Hyla. She was beginning to wonder how long they could go on when the giantess stopped at her chosen campsite, gently laying her new patient to the ground. When they caught up with her, Dreyk and Benna threw themselves to the ground, exhausted, but before they could even regain their breath, Hyla asked them to help her gather wood for a fire. They struggled to their feet and followed her out into the brush.

Nikki watched them go, more than a little suspicious when they didn't seem to be gathering any wood but talking. Her first instinct was to extend her awareness, to listen in on their conversation, then she remembered that she couldn't. Her talent was gone. She sat down in the dirt and stared at her hands, too exhausted to move.

Dreyk and Benna followed the huntress reluctantly, their eyes on the ground. They almost collided with her when she stopped abruptly and turned to them.

"Not wanting to alarm the Mistress, was I, but being followed are we. With such a pace we set today, I thought we might lose him. Also, in grave danger are we if we stay out here in the open. Approaching is another unnatural anomaly, a disruption, they call it. I fear it is something that avoiding is difficult if not impossible to do."

"What, now we have two threats at once?" groused Dreyk, then more quietly, "Why didn't you say something earlier? Who is following us? What is this anomaly?"

"The follower, I fear that there is some transmogrifee to it. I am befuddled. Sometimes when I look back there is a wolf, then a man, or a grella. Once I looked, and there was a lushtree in the desert where there can live no such trees."

"Why didn't you ask Nikki? She a great transmogrifer herself," said Benna.

"Have you never seen one in her condition?"

"She seems fine to me, a little distant, perhaps."

"More than that it is, no? The loss of power can cripple, or even kill a shaper. If her talent she tries to use too soon...anyway, from more stress she must be protected, at least for a time, until her mind can heal itself, if it can. Help her we must. More at stake here there is than you know."

"That's fine," interrupted Dreyk in obvious frustration. "But how are we going to protect her when we can't even protect ourselves? None of us can defend against an attack of transmogrifee, if one is coming. And as for this disruption—I went through a psy storm once. I can tell you that I don't want to go through anything like that again."

"Nor I," said Hyla seriously. "Do what we can, we must. If necessary, my life I will spend to protect you, but to what you believe you must hold tight. That the Gods will grant us luck, or at least not work against us, is all we can ask, no?"

Dreyk said, "I have the feeling that they've been doing a little bit of both, all along, just to see us dangle on the string. I only hope that we're not walking into something even more evil than what I've already seen."

"Nonetheless, we must fight on. Now gather some wood we must and get camp set up before dark comes."

But Dreyk held her arm before she turned away. "There is something I should say, that is—I didn't trust you at first..." he trailed off.

"Apology accepted," said Hyla simply, before turning to her tasks.

Back at camp, they found Nikki leaning over their unconscious guest, who was moaning and fighting Nikki's efforts to keep her still.

"Don't move! You'll tear your stitches," Nikki admonished. In response, the woman only moaned more loudly. Finally, her eyes opened, and she surveyed the group with a look of panic. Dragging her arms from Nikki's grasp with more strength than she should have had with her injuries, she rose, then almost toppled over as dizziness hit her. She turned to run, with one hand clutched to her side, but somehow, the donklet happened to be right behind her and she stumbled into him, giving the others time to grab her and haul her back down.

"Let me go!" she screamed. "What ya holdin' me fer? I's nobody's slave. I'll die a'fer that!"

As she struggled, Nikki could see that she was trying to transform. Her skin color shifted, and her features blurred, but then settled back to her original shape. She was trying to transmoger, but, like Nikki, it appeared that the trauma of the injury had affected her abilities. She felt a strange kinship with their malodorous guest. In fact, there was something familiar about her that Nikki was struggling to define. Perhaps it was just that the girl seemed to be about the same age and height as Nikki, though while Nikki's complexion was light, the stranger's was deep bronze. Nikki wasn't sure how much was natural and how much the result of hours spent in the elements.

Nikki said calmly, "It's OK, dear, we're just trying to help. You were badly hurt. Here. Let her go and get back. Give her some air."

"Gladly," mumbled Dreyk. "In fact, I wish there could be a mile of air between us."

Nikki glared at him, and he raised his hands in surrender.

When the others stepped back, the woman visibly relaxed, but the look of wariness never left her features. Nikki was to learn that it would be a long time before that look finally gave way to something softer.

The woman was now pulling at her bandages to view Hyla's handiwork. When she raised her eyes, they were distant, perhaps trying to recall what exactly had happened to her.

"The forest..." she mumbled.

"Yes," began Nikki. "We found you there, badly hurt. You'd been hit by an arrow and Hyla—"

"Shows it t' me now," she demanded.

"What, the arrow? Why would you want to see that?"

"So's, when I finds its owner, I kin know who ta kill," she responded morosely.

"OK," said Hyla slowly, then began giving orders. "Get to it, folks. Rain is coming tonight, or I'm not Hyla Sdyzy Dkym." The donklet sneezed something that sounded like, "Shees noot, shees noot," then was silent.

Nikki couldn't sleep. Despite the totally dry evening, somehow Hyla had been right about the rain, and it was starting to sprinkle now. The stars were obliterated by dark clouds that had marched in like dutiful troops after sunset. Now, the air was still, but filled with the portent of a larger force to come. Despite her fatigue, the restless air made her uneasy. They had done the best they could to protect themselves from the rain that Hyla had predicted, but Hyla had explained that when it rained in the desert, it was no gentle sprinkle. They were bound to get wet, but somehow Nikki didn't mind. She thought the rain would feel good, cleansing the air and her muddled thoughts at once. At least so she hoped.

She glanced over to find that the huntress had dozed off on her watch. It was just as well, the woman needed sleep as much as anyone, and Nikki couldn't see why they needed a guard anyway; the desert was still. The plants seemed to be waiting with their limbs outstretched as if they reached for the coming rain.

Nikki got up and wandered a little way into the brush, carrying her blanket with her. Something flashed on the distant horizon, below the clouds. Lightning. Then all was dark again. She hoped it wasn't coming this way. If lightning hit the ground near them, they would have nowhere to hide in this flat land.

It flashed again, and this time she saw him on a distant rise, loping toward her. She stood frozen in fear. Why did the wolf frighten her so? Where was Moonchaser? She tried to scream, but she was unable to move or speak. Another flash, and he was right in front of her, looking across at her from a low hillock not twenty feet away. His eyes glowed, little fires in a matted mass of fur. His fangs gleamed yellow in the dark as he snarled at her. Then he spoke in her mind, and his thoughts hit her with searing pain.

"Now you're mine, little one, but there's no need to hurry. I put a transmogrifee on your companions. They may wake by festival time next year." He howled, the laughter of a jackal.

"It's a shame you lost your power," he continued. "I might have made a deal with you. I've got to be realistic. There isn't a chance of gaining the position I want while my mother lives. You could have helped me defeat her, but it's too late now. I guess I'll have to kill you, after all. It's too bad; you really are a pretty little thing, my pet."

He started to advance. Then everything happened at once. It began to rain, great droplets hitting the soil, slowly at first, then with an increasing rhythm that drowned out all other sounds. The wind picked up, gusting through their camp with a wild fury, carrying with it something unnatural, a sucking force that pulled the color from life itself. Very close to her now, the wolf howled again, this time in raging agony, as his power was ripped from him. Nikki laughed, a wild, crazy cackle at his misery. "Now you know how it feels," she hissed, but then she was lost as well in the vortex of the disruption, not even thinking to pull her sword, then when she did remember, she realized that it was back in her bedroll.

As soon as the anomaly hit, it collapsed the transmogrifee that held her companions, and Moonchaser was up, leaping through the night in a blur of speed and fury. Hyla was instantly in action as well. The drawing of her massive sword made a sound that rang in the air as it sliced through the darkness. They arrived almost together at the spot where the wolf had been, but the wolf was already far away, running for the distant hills in a desperate attempt to escape from his agony.

Moonchaser started to follow, but Hyla called him back, screaming over the noise of the wind and driving rain, "Wait! He's gone. We must stay together!" then to Nikki and the others: "The storm will become more disorienting as it intensifies. Form a ring in the center of camp. Hold hands. Don't let go for any reason! Moonchaser and I will stand guard."

The others did as she commanded, and none too soon, as the sky began to moan, warping and folding into hideous, impossible shapes. The screaming entered their minds and tore at their sanity. Nikki lost all senses in her hands. She couldn't tell if the others were still beside her, or if they still held her hands. Her body was lost, her mind on a tortuous journey that seemed to go on forever. She only wanted release. She found herself begging for death, to be let go and freed of the pain, but the sky answered with a grotesque mockery of laughter. The sound grated at her, mocking life itself, ripping at her painfully exposed mind. At one point, she thought she cried out, "Gardland

help us, what is this?" But then a second later, she said it again, not
repeating herself, but as if time had a hiccup, repeating itself and even
jumping ahead and back at times.

Much later—or sooner, she wasn't sure which, Nikki became
aware of sobbing and then realized that it came from her own throat.
She sat alone in the mud. Rain stung her face, and it was cold, so cold.
She hugged her shoulders and rocked back and forth in misery.

After a time, the rain stopped, and the air began to clear. Nikki
stood on unstable legs and looked around her. Their campfire had
gone out in the rain and lay smoking. Pale starlight revealed Dreyk
and Benna, lying unconscious beside her. A short distance away stood
Pollux, looking wet and miserable but unharmed. Of the huntress and
Moonchaser, she saw no sign.

She went first to Benna, rubbing his hands until the sensation
brought him around. He sat up, holding his head and moaning. His
flushed face was covered with mud and tears.

"I hope I don't look half as bad as you do," said Nikki.

"I hope you don't feel half as bad either," he replied.

Seeing that he would recover, she went to the dark-haired girl, who
appeared to have slept through the whole affair and was groggy but
seemingly unharmed. Then she knelt beside Dreyk, who seemed to
have suffered the most from the effects of the disruption. He would
not respond for some time, and then he was withdrawn. When Nikki
was able to get a word out of him, he started sobbing. She hugged him
until the crying passed. He pulled away from her with an embarrassed
expression.

"You're alright now," she said. "Some are just more affected by these
things than others. Usually, they say it's a male transmogrifer who'll
suffer the most. Perhaps you have hidden talent, after all."

"I doubt that," replied Dreyk in a shaking voice. "But thanks."

Nikki turned from him, scanning the glowing horizon with a worried expression. If only she had her talent, she could do a mental search for Moonchaser. She was about to try it anyway, when she heard the rustle of clothing and delicately tinkling bells.

The huntress and Moonchaser stepped out of the darkness and into their camp as if by magic. Hyla looked unchanged, as if she had escaped the effects of the storm entirely. Nikki wondered at this. She was beginning to think that the giantess had more power than she was letting on. Moonchaser's fur was wet and matted, but he seemed unhurt as well. Nikki knew that animals usually weathered such storms better than humans, with their more complex thoughts, but Hyla's seemingly unscathed appearance roused her suspicions.

"The wolf we tracked as far as we could in the dark," said the huntress. "Then very confusing the tracks became, as if we were tracking a distorted creature, part-human, part-wolf, part something I can't define, and would rather not consider. His scent disappeared, says Moonchaser. I only hope that disabled permanently by the storm he was."

Nikki asked, "But how is it that you escaped the effects of the storm?" The giantess answered, a little too quickly and glibly, Nikki thought.

"For this journey the transmogrifer prepared me before I ever left Bay Towne. Many talents she has, as I have said. A potion for protection she gave me. In our dinner tonight I placed it. Much worse would the effects on all of us have been without it."

"But still, you were not affected as much as we were."

"No time for further explanation is there now. Still in danger I fear that we are. Breaking camp and leaving this place, now, I would recommend."

"Now? But Dreyk is ill."

"No, I'm fine," Dreyk piped up with effort, and then aside to Nikki, he said, "I think we should trust her. After all, she's all we've got, and she's been right so far."

"Alright," agreed Nikki reluctantly. "But I still don't understand why she's here. There's something she's not telling us."

"If wasting time we are done with, going now we should, yes?" said Hyla brusquely.

It was a long night. When the sun started to warm the sky, they were still walking, while their injured guest rode the donklet. Repeated questions received increasingly short, enigmatic answers from the giantess, and Nikki gave up, trudging along in silence through the wet terrain in a waking bad dream. Often, they were forced to wade rushing streamlets, newly formed by the rains, and one was larger than the river Cyn that they had crossed earlier in the day. Nikki could well imagine the raging torrent it must now be, and she was grateful at least for the comforting presence of the giantess, and for her seeming knowledge of these wild lands.

At last, Hyla pulled up, surveying the ground with a frown. "This will have to do. We can go no further without rest. My only hope is that we've gone far enough. Over nothing may I be worrying. Unless there are kits to feed, attacking us is unlikely."

"Who has kits to feed?" asked Benna, but the huntress offered no reply, and they all seemed too tired to worry about one more thing. Nikki threw herself down on her bedroll and was deeply asleep in seconds. She didn't even have the energy for dreams, and she was grateful for their absence.

CHAPTER NINETEEN

Daemon Bunnies

The next day, they all trudged along in silence. The injured woman, whose name she had grudgingly admitted was Char, showed incredible resilience, and was already walking on her own. When Hyla checked her wound, she seemed amazed at how far along the healing process had come. Apparently, Char's transmograffic ability was working in the background to heal her.

After a brief breakfast of dried fish and a handful of the pale green bitter grossberries, Hyla insisted that they get moving again. Benna moaned, but Dreyk was uncharacteristically quiet. He looked pale and drawn, his face pinched.

Nikki asked, "Are you up to it, Dreyk?"

"Of course. I'm just a little tired, that's all. Last night took it out of me."

"Tonight, much rest we can catch," said Hyla, and then almost to herself, "Still in the range of the warrens we are. Arising is unlikely it seems, but chances we don't need to take."

"Arising what? Warrens?" asked Nikki, but she stopped herself when she saw the expression on Hyla's face. Was that a look of terror? She couldn't imagine anything that would cause such a reaction in the giantess, who had been stalwart and imperturbable through experiences that might have brought another to her knees.

Hyla whispered to Nikki, "Further I didn't wish to worry you. We've been through so much already. Better to tell you all less, I thought, especially if avoiding them completely we can achieve. To sap the strength of the worrier is worry's only use."

Wren thought better of further questions. With any luck, she would never have to learn more about these warrens. Didn't bunnies live in warrens? What danger could little contails present?

By late afternoon, nothing unusual had happened and Nikki was starting to relax. They were working their way down a gentle slope toward an idyllic vale. Dancing grasses seemed to go on forever, interspersed with small mounds of earth. When they reached the valley floor, Wren found the soil softer than she'd expected. Perhaps the recent rains had caused the sponginess, but she wasn't encouraged by Hyla's expression.

Hyla said, "Traverse this area quickly we should. Firmer ground is ahead."

Wren was more than willing to oblige. Despite the peacefulness of the scene, the ground here had an evil smell, something rotting and living both. It had a sickly-sweet and cloying odor that made her nauseous. Dreyk had drawn his knife. His face was pale, his mouth set in a determined line. Benna just looked confused.

The dirt around them began to emit popping sounds, as of long confined gases escaping. This was followed by a sound like a hundred ripping gowns and the ground came hideously alive. In an instant, they were surrounded by writhing shapes, vaguely leporine, but mostly monstrous.

The creatures advanced on them from all sides, their mouths opened to reveal rows of sharp teeth. They all bore ghastly expressions of anguish, but warped and twisted by some hideous need. Their contail torsos were muscular and too massive to be normal rabbit bodies. Arms were truncated versions of rabbit paws, with brown-tipped claws where paws should have been. Hundreds of the creatures popped out of their burrows at once, fully formed and hideous. Twisted faces grew wailing mouths, and Wren shrank from the sound. It wasn't language, nor song, but some primitive and animal need. They screamed like a hundred babies being tortured. After a second, she realized that they were pleading for help. Nikki leaned forward to listen, to gaze into their faces.

"Listen to them not!" yelled Hyla.

"But they're hurt, or they need something," Benna cried.

Nikki was overwhelmed by a desire to help them, to give them what they asked.

"Yes, food they need!" yelled Hyla.

"But there is green grass everywhere," exclaimed Benna.

Hyla barked, "Boy, born to ask stupid questions were you, or a recently developed talent, is it?"

"Oh," Benna stammered. "You don't mean they eat—"

"Yes, flesh they eat," interjected Hyla, "and dining well tonight will they be if we don't act quickly. Reach that rock outcrop ahead we must, and quickly. If anyone falls, leave them."

"Benna, no!" cried Nikki, as she saw her brother leaning toward one of the keening creatures. "Cover your ears." Benna got her message, and retreated to Nikki's side, putting his hands over his ears.

Nikki had drawn her sword, and when one of the creatures leapt at her, her long hours of practice took over. She lopped off the head of one and split another in two. With a high-pitched squeal, the creatures died. Any concept of cuteness was long gone for Nikki. These creatures were hideous. Then there were more, and her responses became automatic.

Hyla fought at their backs, her huge sword slicing easily through several of their attackers at once. She worked at a constant, unfaltering pace, and they were slowly making their way upward toward a rocky outcrop, but it seemed too far. Nikki's muscles were already burning with pain. Even if the giantess could keep up the pace forever, Nikki knew that the others could not. Knowing that they were as good as dead if she didn't keep moving gave her a burst of energy and she kept on, ignoring the pain in her legs and arms and somehow finding the reserves she needed.

Dreyk was also helping now, stabbing at the aberrations with his knife. Wren took a step backward to escape one that scrabbled dangerously close to her. Her foot hit stone and she fell backwards.

Stone! Somehow, they had reached the rock outcrop. She scrambled up onto a ledge. Another creature lunged at her but was unable to scale the rock. Hyla and Char leapt up beside her, followed by Dreyk, and then the donklet, who was the last to clamber up, as the creatures reached after him with their claws, snapping at his legs with their dripping fangs.

Unable to follow, and realizing that their meal had escaped, the daemon contails began a pitiful wailing at the edge of the stone.

The group scurried higher up to safety and collapsed in exhaustion.

"Why didn't they follow us up here?" asked a breathless Dreyk.

"They're bound to the vale," explained Hyla, "like a fungus in the soil, all are netted together below the surface. One cannot separate itself from the others, any more than a limb can jump from a tree."

Breathing hard, Nikki asked, "Is everyone OK? Benna, did you—"

Turning, Nikki heard a heightened level of frantic screams below them and with horror, she realized that Benna was gone. He hadn't made it up into the rocks with them.

"Oh no!" she cried, "He's still down there!"

"Wait here," Hyla commanded, even as she rushed back down into the deadly vale. Nikki was amazed as Hyla's sword whipped around her with incredible speed, taking out the crazed contails as if she were wiping salt from a table. Hyla disappeared into the bloody tableau and

Nikki was about to follow, when the giantess emerged, a torn, limp form over her shoulder. Wielding her sword now with one hand, Nikki could see that the fighter was starting to slow down. Forgetting her own danger, Nikki rushed out to help her and took a position at Hyla's back, fighting with renewed energy to save her brother. They were finally able to stumble up onto the rocks, both exhausted, but fearing for Benna. Was he still alive? Dreyk gently took the unconscious boy from Hyla and laid him gently onto the stone. Hyla knelt over him, still breathing hard.

"Is he still alive?" asked Nikki in dread.

Hyla felt for a pulse and said, "Yes, but just barely. His heartbeat is weak." The fighter started to tear pieces of her vails to fashion bandages for the largest of his wounds. There were just too many cuts, scrapes and torn skin to cover them all.

"Infection is what we have to worry about now, I fear. Not the most hygienic of creatures are those horrid beasts. On Pollux will we carry him, but get out of here we must, as quickly as possible."

No one argued with her.

Despite her claim that the disruption and fighting off the contail daemons hadn't affected her, Hyla stumbled several times and had to lean on the donklet as they walked. Nikki asked her what was wrong, but she only mumbled something about getting to a cube. Nikki thought the giantess must be losing her mind.

Benna was still unresponsive, and Nikki was wracked by worry for him.

After a miserable hike that took most of the day, Hyla pulled them all up at a promontory. Below them, a line of dust snaked its way across the sparse plain. The giantess pointed.

"Going north is that human caravan. Perfectly safe with them will you be, and in a wagon can Benna be carried while he heals. Medicines might they have that could help with the infection, yes? Below the escarpment will we meet again. Pollux I will leave with you to carry him until you reach the caravan. Then, just let the donklet go and find me he will."

"What?" asked Nikki in surprise. "You're leaving us *now*? I don't understand. You seemed so eager to lead us, now you're abandoning us?"

"For a short time, only. Trust in me, mistress."

Nikki said nothing, but trust wasn't her first inclination.

The giantess leaned heavily on her sword, watching the group as they disappeared behind a rise in the valley floor. She turned to face the cube that had materialized behind her. Hyla began a slow change, growing smaller and losing her many veils and bells. At last Wren stood where the giantess had been.

Beside her, the winded donklet wheezed and stretched his sturdy back. He arched upward onto two legs, becoming the tall, human warrior as he stood.

"Yikes," Trey muttered, rubbing his back. "Who knew being a donklet was such hard work?"

"Oh, I don't know," said Wren in a sardonic tone. "At times, I think being an ass comes quite naturally for you."

"Ha, ha, very funny." As he studied her face, Trey's false humor turned to real concern. "I thought you were faking that dizzy spell, but you don't look so good. Are you OK?"

"I was faking—to a degree—but I do need to get back into the cube. There's no way I'll make the entire journey in real time. Besides,

Nikki needs time to grow into her role as a leader, if she's going to take my place eventually."

"I don't know," mused Trey, "half the time she seems more like a rebellious teenager than the savior of mankind. Why don't we just bring them all into the cube and—"

"No, Trey. I don't think that would work. Despite the shock it would cause them, they need to move at their own pace. There's more to this journey than the hours it will take. It's about what they will become along the way."

"Well, so far, they are becoming impatient, grumpy and distrustful, so things are going as planned."

Wren sighed. "They will change. She'll grow into the transmogrifer we need her to be. She must."

"I hope so. I just hope they'll trust us again after this. Did you see Nikki's expression when you told them you had to leave again? It's been hard enough getting them to trust us so far. Now we'll likely have to start over."

"There's no avoiding it, I'm afraid."

With a sigh, Trey said, "You know I trust you, and I'm with you all the way. I didn't mean to sound like I have doubts about all this."

"I know that, silly." Wren smiled as she said it, that gentle, winning smile that had first made him want to spend eternity with her.

She didn't say what she was thinking, that her doubts were also screaming at her.

Taking each other's hands, they entered the cube.

They stepped out of the cube a minute and one week later and miles away from their starting point. Wren quickly sent the cube away and transmogered into the flamboyant giantess, just as Trey became her beast of burden.

Above them loomed the escarpment that Wren knew the caravan would have descended to reach the valley floor. As they reached the top of a gentle rise, an odd sight greeted them. She had expected to meet Nikki and the group here as they left the caravan, but what Wren had foreseen was not exactly what had occurred. Had her very presence altered events? Every time a little change was made to the present, her calculations had to be redone. The abacusian granted her some foresight, but not omniscience.

To their surprise, the group that met them was larger, having added several dageki and a telepathic worm. And they were running for their lives.

CHAPTER TWENTY

The Keleps Brothers

Nikki surveyed the desert with growing concern. Squinting in the blaze of the afternoon sun, she wondered again about the line of dust ahead of them. It had grown steadily larger throughout the morning, until now she thought she could make out wagons at its head. If it continued in its present direction, it would intersect their course soon, before dark could offer them some cover. Again, she considered what course of action to take. With the water almost as low as their spirits, and the dry lands stretching out in an endless flickering heat dream before them, their options were fading fast. And they needed to get help for Benna, now that the giantess had abandoned them.

Nikki felt anger warm her face. She didn't understand why the giantess had left so abruptly, but she was determined to survive without her help. How could they succumb now, when they'd survived such hardships already? She remembered her mother saying that how your life turned out might never be fair, but when it isn't, you just have to try all the harder. So many things Tya had told her that as a child she hadn't understood, but were now becoming frightfully clear. Only now was Nikki beginning to realize how wise her mother had been.

She turned to Dreyk, and saw her concerns mirrored in his face.

"Well," she began. "It's time to decide. Do we run and hide, or beg help from strangers?"

Dreyk ran a hand through his wild mane of hair. "I don't see that we have much choice. We must ask for help. Our food and water supplies are almost gone. Benna needs medical care we can't provide."

Nikki grunted. She glanced at Char with a questioning look.

"It's yur skin, I s'pose, not mine. I kin be leavin' anytime I wants. These traders, they's mostly harmless, I's thinkin. Unless you's a fruckin' dageki, that is." What sounded like an evil chuckle erupted from an expressionless face. Nikki cringed. She didn't know what a dageki was, but it didn't sound like she wanted to be one. Char continued, "I'll gets meself water an' hunt fer food, when I gets me strength back, a' course. But it's rough goin' ahead. Might be nice to ride fer a bit."

Nikki turned to Moonchaser. "My little heart, I'm afraid you will need to stay out of sight. These men are more likely to try to kill a grella than invite you into their camp. To them you are nothing but a dangerous predator."

Moonchaser growled, as if to agree with her assessment of him, but finally he slunk away to stay out of sight.

Nikki nodded and said with enthusiasm that she didn't quite feel, "Then we'd better get moving if we want to catch them."

It was approaching the hottest part of the day when the caravan at last came close enough that their shouts and waves were noticed. As they approached the wagons, Nikki did a quick head count.

Know the number of your enemy, Tbrin had counseled her.

Perhaps there would be no trouble, but over-prepared was preferable to dead. She counted about twenty armed men and women, but it was their cargo that really caught her eye. Several wagons had large, built-in cages, and in them where the strangest beasts Nikki had ever seen.

Massive heads, vaguely equine, but with rows of gigantic flat-topped teeth, protruding from the cages. Not carnivores, she thought, flat teeth for grinding coarse vegetation. The shape of their bodies she couldn't quite define. Though massive, they seemed to melt into the space they were given, which wasn't a lot in the cramped cages. Those that were able to sit up, sat on massive haunches. Smaller and almost fragile front limbs hung at their sides. They had no skin, at least not in the human sense, but instead were covered with shiny, hexagonal plates that caught the sunlight, each in its own manner. Iridescent colors played in the depth of each plate, predominantly rich turquoise, deep magenta or glowing amber.

Lovely, she thought, and then laughed at the incongruity of her observations. To think such a hulking beast lovely! But she had learned not to pre-judge or assess by looks alone. In Mistra, such a mistake could be your last. She planned to get a closer look at these captives if she could.

The front wagon came to a halt, and a large human clambered down from his high perch. Nikki reluctantly pulled her eyes from the beasts. At the same time, another man dismounted from a sturdy sagehorse and stepped forward. The two were alike in some ways, yet seemingly opposite in others. While they were of similar build and complexion, they were totally different in bearing and dress. The man from the wagon was large, but neat and clean, perfectly dressed and groomed. Nikki had to wonder how he managed it in this dusty environment. He came forward with a mincing step, as if he were trying to keep his shiny boots out of the dirt as he walked.

The other man stepped up to them with an overt expression of hostility on his face, one hand at his hip and the other at his sword belt. Above this he wore a tattered vest that had once been red, adorned with tarnished medals, sweat stains and the greasy remains of several meals. While the two were obviously brothers or close kin, Nikki thought that no two people could look more alike yet seem more different.

The greasy one was the first to speak, and his voice grated at them, suspecting, accusing and condemning in the first word, while his eyes surveyed them with a scathing look, coming to rest on Dreyk, whom he obviously assumed was their leader.

"What are humans doing out here?" he boomed. "The nearest human settlement is Madog, many miles to the north. You people must be very lost. If you are people, and not transmogrifers or daemons in human form." This last he growled at them as if he expected them to jump out of their skins and attack at any moment. It was beginning to look like they might have to fight their way out of this. *Another brilliant idea of mine,* Nikki thought.

Dreyk flicked her a warning look, but she didn't need to be reminded that men of the north were often suspicious of transmogrifee.

She stepped forward to speak and immediately knew it was a mistake. The gruff one looked at her as if he couldn't believe that she would have the temerity to be so bold. Perhaps women were not allowed to speak in his society! Since she had already begun, she saw no choice but to continue and hope that these men would grant her the time to learn their customs.

"I assure you that we are very human, and very lost," said Nikki. Trying to keep her tone casual and soothing, she continued, "Our aim is to reach Kraida to the North. My brother and I are from a small fishing village far south. We are accompanying this man who was shipwrecked near our village. We became lost in the desert and need water and directions. We will repay you in any way we can."

The man's only response was to snort in seeming disbelief and finger his sword. Nikki trailed off into silence. She was beginning again to assess her probable opponents, noting grimly the number of swords, when the other man stepped forward.

"Please, please excuse my dear brother," said the man in an almost whispered rasp. "He lacks proper manners even in the best of circumstances." He shot his brother the briefest disparaging look, then turned back on them with an impossibly wide smile, showing rows of perfect white teeth. *The smile of a hungry jackal*, thought Nikki. The man continued to speak in his effusive manner.

"Let me please present ourselves. I am Master Osli Keleps and this sad excuse for a gentleman is my brother, Zarad. We're just returning from a successful but exhaustive expedition into the dageki lands."

Nikki noted that Zarad's hand still hovered over his sword, and she was beginning to think that they might have to fight after all, when Osli stepped close to her. She was assailed by a mixture of scents so strong that her eyes began to water. She forced herself not to pull away and concentrated on trying to isolate the odors. Most noticeable was a rich, musky-sweet spice that seemed the perfect complement to Osli's overweening manner. It was obviously meant to hide other odors but managed only to mingle with them in an unhappy union. Beneath the spice she detected some scents she knew from Hyla's cooking, ground root, kara spicegrass and cinnamon bloom, and something else, something alien. The closest Nikki could come to it was lizard, or snake. She shuddered, hoping that he hadn't noticed.

He was now close to Nikki, and she could see the gilt on his teeth and the makeup he wore to hide a mole. Suddenly he stuffed his chubby hands into his pockets, nervously fingering something there, then he let out a sigh and a twittering laugh.

Turning to his brother, he said, "Nothing to fear here, Zarad. They are as they appear. No auras. They are as talentless as you or me, except for the beast-woman, but she is a huntress only, and it appears that her talents have been, at least temporarily, diminished. She might be useful in gathering food." At these words Zarad visibly relaxed and for the first time removed his hand from the hilt of his sword.

Osli turned to her, pulling her forward, lifting her hand to shake it vigorously between his two.

"Welcome to our caravan. Welcome!"

Despite her relief, Nikki couldn't help but feel resentment at his statement. Talentless! After years of study, practice, all the hardship, to have her condition spoken of so blatantly. It was some concession at least that her lack of power had certainly saved them a conflict here, and quite possibly saved their lives as well. But how did Osli detect that they had no auras, if he himself was talentless, as he claimed? She didn't trust either of these brothers, but Osli especially would bear watching. With his sickly-sweet manner, he was probably more dangerous than Zarad, with his open xenophobia. At least you would always know what Zarad was thinking. She felt certain she could take Zarad in open combat. The fact that he saw her as no threat would be all the advantage she would need. But there were many others in the troop, perhaps twenty armed men in all. They were badly overmatched. She glanced at Dreyk, as if to tell him to watch his back, but he returned her gaze with one that said that he understood her all too well.

She realized that Osli had been speaking and warned herself to pay better attention. There was something in his voice that seemed to turn off her awareness, the way he rambled, never really saying anything. But she couldn't afford to miss a word.

"...and I will gladly show you our catch this evening, if you can stand the smell. I'm afraid it's not the most pleasant part of our job. But I forget myself. You are obviously tired and thirsty. Zarad, get these fine people some water. No, don't worry about payment now. We'll make arrangements later. It's still a healthy journey to Madog. From there you can follow the pass over the Hartbone Range to the region of Kraida, if that's still your desire.

"We're headed for the Shallow Run," he continued. "It's only a few hours march north. You probably would have found the river yourself once you reached the escarpment, but I insist you travel with us. For safety, you know, and I haven't had civilized company to talk to in weeks."

Osli slid his eyes down her torso with a look so slippery that it made her feel like she needed a bath afterward. So that was it! He wanted her. This she might be able to use to her advantage. Perhaps she was no expert at it herself, as she had always preferred to pick lovers for pleasure, rather than for personal gain, but she had seen how the highborn used lust to gain political power in Mistra. The trick would be to prevent the situation from getting out of control. She wasn't sure that she could fake it with this man. *I'd rather sleep with an eel*, she thought, then realized to her chagrin that she'd spoken aloud.

"What was that, my dear?"

"Oh—I just said, you don't know how much better I feel."

"There, there," he crooned. "You're in very competent hands now. You can put your complete trust in me." He leaned forward to pat her on the shoulder, but his hand lingered, sliding down her back to caress her rib cage. Nikki suppressed a shudder with all her will, and a moment came back to her clearly, from her sessions with Tbrin. His words rang in her mind, echoing with the resonance of croma on croma as their swords collided. *Use your opponent's emotions as a weapon against him. Silence your fears. Become the vessel, and he will pour his life into your hands.*

She returned Osli's smile with one that she hoped would both keep him interested and give her the time she needed.

"I'm afraid we have no coin to pay you, but we were hoping we could offer our labor—"

"Yes, yes, but let's not worry about reimbursement now. I do so hate to conduct business in the heat of the day. We've plenty of time, plenty."

Nikki tried to beam relief, but she wasn't at all relieved by his manner. Most likely, his intention was to stall until he got what he wanted from her, and then eliminate them. Of course, his brother Zarad would do the dirty work, while Osli gave the orders. That much at least was clear. Osli was the decision maker, but he would hesitate to get his own hands dirty. And right now, he had decided to be generous, as long as it worked to his advantage. He had found some playthings to distract him from a long and tedious journey. Nikki only hoped that she could beat him at his game. Right now, she wouldn't bet on her chances.

Nikki was trying her best to make small talk, and her head throbbed with the effort not to make a slip. How difficult it was to make no reference to transmogrifee. She realized more and more how much it had been a part of her life, of her very existence. Well, that would have to change, and this was as good a place to start as any. It probably wouldn't matter if she made a slip anyway. Osli was too busy finding excuses to pat her knee or caress her hand, to pay much attention to what she said. He thought her provincial and unschooled, that much was clear, and Nikki would make no effort to change his opinion. *What your opponent doesn't know about you can often be more useful than your sword.*

Osli had insisted that she ride up on the front of the wagon with him. She hadn't wanted to be separated from the others, but she didn't want to raise the ire of this man. Char had insisted on riding one of the equines in harness, while the others rode in the wagon.

She had a feeling that Osli's sunny disposition would vanish quickly in the face of the slightest opposition, especially from a woman. When she saw that Benna and Dreyk were being shown to the next wagon, she had relaxed just a little. When she looked back, Dreyk gave her a brief, glum look as if to say, "I hope you know what you're doing!" then he turned his eyes out to the desert. Benna lay silent and pale beside him.

Nikki could see nothing but endless, dusty terrain before them, but Osli said that the Shallow Run was at the base of a large escarpment, only a few hours north. All day she expected cliffs to loom before them, but none appeared. In the late afternoon they reached the escarpment, but it wasn't what Nikki had expected. She didn't realize that they had come to the edge until they were practically upon it. Osli pulled up the wagons with a loud whistle, seemingly just in time, although he showed no concern.

To her surprise she found that they were not below the escarpment, but on top of it. To get her bearings, she looked toward the horizon first, where the sun was painting the mountains purple as it slid behind them. Misty and cool, the peaks beckoned to her restless soul. Would she visit these peaks on her journey? She hoped so, they were so beautiful. Just the lack of detail caused by distance, she thought. Up close they were probably cold and forbidding, like every other mountain she'd known.

Her eyes traveled downward through a gray-green haze that materialized into forest as she looked closer, until directly below them she could discern individual trees, the misshapen, twisted limbs of scrub pine, interspersed with tall, stately firs. Through the trees meandered a river wide enough to make crossing a challenge. It followed a general course along the base of the cliffs, but its path was anything but direct. Nikki was intrigued by the many sharp twists and turns it made. It was a wonder it got anywhere with so many side trips.

She bravely stood up to look down the shear sides of the escarpment directly below them. How would they ever make it down to the river from such a height with these wagons? Osli pulled her down and told her to sit and hold the brake while he got down from the wagon for a conference with his brother. The two conversed in hushed tones for several minutes, but all Nikki could make out was "the maze". From the tone of their voices, she had the general impression that something was wrong. When Osli clambered back up, she said nothing although the foreboding must have shown on her face. Osli patted her hand paternally and said, "Nothing to fear, my dear. We've just come a little farther west than I had intended. It won't take long to correct our course." But Nikki noted that he seemed distracted and unusually quiet as they rode on.

At last, they reached the maze, and Nikki could see why it was so named; a narrow, steep series of switchbacks and rough-cut trails wound its crooked way down the face of the escarpment. Nikki wasn't encouraged by the fact that it seemed to be partly man-made and partly naturally occurring, the result of erosion and slippage of loose shale on the steep grade. At the bottom, the trees looked very small.

"We're taking these wagons down there?" she exclaimed.

Osli patted her thigh reassuringly. "Now don't fret, my pretty. We've done it many times. Besides, it's the only way down, unless you want to travel north for another hundred miles or so in the desert. If you have someone like me who knows the correct route, it's easy."

Nikki noted the beads of sweat on his brow and wondered if he really believed any part of what he'd just said. Even having grown up in the formidable peaks of the Drakyn's Teeth, Nikki found the ride a little unnerving, having to trust to the skill of the drivers. Glancing back, she noted that Dreyk's face was pale, and he refused to look down, keeping his eyes trained on the narrow path before them.

Nikki was amazed at how calmly the teams worked their way down the steep trails. After a few switchbacks, she also wondered how Osli was keeping track of the route. From the top she had seen many false trails leading to dead-ends. At the end of one of these, she spotted the skeletal remains of a wagon, its twisted gray ribs stabbing at the air. The contents lay where they had fallen, now a grass-covered mound of decay. She imagined what it must have been like, having to leave the wagon and most of its contents behind, but the trail was too narrow for turning a wagon, unless it could be backed the entire length of the false trail, and up a jagged switchback to the main trail. It looked as if they had decided to try to turn the wagon, when it had tipped. Had they lost the team over the edge?

She could see how they might have become lost in the maze; the main trail was so rarely used that it was as overgrown as the false trails. Apparently Osli had a map in his mind, telling him which course to take. There were a couple of times when he had to stop to consider. Here he paused with a distant expression on his face, his fingers fidgeting in his pocket nervously. Then the way would seem clear to him, and he would continue.

What a disaster it would be to lead all these wagons with their living cargo down the wrong way! Would they just leave their captives to die? Nikki thought so. Although Osli had said that the beasts were no threat, she had seen the way the men avoided reaching into the cages, if possible. She didn't think that these men would risk releasing their cargo where attack would be possible. She only hoped the situation would never arise. She wasn't sure whose side she would take.

But Osli never faltered, and the smile never left his face. Although the wagons progressed with excruciating slowness, the valley floor did seem to be coming closer, and Nikki began to relax, until the wagon suddenly tipped, almost tossing her from the seat. One of the back wheels had hit a soft spot in the trail and began to slide over the edge.

Loose dirt and rock broke away and disappeared, tinkling far below as it came to rest on some lower level. Nikki was sure that they were going to go over. She was poised to jump from the wagon, when Osli yelled and whipped the team ferociously, knocking her back into the seat. The wheel came up and the wagon lurched forward. Once they were safely beyond the slide, Osli yanked on the reins to stop the agitated sagehorses and leapt down to calm them with a speed that Nikki would not have suspected him capable of.

The two brothers conferred over the collapsed portion of road, eventually deciding to continue, but Nikki couldn't see that they had much choice; turning back didn't look like an alternative, especially with one wagon already beyond the gap.

With two wagon side rails serving—hopefully—as a bridge, and steering the wagons partially up the hillside, the entire caravan was able to make it across unscathed. Except for some grunting noises, the beasts in the cages sat unnaturally still and quiet. Were they too stupid to be frightened, or smart enough to know that a sudden movement might send them all over the edge?

When they were all safe, Nikki thought she heard one of the captives shout something to its guards, but she decided it must have been one of the other men. Hadn't Osli said that the beasts lacked the wit to learn language? She was happy at least that these animals weren't being collected for food, but Osli just laughed at her question, saying that cooked dageki tasted little better than dried marm hide. He seemed reluctant to answer more questions about his "catch," as he called it, and would say only that with extensive training on his part, they made passable house servants for those in the northern cities who could afford them.

Nikki was stunned by what she heard. Could these ugly beasts be the creatures of legend that she had learned about in her studies;

the talentless reptilian dageki? She looked back again at their huddled forms and wondered.

Another thought nagged at her. Despite Osli's euphemistic phrasing, she couldn't ignore the fact that they had unwittingly joined a band of slavers. Would their fates join that of the tractable dageki?

She was distracted by another sharp turn that the wagon barely navigated, and she was forced to forget the dageki, and all less immediate problems, until much later.

CHAPTER TWENTY-ONE

A Tale of Lost Tails

G ormz regained consciousness, squinting at the chilly sun through the bars of his cage. He felt sorry for himself. His precious tail hadn't been oiled in weeks. For all he knew it was going to fall off right in front of his peers, and he would be exiled from dageki society forever. He'd heard of court hopefuls who had lost only a tiny portion of their tails and had been banned from the palace of Dmisi until which time the tail could be regrown, a matter of years, in some cases. He wondered how the dageki could be so prone to losing these precious tails, but not for a second did he believe that the legends were true, that the dageki had once been small scurrying denizens of the desert floor, and they lost their tails when grabbed by a predator, thereby saving their lives.

His thoughts returned to himself, as they inevitably did. How had he gotten himself into this position? If only he had realized sooner that Garak Zia Sinz Rentros had been scheming all along to remove him from his post at the university. He needed to be back there where he belonged, especially now, when the long dark ages of dageki science and learning appeared to be nearing an end. A renaissance was coming, and Gormz wanted desperately to be a part of it.

Instead, he had been sent out here to this miserable desert on a fact-finding mission. The only fact he had found was that the dageki race was in real danger. Outside Dmisi itself, whole villages had mysteriously disappeared. At this rate, the dageki were doomed. If he survived this, he would have to report to the sovereign that life outside the dageki metropolis was just too dangerous. No wonder their race had been in decline for years. Why hadn't the dageki leadership done more to prevent this?

He paused depressing thoughts when a creature new to his experience approached. He had to admit that it was perhaps the ugliest creature he had ever seen. Instead of the lovely, durable and protective plates of a dageki, the thing sported only a thin, pale underskin of some kind, with a massive tuft of dark brown moss growing from its snoutless head. The worst aberration of all was that it had no tail. Did it lose the tail in a catastrophic accident or, sovereign forbid, was it born without one? *Poor thing*, he thought with his first experience of compassion.

Only later would he learn the word for this creature: *human*.

CHAPTER TWENTY-TWO

Allow Me to Introduce Myself

As darkness was closing in, they finally made it to the bottom. They went as far as possible, until the undergrowth became thick and the ground uneven, making progress in the dark both difficult and dangerous for the mounts. As soon as Osli pulled up, Nikki climbed down on unsteady legs and walked into the trees, on the pretense of stretching her legs and relieving herself. Behind her, she could hear Osli shouting orders to set up camp right where they were. It was obviously too dark to make it much further, and they could hear the rush of the river to their right. She pitied the men who would be sent to carry water and gather wood in the dark.

Nikki stretched her back and gazed up into the trees. So many trees together were a rare sight in the mountains where she'd spent her life. They usually lived alone, stalwart and noble sentinels who stood against the whims of the mountain climate. Here the trees were more social creatures. In the slight breeze, they danced together, she thought, like newlyweds, caressing, yet never abrading each other. She wondered, with a silent laugh, if their dance would be so convivial when the winter storms arrived, and the honeymoon ended.

Leaving the trees, she wandered casually back toward the end of the caravan and the cages there. She glanced back at the growing camp as tents went up, and a fire began to glow and crackle. She might have a few minutes before Osli realized that she hadn't returned.

Long before she reached the cages, the scent accosted her, and she remembered where she'd picked it up before, on Osli. He said that he trained them. She wondered what this training entailed.

Once near, she found herself unable to step closer. She could just make out the dark masses of their bodies in the moonlight and the glow of their luminous eyes. Still. Very still and quiet. They watched her.

"I mean you no harm, my friends. I hope you survived that trip in better shape than my nerves did," she whispered, only to reassure herself, expecting no answer.

To her surprise, she got one anyway, in perfect diction.

"I don't know what I'm doing, trying to talk to a human. It's all hopeless." The voice paused. Was that a sob? The voice resumed, and Nikki searched for its source. "But it is improper for me to speak without formal introduction."

Nikki looked around, but there were no other humans nearby. She could hear Zarad in the distance, noisily supervising the set-up of camp.

She forced herself closer to the nearest cage and investigated the faces of the dageki inside. In the moonlight, she could just make out one eye watching her; the head tipped like a bird to follow her every movement. It was perhaps smaller than the average of his race. An adolescent? Like the others, it stood very still, but its front limbs quivered slightly.

"You speak?" she asked.

"Of course, I speak!" snorted the creature. "I am a Gormz Ri Tageki Si, a graduate of Dmisi University."

Another dageki grabbed at him and whined in the dageki language, or so she assumed it to be, since this one could obviously speak the common tongue.

"I can't speak with you without formal introduction," said the creature again, even as he *was* speaking to her.

"Is that why your people don't communicate with humans?"

"Yes, it is beneath us."

"But you need to tell these slavers that you are intelligent creatures who don't deserve this treatment."

"It's not that simple. I am different than most of my kind, less prone to following the rules, as my teachers said, but the others will not interact with a species that they deem beneath them."

"That's ridiculous! You need to fight. You all look stronger than any of these men."

"It is not going to happen. It is our way, and one lone dageki cannot change millennia of tradition."

Nikki let out a long breath. She imagined that the slavers had found it all too convenient that the dageki were silent and so gentle they wouldn't even fight back when captured.

"I can't leave you like this. We're going to escape this caravan soon, ourselves, and I'll find a way to take you with us."

Nikki didn't know why she said it but realized that she meant it. She couldn't leave, knowing that these creatures were suffering. She turned away, her thoughts in turmoil.

Behind her, she again heard the other dageki whining at Gormz in their strange tongue, but Gormz made only a brief response. Were they berating him for speaking to her without a proper introduction? How could they be so obstinate when their very lives were at risk?

As she walked back toward the camp, she was reminded that the dageki were the least of her worries right now. Why had she offered to free them? She had said it without thinking, spurred by her indignation at their treatment, but the fact was that she was probably in as much danger as the dageki themselves. And what would the others say about her plans?

She decided to face them at once and get it over with. She found Dreyk near the camp and tried to pull him away as inconspicuously as possible. When she got him aside, he informed her that Benna was responding well to the medicines that Osli had provided, and had even woken up briefly, though he was back asleep now.

"Shall I try to wake him?" asked Dreyk.

"No, let him sleep. I'm just glad he's starting to recover. I can't wait to get away from this caravan."

She described her conversation with the dageki and her offer to free them. She crossed her arms and waited for his outburst, but he only looked at her with an odd, quiet expression, then shrugged his shoulders.

He said, "I didn't know that the dageki could learn our language, but I'm not surprised that they're so intelligent. I've suspected as much for some time."

"Did you keep them as slaves?" Nikki demanded hotly.

"No, I never kept slaves!" shot Dreyk. "But they are everywhere in Bay Towne, the latest fashion in house help," he added bitterly. "They can be taught to do simple chores. They provide some amusement for the aristocracy, then they usually die. But they're given no respect, even in death. I know a tavern in Suz with hundreds of dageki skins adorning the walls, like some proud flag of genocide. I agree with you, Nikki. We've got to do something, at least for these few, if we can."

He was silent for a few seconds, and Nikki could feel the pressure of the space between them.

"What game are you playing here, Nikki? I heard your conversation with Osli. I don't trust him. I don't trust him at all!"

Nikki could see his eyes flickering bright, even in the dark.

"It's a game I've got to play, Dreyk. Of course I'm not interested in Osli, but I don't know how long I can deceive him. You'll just have to be ready. We'll need to leave here in a hurry. Tell Benna and Char."

She turned to leave, but he grabbed her arm.

"Wait, Nikki—" he began, then seemed to think better of what he was going to say. "Just be careful," he finished.

"I will," she whispered harshly. "Don't worry about me, Dreyk. I'll try to do a better job of taking care of myself—and us—than I've done so far."

"That's not what I meant," he retorted. "And if you'd stop being so damn defensive for just one moment, you'd see that I'm on your side!" He ran his fingers roughly through his hair.

"Nikki, I don't think that I would have survived the things you've been through. At least I'm sure I would have complained a whole lot more. But you take so much on yourself, as if the whole world were your responsibility alone, and now you've included the dageki in that equation. I'm not patronizing you. I envy your strength. I just don't want you to push your luck too far. I don't like the idea of you playing games with Osli. He'll just as likely to stab you in the back as—"

"I think it far more likely he'd have Zarad do it for him."

"You know what I mean."

"Yes, I do," she sighed. "I'm sorry, Dreyk. I don't mean to be defensive. It just comes out that way. To this point, I've failed at just about everything, and I've dragged you and Benna into danger with me."

"It was our decision," he said roughly, then more gently, "Just be careful, that's all I ask."

Nikki nodded and turned away. She couldn't help wondering at his concern. It seemed that Dreyk's distrust of her had vanished when she'd lost her power. With his distrust of transmogrifers, would his affection dissolve as quickly if she were to regain her ability?

Her thoughts so occupied her that she didn't see Osli approaching until she almost ran into him.

"There you are, my sweet," he grinned. "I've been looking all over for you. I bet you'd like to freshen up. I have a tent set up over there. And I have a surprise for you before dinner."

I can just imagine, she thought, and this time she managed not to say it aloud.

Osli led her to a large tent near the fire, where he showed her to a table with a basin of steaming water.

"Primitive," he said. "But we must do with what we have out here in the savage lands. I had one of the men heat the water for you."

"Thank you," she replied in all honesty, "this will be a very welcome luxury, but you shouldn't have wasted hot water for me. They probably need it for cooking, and it's a walk to the river."

"Nonsense, my dear. I pay them well. They wouldn't dare complain." With that, he walked out.

Nikki stuck her hands into the water, splashing her face. She moaned unconsciously, luxuriating in the warmth and the silky feel of it on her dry skin. How long had it been since she'd been clean? She scrubbed as best she could, but what she really needed was a bath. The stubborn desert dust seemed to clog every pore. She buried her face in the soft towel Osli had left her. When she looked up, she found Osli watching her, and she wondered how long he'd been there. He held out a neatly folded white bundle.

"I hope you like it," he said, almost meekly as he unfolded the garment.

The problem was that she did like it. She unfolded a delicate gown made from a fabric like none she'd ever seen. Even the most accomplished artisans of Mistra, with all their creative enhancements, had never produced anything so exquisite. It was made of many sheer layers of the softest glowing white fabric. Embroidered among the layers were shimmering birds and flowers in flowing pastel detail. The effect was that of a pale garden of dancing beauty. Her appreciation must have shown on her face, and Osli let out a satisfied sigh.

"It's far too beautiful and valuable to wear!" she exclaimed truthfully. She tried to return it to him, but he pushed it back into her hands.

"Don't be so modest. This dress will be only a poor shadow to your own beauty. I picked it up in the market at Tia Cara from a Belwenieze seamstress. She was a hostile woman, as are most of her kind, but they are unrivaled in their stitchery, if not their business sense. I paid half the going price."

"Still, I don't—"

"I insist you wear it for dinner. We'll dine in my tent in ten minutes."

Nikki heard a rigidity in his tone that seemed to brook no disagreement. He turned and left before she could formulate another argument.

When she donned the gown, she immediately regretted that she hadn't been firmer with Osli. The fabric was far too revealing, the neckline too low. She thought about wearing her own clothes underneath, but she knew it would look ridiculous and would only show Osli that she feared him. She would just have to go through with it.

She compromised by leaving on her boots. They barely showed beneath the long gown, and she could claim that she had no other footwear. Besides, the tall boots made an excellent cache for her slender knife. She wouldn't be foolish enough to go into this man's tent without at least one weapon. She only hoped that she wouldn't need it.

The tent's furnishings consisted of a few makeshift tables, two low stools, and a seagrass mat. Seeing the bed, Nikki suddenly remembered that there had been none in her tent, and her apprehension grew. Osli apparently wasted no time when he wanted something. She would just have to stall as best she could until Benna was well enough to travel.

Only when she sat down at the table, did she realize how ravenous she was. The meal consisted of traveler's lettuce, dry waybread, and hard cheese. Osli also offered her a slice of oily, sweet-smelling meat, but Nikki refused it. Even though Osli said that he didn't find dageki flesh palatable, she wasn't sure that she believed him, and the anonymous meat didn't have an appealing smell.

She concentrated on her meal while Osli nibbled at his food, watching her. He opened a bottle of some tangy liquor and never let her cup get below half full. Nikki noticed that he seemed able to down prodigious amounts of the drink himself. She didn't think it necessary to point out that she had always had a high tolerance for alcohol.

"Tha' dress looks like i' were made for ya, m' dear," he slurred. "From now on, you're t' wear only white 'r nothin' at all! I knew there was a lovely flower hidin' under those dirty travelin' duds. Like the dress, you got layers. Can't wait to discover 'em all!

"Now, let's toast our sera–serendipitous meeting. Here, yer cup's almost empty ag'in." He tried to fill it, but most of the liquor spilled onto the table and floor.

She was beginning to feel a little tipsy herself. The drink was stronger than she had at first thought. Fortunately, Osli was far enough along that he didn't notice when she occasionally tipped her cup into the dirt under the table.

"Le's dance," he slurred, knocking over the empty bottle and tipping the table as he stood, weaving like a tree in the wind.

"I'm afraid I can't dance," she lied.

"Teach you," he mumbled, grabbing her arm and pulling her to her feet with more strength than she would have given him credit for. "Bet there's lots a' things I could teach ya, li'l flower."

Nikki wasn't feeling threatened; Osli was too drunk to follow through on any amorous intentions he might have. She was more afraid that he would fall on top of her, which he almost did. His head slowly wilted to her shoulder, and she could hear the soft rumble of his snoring. Fortunately, they were near enough to the mat that she managed to steer him down to it without mishap. He was awake again and giggling now.

"Can't wait any longer, eh? You misled me, little minx, pretending to be so shy." He tried to drag her down on top of him, but she managed to pull away.

"Just a minute, lover," she soothed. "We wouldn't want to wrinkle this dress, now, would we?"

But Nikki had no intention of removing her clothing, and as soon as she was able to escape his grasp, she headed for the door. When she looked back, Osli was snoring again peacefully. She wondered if she would be able to convince him tomorrow that they'd had sex after all. *Probably the type who remembers every detail, despite the drink,* she thought morosely.

She was beginning to think that Dreyk was right; she might be stirring up more trouble than she could handle.

She crept back along the wagons, stealing a loose blanket from among the baggage on the way. In the distance, a grella howled. Moonchaser? She knew he was out there somewhere, but she missed him. She missed the touch of his fur and the way he curled up at her feet.

When she reached her tent, she wrapped herself into the blanket and slumped to the dirt floor where dizziness and sleep enveloped her in welcome numbness.

The next day was a nightmare. She woke with a throbbing headache that only grew worse as the day wore on. The caravan was packed up and ready to move early. Osli was in an ugly mood and seemed to want to take it out on his men. Nikki could only imagine what his head must feel like. He had drunk twice as much as she had. Mostly, he ignored her, except when he was glaring at her. She had taken off the dress and returned to her own gear but still didn't feel comfortable. He said very little to her, but his looks showed his anger. Apparently, he felt that she'd made a fool of him, and that was a thing that wouldn't go unexcused.

By noon Nikki was exhausted with the effort of always being ready to fight while trying to appear relaxed and friendly. The more she plied Osli with small talk, the more reticent he became. Finally, she gave up and sat miserably in the brooding silence.

The afternoon wore on as they followed a rough trail along the river. The terrain was, at times, difficult to navigate, being conversely muddy or rocky. The wagons creaked and groaned with the strain. Toward evening, as they were making their way through an especially rough spot, Nikki heard a loud snap behind them. One of the wagons carrying the dageki tipped wildly as a wheel splintered and disintegrated. The wagon ground to a halt, its axle burying itself in the dirt.

Osli jumped down and began yelling at the dageki in incoherent fury. Some of the creatures were yowling in excited tones, others in painful squeals as they were crushed under the weight of others in the tipping cage.

Zarad came up beside his brother and shouted orders for his men to right the wagon, while Osli continued to scream at the dageki. Osli seemed to believe that the dageki had intentionally caused the accident in an escape attempt. Sensing his rage, the dageki grew quiet, except for one who was ill or in pain. It continued to whine in a grating nasal tone. For a moment, Nikki thought that Osli might order them all killed that instant. His face was livid with rage, but instead, he stood still with his hands in his pockets. After a moment, she became aware of a barely audible sound. It was an ethereal music in sharps and flats that made her shiver. The dageki responded to the melody, becoming even more still. The one who had been whining ceased and began to crawl to the back of the cage, one leg trailing uselessly behind it, but the creature's face held no pain, just a blank expression.

Zarad opened the cage door, and the injured dageki tumbled out. Osli stared at the creature in silent malice while warring expressions crossed his face. Was he having second thoughts about harming these docile creatures? Nikki hoped so. She wasn't sure that she had the strength to save them. Osli was already angry with her. She sat frozen in her seat, afraid of what might happen if she interfered.

Osli looked up and down the line of cages. Nikki could see the sweat on his brow. "It's time you new ones understood," he began in an unnaturally calm voice. "When I say quiet, I mean quiet. Disobedience will not be tolerated. Zarad, kill this one."

"No!" screamed Nikki as she launched herself from her seat, but she was too late. She heard the scrape of Zarad's blade on the plates of the dageki's breast. The dageki took a deep, slow breath, then let it out finally and peacefully, as if death were a relief. Before she could say more, Osli turned to her.

"You will be at my tent at sunset, and you will wear the dress. Is that understood?"

He didn't wait for her answer but stalked off as if there could be no question as to her response. And what choice did she have? Zarad leered at her through the corner of his eye as he cleaned his blade in the grass, then left her standing over the body.

She watched the iridescence fading from the dageki's body plates and felt her hope draining with it. Dark blood was seeping into the porous ground, irreplaceable hope draining away.

Osli had merely been taking his anger for her out on them, and because of her, this dageki was dead. Perhaps the poor creature had been right to welcome death. Better to die than be the cause of it, and yet live on. There were worse things than dying. Far worse.

Nikki suddenly felt the weight of her decision to leave Mistra. She was learning fast that the world was not a pleasant place. *Lesson number one,* she thought bitterly, *but will any of us survive to learn lesson number two?*

CHAPTER TWENTY-THREE

The Worm Turns

The sun set and the wind picked up in the trees, as cool breezes moved in from the south. Drakonia's lesser moon rose and filled the river valley with delicate blue light. Nikki sat on the floor of her tent, fingering the white gown in her lap.

She couldn't clear her mind of the memory of the dageki, how easily it had died, how easily it had let itself be killed. Osli had transmograffic power—that much was clear—and Nikki had nothing but a slender knife and even more slender hopes of them escaping this nightmare. But she had to try. Especially now. One more death on her hands would be more than she could bear.

Gathering her courage, she rose and put the dress on, again slipping her knife into her boot, and picked up her pack and sword. She made her way reluctantly toward Osli's tent. She slipped through the camp with her head bowed, ignoring the gazes and whispers that followed her. Dreyk and Benna were at the far end of camp, and she was glad that she didn't have to face them. She didn't think that she could bear the accusations that she would surely see in their faces.

Working her way around to the back of Osli's tent, she silently deposited her sword and pack in the shadows, then backtracked and came around to the front, where a guard stood at the entrance. He pulled the flap aside, motioning her in without expression.

The tent was dark inside, and Nikki stood for a second, waiting for her eyes to adjust to the low light. This time Osli made no pretense of offering her dinner. He came up from the shadows behind her, grabbing her shoulders roughly.

"You're late," he growled and started to drag her toward the mat.

"Wait! What about dinner?"

"Later."

"We need to talk about the dageki. They are very intelligent and don't deserve this treatment. One of them told me—"

"The dageki don't speak," he interrupted. "Shut up and get that dress off. We don't have all night."

Nikki struggled, but again Osli proved stronger than she expected. He forced her down, and his weight pinned her. She struggled to reach the dagger in her boot, but he grabbed her arm and knocked the weapon out of her hand. She heard the dress tearing and was oddly more worried about the dress than about herself. How could he destroy something so beautiful? She found herself thinking in defeat that beautiful things were created for people like Osli to despoil.

Nikki wanted to scream, but where would it get her? Dreyk and Benna would certainly try to come to her aid and almost as surely be killed for trying. Besides, she felt almost embarrassed that she had allowed herself to be put into this position. What would Tbrin have to say about her fighting skills, if he could see her now?

Osli pulled back for a second, stuffing his hand into his pocket roughly. She put all her thoughts into a last desperate prayer, and it seemed that almost instantly, her prayers were answered. Osli became very still and stared at her with glazed eyes of terror.

"No!" he screamed, gripping his head in both hands. Nikki watched in amazement as his skin grew flushed, his eyes bulged from their sockets and his mouth opened in a silent scream of agony. He fell away from her, and bloody saliva gurgled from his lips. He struggled through a few gasping breaths, his body convulsed, then lay still.

Nikki watched in horror as something began to crawl slowly from the pocket of the dead man. Before her squirmed a soft, segmented worm as large as a man's foot. It was a sickly yellow color, with purple blotches along its length. With obvious effort, it raised its quivering head and looked up at her with tiny, black beady eyes.

She grabbed for her knife and raised it to kill the abomination, but the blade never reached its intended target, as searing pain blinded her, physically knocking her backward. She fell, clutching her head as Osli had done, and wondered if she would share his fate. The pain filled all her being, making coherent thought impossible. Through the pain, she felt her mind being invaded, and she was completely powerless against it.

As suddenly as it began, the pain stopped, and she lay gasping on the ground. It took her a while to realize that she heard a voice, a clear signal in her mind; the kind of signal that only a psy adept could send.

Please forgive me if I hurt you, the voice was saying. *I didn't mean to react so violently. I'm afraid it's a natural defense mechanism. The probing thought was necessary also. I had to know that I could trust you.*

Nikki crawled forward, not trusting her legs, and looked into the glossy depths of the worm's tiny eyes.

"You?" she rasped.

Don't look so shocked, spoke the voice clearly in her mind. *Size isn't everything, you know. Psy ability is inherent to my race, with the Herb, of course. My name is Dweeba. Pleased to meet you. Now let's get out of here before Zarad decides that it's his turn.*

"That's how Osli did his tricks; you did them for him, controlling the dageki, and finding the trail down the escarpment."

Yes, but I now regret much that I have done. Osli was always on the edge, and today he went too far. Killing the dageki was unnecessary. I refused to help him again tonight, and he tried to hurt me. He won't do that again.

"Remind me never to offend you! But why did you help him? Did he pay you?"

Of course not! What would I do with money? Do you know nothing of the Mei? We require a constant supply of the Herb to maintain our psy abilities. When we grow older and are unable to gather it for ourselves, we often make pacts with other races, a symbiotic relationship. I have always chosen humans. I find them interesting.

I made a mistake, joining the Keleps brothers, but when you and your friends arrived, I saw a possible way to redeem myself. I will help you if I can. It will be a small payment for the ills I've already caused you.

Nikki didn't know quite what to think. There was no doubt that they could use the help that a psy adept could provide, and she didn't know what he might do to her if she refused. On top of that, she probably owed him her life.

"Alright," she said at last. "But we've got to get out of here now."

Isn't that what I've been trying to tell you? She could feel the amused exasperation underlying his thoughts. *Pick me up,* he continued. *The closer I am to you, the better we can work together.*

Nikki reached forward tentatively, not at all sure she wanted to touch the thing, much less pick it up.

Don't worry, I'm not the least bit slimy, and if it makes you feel better, I promise not to squirm.

Embarrassed by her fear and the mocking tone of his thoughts, she forced herself to reach down and pick up the creature. To her surprise, he felt neither cold nor slimy. Instead, an astonishing sense of warmth and well-being flowed through her, a tingling that crept from his skin to hers and into her thoughts. She gasped and held him close as visions began to flow through her. She sensed the camp, the bored thoughts of the watchman outside. She extended herself into the sailing dreams of her brother as he slept, and for a moment, the cool spray from the prow of a sailing ship touched her face, as Dreyk dreamed of his home waters. Even the strange, alien thoughts of the dageki reached her. She searched for Moonchaser and found him watching on a ridge not far from the camp. She pulled away, forcing herself back into her own body, where she still stood looking down at the worm, gently cradled in her arms. His image was blurred, and only then did she become aware of the tears that streamed down her face.

I'm so sorry, he thought to her. *Only now did I become aware of the full extent of your loss. You had a great talent. But it is so easy with you, so clear. As if we were made to be a team. I could be some of the talent that you have lost.*

She put Dweeba into her pack quickly, as much because of her need to adjust to this strange new awareness, as their need for speed.

Once Dweeba had slipped the camp into a psy-induced sleep, she crept out and to the back of the tent. Not wanting to take the time to change, she slipped her own gear over the torn gown, tying the loose ends of the delicate garment around her waist so that it wouldn't trip her. She crept out to wake Benna and Dreyk.

Dreyk stared for a second at her strange garb. The lesser moon was still overhead, casting just enough light to see shapes and pale shadows. He had his pack and was up before she said a word.

"Osli is dead," she whispered. "We've got to get out of here, *now*."

"I've been expecting something like this," was his brusque reply.

They woke Benna, and together they went to the picket line of sagehorses, where Char sat atop one of the equines, as if she had been waiting for them.

"Char, do you think that sagehorse will slip out quietly with us? Benna needs to ride until he gets his strength back."

"This one 'ere, he's a good 'un. I's thinkin' he understands what we needs of 'im."

They started out of camp and the equine followed peacefully behind them. He really did appear to understand the need for quiet, as he let out not even a wicker as they led him from his companions.

We must hurry, thought Dweeba to Nikki. *Zarad is getting restless. My range is limited, and I can't keep them all asleep forever. He will soon discover the body. We must be far from here by then.*

"I've got to go back," Nikki suddenly blurted. "The dageki—I promised."

I wouldn't advise it, he thought back to her. *The dageki are not rational creatures. They live by social rules as outdated as their parochial view of the world. That's why they are so easily swayed by psy suggestion. They have no individual wills and are therefore very dangerous. Leave them.*

"I think you're wrong, and anyway, how can we condemn them to slavery and death because of their views?" Nikki suddenly realized that she had been responding to Dweeba aloud. The others were looking at her as if she'd gone mad.

"Dweeba says that the camp is beginning to wake from his transmogrifee," she said to them. When they stared at her blankly, she added, "I'll explain Dweeba later. There's no time now. Just trust me. I've got to go back for the dageki. Don't wait for me, I'll catch up. Moonchaser is just ahead. He knows we're on our way."

"I'm going with you," said Dreyk. "And who is this Dweeba?"

"He's a psy adept. I'll explain more later. You'd better go on ahead with Benna and Char."

"No."

Nikki was about to argue, when she saw the fierce look in his eyes and decided that she didn't have the centuries it might take to change his stubborn mind.

"Alright, but we've got to hurry," she said to the empty space where Dreyk had been. He'd already disappeared into the darkness.

She caught up quickly, and they reached the cages together. The glow of bright eyes met them in the dark. The dageki were all awake and ready, as if they had been waiting for her, too.

She ran to the first cage and struggled with the latch, only to find it locked. Why hadn't she noticed the locks earlier? After all this—if she couldn't even get them out!

"Here," said Dreyk, coming up behind her. "I managed to lift these keys from the guard's tent. Hope I got the right ones."

"You think of everything!" she exclaimed, as she slipped the first key into the rusty mechanism and was rewarded by a resounding click, as the lock fell open. She returned the keys to Dreyk, and he continued down the line of cages.

"Gormz?" she called.

"I am here," was the response from the dark. Then the dageki was out on the ground in front of her, and she was struck again by the great mass of these creatures. Gormz towered over her, and his great bulk obliterated half the horizon behind him. *And this was a small dageki.* She only hoped they were as docile as they appeared. She didn't want to have to use Dweeba's powers against them; they had suffered enough subjugation already. She steeled herself against her fear, forcing herself to speak calmly.

"Do you know this area?" she asked.

"Only from travel primers," he replied. "But I have a fair idea of our position. We are in the river valley of the Kgyk. Dmisi is directly Northeast over open terrain. We need only follow the star of Glemedi, there." His stubby front limb pointed to a bright red star at the horizon.

"Then you intend to come with us?"

"I will take you as far as Dmisi, our capital city."

"That's all we can ask. Now we must hurry. Our friends must already be far ahead of us. Can all your people walk?"

"Yes, I believe so. Of course, Giaranu Wiyhe Mageki Ky Sizi now walks among the stars, no more troubled by the pains of this life." He spoke these last words without any sign of emotion, at least that Nikki was able to detect, and somehow his lack of feeling only made her own guilt cut deeper. Did he blame her for the death? How could he know that she had been the cause of Osli's anger? These thoughts troubled her as they hurried forward in a loose group.

They hadn't yet reached Benna and Char, when the frightened screeches of the dageki ahead of them rang out.

"Moonchaser! I forgot to warn the dageki about him. I hope he hasn't eaten any of them yet!"

Nikki rushed forward to meet her friend, encircling his massive neck with her arms and burying her head in his mane, wishing she could remain there indefinitely.

"No time to catch up now, but you must understand that these creatures are our friends."

"Lizard flesh is tough and stringy, anyway," he growled.

"You haven't!" exclaimed Nikki.

"No. Dweeba explained to me. Besides my stomach is contented. Good hunting last night."

Nikki was still trying to calm the dageki when they heard angry shouts echoing from the direction of camp.

Zarad has discovered the body of his brother, spoke Dweeba in her mind. *He will soon be on our trail. The dageki make prints that anyone could follow.*

"Dweeba, can you confuse him?" asked Nikki. "Protect us until we can get away?"

Zarad is now far ahead of the others. I don't believe that they will follow him any longer. He's in a murderous frenzy and has already killed two of his own men in his wrath. They already had little reason to be loyal. When he returns, he may find his camp looted and his men gone. But he is in a wild mood. Apparently, I underestimated his dependence on Osli and how his brother's death would unhinge him. I cannot control a mind that has no rational thought. He is like an animal.

"Are you telling me that we'll have to fight him?"

I'm not as young as I once was, and Osli withheld the Herb, trying to force me to put you under his control. I used most of my remaining strength against him. We must find more of the Herb, and I need rest.

"Great. So much for a clean getaway!" she huffed aloud.

Dreyk came up beside her, watching her with a puzzled expression.

"Zarad is pursuing alone," she offered. "The others have returned to camp. Don't ask me how I know, I'll explain later. I'm going back to intercept him, if I can."

"I'll go with you," said Dreyk.

"As will I," said a quiet voice from behind, and Nikki jumped, startled to find the dark shape of Gormz's aquiline head looming out of the darkness above her. His voice held so little expression, and if his face told more, she was unable to read it. Did the dageki plan to kill Zarad himself in revenge for the death of Giaranu? Well, maybe he deserved his revenge, but Nikki couldn't imagine these docile creatures being capable of violence.

They were now coming into an area of many large, jutting boulders, looming up from the dark before them. They were silent, brooding guardians, their angular placement at odds with the plain's flat monotony. The night was cooling, and a swirling ground fog began to gather about them. Nikki called ahead to Benna astride the sagehorse at the head of the ragged line, drawing the group together.

"Benna, we've got a pursuer behind us. The three of us are going back. I'm going to leave Moonchaser with you for protection. If we fail—"

"Let me come with you," Benna pleaded, "I can't let you go off alone."

"Don't be silly, little brother," said Nikki in her best authoritative voice. "He's outnumbered and acting irrationally. We're in no real danger. Besides, someone needs to watch the dageki and keep them moving. Follow that red star as long as you can see it. Agreed?"

"Alright, but—"

"You saved our lives once already with Hawkwind," said Nikki, then quietly to Benna alone, "No need to be a hero so soon. The night is young."

"Message received, big sister," Benna replied in a dry voice, but the worry remained on his face as he moved away from them, leading their odd group into the dark.

Gormz said a few words in the dageki tongue, and the dageki obediently followed Benna, disappearing into the darkness as well.

The three moved off the trail, careful to hide their tracks, then they too faded into the ground fog between the stones. Nikki saw a shadow following them. Char, she assumed, moving with the stealth that made her a great hunter.

It was no difficult task to locate Zarad. His labored breathing carried through the fog, reaching them long before they reached him, but again, Nikki was surprised by the hidden talents these two brothers possessed. Perhaps years of pursuing and tracking the dageki had given Zarad a fighter's sense, that anonymous faculty that gives some advance warning of danger, or perhaps it was the unmistakable scent of the dageki that gave them away. Whatever the reason, Zarad was ready for them.

Suddenly, Nikki heard a whistling, then a crack as an arrow hit the rock next to her head and clattered to the ground. Ducking, her subconscious registered something about the arrow that was familiar. Later she would realize that the fletching was a bright yellow.

Nikki had pulled her sword from its sheath as they approached, or
his first attack might have removed her head. As it was, his heavy sword
glanced from her raised blade within inches of her neck. Somehow, he
had been able to drop his bow and pull a long sword from its sheath.
He had come around one of the tall stones behind them, while they
still heard him in front of them. Nikki had little time to wonder what
trick he had used, as she was busy defending herself from the onslaught
of his attack.

Dreyk had fallen back and pulled his slender knife. It might not be
much use against a long sword, but at least he might distract Zarad
long enough for Nikki to inflict a fatal blow. Perhaps it wasn't perfect
fighting etiquette, she thought, but when had the Keleps brothers
played fair?

Of the dageki, Nikki saw no more, but she couldn't blame him for
wanting to avoid this confrontation. Zarad's eyes burned red, glowing
with wild rage even in the dark. Without a word, he screamed, lunging
at her with ferocious speed for such a large man. Their blades rang
out in the moist cold air as Nikki diverted his blade, using the whole
strength of her body, instead of just her arm, as she had been taught
to counter an opponent with superior strength. But never had that
opponent been human, only illusion.

She thought with black humor that this was not a good time to
consider the possible shortcomings of her training. Instead, she forced
herself to concentrate on the battle at hand, releasing her fear and
focusing her awareness. She did manage to score a slashing hit to his
sword arm as he twisted around toward Dreyk, who was doing his best
to pull Zarad's attention from her.

For a fearful second, she thought he might rush Dreyk, even
though such a move would allow her a clean hit, but however irrational he might be now, his wrath was clearly focused on her as he
twisted another full revolution, bringing his sword around in a daring

two-handed arch. Only a quick reaction prevented her from being decapitated again, but she didn't pause to think about her near miss. Since she was down already, she used the opportunity to slash at his legs, but he reacted quicker than she thought possible, jumping back from the flash of her blade with the agility of a dancer.

Again he came at her with a series of lightning-quick thrusts, and although sweat streamed from his face, and his sleeve was drenched in blood, Nikki knew that his mind was clearing. Perhaps it had finally occurred to him that he might lose his own life if he didn't control his rage over Osli's death. Nikki remembered the words of her teacher; *Don't fear your opponent's anger; it's your best weapon against him. Use it to its fullest potential.*

Nikki felt the familiar burning of exhaustion in her arms and sensed the stone looming behind her as Zarad's attack forced her back. She had underestimated his skill and stamina. Even with Dreyk behind him, he might be able to kill her before Dreyk could be of any help. She knew she had to act quickly.

"Zarad," she sneered. "How would you like to die? Quickly? Or slowly and painfully like your poor brother Osli?"

Her remarks created the effect that she desired. Zarad was a wild beast again. He roared, rushing at her with all his speed and strength. Nikki pulled away with only inches to spare, and Zarad came up hard against the stone, bruising his already bleeding right arm. But the pain seemed only to fuel his rage. Bellowing, he grabbed at her with his left arm, getting a piece of the white gown before Nikki could get her sword up between them. Together they fell to the ground. Nikki's head hit the dirt with a thud and her vision darkened.

What followed was a blur to Nikki. One moment Zarad had his hands at her neck as she struggled for breath, then she saw Char running and Dreyk coming forward with a knife in his hand, until her vision was filled by a dark mass hurtling down from above. Zarad was knocked away from her. She lay, dazed, as Zarad and the creature thrashed and rolled on the ground next to her. She heard a rending sound as Zarad's head disappeared into something dark and huge. There was a muffled, truncated scream, followed by the grinding and crunching of bone.

Nikki pulled away in horror, as a lacerated, crushed skull peered from the mouth of the attacker, dropping to the ground before her with a dull thud. Purple blood spurted from the suddenly lifeless body, and the air reeked with the stench of death.

She sat paralyzed by terror as the monster that had done this grisly killing pulled away from Zarad's body and stood up, towering over her, cool and remorseless as the standing stones. Blood and hair clung to its teeth and quivering lips. Glossy eyes darted, coming to rest on Nikki with a look of vacant, unfocused malice.

Behind them, Char commented, "Nice! Couldn't a' done better meself."

Still, the beast advanced on Nikki.

"Gormz, is that you?" Nikki croaked. "Don't you recognize me?"

The creature said no word but came toward her with its claws outstretched, its great bloody maw opening and closing slowly to the accompaniment of grinding teeth and heaving chest.

Then it reached down for her with the acrid perfume of death on its breath, and mercifully, the darkness took her first.

CHAPTER TWENTY-FOUR

From Ruin to Renaissance

Wren, as Hyla again, looked them over in disgust as they pulled up, panting and looking behind them for signs of pursuit.

"Into what have you gotten yourselves now, and who be these new recruits?" she asked with her hands on her massive hips.

Nikki gulped, and breathing hard, said, "I can explain, but it's a long story."

Hyla just sighed and said, "No helping it now, is there. Pull their own weight they must."

Nikki looked distracted for a second, then with a puzzled frown said, "Dweeba says that he knows of your mission and approves."

Hyla looked, if possible, even more irritated.

"Well, so sweet isn't that?"

"But what does he mean?"

"Beyond our ken may be the delusions in the mind of a psy adept worm, yes?"

"But Dweeba says—"

"Enough! Out of here must we get before organized these slavers become. With your magic worm we can discuss matters of high import at a later time."

As they traveled, the road to the dageki capital improved, making it easier for them to navigate as it grew wider and more maintained.

Hyla seemed to know a lot about the dageki and had many questions for Gormz, who obliged with lengthy dissertations on dageki history and culture. The other dageki trailed behind, their considerable noses in the air, seemingly aghast that Gormz would break tradition by conversing with their "inferiors."

"So," explained Hyla, "of dageki history my knowledge is limited. Very old and incomplete I'm afraid our records be. The scientific advances of your race I assume have only increased over time."

Gormz was silent for a moment, then he spoke hesitantly. "It is true that dageki scientific and technical expertise reached a high point several centuries ago, but since then, I fear that we have not lived up to our potential. Dageki culture experienced what I believe humans call a period of "dark ages." The university was closed and contact with other species was curtailed. It was as if the thirst for knowledge was lost."

Gormz was silent for some time, as if contemplating what might have been. Finally, he said, "But there is hope for the future, now. The university has been reopened and our society is entering a renaissance, if that is the word, where knowledge has a chance to grow again."

"Good news that is," said Hyla, but Nikki could sense her disappointment, as if she'd had high hopes for the dageki, and they had failed her somehow. She wanted to ask Dweeba what he knew, but he was uncharacteristically silent.

When they camped that night, the dageki set themselves a little apart from the others, and Nikki wondered if they stayed with the group only for the relative protection it offered. Except for Gormz, it seemed they would rather be left to themselves. She assumed that all the dageki would be leaving their group soon anyway, when they reached Dmisi.

She also wondered how long Char would accompany them. She had little patience for polite chatter around the campfire. Though she had washed up in the river, she still managed to collect dirt and grime like a magnet, and the others gave her a wide berth. Though even without her transmograffic ability, she was the best hunter and gatherer among them, providing most of the food for them all.

Now she sat by the campfire, carving on a strangely twisted piece of wood. Nikki wondered if she was making some kind of bird. It did appear to have rudimentary wings.

"What are you shaping?" asked Nikki, when her curiosity wouldn't let her be.

"It's not much yet," said Char proudly. "But it's gonna be an arbalest."

"What's that?"

"Just the meanest weapon you's ever seen. Take down an elkin at two-hundred yards, an' drop it dead in its tracks."

"I never heard of such a weapon."

"It's like a crossbow, only way more skookum. You'll see, once I gits me powers back, I'll be addin' the steel shaft and you's gonna be amazed at what this 'ere baby can do."

"I hope we get to see that. You've been a real help to us so far, making an uncomfortable journey bearable anyway."

Dreyk mumbled, "Ya, and since you had a bath, it's way more comfortable for me, too."

Char heard him and explained, "Doe urine. Not much of a hunter, is ya?"

"What are you mumbling on about now?" asked Dreyk, irritation in his tone.

"You's just a idjit, ain't ya? I uses it ta blend inta the forest, eh? Them deer an' elkin live by smell, an' hearin' a' course. They's far superior t' us, ya know. Ghosts o' the forest. Soon as I gits me abilities back, that's where I's headed, you can bet yur purtty little city arse on that!"

Dreyk said nothing, but Nikki could hear his unsaid "good riddance," loud and clear. For herself, she hoped Char would stay with them a little longer. She was curious about the transmograffic talent Char possessed, a talent far different from her own, and she thought that beneath her prickly exterior, there was more to Char than they had yet seen.

She was distracted from her thoughts when Dreyk whispered in her ear, "Can you please talk to her about that?"

Confused, Nikki looked around to find Char squatting at the edge of camp, the sound of urine trickling to the dirt. Nikki giggled. "What, Dreyk, does it bother you?"

"Of course it bothers me! Why can't she at least go out a little farther from camp?"

"All right, I'll talk to her, but I can't say she'll listen to me any more than she does you. Our Char seems to have a code of her own. Perhaps she's marking our camp to keep predators away."

Ignoring her, he continued, "And there's another thing. What kind of name is Char, anyway?"

"Oh, I don't know. Maybe it's short for something; Charlotte or Charlene maybe."

"Or maybe it just means she was formed from an ash pit."

When Char returned, having gathered a few more sticks for the fire, Dreyk asked her casually, "So what does Char stand for, anyway?"

"Nuttin, just Char," she answered abruptly.

Nikki said, "But Char must be short for something, Charlie, Charmain—"

Benna interjected, "Dreyk told me that the char is a fish of the northern isles. Said it tastes like—"

"She was not named for a fish, I am certain," said Gormz.

"All right!" said Char loudly, then, very quietly, "It's short for Chari..."

"What was that?" Nikki leaned forward to listen, as Char covered her mouth and almost whispered the word.

Char, obviously irritated, said loudly, "It's Charisma, all right? Me fruckin' name's Charisma."

Nikki almost laughed before she could stop herself. Dreyk was chuckling.

"Charisma, that's your name?" he said raucously. "Doesn't that mean 'charming?' Yah, a real people-person you are. Mistress Charisma, ha!"

Nikki gave him a dark look and he went silent, but too late. Char turned red and threw down her sticks with disgust and embarrassment, then stomped out of camp without another word.

"You've done it now," said Nikki. "She'll likely never speak to you again."

"There's always hope," said Dreyk dryly.

When they at last reached the crossroads and bridge overlooking the dageki realm, Hyla surveyed the bleak, fallow fields and run-down rural structures. She frowned.

"What is it?" asked Nikki.

"Oh, nothing it is, just not exactly as I remember it."

Gormz said, "How long has it been since you have seen the Dmisi territories? I think not much has changed here for centuries."

Hyla laughed, appearing a little nervous, an expression that Nikki couldn't remember the giantess ever showing.

"Well, of course *centuries* it hasn't been," tittered Hyla. "Spring was perhaps when I was last here. That's it, I'm sure. In such a state of disrepair are the fields and farms, yes? So efficient are the dageki, you know, so regimented..." She trailed off and Gormz turned his head in that vaguely avian way he had.

"Efficient? Regimented?"

Pollux nudged her in the back with his wide head and Hyla seemed to come to her senses.

"Never mind that. Gormz, where we part ways is this—"

Hyla was interrupted when one of the other dageki came forward, yammering at Gormz for several minutes. As they spoke, the young dageki's hexagonal plates gradually lost their color. Finally, the other dageki waddled away and Gormz stood silent, gazing blankly across the bridge toward his homeland.

Nikki asked, "What is it, Gormz?" When he didn't answer, she began again, "If there's something we—"

"No, there is no hope for me now. I am to be exiled from the dageki nation for my transgressions."

"What transgressions?" asked Benna. "You saved us all from Zarad back there. What could possibly be wrong with what you did?"

"Well, killing Zarad was of course a slight offense, but the main reason is that I have been conversing with an inferior species without formal diplomatic relations being established."

"Inferior species?"

"Sorry, not my words."

Nikki said, "What will you do?"

"I do not know. I need to ruminate on this."

"Then come with us. Hyla has suggested that the Leijong may be able to help us get over the mountains to Kraida. It would be an adventure."

In her pack, Dweeba thought at her, *Ooh, I've always wanted to see the Leijong empire.*

"I have in the past considered a sojourn to the Leijong nation," mused Gormz. "It is said that they have an advanced social and technological system, like nothing else on our world."

Hyla gave him a strange, wondering look, but said nothing.

"Plus," continued the dageki, "if you are heading north, that may be the one place where I would have a chance of redeeming myself. It is said that is where the majority of dageki slaves are kept. If I could find a way of freeing them, surely the sovereign would consider my reapplication to personhood."

Personhood? thought Nikki, bemused.

Dreyk interjected, "You might want to rethink that plan, once you see Kraida. There are hundreds—maybe thousands—of dageki slaves there."

Ignoring him, Nikki said, "It's settled then," with as much false cheerfulness as she could muster.

When they turned away from the bridge, Nikki noticed that the dageki group had already passed over, not even acknowledging Gormz as they left. What strange creatures they were. She wanted to spend more time here and see Dmisi, but Hyla seemed in a hurry to lead them away. Somehow Nikki knew there was more to this than Hyla was willing to tell them, and she vowed to get the story out of the giantess, one way or another.

CHAPTER TWENTY-FIVE

Freedom Bound

Nikki woke the next morning, groggily rising and stumbling over to stoke the fire. It wasn't until her eyes were fully open and she had started to heat water for tea that she noticed the empty bedroll where Char had lain the night before.

"Oh, no," she breathed. "She's gone."

Benna rolled over with a groggy, "Whaa—?"

"Char—she left us. I wondered when it would happen. She must have gotten her talent back. I just hoped we'd have more time."

Benna heard the melancholy in Nikki's voice.

"Maybe she'll be back. You never know with that one."

"Would you come back to this miserable, dusty camp full of hopeless, untalented shlubs like us if you could run as an elkin, or fly like a falcon?"

Benna sighed, rolling up his blanket with a distracted air.

There was a subdued feeling to the camp that morning, as even Dreyk seemed to consider what Char had done for them and what her loss would mean as they traveled on.

Around noon, the wind picked up and high clouds streaked by far above them. Nikki saw a dark spec on the horizon, a large bird of some kind, growing closer as she watched. Hope filled her for a second, then deflated like a needle to the stomach of a bloater fish when the spec faded away, floating with the winds and disappearing into the south.

Having given up on the idea that Char might return to them, Nikki trudged on through the day, not paying much attention to her surroundings. She was lost in thoughts of what might greet them at the nation of the Leijong, when a brittle screech rent the air. Starting, Nikki fell back as giant black and silver wings filled her vision. She stumbled and almost fell. Reaching out for support, she leaned heavily on a rocky outcrop to steady herself. Upon the rock beside her alit a massive bird of prey, mostly black with elegant silver stripes decorating its wings. As she watched in awe, the creature stretched and the feathers melted into pale skin, except on its head, where the feathers elongated to form a rich cascade of raven hair. A naked human woman sat before her on the rock, grinning at Nikki jauntily. The woman reached down and gathered a handful of dust from an indentation in the stone. As she tossed it into the air, it formed a cloud around her that settled into Char's familiar leather vest, whitish shirt and grungy pants.

Nikki had to wonder, if Char was transmogering her clothes anyway, why didn't she reform them clean and new? It was in this moment she first realized that perhaps everything they knew about Char might be just an act, a game she played to hide her true nature. What she presented to the world was just a facade. Nikki had to wonder what the real Char sounded and looked like, and why the woman felt the need to hide who and what she was from the world.

"Char!" Nikki exclaimed, ecstatic at seeing her friend again, but trying to hide it. "You're back. And look at you. Your talent has returned. I'm so envious. Are you going to stay with us for a while?" Nikki added hesitantly.

"I don't know," said Char, her voice flowing down the scale from an avian screech to her more melodic human tones.

"I's thinkin' you folks need me ta help out jus' a bit longer. Besides, I been meanin' to check out the Leijong for a while now. I heard lots about 'em. Legends among transmogrifers, they is. And it's said that, in spite a' their advancin' in science and society, they's still wild inside, like me, sorta."

"Well, you're welcome to continue with us, as far as you're willing to go. We could really use your help," said Nikki matter-of-factly. What Nikki didn't express was her complete joy and relief on seeing the huntress again. Somehow the tactless, brusque and demanding woman had found a way into her heart. Nikki knew she needed time to consider what that meant, but for now she was just happy to have Char back with them.

Dreyk came up beside her and studied his feet. Char said, "Yah, course you's glad to be seein' me too, eh, but don't you overdo it now. I can't stand it ta' see grown men cry."

"Yah, I guess," drawled Drake, obviously having difficulty explaining that he too was having a change of heart concerning Char.

"Truth is," he began reluctantly, "you're a passable hunter, and we could use your help on this journey. You know, that mushroom and contail soup you made the other night—I guess I'm trying to say—I guess your smell is starting to grow on me, too."

"Oh, stuff it, ya' idjit," growled Char, abruptly sliding from her rock and leading the way down the trail.

"I guess things are back to normal," mused Benna.

Behind him, Hyla just shook her head.

CHAPTER TWENTY-SIX

Prophesy, Part Two

The watercourse they followed upriver seemed gentle enough, until the land grew steeper. As they struggled uphill, the rapids picked up and the river began to roar.

Nikki was looking down, watching her footing on the rough trail, when the sound of the river suddenly dropped away. She looked to her right, but the river was gone. The riverbed was empty except for a bed of dry stones with grasses, shrubs and even small trees popping up here and there between the rocks. Doing a double-take, Nikki almost fell. From her pack, Dweeba laughed. *Look up, silly human.*

"What?" she asked, but she did as she was told. Above them, the river flowed through the open air with no support to hold the water in place. Astonished, she stumbled and ended up on her knees.

Dreyk bent down to help her up. "Are you OK?" he asked solicitously.

"I'm fine, it was just a shock."

"Yah, I should've warned you. I've heard of this. To tell you the truth I thought it was just an old fishwive's tale. Apparently not."

They continued their trek, and eventually, the river settled down into a normal position.

Nikki asked Hyla how the river had become like this.

"No one really knows. I think it was an after-effect of a transmogrifee battle. Apparently, the Leijong are also such an effect. No one knows if they were originally human, raptor or lepidoptera, but they have their own identity now, and breed true to form, just like an original species."

Nikki looked at her, disbelieving.

"You will see," was all the giantess would say.

They continued until they came around a curving rock wall, where an amazing vista opened up. A huge city towered before them, with many tall wooden buildings, several stories high. The structures were even and straight like nothing in nature. Every window was open, and many balconies were occupied by elegant, winged creatures, their limbs and bodies works of natural art, iridescent, living beauty. Even Hyla was incredulous. She stopped in her tracks and her mouth fell open. "It can't be," she muttered.

"I thought you knew this place," said Nikki, again suspicious about what Hyla actually knew.

"I did, I mean, I do. It's just—there have been some changes since I was last here," she ended lamely.

The group stood for some time, in awe of the graceful Leijong city. Eventually, some people came out to meet them. They were even more amazing close up, tall and aristocratic in bearing, yet adorned in luscious colors beyond the rainbow that filled anyone near them with awe. Their wings were living, powerful curves that glittered with every movement, highlighting shades of cerulean blue, iridescent purple and luminous magenta, all in flux, ever morphing into shapes and hues even more enthralling.

The males wore a sash of cyan, the women one of cardinal red, but most of their clothing was hidden by their arching wings, limbs that they displayed with pride as they curled around their athletic bodies.

One of the males stepped forward. With a proud, aquiline face, and a melodic voice, he greeted each visitor in turn by name, then introduced himself as Flohandri, eleventh heir of Aquilinus.

Hyla seemed unable to speak, staring at the amazing city, so Nikki stepped forward.

"How is it that you know our names?"

"It was written by the great seer Aquilinus that you would come. Wren should have told you." With that he looked to Hyla.

"Who is Wren?" asked Nikki, suspicion evident in her tone.

Hyla finally found her voice. "An old name they know me by, it is. Pay no mind. Down to business, shall we get? We seek transport over the Hartbone Range, to Kraida."

"Yes, we know of your quest and are willing to transport you all, for a price."

"Here it comes," mumbled Benna.

Hearing Benna's mumbled remark, the leijong man chuckled. "It won't be that dear a fee, young Benna. We only wish you to spend a pleasant evening in our humble central garden, to sit by a primitive fire, much like the one where our ancestors first met with your kind, eight centuries ago. Tonight, we will bring a new prophesy to the present heir of the abacusian. Tonight, we will change life on Drakonia forever."

"Oh no," whispered Hyla, her eyes bright and glazed over with something that had become familiar to all of them. It was a look of foreboding.

They came together by the rock-encircled campfire. A manicured lawn dotted with blooming clover and wildflowers led down to the river that flowed gracefully, its sides decorated by the sparkling, redolent flowers of lilacs and hydrangeas. Nikki was enthralled by the scene, but worry nagged at her.

Dweeba said in her mind, *How fascinating. These people may be the most advanced on all Drakonia, yet they have also retained their instincts and honed their psychic abilities to a degree I have never experienced before in another race. I must study them.*

Nikki replied out loud, "I don't know about this conclave and prophesy reveal they are planning. Something about it has me worried."

What could possibly go wrong? asked the worm innocently.

Nikki wanted to glare at him but didn't know how to do that mentally. Finally, she commented aloud, "Everything."

Her companions said nothing, now well inured to her one-sided conversations with the psychic worm.

Ilyla seemed nervous as well, and Nikki wondered what might be bothering her.

The group sat on logs that ringed the fire, awaiting the Leijong contingent. They had been provided with drinks that tasted of peach nectar and a delicate cake that was sweet and delicious. Near dusk, when the Leijong finally arrived, Nikki was impressed by the beautiful robes they wore, fashioned of a feather-light, iridescent fabric that flowed and danced around their bodies as if powered by their thoughts and moods. One carried a cylinder adorned in colorful gems, with a brightly colored tassel at one end. Again, Flohandri was the one who stepped forward. Taking the cylinder from an unusually tall, bronze-skinned Leijong beside him, he held the piece reverently, as if it were a religious relic or talisman of great significance.

With a flourish, he flicked the cylinder into the air, where it spun.

Nikki gasped, as she feared the lovely object might break on impact with the ground, but that never happened, as the cylinder hung in the air instead, unraveling itself as it spun, revealing a transparent fabric or papyrus that floated like dandelion fluff on the gentle breeze. It was covered in marks that looked to Nikki like the scratches of seedeater songbirds in the dirt.

"Before us is the prophesy that we have kept for centuries, awaiting just this moment to be revealed, only to this group; the Seekers of the Great Terraformer."

What the fruck is a Terraformer? thought Nikki and Hyla, had they known it, at the same moment. For a second Nikki wondered if they had been mistaken for a different group, but before she could question him, Flohandri continued.

In a rhythmic, formal voice, he read, "It is written that every thousand years, the Great Terraformer will wake, blooming with the seeds of stability that have long kept our world in balance. When, for the first time, the tree failed to come forth in a timely manner, the Peacemaker was born to maintain the continuity, until which time the tree should be woken again by the Heir of Power. Together, the Peacemaker and the Heir of Power are here today.

"Here are your instructions:

"For the Peacemaker, your time is done, but for this one task. Faithful binder of the continuity, you have completed your duties, and a well-earned rest is your reward. But before you return to your time, there is one final task you must fulfill. To you is given the burden of bringing forth and teaching the Heir of Power what her abilities and duties entail. Plus, you must ensure that she fulfills her monumental task."

Nikki frowned, now more confused than ever. Beside her, she noticed that Hyla was frowning as well. *Did this make sense to anyone?*

Flohandri continued, "To you, Heir of Power, falls the greatest burden. It will take all your considerable transmograffic talent, strength and willpower to achieve, but it must be done, for the sake of all the races of Drakonia. To fail, is to bring death—or worse—to all sentient beings on our world."

Nikki thought, *What could be worse than death?*

"You must return life to the sleeping, thought to the heedless, and hope to the darkness. Malgryn, the worldheart must be healed, not destroyed."

When Flohandri said no more, the Leijong turned away as one and left the group on their own to ponder this inscrutable prophesy. No one said anything for a while, until, Benna, true to form, piped up.

"That clarifies everything now, doesn't it?"

Chapter Twenty-Seven

Someone a Drakyn Can't Defeat

The road to Tia Cara was overgrown and pitted. To Nikki, it was the most beautiful solid ground in the world. Even though she'd lived her whole life in the heights of Mistra, there she'd had control. With her talent, she could transform at will. Talented Mistrans rarely fell to their deaths, but being ferried by the leijong was another matter. She just had to trust that her carrier didn't lose his concentration, or his grip on her.

"Anything would be preferable to being carried like a sack of taters by the Leijong," she exclaimed as she tripped over another errant tree root.

"I didn't think it was so bad," interjected Benna. "Once you got used to it."

"Well, you can have it!" she retorted, adjusting her pack. "Next time I'll walk—or transform and fly myself." Then she remembered that her talent was gone. She looked over to Char, who had transformed back into human form to walk with them. She was grateful that Char at least understood her loss. She had to admit to just a little bit of envy, that Char had her talent back and she did not.

Dreyk snickered under his breath until she turned on him with a glare.

"You did quite well for your first time," he said contritely. "I only wish that riding with the Leijong was the greatest danger we might face. Without Hyla and that psychic worm along, we might be a tad bit more vulnerable."

Nikki hadn't been surprised when Dweeba decided to stay with the Leijong. From the very beginning he had been enthralled with their culture, and he was, as he himself admitted, getting too old for another adventure. Nikki had wished him well and hoped they would meet again.

Hyla had disappointed her again, claiming that the Leijong couldn't carry her weight, although they didn't have any trouble carrying Gormz, though it took two of them together to haul the reluctant dageki into the air.

Hyla had explained that she and Pollux would find transportation to Kraida on their own. When she said she would meet them on the outskirts of Tia Cara, Nikki had to wonder what form of transportation the giantess could find that would get her there faster than flying, but she didn't bother to ask. Something was not right about Hyla and her donkey-donklet. Nikki was almost relieved to part ways with the strange duo.

It was a bit surprising to Nikki that Char was continuing with them. She'd been in awe of the Leijong and asked so many questions they'd started to avoid her. But Char claimed to have visited both the northern cities of Tia Cara and Bay Towne in the past and said she wouldn't mind going again to "soak up a bit o' northern culture," or so she claimed. Again, Nikki wondered what the truth was about Char and why she chose to keep her true nature hidden from the others. She intended to learn more about her and her past.

Nikki realized that Dreyk was still talking. "This road looks innocent enough, but it can be dangerous for unwary travelers. We're a large enough group that we shouldn't be bothered by thieves. They're generally unorganized and opportunistic. They're more likely to steal your mount while you sleep than attack a large group in open daylight.

All the same, we'll need to post a watch tonight, and be on our guard during the day. Also, there have been rumors that wolf packs have returned to these woods."

"Surely wolves wouldn't attack here," said Nikki, unbelieving.

"If they're hungry enough," said Dreyk. "They've been known to attack humans and livestock, but usually they'll only attack a lone individual. We should be safe."

"I can't believe there's any danger on this road," said Benna. "It's so quiet and peaceful. We haven't seen a single traveler since we landed."

"It's strange," added Nikki. "This track looks like it was once well-traveled. The ground is packed as if from years of wagon travel, but now the trees and brush have almost reclaimed it."

Gormz knelt, picking up a piece of crumbling roadbed. "At one time, there must have been a great deal of trade between the dageki who populated this area and the humans to the north, but it must have been ages ago. This road looks like it hasn't been used regularly in many years. No dageki would now venture out this far. My people have been slowly isolating themselves from the rest of the world."

Without warning, Char pulled up in the road, looking back the way they'd come. "They's someone coming up behind. Let's get off the track and let 'em pass."

"You must have better ears than I do," said Nikki. "I don't hear a thing."

"On a sagehorse, I'm thinkin'."

Dreyk said quickly, "Let's get down over the edge here."

They scrambled down the bank into the brush, where they waited in silence. Nikki grew impatient and was about to speak, when she heard hooves on the trail. Soon a dusty sagehorse came into view. His rider hung forward over the neck of his mount and appeared to be asleep, drunk or ill. The sagehorse stopped in front of them and nibbled at a tuft of grass in the middle of the trail. The rider made no move to urge his mount on. Nikki was about to spring forward when she felt Dreyk's arm on hers. He whispered in her ear, "Wait! Let's be sure he's alone."

"Don't be ridiculous," she snapped. "There's no reason for all this caution. The man is obviously hurt and in need of our help."

"He could just be drunk," said Hyla. "And not want our help."

"Well, we can at least ask him," said Nikki, exasperated. She sprang up and over the bank. The sagehorse started, and the man fell from his back, hitting the turf with a wheezing thud. The sagehorse bolted away down the road, then stopped and looked back at them balefully. The man groaned but made no attempt to rise. As Nikki approached, she saw the crusted blood and ragged cuts on his neck, arms and hands. As she knelt beside him, the man's eyes opened to stare at her with vacant horror. She called to Char, who came forward to look at his wounds.

"No broken bones as I can tell," said the huntress after a cursory examination, "but these 'ere cuts 'll git infected if'n we don't clean 'em. Wolf bites is nasty."

At this last, the man's eyes opened even wider. "Wolf!" he rasped.

"Wolf, yes, but a beast—almost a man..." His voice trailed off.

"He's delirious," said Nikki. "Not making any sense. Char, how do you even know that those cuts are from a wolf attack?"

"I've seen 'em afore, ain't I? But not usually on a still livin' body. Lucky, this one."

The man grabbed Nikki's arm with surprising strength. "Not delirious," he said. "Or mad. Saw it—saw it all from the bushes. I crawled off and he was too busy with the others to notice me, maybe." He shuddered.

"It's all right now," said Nikki gently. "You'll be safe with us. Just try to relax and tell us what happened."

The man was silent for a long time, and she began to think that they would get no more out of him, when he began to whimper softly.

Snuffling and inhaling deeply, he seemed to muster some control. He looked up at her and his eyes cleared.

"You need to get away. It's too strong for you. Escape while you still can."

"Escape from what?"

"The beast. Took five strong men. It came out of the dark like a psy storm, only worse. I think I was the only one to escape alive." He began to cry softly again. "That sound—I'll never forget. Ripping and shredding and all the while that gurgling laugh—and the smell." His voice cracked, and Nikki could get him to say no more. He lay with his eyes open and vacant as if unaware of his surroundings.

Dreyk pulled Nikki aside. "Nikki, did you hear what he said? Not a pack of wolves, but one creature. Almost a man, he said. Maybe it was the transmogrifer who attacked us in the desert. Remember after the disruption? Hyla said the tracks were half-human, half-wolf."

"That's ridiculous," she retorted. "He's just delirious. Obviously, he's been through a terrible ordeal. It must have been a huge pack, to kill five men."

"That's just it, Nikki, they wouldn't do that. It's not the way wolves hunt. Their way is to isolate one animal from the herd and run it down as a pack. I've never of heard anything like this. And I've never yet heard of a wolf who laughed!"

Nikki had to admit that he might be right, but after everything they'd been through, she didn't want to think they were still being pursued.

"But if it's true, and the transmogrifer is still following us, why hasn't he attacked before this?"

"I don't know. You're the expert on transmogrifee. Perhaps the disruption was harder on him than it was on us. Didn't you say that the greater a person's talent, the more the storm might damage them?"

"Yes, but—"

"Maybe he was trapped in wolf shape, or what if he were transforming when the storm hit? Could he be caught between shapes?"

"I guess it's possible, though I've never heard of an actual case. He would probably recover his power and shape-changing ability in time."

"What if he's been waiting for that, just following us. And we've been in larger groups since his first attack, first with the Kelep's caravan and then in the Leijong city. What if he's just been biding his time, waiting until his power returns, and when we're alone and vulnerable?"

"You mean like now?"

"Yes," he replied in a thoughtful tone.

They decided to pull off the road into the trees and camp where they were. Benna found a stream down the hill and brought up water. The stream was barely a trickle, but it was enough to give Char water for her herbs. After discussion, they decided to risk a fire.

"The poultice won't work without heatin o' the water," said Char. "Find the driest wood ya can, and the smoke'll be hardly anything." After her poultice was applied to his wounds, the man seemed to rest more peacefully.

"I's done what I can fer 'is body," she mused. "But the mind be takin' longer to heal, me thinks. It'd be best if'n we could rest the night. Better we be rested an' travel tomorrow. Besides, it's the battle ya run from that ya don't see comin'." She laughed at her own strange humor. "If'n he does attack tonight, we'll be as ready now as later."

"I agree with Char," said Dreyk. "I'll stand watch."

"We'll take shifts, and sleep lightly between," Nikki added.

Nikki found she couldn't sleep at all, even though she knew that she would undoubtedly need to be rested and at her best tomorrow. Instead, she lay awake, staring up through the gently stirring branches at the high, pale stars, trying to understand all that had happened to her since this nightmare began. She thought of Tbrin, wondering again if he was her ally, or her enemy. Through the night, she heard no wolves howl, only the distant call of a lone grella. Moonchaser growled in his sleep, as if in answer, but didn't wake, then all was quiet again.

When her watch came, just before dawn, Nikki saw the sunrise slanting narrowly through the leaves, turning them to speckled shreds of dancing gold. Slowly, the flitting songbirds began to practice their tunes. Char got up and sat beside her.

"It looks as I were wrong 'bout an attack comin' last night," Char said quietly. "And we been cautious for nothing."

"This is one time you should be glad to be wrong," she replied. "But we have yet to reach Tia Cara safely, and you could still be proved right." She paused for a moment. "There's another thing to worry about." At this Char snorted, but Nikki ignored her, continuing, "I've been thinking about everything that's happened since this began. Now I know why Tbrin spent so much time teaching me how to fight long-dead enemies, though how he knew they would return, I don't know. I believe that I'm the shaper's intended target, and that Jelebron sent him to kill me, far away from Mistra, where my untimely death would have no 'unpleasant political repercussions.' If he is what I think he is, he will attack when I'm alone, or defenseless. He will use treachery before force, if possible. It was always their way."

"Their way?"

Nikki hesitated, not knowing how Char would take her response.

"Drakyn. The drakyn."

"But you said there was only one, this woman you said was in disguise at Mistra."

"There are two, and it's not a disguise. They actually become the shape they take. They could live in human form for centuries, and we might never know."

"You mean there could be drakyn still alive, livin' all around us?"

Nikki heard the panic in her voice. "No, I don't think so. I can't believe they would have waited this long to reveal themselves. Patience was not in their nature, or so Tbrin told me. I believe that Jelebron was recalled, using transmogrifee, by a human who may have waited for centuries for the right moment to recall the beasts and renew the war between human and drakyn."

"Why would anyone do that? They almost destroyed us humans, right?"

"For power. This is one time, I think, that I understand the situation better than you. I have known those in Mistra who would risk everything to gain power. And while I live, I must be considered a constant threat."

"Then why hasn't he attacked yet?"

"I don't know. The only thing I can believe is that there's someone in our group that he doesn't want to face, that he feels he can't defeat. It seems that someone is aiding us. Why else would he bide his time so?"

"Someone a drakyn can't defeat? Who could that possibly be?"

"I don't know. There are only two possibilities that I can think of; one would be an immensely powerful human transmogrifer, the other..."

"Why're you hesitatin'?"

"The only thing I can imagine would be another drakyn."

"No. It ain't possible," said Char, but she turned to regard their sleeping companions with a face that was pale with fear.

CHAPTER TWENTY-EIGHT

One-Shape Abominations

He realized too late that he'd opened a gut. Now the scragling meat would be tainted, but he didn't really care for the meat anyway, not when there was plenty of blood. It was a good vintage, this one, if a bit rangy, and it smelled a tad too much of garlic, for his tastes.

He tossed aside the stinking carcass and grabbed another squirming body. Raising it high over his head, he opened the neck deftly with a flick of one infinitely sharp claw, letting the still-beating heart pump the delicacy into his throat. He laughed at the sheer joy of it, then choked on the thick liquid, which made him chortle even more. His laughter gurgled up through the blood, creating delicate bubbles of pink froth. He shot it out through his nose, and the fine spray tinted the air with the perfume of death, that smell that he loved above all others, that transitory art form that he both created and appreciated. Nothing in the world could compare to it, not sex, not flight, not victory or torture. Nothing.

He tossed the body aside and stretched, flexing his claws and rubbing at his sore palms. It was so good to be back in true form—no more scrabbling in the dirt like a rodent. He could be whatever he wanted, but any shape would be preferable to the half-human, half-wolf monstrosity he had been trapped in by the disruption.

She would pay for that, and he'd had plenty of time to think of just how she would.

They weren't far ahead of him now, and by tomorrow the job would be done. Then to find the Tree of Malgryn and claim the power of the eye, and the throne of the queens would be his.

Wouldn't Jelebron be surprised. Of course, no male had ever held the throne, but he would be the first.

Then, once the farms were set up again, the blood would flow in rivers. The thought of it made him giddy.

He rolled over on his back and howled at the evanescent daytime moon, then swore at himself. Some habits were hard to break. Never again would he be trapped in wolf shape, though he might have to take on human form again. He had to admit that it was good for some things, all naked skin, and so sensitive. There might be a chance for some recreation first. He'd like that. He'd made the mistake before of rushing. That wouldn't happen again. That last encounter had surprised him, but next time he would separate them. No need to fight that one, when, with a little patience he could kill them all so easily, one at a time. He laughed again, rolling in the blood and dirt, and picked a bit of cartilage from his teeth. No need to hurry now. He could take wing at first light and be in the city long before them. Tomorrow eve, the fun would begin. He roared in joy, and the scraglings around him—those who still could—whimpered.

He heard rustling in the brush, something crawling away.

Disgusting vermin, did I miss one? No matter. Let it crawl off and die. There are plenty more.

He had all the time he needed to revel in the sticky red wine of death that he loved so much. It was really all they were good for, these alien, primitive creatures. To think that they actually put the dead in the ground with the blood still in them. Sacrilege and waste.

Not born to transmoger, as the superior drakyn were, but barely able to learn it, if they could at all. They were wingless, hairless rats; mere herdbeasts, to be consumed and their carcasses discarded to rot, these one-shape abominations, these humans.

CHAPTER TWENTY-NINE

Cities Stink

They reached the promontory overlooking the city of Tia Cara at dusk. Nikki surveyed the bay but could see only a few shadowy forms of fishing boats returning to dock. The docks themselves were a dark mass of boats, interrupted by the occasional jutting point of a mast. Nikki was startled by the calm water here, but Dreyk told her that the bay was long and protected from the tides and storms, though she noted that the docks seemed to have mooring spots higher up the bank as if they were moved up as the water rose, and the city was far above the waterline.

Tia Cara was smaller than she had expected and more ragged. Buildings sprawled randomly throughout the hills above the river and the bay, becoming more compact near the water's edge. The streets seemed to follow no pattern or design, and what she could see of the houses themselves looked haphazardly constructed and poorly maintained. As they drew closer, she heard the occasional bleat of a goat, or the cackling of geese and chickers. Even from here, she could smell the city. It was a recipe for human misery; sweating residents in cramped quarters, living too close to their animals and in-laws, topped by a generous dollop of rotting food and fish guts, all zestfully over-seasoned by the indelicate bouquet of poor sanitation.

"Cities stink, but you'll git used ta' it," counseled Char, as if she knew everything they might need to know about cities. "And they's always good ale and cheap sex if you know where ta' be lookin'. There's this little inn—"

"Char, let's not forget that we're here to get a boat," interrupted Nikki. "I think that after we take our patient to the medic's tent, we should go straight to the docks."

"There's something you're forgetting—" began Dreyk.

"And I need to see where the slaves are kept," interrupted Gormz.

"I want to see the boti—I mean the crendas," added Benna.

"As I was saying," Dreyk began again, louder, and more stridently. "This may not be as easy as you think. No one is going to just give us a boat, and I lost everything when *Windsinger* went down."

"Couldn't we offer to crew for someone?" asked Nikki.

Dreyk gave her a sour look. "With this lot? What skipper's gonna take on a bunch of landers who wouldn't know an emergency boom if it hit 'em in the face, which it probably would, first thing. Plus, there's the fact that Char's smell alone would drive the crew overboard."

"Then what do you want to do?" she asked, ignoring the Char comment, with Char bristling at her shoulder.

"I thought I would go down alone and check it out. There's a guy I know—he kinda owes me. Besides, he controls most of the interest in the boats 'round here. I'd probably have to deal with him sooner or later anyway."

Benna looked crestfallen. "Can I go too?" Nikki almost laughed. He sounded like a puppy begging for a treat.

Dreyk hesitated, then sighed. "I don't see why not, but let's not make this a party. These are simple people. They'll be suspicious of a group, especially one as strange as this one. I think you'd better leave your feline friend up here, Nikki. You don't often see grellas being kept as pets in a city as small as this. If we get a boat, we can sneak him onboard later."

Moonchaser growled, and Nikki rubbed his chin. "He's probably right, my friend. You could take a nap. We won't be long."

Dreyk gave her a dubious look. "If we get separated, let's meet at the camp we set up last night." He pointed to the high valley they'd come down that morning.

Nikki followed Char into the noise and smoke of the busy tavern. Char pushed her way to the bar, and Nikki followed, feeling foolish. How had the huntress talked her into this? Was this the northern culture Char had gone on about for days? If so, she wanted nothing to do with it. There were rough men at barstools that smelled of days-old ale and other, more mysterious things. Earlier, they'd watched Dreyk and Benna disappear into a ramshackle building near the docks. They'd waited patiently, until patience at last ran out, then they'd wandered the streets aimlessly. Gormz was disappointed when they didn't see a single dageki slave. Char stopped to buy fish on a stick, that to Nikki, smelled and resembled dried weeberdung more than anything edible. Char passed a coin to the street vendor, using a gravure that appeared miraculously from her pocket. The vender looked at the coin critically and bit it, but apparently it passed the taste test, and he was fooled by Char's transmogrifee. Nikki asked the man why they hadn't seen any dageki slaves in town.

"You probably won't be seein' many," replied the man. "'Cept maybe up on the hill. A couple o' 'dem rich traders might 'ave 'em. Most folks can't keep 'em no more. Price's gone up so that us normal folk just can't afford 'em no more. They bring 'em through here, but they's all headed for the bigger cities, like Bay Towne. That's where the money's at these days, 'parently."

The man looked Gormz up and down with narrowed eyes. "You must be purtty flush y'urselves. Y'ur boy looks to be in good shape. If y'ure here to sell, I can hook ya up with someone what might be interested, fer the right price, o' course."

Gormz seemed about to respond indignantly, when Nikki replied that they weren't interested in selling, but she'd keep it in mind, then rushed them off before Gormz could say anything.

Nikki looked back at Gormz now, as he sat quietly by the open door. Char had warned that slaves would not be welcome in the inn, but Nikki couldn't believe it, seeing what kind of shady characters they *did* allow. Leave it to Char to drag her straight into the most disreputable part of the city. The worn sign outside read, Rat's Nest Inn, but Nikki didn't believe that any self-respecting rodent would reside in a place like this. The smell of stale beer and vomit would surely drive them out.

Before Nikki could stop her, Char had ordered them both glasses of some dark liquid. At her first taste of bitter Tia Caran ale, Nikki grimaced, but after a few sips, it seemed to improve, and she began to relax. Char downed a few glasses before Nikki could drink half of hers, then the huntress wandered off toward a noisy dice game in the back. Nikki sat alone for a few minutes, when she felt the hair rise on the back of her neck. Even without her transmograffic senses, she knew that someone was watching her. She turned to face a tall man in dark clothing, with a handsome, tanned face and long black hair. But all this she saw later. It was his eyes that captured her first. They were not striking in color, just brown, but light as honey, with depth, mystery and intelligence. They glowed with joy, and she knew she'd met a man who loved life. When he smiled, they glowed even brighter. Nikki was entranced.

"Wren, is that you?" he said softly, and Nikki thought his voice matched his eyes; deep, but playful.

"No, I'm sorry," she said, "you must be mistaking me for someone else. I'm Nikki."

"But you look just like her," he said, and Nikki saw the disappointment in his face. She found herself wishing she was this woman, Wren, just to make him smile again, then she realized that she was being silly, and dangerously foolish. No doubt he'd made up this woman, just to meet her. If she let him, he'd probably try to steal her wallet—or worse. But she couldn't quite bring herself to believe him capable of petty theft. No, she told herself, if this man steals, he does it with more style than that. She smiled into her beer, and he looked at her curiously.

"Did I say something amusing?" he asked in his honeyed voice.

"No," she replied with a smile she couldn't quite prevent, "I was just thinking that if you're going to try to steal my wallet, you're in for a disappointment; it's empty."

He laughed at the ceiling, then said: "I would much rather steal your heart, but right now I'll settle for your company. Will you join me?"

"Where?"

"My table's right over here. Another ale for the lady Nikki, please," he barked at the barkeep.

Nikki thought better of it, then found herself following him anyway.

"It's just Nikki. No ladies here, I'm afraid."

"But it's a lovely name, as you are lovely. If it's possible, you are even more beautiful than Wren. I am enchanted."

"And I'm sure you told her the same thing about some other imaginary woman," replied Nikki, realizing too late the paradoxical nature of her statement.

His laughter made her stomach tingle. "You are a cynical woman, Nikki, but I forgive you. It's better to be cautious these days. Rumors have been spreading about someone they brought in this afternoon—something about a drakyn stalking the south road. That's ridiculous, of course. We know they've all been dead for centuries, but there are wolves out there, and some of them find their way into town."

"And how do I know you're not one of those wolves?"

Laughing again, he looked into her eyes. "I guess you'll just have to trust me," he said, and she did. The ale made her dizzy; she felt confused and lost for a second, then suddenly free. She'd worried for so long, and she couldn't worry anymore, at least not tonight. She let her fear go, and she was falling, falling for this stranger.

"Let's go out for some air," he said. "You're looking a little pale."

"I feel fine," she said, but she followed him toward the door. As they stepped out, she realized that Gormz wasn't there, or Char.

"I forgot Char," she blurted, ducking back into the inn. She searched through the smoke but couldn't find her friend.

"Only I could lose a woman as obnoxious as Char," she grumbled.

"I think I saw your friend leave with her dageki earlier. She's probably gone down to the docks for the festival."

"What festival?"

"I thought that was why you were here, to see the parade. But there's still time, if we hurry." He led her through a maze of streets until she was hopelessly lost. She wasn't sure she could find her way back to the inn if she had to, but she told herself not to worry. Char and Gormz would eventually show up. They rushed around a corner, only to come face to face with a huge, roaring drakyn. Nikki sank back in fear, then felt very foolish.

Instead of laughing at her, her companion said soothingly: "Easy, easy, it's only paper and sticks, you know. But we'd better get out of the way, so they don't trample us. I think it's pretty hard for them to see where they're going inside there."

The paper drakyn was coming right toward them, and Nikki had to hurry to get out of the way. Breathless, she struggled to keep up, as a crowd of dancing revelers surrounded them. The imitation drakyn led them all down towards the bay, and Nikki was caught up in the excitement. She looked at the people around her and found that many were wearing masks, some intricate and cumbersome caricatures of drakyn. Others were simple, handheld masks that covered only the eyes.

At the water's edge, the drakyn stopped and turned, letting out a roar. Its sides heaved as the men inside tried to hurry the massive, if hollow creature. The crowd broke into a frenzy, rushing the drakyn en masse. All that Nikki could see were shreds of paper flying as the drakyn was torn apart. Those inside broke free and ran. While they watched, the pieces of shredded beast were set on fire and tossed into the bay. Feeling it suddenly difficult to breathe, Nikki tried to work her way to the edge of the crowd.

"It gets pretty wild from here," shouted her companion. "We might want to get out of the way." He started to lead her along the water's edge, and Nikki followed, glad to be away from the noise, confusion, and smoke.

"It seems so primitive, almost feral," she said.

He looked at her strangely. "I was thinking the same thing. The drakyn couldn't have been so bad that we ourselves need to become beasts to remember them."

"I suppose you're right, but if the legends are true about the farms, the atrocities... They kept humans like livestock, just for their blood."

"Legends are exaggeration, by their very nature. Surely, the reality would not seem so horrible. We look on another species as beasts, when to them we may be the beasts ourselves. But enough about drakyn, let's just walk."

Nikki agreed, feeling light-headed. She didn't want to think about drakyn, or Mistra, or her lost abilities. Perhaps she could stay in Tia Cara, cleaning fish or serving ale, and never have to face her fears.

As they walked along the water, the noise of the crowd faded away behind them. Gentle waves lapped at the shore, setting up a rhythm in her mind. She felt good; she felt free for the first time in a long while. She giggled. Her companion laughed.

"It's good to see you smile," he said softly.

"Who are you?" she asked suddenly.

He turned toward her sharply, then let his shoulders relax. "That's right, I haven't told you my name, have I?" He stopped, as if thinking. "We're near my boat. It's just down here, at the end of the docks. Would you like to see it?"

"You have a ship?"

"It's just a little skiff, really, but it's been reliable transportation."

"You're a trader?"

"Sometimes. I have enough to be comfortable. I do a little trading to stay busy."

"It sounds like a wonderful life."

They followed the dock out to a large boat. Nikki could just make out bright new paint on the hull.

"It's beautiful!" she exclaimed. "But I thought you said it was small."

"Well, by some comparisons, it is. Would you like to come aboard?"

Nikki hesitated.

"My name is Semli, and I promise not to bite," he said. She laughed.

"It's not that," she said. "It's just that my experience with boats is quite limited, nonexistent to be exact."

"Well, this one isn't going anywhere, and the water in the bay is calm tonight."

He offered her a hand, and, despite her trepidations, she climbed aboard. He disappeared into the lower deck and Nikki was left standing alone. He returned in a moment with two glasses of golden wine.

"A toast to new friends, and old," he added wistfully.

"You really do think I look like this Wren?"

He downed his glass, tossing it overboard as he did, then looked at her with a teasing glance, daring her to do the same. She followed suit, laughing, and the wine went down cool and yet not cool enough to quench the fire that she felt.

He touched her shoulder, stepping very close. He kissed her gently on the cheek, then ran his tongue down her neck, kissing her collarbone. She shuddered, and he laughed, pulling her close. She felt the strength in him, his body hot and powerful, as if he were barely in control at all times. His skin was smooth and tight, his muscles straining, as if that power could burst out at any second and reveal a much larger creature, an animal of immense strength and wild passion, a lover who would tear at her resistance until she would gather her wings and break out of the sickly mold of humanity and into the bright, cool air of remorseless power. Suddenly she realized that he was the creature in her dreams, the one she fought but could never kill. In that instant, she saw him as he really was.

"You are the drakyn," she rasped into his chest.

"What did you say, little one?"

"Semli. Semli is a drakyn name. You are the one who attacked us at Mistra and in the desert."

At this, he laughed, nonchalantly pulling back from her. Too casually, and she knew with a sinking heart that her guess had been all too correct.

"Your eyes were always too sharp for your own good, dear Wren."

"I'm not Wren, I'm Nikki," she said, trying desperately to think of a way that she could avoid the death that surely loomed in her near future, but all she could think of was that Dreyk and Benna would think she had acted a total fool, and they would be correct.

"Yes, but you are so alike," continued Semli. "It's hard not to remember her, looking at you. When you first walked into the inn, it was as if she were alive again. It's been too long for her to still live, of course. Humans are so fragile. But to meet you in my human form was a mistake. I'm afraid you've captured my soul, as she did, so long ago."

As he spoke, he backed away from her and she saw the narrow glint of his croma sword as he flicked it forward, but she was no longer under the spell of his words, and when he struck, she was ready. She pulled her own weapon in a flash, and the two met with a sharp clang in the cool air. He laughed, but now the sound chilled her.

"You are swift as well as discerning, little Nikki. I think I'll enjoy toying with you."

Even as he spoke, his arm shot forward with a thrust so fast her eyes couldn't follow it. Nikki responded, but barely in time to deflect his blade. As they fought, Nikki was forced backward until she felt the boat's damp rail on her thigh. Her panic rose, and for a second, she lost concentration. His blade struck hers with painful force, and her weapon clattered to the deck, shattered in two. There was a flash of light and heat at her neck, where the useless St. Murphy medal lay. She frowned at the pieces of her precious sword, broken on the deck, useless to her now.

He laughed, drawing in a ragged breath.

"You make me work too hard, pretty one."

He stepped forward, and the air caught fire, exploding in her face. Nikki was blinded as she reeled back, expecting death, but instead, she found herself tumbling backward, then the shock of cold water. She struggled, trying to remember what little she knew about swimming. Suddenly air filled her lungs and she coughed, spitting water. Still unable to see, she struggled against something like rock that held her upside down, trying to shake her to death.

"Let me go," she yelled, but the beast that held her ran on and on, until Nikki remembered no more.

CHAPTER THIRTY

The Palace Remembers

Nikki woke with a tree root stabbing her in the back like a sword blade. She rolled over to find a more comfortable position, but rising even slightly, started her head throbbing. The pain brought her completely awake, and she recalled ugly bits of the night before. She sat up with a groan and looked around her with bleary eyes.

She sat in a small clearing, surrounded by twisted brush and tortured scrub trees. Nothing looked familiar. She wondered where she was, and how she'd gotten here. Then, she heard a sigh behind her. She turned abruptly and found Hyla leaning against a tree, picking at her teeth with what appeared to be a small tree limb. Moonchaser drowsed beside her, and she, Nikki, squinted at the sky, waiting for her world to stop spinning.

She rasped, "The others?" The words barely escaped her. She coughed and started again, but Hyla understood, anyway.

"No sign yet," said the giantess gruffly. "But coming soon they will be, I'm sure. Watching the road are Gormz and Pollux, of course."

As if on cue, the bushes rustled. Hyla drew her sword, listening, then sprang forward.

"Pollux!" she exclaimed, as the donklet stepped out of the brush and surveyed them with a bored expression, as if he'd just been out for a stroll. Hyla grabbed his one floppy ear and slapped him loudly on the back. Dust rose.

"There you are my dear," said Hyla. "Are the others coming?" As if in response, the animal curled his lip and snorted loudly. Hyla laughed.

Watching them interact, Nikki was even more worried about the others. She groaned again. "I really did it this time, Hyla. They could be in any kind of danger, or dead. Why did I let things get so out of hand?"

"A suggestion on you he must have used," Hyla replied. "Myself I blame for what happened. Never should I have left you alone to fend for yourselves. Should have known trouble would find you, yes?"

"How could you have? And what did you do to Semli? Hyla, I know you're not who you appear to be—and I really don't care who you are—I'm just glad you're on our side. I know you are. I can feel it, despite your behavior."

For the first time, Hyla showed some emotion. Her eyes turned glossy, then she spoke quietly: "Only a noble heart would give trust without knowledge."

"Or a fool," Nikki retorted.

Hyla snorted. "Extremely foolish what you did last night was, but under great pressure you have been." Hyla paused, as if considering how much she should say. "A great deal that you still don't know, there is. My true nature I will be able to reveal to you in time, but until then, trust me you must. My loyalty you will always have."

"I appreciate that, but I must admit that it's not totally blind trust, but logic, that drives me. If you'd wanted to kill us, you could've done it any time along the way, and your best chance was at the beginning, when you first found us in the desert."

"True," mused Hyla.

"Then I owe you my thanks," said Nikki as she rose to stretch her unstable legs. "And more, I owe you my life, twice now."

"My duty I am doing, mistress. Great work ahead for you there is and my job it is to ensure that you survive to accomplish it."

Before Nikki could respond, Hyla had disappeared into the brush. Nikki found her pack on the ground beside her. How considerate of Hyla, to not only save her life, but collect her belongings along the way. She pulled out a piece of dry bread and chewed noisily, trying to ignore the pounding in her head.

"No more Tia Caran ale," she said aloud, rubbing her temples. "You deserve a hangover for being such an ass! You almost ruined everything, and for what? Stupid, stupid, stupid."

"Do you always address yourself so rudely?" asked a teasing voice behind her. Nikki had risen and was reaching for her absent sword, before she realized that the voice was familiar, as was the tone.

"Dreyk, you're alright!" She sprang forward, as Dreyk appeared out of the trees. Benna came up behind him with a sheepish grin. He looked pale and sweaty. Nikki ran up to hug her brother, but he fended her off, claiming that his head hurt too much for hugs.

Dreyk looked at her apologetically. "I'm afraid that Benna and I got into a larger dose of Tia Caran hospitality than was good for us. I'm sorry, Nikki, we couldn't get a boat. I guess you'll have to come to Bay Towne with me, unless you, Char and Gormz fared better?"

"Not exactly," she began. "We—"

Hyla interrupted her, as she stepped into the clearing.

"Time to chat now we do not have. Keep moving we must." Nikki, hearing the warning tone in Hyla's voice, realized why Hyla might not want the whole story told. They would depend on Dreyk to get them a boat. With his fear of transmogrifee, what would he do if he knew he was traveling with such a powerful transmogrifer as Hyla obviously was? Would he leave them? She didn't want to test that theory just yet.

"But we haven't slept all night," moaned Benna. "My head is pounding like you wouldn't believe."

"Whose fault be that, then?" monotoned the giantess, standing suggestively with her switch in her hands, though they'd never once seen her use it on the donklet. Nikki suppressed a smile at the efficient way Hyla had turned the conversation away from her own activities last night, but secretly, she felt more guilty than ever. Dreyk, however, wasn't completely fooled. As they were shouldering their packs, he said: "I'm sure we'll get a full account later of what you two did last night."

"Sure," said Nikki, with as much false sincerity as she could muster.

Nikki was still worrying about Char when a huge black and silver falcon flew overhead.

Nikki waved to Char, and they headed out on the road to Bay Towne.

Fortunately, the trail took most of their attention that day, being even more pitted and narrow than the worst of the route into Tia Cara had been.

"Worse from here it gets," warned Hyla. "Crossing an arm of the Hartbone Range we will need to do to get to Bay Towne. The fastest route takes us near the ocean, and into ancient drakyn territory. At least robbers we won't have to worry about. Rarely visited is that place. Why the stigma still exists, after all this time, I don't know, but few humans venture there."

"Why?" asked Benna. "Did the drakyn leave traps?"

"No," replied Hyla. "At least not any that would still exist after so long, but up in the hills there are drakyn ruins. From just about anywhere you can see them. Just a little spooky it is, though only rats have inhabited the palace in centuries."

"The palace?" asked Nikki.

"The palace of the queens," replied Hyla. "The drakyn queens. They had a strictly matriarchal society, yes?"

Hyla grew quiet, and Nikki wondered how she knew so much of the ancient drakyn.

They slipped into the rhythm of the trail. Before Nikki knew it, the day was already fading into dusk, and they pulled up at a spot where a stream crossed the road. A rotting bridge spanned the narrow waterway.

"Follow this stream up into the trees we will," said Hyla. "Safe from attack we should be and better able to see and hear anyone coming up the road behind us." Nikki glanced at Hyla, suddenly worried. While the others were setting up camp, she pulled her aside.

"Why are you so jumpy, Hyla? Don't you think you killed the drakyn back at Tia Cara?"

"Almost impossible is such a creature to kill, as you know. The power I don't possess. That my shaping worked as well as it did was I amazed. Recover and follow us, he will. Though slow him down a bit was I able to do. Were he able to transmoger and fly, he would have overtaken us long before now."

Nikki shivered. "How were we ever able to defeat them, Hyla?"

"We didn't, though, did we? At least that's what my granpapa believed. Fascinated he was by their history and used to ask strangers for any legends they knew of the drakyn war. That they defeated themselves he believed—that there was a faction within their ranks who didn't want the humans destroyed and fought against their own."

"But that would mean that all the stories I learned as a child in Mistra were untrue, that Wren Weatherspring and Trey never existed, never defeated the drakyn as legends say. I can't believe it."

"What the real truth was probably doesn't matter now," replied the giantess. "Never know for sure may we. That you will be able to reach this island before he recovers and attacks again is what matters. They will multiply, will they not, if we fail to stop them here? No one else to save us now is there. Only you we have."

"Hyla, I appreciate your faith in me, but I'm not sure that I can defeat them alone, even with the power of a new drakyn's eye. I'm not even sure I will regain my own abilities. It's been too long. Even Char recovered before me. I'm not sure I'll ever be able to transmoger again."

"Then hope we must, because not just our own lives may depend on it, but the lives of everyone on Drakonia." Hyla let out a long sigh. "Getting to Bay Towne as quickly as possible now must be our goal. To ensure defeat, all we need do is not to try, yes?"

"You're right, of course," said Nikki. "Hyla, let's not tell the others about my confrontation with the drakyn in Bay Towne. Perhaps it's unfair, but I don't know how they'd take it—especially Dreyk—and we need his cooperation. Is that wrong? We're putting them all in danger, and Dreyk may never forgive me if he finds out that I lied to him."

Hyla snorted. "More at stake there is than the hurt feelings of one obstinate, wood-headed sailor!"

Nikki watched her walk away and realized that Hyla knew much more than she was sharing. Who was this woman? Nikki had a feeling she might find out before long, and she wasn't sure she wanted to see Hyla's awesome power released again. She hoped that if she did, they wouldn't be pitted against each other. She hoped that she was trusting the right person. For a second, she thought of going to the others and telling them everything, but even as she walked, she knew it was the wrong thing to do.

Not yet, she told herself. *Not until I know more.*

One night, far along on their journey to Bay Towne, Nikki woke to the sound of distant bird song, but she opened her eyes, not to dawn as she expected, but to deepest night. Both moons, Beckle and Meika, were full and bright, laying competing shadows across the land. She looked around at her sleeping companions, but none stirred. Char was missing, but she often hunted at night, arriving at dawn with a prize that would feed them well for days.

Now fully awake, Nikki rose as quietly as possible, and stood waiting for the sound to recur. After a time, she began to think that she'd dreamt it. Then the sound came again, faint and fleeting, but undeniably real.

Their camp looked different by moonlight. Things were not as she remembered them. Which way was the road, and where did that path lead? She didn't remember seeing the path at all in daylight, but now it seemed to glow with cold fire, leading up the hill behind their camp.

Just as she realized it was foolish, she knew she couldn't resist the urge to follow it. She slipped out of camp quietly, stepping gingerly past the sleeping forms of her companions, and headed up the trail. Soon, she was breathing hard, as the trail became even steeper. In spots, neither moon could fill the shadows and she stumbled. She thought about turning back, but when she did, she heard the distant song again, and it led her on. The trail began to smooth out as she climbed, until it became a path with tightly packed pebbles that seemed to fit together perfectly, like tiny, many-sided tiles. Once, she heard a sound behind her, like a piece of gravel slipping underfoot. She turned and stood very still for several minutes, but she heard nothing more. Her breathing leveled. She could hear her heartbeat in her throat like a beating drum, but no one appeared on the trail behind her. She turned and walked the last few yards to the top of the hill.

She gasped and stepped back in awe. Before her was a palace of crystal, like Mistra, but opposite, darkly ancient, harder of design, almost cruel in the cuts and angles of semi-transparent onyx stone. Ferociously beautiful, it was a tower of strength and enduring power. Nikki felt her skin tingle.

"This must be the palace of the drakyn queens," she whispered to herself. "How could a race capable of such ugliness also be capable of creating such beauty?"

The music now reached her clearly. It came from a swirling black fog at the top of one of the semi-transparent spires. As she looked closer, she made out a celadon glow, dotted by dancing flecks of black. The song it produced tugged at her. It spoke of power and dominion, but in a voice that held a tragic melancholy. It was a story of great struggle and the triumphant final victory to come. It was the most forlorn, yet enthralling music she'd ever heard, and it called to her, pulling her inexorably onward.

She stumbled forward, following a well-worn route, as if her feet knew the way, even when she did not. She took many stairs, winding and twisted and set to a rise and run not made for human anatomy. In places, the steps suddenly changed size and position, as if to test the unwary. In one spot, the stairs dropped away, and she fell, but she had no fear. She knew this place. It wasn't far, and she landed dexterously on her feet, continuing on her way as if nothing out of the ordinary had happened.

Then she was in the great hall. Her steps echoed. She was speaking a language sacred and ancient, and her voice mingling with the voices of the other revelers. Torches flickered, but there was no light. Leaves scratched across the floor's inlaid stone, like a thousand gowns, rustling across its surface. They were all lost in the dance. She heard voices, whispered laughter, a lewd comment in her ear. She laughed diplomatically. She heard them, almost saw them, the nimble dancers with huge shadows, so agile for beasts so large. She was one of them, and yet not, for she was the Queen. She turned from the dreamers, still lost in the last reverie, and her partner was there. Tall and regal, in a living dress of gossamer bride's maid moss and silver lichen streamers. Her hair was a cloud of the purest ink black, tied up in an intricate, firefly-decorated bun on the top of her head. A graceful, perfectly proportioned set of antlers adorning her brow. Her mask was that of a chroma hawk, every feather defined in colors ranging from hunter green to honey ochre to burning rust, complimented by shards of cerulean blue that matched her eyes, eyes bright as cool burning suns, slow but eternal. Nikki looked into those eyes and knew that this was her destiny—had been from their first moment together. She touched a white-gloved hand and sparks flew, delicate showers of sparklers that followed their movements as they entered the dance. The room swirled around them, the magical aria filling her with an effervescent laughter, her joy apparently contagious, as her partner began to laugh with her. They twirled, and Nikki's head spun. When the dance ended, their skin was damp, and their breath came in gasps. Char drew her to the side and whispered in her ear, "It isn't real, you know. It's just a memory. The flets can amplify emotion, create visions that bear no likeness to reality. But it's still fun, eh?"

Suddenly confused and embarrassed and angry, Nikki pulled away and ran out through the wide doorway and up a dark stone stairway. She hated to leave the dance, but they would understand. *Besides,* she thought as her heartbeat began to slow, *it is time.*

She knew the way. She'd done it a thousand times before and would do it a thousand after. Anticipation rose in her throat, and she was frantic to reach it, to have it. They were waiting for her.

She broke out into the tower room at last, and the song was overwhelmingly loud and strident, not just in her ears, but deep in her chest. It filled her, became her. She rushed through the black fog, now revealed as dark wings and thousands of tiny golden hearts, her allies, her messengers.

She climbed the throne. It was too large for her now, but she'd been hiding, shrinking, and she would rise to fill it now. It took all her strength, but she pulled herself up to where they were waiting for her. Where there had been the song of glory and loss, now her mind was filled with faces. All along, they had guided her. Old friends. Dear comrades who had waited so long for her return, for her to listen to the story, to oversee the battle they were waging.

Then she was there, in the dream, as it had always been, but now clear and sharp. The battlefield stretched out before her, and she could see the bodies, smell the fear, death, blood, piss, and loosed bowels.

Nothing noble in this, she felt herself thinking, but the thought was distant, detached. She lifted her sword and struck. Another head rolled away into the muck. She looked away in disgust and regret. The battlefield faded.

So long waiting and no one listening. Only hollow ghosts and empty shades of dreamers. *Where have all the dreamers gone?* they asked. *There are stories to tell, messages to deliver. The war is going badly, very badly, since the traitor turned on you. No nightsong at doublemoon. No dancing until moonfall, no rewards, but still we return. At moonfall we fly. Where are all the dreamers?* they asked again.

"We're dead," she screamed. "We're all dead!"

Her words broke the spell that held her, and she started, wondering where she was and how she'd gotten here. She sat in an oversized, black crystal chair with no idea how she could have climbed into it. It floated in the air at least ten feet off the floor. Around her head, a thousand dark-winged bat-like creatures danced in frantic confusion. Their song broke into cacophony as they realized at last that their dreamers would not return.

Imposter: not of the dream, they hissed at her. Their leathery wings flapped at her face, blinding her. In sudden terror, she crouched low in the chair, shielding her face. But the anger of the flets was unfocused, dissipating into confusion, as they flew from the tower in a thousand different directions. The song ended, fading into distant hysterical cackling, leaving Nikki feeling hollow and cheated, and somehow inadequate.

Tears streaming from her face, she lowered herself from the chair and ran from the tower, but while before she had known the way unerringly, she now faltered, finding one dead end after another. She began to panic and forced herself to be calm. She stood still and felt the direction of the breeze on her face. With a ragged sigh, she turned and followed the air.

She spied a light ahead and followed a long corridor down to the open sky. It opened to the outside, but the view was unfamiliar. She must have gotten turned around and come out on the back of the palace. Far below her, the ocean slept in a quiet bay, while here above a deciduous forest danced in the midnight breeze. Directly in front of her was a glassy pool, lit by the light of the double full moons and decorated by the lacy shadows of giant fine-leafed ferns. Around the pool was a bed of fine moss, and she had the sudden urge to take off her boots and see if it was as soft as it looked. She stepped forward, enchanted. She felt a hand on her shoulder, and she whirled, prepared to fight.

"You!" she exclaimed. "Do I need looking after so badly?"

Char lifted her hand from Nikki's shoulder as if it burned, and Nikki felt a surge of regret at her outburst, and something else, the shiver of some unfamiliar emotion.

"Hasn't it occurred to you that I might also be curious about these ruins?" said Char harshly. "It might help us to know a little more about our enemy, if this was indeed their palace."

"Char, I'm sorry. I guess I can be a little defensive, at times."

Char gave a snort and seemed about to respond, but as if thinking better of it, she turned abruptly, facing the pool.

"There's nothing here," Nikki said. "Just an abandoned tower and a crumbling ballroom filled with some curious flying lizards."

She didn't want to discuss what they had just experienced, wanting to get it clear in her own mind first. Had Char really danced with her, or had she imagined that too? She still wasn't sure what had been real and what had been a dream. Had she wandered into an ancient drakyn trap?

"They're just flets, silly. They're a kind of flying reptile that live in caves, mostly. I guess this place is cavernous enough to draw them in. This flock does seem to be imbued with some kind of psychic connection. To what or whom I can't tell."

"I've heard the term. I mean, who hasn't said 'fletshit,' when something goes wrong, but I had no idea what they looked like. I think this is the drakyn palace that was abandoned centuries ago. The flets still wait for their long-dead masters. I felt drawn here, as if I belonged."

Char sighed. "I couldn't stay away either. It's so peaceful up here, isn't it? And look at that pool. It's really a shame this place isn't used. Far from seeming a haunt for ghosts, it feels more like a safe haven, a place you could come to rest."

Nikki started at this reference to ghosts. Did Char feel them too? The images in the tower flooded back to her, and she realized that in the short time she'd been up there, she'd changed. She saw the past now as their possible future, and it wasn't a pretty picture. The transmogrifee wars had been horribly real, the death and destruction horrific for both races. She felt suddenly old and tired.

"I don't think there will be any rest for us," she sighed. "At least not while even one drakyn lives. And one is more than I can handle. I'm just a burned-out transmogrifer. I'm a fool to even attempt this insane quest."

"No, you're not," Char replied with heat in her voice. "You're a hell of a fighter. Give yourself more credit. Look at how far you've come without any transmogrifee at all! Besides," Char added softly, "if there is any way, by life or death, that I can help you, I will."

Nikki heard the serious tone in her voice, realizing that Char hid behind her gruff exterior and how hard it must have been for her to express her feelings. Nikki was deeply moved, but more, she was relieved, finding the same emotions in Char that she now saw in herself.

She studied Char's profile, etched severely by the moons. Her own silver tresses were at odds with Char's dark mane, seemingly alive as it was lifted gently by the breeze, but despite the hair color, they were much alike. They were both fighters. Both would do anything for those they cared for. Nikki saw Char clearly at last, both dark and light of wing, a hunter, a hawk. A transmogrifer with skill and imagination like nothing she had ever seen, or ever would see again. No wonder Char hid her true talent, it was indeed impressive. Who wouldn't feel threatened by that? It was sure that Char's childhood had not been an easy one.

Nikki turned to catch Char watching her, her lips turned up in a wry smile.

"I wondered if you would ever get around to seeing me," Char said softly.

Nikki looked down, suddenly ashamed of her failure so far to really understand the huntress, and indeed her own feelings toward her.

"I just realized that your dialect has changed," mused Nikki. "I knew you were hiding your identity, but—"

"People see me as less of a threat if they think I'm a rube."

"Well, sometimes you *are* a rube," laughed Nikki.

Looking skyward, Char snorted and said, "Those two moons have defined my life, you know."

"What?" asked Nikki, not following the non-sequitur.

"They say that those born under the lesser moon, when both moons rise, and the larger one sets, leaving the lesser moon on its own, are born to either greatness or great evil. A child born at this time is destined to great works of either creation or destruction. Judging by my life so far, I'd guess that my destiny is leaning toward the destructive side."

"Surely not!" said Nikki indignantly. "It's the opposite, I know it! It's you who doesn't see yourself truly. I have faith in you Char. I love you for who you are."

Nikki found suddenly that it was too late to turn back, or even alter their course, and somehow, she didn't care. She felt Char near her, inhaled the dusty, clear scent of her, and felt dizzy with the need to touch that tanned skin. Nikki raised her hand, caressing Char's cheek gently, but there was fire in her touch and her fingers trembled. She laughed, suddenly giddy, and Char's smile broadened to match hers.

They kissed in the soft moss, gently and tentatively at first, and then with mounting passion, until Nikki had no more energy for fear, no more need for anything. Afterwards, they lay silent beside one another, looking up at the sky in contagious peace. Nikki felt the tickle of the moss on the her legs and back. The midnight breeze touched her skin with infinite gentleness and care. Nikki lay unmoving, feeling everything and nothing. Finally empty.

"I think I would like to come back here, someday," Char mused. "When all this is over. It's so quiet. Maybe there is peace to be found here. I hope you find what you seek, Nikki, but I also hope to be a part of your future."

"Now, don't you be silly," she teased, "of course you will." But Nikki secretly wondered if Char would feel the same way about her if she regained her power. What if she succeeded in this ridiculous quest? Would she be the same person she was now? Newly born questions knocked about her brain like flets gone crazy in the tower. *Would she and Char stay together? Would they both even survive?*

CHAPTER THIRTY-ONE

Dead Slaves Can't Bring the Wine

Semli rolled over, stretching languorously as the sun's late morning warmth touched his face. It had risen high while they slept, finding a place in the dusty window of this tiny second-story room. Outside the window, hinges creaked as a sign that read, Bay Towne Inn, gently twisted in the breeze. He smiled, caressing the hip of the woman who still slept. She moaned in her sleep, curling deeper under the blankets. He decided to let her sleep a little longer. They had stayed up late into the night, and the wine was still in her blood. Rising slowly to a sitting position, he pulled on his pants. He heard the rustle and felt the weight of coins in his pocket. Vaguely he remembered the dice game that had produced his winnings and the woman from whom he had won them. She had been an exceptionally good sport, but she could afford to be. If the hints he'd gotten were true, she was the daughter of one of the wealthiest families in Bay Towne. And she had proved herself to be much better at lovemaking than at gambling.

Already he liked this town. It had everything he could want, at least for now. Besides, he was growing tired of this game his mother had thrust him into. This Nikki had too many allies, and they had the disgusting habit of showing up at the worst of times. Better to let someone else wear down her resources, then he would step in to claim his winnings.

Patience, he told himself. Patience is the key to victory.

And now he had all the time in the world, if Jelebron was busy in Mistra, trying to convince those hidebound mountain dwellers to back her in battle. If he were fortunate, Nikki might take care of the problem of Jelebron for him. With a little maneuvering, it might be possible. Lost in the intricacies of his plot, Semli did not see the shadow that fell across the sun, but he heard the scream. The next instant he caught the red blur of his lover's body as it hurtled out the window, hitting the ground below with a conclusive thud. He spent no time at all on remorse. He was more concerned now that he didn't join her there.

He backed away from the bed while his mother took on her true shape. The room was far too small for her, and he thought for a second how ridiculous she looked, her head cocked at an angle against the ceiling and blood dripping from her glistening teeth onto the delicate lace coverlet of the tiny bed.

"Mother, you still have much to learn about the proper deportment of a queen," he chided. "They must fear us, of course, but dead slaves can't bring the wine."

"You know nothing of ruling, Semli. You are nothing but a male, and a weak one at that. You are an embarrassment to the memory of the Queens. I should have killed you at birth, as Kyrun and the others counseled. But you will fail me no more."

Jelebron stepped forward, and Semli knew that he would have to think fast if he wanted to live. He felt a rush of excitement—almost joy. This was when he was at his best—when everything hinged on one last bet. He had no chance of defeating his mother in battle, but he knew her well. It gave him all the weapons he needed.

"But I haven't failed you, Mother. Nikki is not dead, but she is talentless. Why should I waste my strength on killing a thing that is as good as dead? I found the way to the lost isle and the tree from which the eyes are born. The eyes will ensure our domination of this world for a very long time to come. Something must have gone wrong for you in Mistra, or you wouldn't be here now. Is your power failing you? Did that rabble refuse to join you, or did you kill them all in a fit of pique? It was a waste of your time anyway. You won't need them now. Are you not the least bit interested in ultimate power?"

Jelebron's eyes narrowed. She hesitated, but only for an instant.

"You lie, Semli. I know you. If you knew the location of this tree, you would not wait for me to find it, you would claim it for yourself. Don't think I am unaware of your true ambitions or the depth of treachery in your heart."

"I didn't say that I knew the location of the tree, only that I knew a way to find it. Nikki will lead us there. Then I will kill her. With a new eye, no one in the world will not bow to you, no pleasure can be denied you. You are the One Queen, Mother. You are a great power of the world, but how would it feel to be a god?"

Jelebron made an infinitesimal movement, the slightest lessening of tension as she rested the ball of her clawed foot back onto the floor.

Semli let out a mental sigh. With this slight movement, he knew that he'd won.

CHAPTER THIRTY-TWO

Hyla's Homecoming

Nikki and her companions trudged up the road, too tired for conversation. Everyone was beginning to show signs of exhaustion. The nights had been growing colder as they rose in elevation. Nikki woke with stiff joints and aching bones. Benna had developed a cough, and Nikki was worried about him.

Gradually the land began to level out, and the road widened, showing signs of increased travel. Nikki knew they must be approaching the city, but she trudged on with the others, too tired to ask. Without warning, Hyla pulled up in the road, turning to the group.

"Bay Towne lies just a couple miles over that ridge. From the road I must turn here to my cabin to complete a crucial task. Not far up this draw it lies. All would be welcome to spend the night by a warm fire."

Nikki was relieved, until Dreyk turned away from them.

"I have no desire to spend another night out here when my home is so close," he said. "You'll have to go to this cabin without me."

He started on alone, and Nikki had to hurry to catch him.

"Dreyk, wait," she exclaimed, grabbing his arm. "Don't be silly. We must at least thank the woman for all the aid she's given us. Besides, we all could use a rest."

"You know what she's like," Dreyk whispered. "Has she ever followed through on anything she promised? There's some self-serving scheme involved, I'm sure of it."

"Please come with us," she whispered. "You know that Benna will follow you, not us. He doesn't want to lose the chance to sail. It's all he talks about, but he needs rest. Can't you see that he's ill?"

Dreyk looked at her for a long moment, and Nikki could see conflicting emotions warring in his thoughts. "Alright, I'll go with you, even though I know you're magnifying Benna's little cold into the plague of the century. But we leave at first light tomorrow. Agreed?"

"Agreed."

The house of the transmogrifer did not impress. It stood in a secluded meadow where weeds grew almost to the roofline. Loose shingles poked out from the roof, flapping in the breeze, and the walls looked as if they stood as much from habit as anything else.

Nikki said, "I don't mean any disrespect, Hyla, but your house doesn't exactly emanate power."

"Remember where you are, mistress. Much feared is transmogrifee here. Not wise would it be to have too obvious a presence, no?"

"OK, your secret's safe with me."

Hyla gave her a sardonic look. "Your silence I appreciate. More at stake is there than you know."

Dreyk made a nervous noise in his throat. He was the last person to the door, and he didn't seem eager to take another step.

"I'll just wait out here," he said.

"Nonsense," said Nikki, exasperation showing in her voice. "You can't just stand out there."

Hyla sighed. "Out there can you wait if you choose, fisherman, but missing the whole story you'll be, and let me tell you, a doozy it is."

"That's it!" shouted Dreyk, suddenly exploding. "It's some kind of trap. I knew it!" He started to back away.

Nikki too, was becoming suspicious, but she still trusted Hyla. The giantess gave them a long-suffering look, then sighed again.

"Follow me," she instructed Dreyk in a tone that vibrated with power. Dreyk nodded vacantly and stepped over the threshold behind the others.

At once, Nikki could feel the hair rising on the back of her neck. Even without her power, she could sense it. The room crackled with the energy of transmogrifee being worked. She wanted to turn and run, but it was too late. Hyla stepped into the room and toward a woman standing in the corner, but as she neared the other woman, she began to stretch. Her image blurred, and Nikki could feel a wind tugging at her as well. Then there was a roar and a flash, as the two people became one. Nikki covered her face but could still feel the light and the power on her eyelids.

When she dared to open her eyes, Hyla was gone. Before her stood a beautiful woman, with a long, flowing mane of silver hair. Her eyes were gray with hints of the brightest sea green and a great depth of mystery. If it were not for the dark circles under her eyes and the paleness of her skin, she would have been the most amazing woman Nikki had ever seen. She looked familiar to Nikki, but for the moment, she couldn't place what it was that seemed to call to her.

"What have you done to Hyla?" Nikki demanded, when words at last returned to her.

"I have done nothing to Hyla," said the woman in a calming voice. "Nothing but to create her. She is here. She is a part of me. I'm sorry I had to deceive you, but it was necessary. Dreyk would never have accepted my help if he'd known in the beginning who and what I was."

"You're damn right, I wouldn't!" he exclaimed, "and it's not that you use that gardamn transmogery. Char uses it and we've accepted her, but she didn't lie to us from the beginning like you did. I don't know what you've been up to, but I've had enough."

With these acerbic words, he stalked from the room.

"He's gone for good, this time," Nikki exclaimed in a worried tone.

"I don't think so," said the transmogrifer with a sigh. "It seems that all roads lead back to this cabin. I regret having to hold him here, but it's for his own good. He wouldn't have a chance against a drakyn alone, and my protection can only extend so far. Let him walk it off."

Nikki could understand why Dreyk might be angry. She was upset herself that they'd been deceived, and she'd really grown to like Hyla. It would be hard to accept her in this new form. But Dreyk seemed angrier than the situation warranted. She planned to get it out of him later. She too was tired of mysteries.

As if reading her thoughts, the transmogrifer said, "I know you're tired of all these tricks, but we had to be sure about you. I didn't want to give myself away by showing my power, and I almost got you all killed as a result. But a drakyn can take many forms, and you might have been able to deceive me. There is something about you, Nikki, about your essence, that still disturbs me—"

"Wait. You said 'we.'"

"Oh dear, I almost forgot." As she spoke the cabin door opened and Pollux stuck his head in, braying loudly. When the donklet started to push his way into the small room, Nikki groaned and started to rise to stop him. It had been hard enough to stuff Gormz into the cramped space. But her worries were for naught, as the donklet disappeared with a gentle "ploop" sound. The tall blond and almost painfully handsome man who stood before them beamed and said, "I don't go in for all the drama and showmanship that my dear wife is prone to." At this Wren snorted.

He bowed gracefully, arching his dusty hat through the air.

"Let me introduce myself. I am Trey, nee Kodo, nee the Wastrel. I never liked that epithet, but there you have it."

Benna sat by the fireplace, his mouth open and moving as if words were on the way, but none arrived.

Char whispered, "Ooh, nicely done."

Benna frowned bemusedly, while beside him, Gormz sat raptly, like an oversized child waiting for story time.

"Sorry for interrupting, my dear, please do continue," said Trey with feigned formality.

"Oh, yes," purred Wren, "Where was I?"

Benna said, "You were saying how you, you... you..." he sneezed, then continued, "...can tell that Nikki is different."

"Yes. While the abacusian gives me—"

"What's this abicuserum, then?" interrupted Char.

"Abacusian. It's a device that amplifies transmograffic power, for certain people, but I'll get to that later. If you keep interrupting me, I'll never finish this story."

"OK, sorry," muttered Char. "Git on with it, then."

"Our story actually begins when humans first arrived on Drakonia—"

"Arrived? I thought we were always here," blurted Benna. Then, at her glare, he mumbled, "Sorry," and hung his head.

"My granpapa told me this story, as he learnt it from his elders, and so on and so on, back into time. It's also in the primers, of course, but few can read them anymore, unfortunately. My mama and her papa were primer-keepers, as am I. It's our job to preserve the history of mankind on Drakonia.

"Our people—humans that is—came from the gardlands. It was a land filled with so many laws and rules, that you couldn't breathe without breaking one."

"I couldn't live like that," interjected Char.

"Well, neither could our ancestors. The lawmakers controlled everything. Your life was laid out for you even before your birth; how tall you'd be, the color of your hair, where and how you'd live, even whom you'd join with when you came of age. Now be quiet, so I can tell the rest of this tale."

Char opened her mouth to interrupt again, but at a look from Benna, remained silent.

Wren continued, "When someone started to show signs of creativity, or be skilled in making things that were not completely utilitarian, they were branded as artistas and thrown into great stone barns called prisons. But, over time, more and more of us were born in the gardlands, until the prisons overflowed. That's when one of the technologists got the brilliant idea to send us to this place through the cubes—"

Gormz interrupted excitedly, "I've seen one of these cubes, on a university expedition. We couldn't find any purpose for them, but they are so perfectly formed as to be impossible to duplicate using the technology we have today. Even the Leijong have not been able to crack the mystery of these stone boxes, and—"

"But what happened next?" interrupted Benna.

Wren continued, apparently having given up on preventing interruptions. "Humans were sent here to live out our lives in exile on Drakonia, never able to return to the gardlands. Here's the part where my granpapa always laughed, because we had the last laugh on the gardlanders. Though surviving here was hard, especially in the beginning, before the seeds and animals they sent with us multiplied, our people were free to live as we chose, go anywhere on Drakonia we wished and create new lives for ourselves. Then we started to learn to transmoger too.

"Apparently, in the gardlands, transmogrifee wasn't even possible. If you wanted to build something, you had to do it from scratch with your bare hands."

Benna exclaimed, "Wow, just like me. I would pity these gardlanders, if they weren't so evil."

"Well, the theory is now that the civilization of the gardlanders must have collapsed, because no one has been sent through the cubes for millennia. It's believed that when all the creative thinkers were purged from their society, the culture grew so stagnant that their civilization collapsed. We think that the gardlanders stopped sending artistas through because there are no more gardlanders left to send them."

Wren's rapt audience was silent for a change, apparently processing this tale.

"My granpapa told me that, at first, we lived in peace on Drakonia, at least here in the south. When the drakyn began moving down this way, the transmogrifee wars between drakyn and human began.

"Now let's jump forward to my time, eight-hundred years ago—"

"What do you mean?" asked Gormz. "Are you saying you lived in the past and somehow were transported forward to our time? That is not scientifically plausible."

"With the abacusian, it is. Both Trey and I lived a long time ago—are still living there in a way. By the way, this miraculous device was created by your people, Gormz, over eight centuries ago."

"I cannot believe this."

"It's true. I'm afraid that rather than advancing, as I had hoped, the dageki have lost much of the expertise and knowledge they had back then, unlike the Leijong, who have come so far. It's really a shame."

Gormz seemed to ponder this deeply. Finally, he said, "It is my hope to be able to recover at least part of the knowledge that was lost, to bring my people out of this abhorrent slavery and renew our place in the advancement of science."

"That's a lofty goal, Gormz, but if you're anything like the dageki of our time, I have confidence that you will succeed."

Gormz was silent, and Wren continued, "Anyway, my journey to Dmisi and how I obtained the abacusian is a long story. You can read about it in my primer, *Chronicles of the Drakyn War.*"

Nikki sat up in excitement. "We have a copy in Mistra, but it's so ancient, many of the pages are lost. I fear it paints only a partial picture of your experiences."

"If I can, I'll bring you a fresh copy from the past, when all this is done."

"A copy?" asked Gormz. "Each one must take years for your scribes to reproduce. That is a very generous gift."

"Not really," laughed Wren. "In the back of the book is a diagram of another dageki invention, the printing press. I'll bring you a copy too, so hopefully your scientists can build one for themselves."

"I will treasure this volume as more precious than my own tail," intoned Gormz, almost reverently.

Wren laughed again and continued, "The abacusian gave me the power to defeat the drakyn, but I chose to transform, instead of destroy them."

At this, Char looked at her oddly, saying under her breath, "Must not 'a been born under the same moon as me, then."

Wren appeared not to hear the huntress and continued. "It may or may not have been the right choice. I've had a while to consider my actions, and I'm still not sure it was the proper course."

"But what did you do to them?" asked Benna.

"I sensed that more than just human survival depended upon the decision I would make. The entire balance of nature could have been upended by the incredible power of the abacusian. If I were to obliterate the drakyn, our whole planet might have been destroyed with them. So, I bound them to human form, reasoning that in the bodies of a less aggressive species, they might eventually lose their incredible thirst for conflict. And it worked, but with a price, a heavy price."

She stopped talking and shared a melancholy look with Trey. When she continued her tone was somber. "Even with the abacusian, it was a constant travail maintaining the drakyn in their new forms. Over time, we learned that the abacusian could be deadly to humans, and that using it was killing me. When I succumbed, the drakyn would return to their true forms and warring ways, since there was at that time no one else with the talent I possessed to operate the abacusian."

"No!" breathed Benna. "Then why are you here now? What happened?" Then he sneezed.

"I discovered that the abacusian also gave me the ability to activate the cubes and move through time, since apparently, the cubes transported their human cargo through space, *and time* to get them here. I could also slow and even stop time for myself while within the cube. I decided to enter the cube and stay there, maintaining the balance in the world, until the day that someone else was born with the power to control the abacusian and take my place. By stopping time, I also stopped the advance of the illness that will eventually end my life forever. Every time I leave the cube though, my death creeps nearer. That's why I had to keep leaving the group. I must return to a cube frequently to extend the time I have left. Nonetheless, that time is finite, and my end is very near now."

Nikki said, "I'm so sorry."

Gormz mused, "It must be like finding a grain of sand in the desert, finding one who has your talent, especially if it is as rare as you say it is."

"Yes," Wren replied. "But when I was about to enter the cube for good, we—Trey and I—learned that I was with child. The great Leijong seer of our time, Aquilinus, prophesied that our daughter would have the ability in an even greater degree than I possessed, and be immune to the detrimental effects of the abacusian."

"Not our daughter," corrected Trey, "our *progeny*."

"Yes, that's correct," Wren added wistfully. "So, when we found that our daughter was not the chosen one after all, we began searching through time to find the one who was destined to take my place.

Fortunately, I was able to place a seeker stone–you call them drakyn's eyes–with my daughter so we could track our descendants."

"And?" asked Benna, sniffing impatiently.

"And they've all been without the talent," explained Trey. "This is our last chance. Wren's ability through the abacusian to sense the future ends soon. That means that either the abacusian is destroyed—unlikely, since it is hidden in a practically impervious redoubt, or..."

"Or what?"

Wren answered for him, "Or time itself ends."

"When?" asked Char, her voice cold.

Wren sighed. "In about a month."

They were all silent for a long time, lost in their own morose thoughts of the pending apocalypse, when Char asked, "So if you're following us—us specifically—then the heir to this power must be here, within *this* group, correct?"

"Yes," Wren admitted.

Benna gave Char a sidelong glance, perhaps amazed that the huntress knew a word like "specifically." It appeared that he too was beginning to see beyond the wall that Char erected against the world.

Char spoke again, in a voice filled with certainty, "I'm sure I'm not the only one who has noticed how much Nikki resembles you, Wren."

Nikki stood up so suddenly that Benna, who had been sitting beside her, fell over backwards. Then he sneezed. Not noticing his turtle-like attempts to right himself, Nikki's eyes flitted between Wren and Trey in sheer panic.

"There's no way. No, it's not me. I don't even have my own powers anymore."

Wren said, "But you will get them back. Nikki—listen to me." But Nikki was already halfway to the door.

Trey said calmly, "Nikki, show us your necklace."

Nikki stopped as if suddenly turned to stone.

"Her medallion?" asked Char. "I've seen it. It's just a cheap Saint Murphy medal, whoever that is. It isn't even real croma. It's some kind of joke. There's no Saint Murphy; no patron saint of 'What can go wrong, will go wrong.' But it does seem appropriate to the luck we've had on our journey so far."

"Let us see it, Nikki," repeated Trey.

Finally, with reluctance, Nikki relented, pulling the chain from her tunic. It appeared to be as described, just a cheap metal coin on a chain.

"Here, take it," said Nikki roughly, as she pulled the chain from her neck with such force that it broke, sending the coin skittering across the cabin's wood plank floor.

As the coin rolled and spun, Wren raised her hand. To their amazement, the coin started to grow and change color. When it stopped, the coin was gone, replaced by a large, round stone aglow with sparkling, swirling colors.

"That's the drakyn's eye. It's imbued with a transmogery to ensure that it will always be drawn to our female descendants. The stone will find a way to be near her, or she will be drawn to it. There's no question. Nikki, you are the chosen one. You're our last chance to save the world from the total annihilation that will surely occur soon, if we do nothing."

"No," Nikki said emphatically before stomping from the cabin.

Char said, "She's not ready for this."

"Are any of us?" asked Benna, but no one had an answer to that. He sneezed.

CHAPTER THIRTY-THREE

Voluntary Captivity

L ater that evening, Wren found Nikki alone, sitting on a log and gazing absently down the valley towards Bay Towne.

Nikki was reeling from the events of the afternoon, when Wren had taken her to the unusual glass-walled sunroom at the back of the cabin. Almost the entire space was taken up by a huge, brightly colored mechanism. Twisting, spiral staircases made up of multi-colored beads spun, as the device itself shuddered and groaned.

"What is it, a giant organetto?" Nikki had asked.

"No," replied Wren with a chuckle. "The is the abacusian. We brought it with us from our time."

Wren proceeded to instruct Nikki on how she used the abacusian to alter matter, but when Nikki touched the black handle of the machine, nothing happened. As she had expected, she felt nothing, no great power, no omniscience. She'd run from the room in embarrassment and disgust.

Now, Nikki turned to Wren with a look of apology.

"I'm sorry," said Nikki simply.

"There's nothing to be sorry about. I understand your reticence. My own insecurities plagued me at first."

"What changed your mind?"

Wren was silent for so long that Nikki thought she might not answer.

"My friends. Kodo, and Trey, and even the Wastrel. Mala, the marm turned human, Poppet, even Teeka, the crazy French cook. The whole human race. In the end, I just couldn't let them down."

"Sounds like you had some interesting friends, too."

"You don't know the half of it."

They laughed together.

"The thing is," said Nikki, "I really don't think I'm your hero, or 'chosen one' as you call it. Even though all the evidence seems to point to me. It just can't be. What if I fail? I don't even know what it is I'm supposed to do. You saw what happened when I touched the abacusian—nothing."

"If you're like me, the ability will come along with the need. Don't worry. We'll all be there for you. I won't leave you again."

"But what about this illness that the abacusian gave you? It's going to kill you eventually, isn't it?"

"That's not what you should worry about now." Wren frowned.

"What else?" sighed Nikki. "I can't take much more."

"Two drakyn have returned to the world."

"Two?"

"Yes. I believe that there are two; a female, and a male, the one who follows us."

"Then I was right about Jelebron. She really is a reanimated drakyn. But why haven't they summoned others? Why haven't they attacked?"

"I don't know, but I know a little bit about how they think. Before the war ended, they constantly fought among themselves for power. They may hesitate to recall others, even if they know how, until they can solidify their own positions."

"Do you really think that this new drakyn's eye will give us the power to defeat them? And if it's so powerful, why didn't you just get it yourself?"

"If we're lucky, the drakyn will hold true to form and fight amongst themselves first. That may give us the time we need. As for what and where the drakyn's eye is, I don't know any more than you do. It's as if the eye and this tree are hiding from me. No one now alive knows where they came from. The Leijong mentioned this Terraformer on an island to the north. I believe it is the tree from legends. From what they say, I believe that this tree is about to bloom. Until you came along, we had no idea how to find this thing. Now time is short. We must hurry, before it's too late. Disaster seems inevitable unless we can get to this isle first."

After they had settled in for sleep, having shoehorned five guests into the tiny cabin, with Gormz relegated to a makeshift pallet on the back porch, Nikki went outside to assimilate all that she had learned. With Moonchaser at her side, she breathed deeply of the crisp night air, trying to focus her thoughts. Why did the responsibility have to rest on her shoulders? Like a child, she found herself wishing that she could just run away or find a new game to play. She didn't want any part of this one, especially since her future looked darker every minute.

Dreyk interrupted her thoughts as he shuffled his feet in the weeds beside her. Most of the anger seemed to have dissipated from him, leaving only concern and resignation.

Nikki said, "I'm glad you came back."

He harumphed. "Well, I didn't get too far. Every trail led me right back here. I listened to everything outside the window, so I know *why* she did what she did, I'm just not sure I can accept it, not yet anyway. After I calmed down, I realized that I couldn't leave you and Benna alone in her clutches."

"I still don't understand why you were so angry with her. She saved our lives many times over."

"I don't like being deceived, that's all." But Nikki could see that there was more to it than that.

"Something like this happened to you before, didn't it?"

Dreyk hesitated, as if even talking about it was difficult for him.

"Yes," he began haltingly. "There was a girl I wanted, but she would have nothing to do with me. We were both very young. One night she came to my room. She seemed a little different, but I was in love; I didn't notice. In the morning, she showed me who she really was, Westry the transmogrifer. I haven't spoken a civil word to that witch since that day."

"Don't you think it's time you forgave her? You were both very young and inexperienced, as you say. Maybe she too was in love. What would *you* have done if you'd had the power she had?"

Dreyk didn't answer, but Nikki could see that it was something he'd never considered.

Much later, or much earlier in the morning, when Nikki still couldn't sleep, she went to a window and saw Char standing in the moonlight, very still. Creeping out as quietly as she could, she stood beside her friend in silence. Finally, Char said, "So, it seems our time is short, one way or another."

"I hope it won't be, Char. I don't know how you feel, but to me what we had at the palace of the queens—"

"You don't have to say a thing. It was wonderful for me too. It's just that now—this new power of yours—we don't know where it will lead and—"

Nikki responded in frustration, "What new power? I don't even have my *old* power! Now everyone expects me to come to the rescue. It's pure fletshit!"

"At least now you know what a flet is," Char remarked with a teasing voice.

"Yah, there's that," said Nikki, dryly.

Nikki said softly, "You bring out the best in me, you know."

"Same for me."

"Look, let's just play this by ear," said Nikki. "For all we know, *you're* the chosen one, not me."

Char burst out laughing, then, worried that the others might wake, said quietly, "The gardlands will freeze over before Char the huntress rescues anyone, especially that wood-headed fisherman you mistakenly befriended."

They both laughed loudly, now not caring who might wake.

In the morning, they gathered their belongings, and to Nikki's surprise, Wren shouldered Hyla's pack. It looked incongruous on so small a woman, but somehow Nikki doubted that Wren would have trouble keeping up.

"Are we going to make it in time?" Nikki asked the transmogrifer hesitantly.

Wren's eyes seemed to lose their focus for a second, then she said: "I believe that the drakyn is following us. In fact, I can't understand why he hasn't caught up already. I expected another confrontation before now."

Nikki shivered despite the warmth of the morning sun.

"The only thing we can do is keep moving," continued Wren. "We must reach this Tree of Malgryn before he catches us. He must not know its location, or he would already have reached the isle himself. Perhaps he's just waiting for us to lead him to it. That's something I would expect of him. Also, he will probably try to separate us, get one alone and unprotected. Please stay close to the group. Believe me, under the interrogation of a drakyn, no one can hold out for long."

"But we don't know the location of the isle ourselves," interjected Dreyk. "All we have is Nikki's needle and a very incomplete map. I've been up in the Thousand Isles. It could take years to find one small atol in that maze. Maybe we should split up and try to gather more information on our own."

"The drakyn would torture you to death before he realized that you lacked the knowledge he needs, or he might do it just for sport," warned Wren. "And there is always the possibility that you might give away some information that would help him find the isle for himself. The beasts are extremely clever. We must stay together."

"Alright, I think you've made your point," said Dreyk. "So, let's get going. It's going to be hard enough to get another boat at this season, especially since word has probably reached here that I didn't leave my last one under the best of circumstances."

"If we have to, we'll use force," said Wren with conviction. "Too much is at stake here to worry about convention now."

Dreyk was silent, but Nikki could see the chagrin on his face. She could well imagine how he would feel if he were forced to steal from his own friends. She only hoped it wouldn't come to that.

They reached the trail and continued towards Bay Towne. After a couple miles, the trail broke out onto a smooth, well-traveled road. At the crest of a hill, the city opened up below them, and Dreyk showed his first smile in many days. Nikki was surprised by the size of the city. Tia Cara would have fit within it several times. It rested on a broad plateau above the bay. Two Moon Bay itself was huge, made up of two large circular coves, well-protected by jetties that almost touched at a point far out from shore.

As they entered the city, Nikki was first struck by the noise. The farther they walked toward its center, the more the noise level increased until it seemed to surround them on all sides. Children laughing, barkers and fish sellers hawking their wares, and the constant drone of conversation filled the air.

As they walked, she realized that they had entered a large open-air market. Goods of every imaginable kind covered tables and carts around the square. At the very center of the square was a large platform, where some kind of auction seemed to be going on. Then Nikki saw them, and her heart began to pound in anger. Here stood a group of the docile dageki, tied in a line like herdbeasts awaiting slaughter. She looked up at Gormz, but she couldn't read his expression. He was very still.

They worked their way toward the line, and Gormz stepped up to one of the dageki, who ignored him as he spoke. Nikki couldn't understand what Gormz was saying, but she knew that he was getting agitated. The other dageki let out a desperate sob and began replying to Gormz.

Their speech caught the attention of the auctioneer, who called down to her. "Sorry, mistress, but these are already sold—to that man there."

He pointed to a slim, gray-haired man at the edge of the crowd. He was neatly dressed in a tunic of sky blue vivimoth silk.

Suddenly Gormz was frantic in her ear. "Tell him that you wish to sell me as well, to this man."

"What?" she cried. "You don't know what you're saying, Gormz. This is slavery!"

"I know what it is, but how am I going to help them, if I can't get near them? This female is pregnant. She probably won't survive without attention. At least I can communicate her needs."

Nikki stared at him in disbelief. Wren came up beside her and said quietly, "Maybe he's right, Nikki. This may be the best way. Who are we to judge the wisdom of this?"

Nikki looked at her, wondering if the transmogrifer saw more of the future than she was telling, but she had to admit that Wren might be right. She looked again at the man the auctioneer had pointed out. How could she know if he were a good man or a beast?

"I'm not here to buy," she said reluctantly. "But to offer this dageki for sale to the man in blue. This dageki is related to these others, and they survive much better if the family is kept together."

"What's your price?" asked the man.

Nikki was about to reply when Dreyk said in her ear, "Not too cheap. He'll think you're trying to pass off a sick one."

Nikki took a deep breath, wondering again if she was doing the right thing. Then she saw the expression on Gormz's face. Was that fear, resolve, or both? Seeing his courage and determination, she couldn't refuse him what he wanted.

"I'll take half of what you paid for all five," she said, and then feared it was too much. But instead of turning away, the man came toward her. He looked Gormz up and down.

"He looks healthy enough," said the man. "Does he have any special skills?"

"I think you will find this the most exceptional dageki that you have ever known," she replied in all honesty.

The man seemed to think for a second, then he said. "I'll give you half what you ask: twenty croma pieces and not a fraction more."

Nikki sighed. "I'll take it," she said.

She pulled Gormz aside. "Are you sure you want to do this, Gormz? This man could be cruel, or at best inconsiderate to dageki needs. Isn't there another way?"

"I don't think so," replied the dageki slowly. "I've been thinking about this for some time. It's the only way for me to get close to them and find out what conditions they're living in. And this one needs me. She decided to let the child die inside of her rather than let it be born here. If she does that, she will die as well. I can't let that happen. Please understand."

She looked at Gormz in bewilderment. In a very short time, he'd evolved from a timid court acolyte to the aspiring savior of the dageki race. She thought he might find a way to free the dageki after all. She also had to admit that he'd become her friend along the way, and she didn't like to think that she was putting him in danger.

"This is only going to be temporary, Gormz. When we get back, we'll get you out of here. I won't leave you like this."

Gormz looked down on her with an unreadable expression in his deep eyes. "You have done much for me already." With this, he turned and joined the line of dageki without looking back. She watched Gormz walking away from them and had to wonder what would become of him if they were unable to return for him. She'd vowed to come back if she could, but she had to admit that they were undertaking a dangerous journey that none might return from. Perhaps Gormz had better odds than they did, after all.

CHAPTER THIRTY-FOUR

Tbrin Steps in

T brin bent over the table in the chamber of stars, sweat dripping from his nose, despite the coolness of the night. He was getting too old for this. He looked up nervously to the high window as the wind howled. Outside, he could feel nothing but swirling snow and ice particles. Winter was bearing down, and the last of the high mountain trees were giving up their leaves to the harassing wind. A few brittle leaves littered the floor and danced at his feet. He struggled to concentrate on the projection on the table before him. Tiny figures wavered as they fought, their swords ringing out as if from a great distance.

How could he have known that she would bring that abomination Semli back into the world? She should have realized that she couldn't control him, even with Jelebron's help. Akriast was growing reckless, becoming more and more irrational as her latest lifeforce ran out. He knew that this might be her last one, but what good would her final death do him with two drakyn still threatening everything he had so carefully planned?

Desperation and guilt warred in his thoughts. He still had not found the right transmograffic formula that Akriast had used to recall the long-dead drakyn Jelebron, but he was close. If he helped Nikki now, it would surely draw attention to himself. Akriast was already suspicious. To play his hand so openly could mean disaster, yet Nikki was in real danger now and needed his help.

He recalled again the delicate face of Greshna, the expression he'd seen mirrored in young Nikki. But the physical similarity was not the only reason he'd taken Nikki on as an apprentice. From that first day, he'd felt the power in her, and while Nikki was at his side, Akriast had not dared to challenge him. Now the girl was far away, in mortal danger herself.

He looked down, as the two minuscule combatants labored. Their swords collided making sparks skitter across the table surface. She'd made a grave error, leaving the inn alone with him. It took practice to see through the complex masks they could wear. Too late, she'd seen her error. Too young for this. And all the training in the world could not prepare her for the trials she must now face. He felt partly to blame. He could have told her more, prepared her better for his treachery. But if he had, would she have understood? How could he explain the wisdom of history to one so young?

These thoughts took him back to Greshna: the softness of her skin and the sparkle of her laughter, the strength he'd seen in her eyes on that last day when they'd been together before she disappeared. He couldn't allow the beast to take another that he cared for. He'd been weak the first time, letting his Greshna go off to die so that many others could live. At the time, he'd thought it wise and gallant, the greatest sacrifice that he could make. But now he wasn't so sure; he'd had eight-hundred years to think about such abstract concepts as honor and duty, and he now believed them to be only hollow and bitter words, while his love for the dead Greshna lived on with a color and vitality that defied time itself. He now thought himself arrogant to believe he could make decisions of life and death. Who was he to choose? Perhaps one soul could be worth many. Perhaps Greshna should have lived while others died.

If he failed to help Nikki now, he might survive and eventually discover the transmogrifee that would return his Greshna to life. But he was tired and afraid, and he wasn't sure that his fear wasn't the real reason that he hesitated now. Once before, he'd hesitated, and Greshna had died. And what would Greshna say if he told her that he had sacrificed another just to have her with him now? This time he knew he must decide to help the living.

Once he'd made the decision, it gave him new strength, and he poured that strength into a potent transmogrifee of protection and warding. Almost tenderly, he waved his hand over one of the figures below him. There was a flash of light, and the figures disappeared.

Exhausted, he leaned over the now-empty table in the darkness, trying to gather his strength. As he turned, he began to feel a presence, something thick and oppressive in the air behind him. He searched around him but faced only the darkness and the premonition of danger.

Then she spoke, and he knew that his life was in mortal danger. It mattered little to him now. Peace filled his soul for the first time in many, many years. He held his head high and prepared to face his enemy, knowing that he had chosen well.

"What are you doing up here, old fool?" rasped Jelebron. "You can't help them—any of them. Soon you and all your kind will be my slaves. You can't take this victory from me with your ineffectual transmogeries."

Tbrin turned sharply, searching her face in disbelief. "You call this a victory? Look at the Mistrans. What have you done to them? The aerie is a shambles. Where there isn't unrest, there's confusion—and the mutations—I saw a baby born yesterday that should never have been. What have you done?"

He saw the confusion in Jelebron's face, and for the first time, Tbrin wondered. Perhaps she wasn't behind the strange occurrences in Mistra. Jelebron seemed almost as disturbed by them as he was. But if it wasn't Jelebron, then who? Did Akriast hate the Mistrans enough to do this?

Jelebron said, "We will regain order. It's natural for there to be some disturbance. Humans are so weak and resistant to change. Once I have total control, it will be different."

Was she trying to convince Tbrin or herself?

"But you'll never live to see it, old man. It's time for you and your meddling to end." She stepped forward, and Tbrin could hear the rustling of her robe on the cold stone floor and see the glint in her eye. In the half-dark, her shape was growing, changing. In that second, he reacted, knowing that it was all he had. She would expect him to attack, but he knew exactly what he needed to do. The Mistrans would have to take care of themselves. He had to reach Nikki and help her find the isle. The drakyn must be purged from the world for all time, and only the strength of a new drakyn's eye could do that. The cold stone of the chamber closed in on him like a vice. There seemed no way out, with only the tiny ventilation window and Jelebron's form blocking the doorway.

Jelebron leapt forward, but her prey was gone. Only leaves swirled around her. Nor did she notice when the wind picked one up and casually tossed it up through the high window. In exasperation, the drakyn twisted in the narrow room until realization dawned on her. Pulling back into human form, she hurried from the chamber and out to the cliff's edge. Here she peered silently into the mists below her. Still as a stone, she stood, deep in thought. Once, she thought she saw a vague shadow of wings far below, heading away from Mistra.

She spoke to herself, "Run, fool, run!" She turned away from the ledge and was surprised to feel relief. Why had she failed to kill him? Why had she given him even a moment's warning? She didn't like to think about Tbrin. Though her memories of the time before the war were cloudy, something about him disturbed her deeply. Akriast would wonder why she hadn't eliminated him for good. But he was out of the way. What harm could he do now? Besides, Akriast herself was growing weaker every day. Jelebron knew that the transmogrifer was too power-hungry and unstable and would eventually have to be removed. She felt no compunction against killing the one who had brought her into the world for the second time. Parents often ate their children, and children assassinated their parents. It was the drakyn way.

CHAPTER THIRTY-FIVE

Foul Wings and Harrowing Seas

The noisy, disorganized and densely packed city seemed to go on forever, and it took them a long time to reach the docks. Once at the water's edge, they saw that the piers were extensive, with masts and sailfish harnesses poking up everywhere. Nikki wondered how they would find any one boat among so many, but Dreyk seemed to know his way, unerringly, even after his prolonged absence.

Picking one of the long walkways, Dreyk left them to wait for him and followed it out to a line of sailfish boats, until he reached a small, brightly painted craft of an intense sky-blue color. On its hull, the name *The Lesser Moon* stood out in black calligraphic detail. A compact, powerful-looking man was scrubbing the deck with a mop. At the sight of Dreyk approaching, the man stood up and shouted. With an athletic leap onto the dock, he ran to Dreyk, hugging him.

"Dreyk! What the fishgutter's luck sent you home after all this time? I didn't see you sail in. Cida has done nothing but ask after you."

Dreyk looked at his shoes. "My crew is gone, Bacha. We ran aground far to the south. The ship broke up on the rocks. All hands were lost in a psy storm."

Bacha looked at him in disbelief. "I can't believe you survived, too."

Too? thought Dreyk.

"Surely, not all hands were lost?" continued Bacha.

"What do you mean?"

"Your first mate—and life mate, if you don't mind my assumin'—Chendri—arrived some time ago with y'ur sailfish. Shortly after, she gave birth. She's told us a little of her adventures, but—"

Dreyk interrupted hastily, "What? She survived? But how? Any other survivors? Boy or girl? I want to see them now!"

"Whoa!" exclaimed Bacha. With a laugh, he raised a hand to ward off further questions. "Cida and I are having them over for dinner tonight. Why don't ya' join us? That'll give us time to warn her that you survived 'afore the shock hits her and gives her a fit—not unlike the one you're havin' right now."

"I guess I can wait another hour or so, but I'm afraid I have my companions to worry about," said Dreyk, pointing to the waiting group.

"That's fine, mate, bring 'em along too. The more the merrier, as they say. Anyways, we had a good haul yesterday; got into a flock of flyin' fisherbuns an' gutter stripes and the kitchen's overflowing with Cida's sea biscuits and ferky. An' you know how she loves to entertain."

Dinner was delicious. After an extended fireside diet of charred groundroot and scrawny contail, Cida's cooked and smoked seafood was a revelation. Char especially liked the oystems in the shell, quickly picking up the technique that Bacha called "shuckering" to open the shells and reveal the delicious shellfish within. Bacha and Cida's house wasn't huge, but it was warm and homey. Cida graciously made room for the extra guests at their rough wooden table. Some had to sit on crates, but no one complained.

Dreyk had briefly explained to them how Chendri had survived the sinking of their ship, but he asked her to tell the whole amazing tale to the group now. She cradled her baby girl in her arms and rocked her rhythmically as she spoke.

"I swear to the gods of gardland that this story be true, but you might have cause to doubt me. I would if I heard it from another. Anyway, it was like this; That ass Krin pulled me overboard and I got caught in Kakuni's harness as she was divin'. As I was sinkin' I was thinkin' that this 'ere baby would be cursed to the half-life of a mergirl ghost. But then somthin' amazin' happened. Somthin' started pushin' me up. 'Afor I knew it, I was floatin' on the surface, on top o' the sailfish an' far from the shipwreck.

"I saw the ship hit the rocks an' I knew you all was dead, but apparently not."

She paused to smile wistfully at Dreyk. Her look said that she was happy to see him, but sad for the loss of his crew and crenda.

She continued, "See, what happened was, when I set 'er free, Kakuni dived. That's what they does when they's in real danger." She said this aside to the newcomers. "But what I didn't realize was that Kakuni had grown attached to me. It happens, ya know, sometimes, with a sailfish and a mate. So, she come up under me and we escape the worst o' the storm. It wouldn't a gone much farther than that, if it weren't fer the fact that I been workin' on a way o' communercatin' with a sailfish, remote, like. I hadn't really tested it yet, so the fact it worked—well anyway, it did—an' she un'erstood where we needed to go. Maybe it's like a sagehorse what always returns to the stable on his own, too. It was a long and nasty journey, le'me tell ya, but we made it. By then I was huge with dear Juni here an' I didn't know if we'd make it all the way back home. But we did an' Bacha found us at the dock, dirty an' sunburnt and exhausted. Juni was born that night and we both lived, an' that's my story. Believe it not if you want but it's all true. All true."

"I believe you," said Benna. "No one could make up a story like that."

The group laughed and then grew serious, sensing that there were important things to discuss.

"Bacha, I'm sorry to have to talk business at dinner," said Dreyk, "but I must find another crenda as soon as possible. We need to get to the Thousand Isles soon. We're putting you all in real danger as long as we're here."

After a moment, Bacha replied hesitantly, "Take your father's boat. It, and his house, are now yours."

"Don't kid yourself, Bacha, my father would never loan me his precious *Prophesy*. Wait, you said his house too?"

"Ya haven't heard? Well, a' course you couldn't 've. Dreyk, your father died a few months ago."

Dreyk stared at his friend. "I knew he was sick," he began slowly. "But I never thought the old bastart would die. He was too stubborn to die. Gardamn him!" He threw his fork down as if it burned, then stood and walked out the back door, slamming it behind him as he stalked out.

The baby started to cry and Chendri shushed her. As soon as the infantile tirade began, it ended in hiccups and a gurgled laugh.

Bacha said to his wife, "I didn't want to tell him tonight, thinkin' he's had enough shocks fer one day."

"Yah, but one is sad, but t'other is pure joy, me thinks," said his wife gently. "He had to find out about his papa sooner 'er later, m'dear."

"Yes, you're right o' course."

Chendri said, "I'll let 'im stew fer a bit and then take his daughter out fer a visit. That should cheer 'im up—at least some 'ut. I think we all got some adjustin' t' do."

Wren sighed, "It changes things for us, too. We can't expect Dreyk to help us now that he's found his family. We'll just have to find another way to reach the Thousand Isles."

Chendri cackled. "Ah, you obviously don't know 'im like I do. Once Dreyk commits to something', he's gonna follow through on it, come gardland or high waters. He'll take ya, an' I won't try to stop 'im. Jus' do me a favor an' keep 'im alive, won't ya?" Chendri appeared to be joking, but Nikki could see the sharp glint in her eyes. Seeing Chendri's muscular arms and athletic demeanor, Nikki didn't think she wanted to get on the first mate's bad side.

Nikki looked at the crenda that Dreyk had pointed out to them, and suddenly realized that they really were going to sail on the ocean. She didn't know if she could do it. The boat looked less than seaworthy, and she wondered at the faded name on its side, *Prophesy*. Was this serendipity, fate, or just bad luck? She had to admit to herself that she didn't know much about boats, or crenda as she kept forgetting to call them, but even she could see that this one hadn't been maintained as it should. The paint was peeling away from the hull in huge flakes, and what Dreyk had called the emergency sails, hung in tatters. The harness for the sailfish was half rotted away. Of the sailfish, she saw no sign. She wondered how long it would take them to make it seaworthy and whether they had the time it would take.

Char and Benna were listening attentively to Dreyk explaining how the sailfish was lured and harnessed. He was showing them illustrations in a parchment with the title "*The Care, Feeding and Control of the Northern Isles Sailfish for Nautical Purposes.*"

Bored, she and Moonchaser wandered up the dock alone and back into the city proper, finding herself in the busy outdoor market. Although some stared at the big cat, Dreyk had said that grellas were sometimes kept as pets and for hunting in the mountains, and the presence of the cat would draw little attention, if he wore a harness and didn't reveal his enhanced abilities. Moonchaser scratched at his leather harness incessantly and Nikki wondered how much longer he would put up with it before he tore it off in frustration.

She was enjoying the noise and chaos of the city. After many days on the road, she found that she craved human companionship. Just to be surrounded by so much sound and color made her feel a strange sense of peace, as if this market and its daily rituals could eliminate the fears she felt. How could the horrors she had seen reach such a joyful place?

She was starting to relax and enjoy the sights of the city when a familiar scent assailed her. A feeling of dread spread through her. Beside her, Moonchaser growled, scanning the crowd with hunter's eyes. Around her, people backed away from the big cat. Nikki looked around but could see nothing to verify her fears. She started to move on again, sure that her over-active imagination had been the cause of her alarm, but Moonchaser resisted, pulling back on his harness. Then, before she could stop him, he was launching himself forward. With a prodigious leap, he landed howling in the arms of a tall, richly dressed woman in a long velvet gown. Beside her, walked a dark-haired man in a finely crafted purple doublet and long wool cape. Nikki was mortified that the cat would attack for no reason.

"Moonchaser, what are you..." The words died on her lips as she saw the woman change before her eyes. Grasping the grella by the fur, the woman held him away from her as her features transformed. The delicate veil she wore disappeared, replaced by a cape of blood-red cartilage, while her face stretched to accommodate rows of deadly teeth. Her stately gown was replaced with the blotched, dull-gray hide of a drakyn.

Moonchaser howled in rage, his great paws tearing ineffectually at the air. Nikki watched in horror, as the drakyn lifted Moonchaser high in the air, tossing him away as if he were a toy that was no longer amusing. Moonchaser hit a stall stacked with fruits. It collapsed beneath him, scattering fruit across the square. He lay where he fell, unconscious, or worse. The crowd screamed in wild panic. Runners tumbled over each other in their panic to escape the beast. Nikki had never felt more alone, or more frightened.

The drakyn lurched toward her. Even though she had already guessed, the voice told her that this was Jelebron.

"I hadn't expected to meet you so soon, Nikkitheis TyaBorne, but this place will do as well as any other. Such a shame that you lost your power. Better that you had died at Mistra, don't you agree? You have the information I want. You will give it to me now, or you and all your friends will suffer. Where is the tree?"

"I don't know what you're talking about."

"This is no time for games, little fool. I am told you know the way to the Tree of Malgryn. Tell me now before I lose patience. You have no idea what pain really is. I will teach you."

Nikki stood transfixed as the drakyn towered over her. How could she resist? She had no power, no strength to fight. The beast grabbed her, pulling her close, and the stench of rotting flesh made Nikki want to retch.

"I don't know where it is. All I have is a map and a needle," she whimpered.

The drakyn laughed, a grating sound.

"I can hardly believe it. Semli, you little bastart, you actually told me the truth this time." Jelebron turned, as if to speak to her companion, but there was no one beside her. "No matter, I'll take care of you later." She turned back to Nikki. "Let's get this map and needle, shall we?" Jelebron started across the square, dragging Nikki like a rag doll beside her.

Nikki's head reeled as she tried to think of something she could do, but all she could imagine was what this beast might do to her friends if she resisted. It was a moment before she realized that the drakyn had stopped. Nikki looked up.

It was Tbrin. Nikki didn't know whether to be hopeful or despondent. Was he here to save her or help kill her?

"What do you want, old man?" hissed the drakyn. "You ran from me last time like a sniveling, frightened child. Have you gained courage, or just lost your senses?"

"I couldn't defeat you alone at Mistra, Jelebron. I didn't have the strength. But now I have an ally."

Tbrin stepped aside, and Wren stood beside him. Jelebron stood her ground and looked at them defiantly, but Nikki, so close to her, smelled a new aroma. It was bitter and acrid. Was this the smell of drakyn fear? Nikki knew that this was her only chance. If the drakyn had her as a hostage, she might be able to force the others to give up the map. It was more than worth her life to thwart the desires of this beast. Sudden anger gave her strength, and she struggled out of the biting grasp of the drakyn. Jelebron reached for her, but her attention was drawn away as the sky erupted with light.

Nikki's nose was assaulted by another smell, the stench of burning flesh. Jelebron screamed out the words of a curse or a transmogrifee, but too late. The combined transmogrifee of both Tbrin and Wren burned the flesh from her bones, exposing tendons and melting organs. With her last strength, the drakyn transformed one more time, turning what was left of her mass into wings. She lifted herself into the air with amazing speed and was soon far away. The curse turned into a primal screech of pain and fear as the drakyn became a distant dot in the sky. Before Nikki knew what was happening, she was running, and soon the docks appeared before her. Dreyk waved at them frantically from the prow of his father's boat.

"Hurry, Nikki!" screamed Wren. "We must get out of here before she can heal herself."

They pulled her aboard, and Nikki struggled, trying to go back up the dock.

"Wait! I must go back for Moonchaser!" she screamed, but the cat answered her, growling as he stumbled beside her into the boat.

In the general confusion, no one noticed the small, scraggly looking rat who jumped aboard at the last second, scurrying into the hold.

Nikki lay down with Moonchaser close, and her energy seemed to drain away. Tbrin was beside her, attending to a gaping cut on her arm. He smiled down at her with what Nikki imagined was an apologetic look.

"You have a lot to explain, old man," she growled, then she laughed and tried to hug him, despite the pain in her arm.

"I know I do," he said quietly. "But I hope that my interrogation can wait until you're rested."

When Tbrin finished bandaging her arm, she rose and stood at the rail, not at all sure about this trip, and feeling less than brave right now. She was distracted by shouts and looked up to see Dreyk yelling instructions to Benna and Char, who were positioned on either side of the prow, grappling with lines of leather harness. Between them was a large basket of bluefish, their sparkling cerulean scales almost blinding when they caught the light.

Nikki had been wondering why they'd sailed out of the bay, and when the sailfish would enter the picture. Now, she had a feeling she was about to find out.

Dreyk pointed, shouting, and Nikki strained to see what he was indicating. Then she saw spouts of water and several huge, gray backs curving gracefully as gigantic creatures made their way through the water. Dreyk made an adjustment to the tiller, and the crenda turned towards the waterspouts.

Before she knew it, they were within the pod, and Nikki worried that one of these amazing animals might capsize their boat, but Benna had explained to her that the sailfish were incredibly gentle creatures and would never knowingly harm a human. She worried just a little bit about the "knowingly" part, as she clung, white-knuckled, to the rail.

Suddenly, one of the creatures surfaced right next to her, and she could see the gigantic, bulbous head with its blowhole and barnacled, scarred hide. A huge eye gazed at her, she imagined, with a look of ancient wisdom. Suddenly in awe of these amazing beings, her fear slipped away, and she marveled at the magic that nature had designed for this world. She felt a great desire to preserve it, if she could.

Beside her, Tbrin had been talking excitedly, "...and they're not really fish at all, you know. They're warm-blooded. Their nearest cousins might actually be the pachyderms of the southern deserts. Another amazing creature. In fact, one time—"

Nikki stopped listening, as Benna and Char started tossing bluefish into the water. A minute later there was a resounding thud. Nikki grasped the rail even tighter, and a cry of alarm escaped her lips. Dreyk spared her just a quick glance and reassuring smile before rushing forward to help Benna and Char attached the harnesses correctly.

"Kakuni!" he cried, "I hoped it would be you. Are you ready for another adventure?" He slapped the skin of the sailfish with a laugh of pure joy. He really did love the sea, Nikki saw, but she was not so sure about this new element. As the sailfish responded to the reins he held, their speed picked up, and land soon fell away behind them. She only hoped that the drakyn were far behind them as well.

Much later, Nikki stood up, looking around her with bleary eyes at the creaking, leaky boat, the wildly pitching ocean, and wondered if dying at the hands of a drakyn might not have been a gentler fate.

The boat pitched again, creaking against the slap of the chop, and Nikki thought she would be sick. At least the nausea distracted her from her fear of the water. By the looks of this floating disaster, they shouldn't have made it this far.

"Another three days is my guess," Dreyk had said. How could she make it another three days on this tilting nautical accident waiting to happen?

She looked over at Dreyk and Benna. Benna was bending over a length of line while Dreyk gave instructions. Nikki had to smile at Benna's intense concentration.

"A natural sailor," Dreyk had said, causing Benna to beam with pride. He had taken to the water with amazing alacrity.

"How could we come from the same mother?" she growled to herself. Benna hadn't been the least bit seasick, and he seemed to have a knack for keeping his footing on the wildly pitching deck.

Nikki had to admit that she was feeling better at last. On the first day, Wren had given her an herbal tonic, but she couldn't keep it down long enough for it to be of any use. Dreyk had said, "Just leave her alone. In a couple days, she'll get her sea legs." Nikki had gathered the strength to retort that in a couple days, she might be dead, but ever so slowly, she had improved.

She gazed at the brooding water, hoping that she wouldn't lose her first meal in days. How could she face the drakyn like this? She felt hopelessly inadequate for the task, while each crest of wild water brought them closer to her final test. Would the Isle of Malgryn hold the secrets of power that she so desperately needed? These thoughts brought her reluctantly to the question she hadn't wanted to ask herself: What if the drakyn's eye wasn't enough to restore her power? And even if it did, what if she just wasn't strong enough to defeat them?

"You're looking much better," said a voice in her ear. "It's good to see that you could make it out of bed today. How do pickled pig's eyes and sardines sound for lunch?"

"Damn you, Char," she croaked. "If there were another way to get to the Thousand Isles, I would tell Dreyk to stuff this floating piece of—"

"Now, now," she soothed. "Let's be nice. Dreyk's father loved this boat, but you're right, it is a pile of junk."

"I'm sorry. I just don't feel very brave right now, and I'm taking it out on you."

Dreyk, coming up beside them, said, "You're both right, it is a pile of junk."

"Oh, Dreyk, we didn't mean any offense," said Nikki.

"None taken. He wasn't a good man. He used people, then discarded them after he'd worn out their patience, or their spirits. It took me a long time to see it, but when I did, I knew I had to get away. I shipped out on the first deep-run fishing boat available, and I never looked back. I guess that, in the end, he just ran out of people to use. Look at this boat. She's probably lucky to still be afloat."

Dreyk saw Nikki's expression and laughed. "Don't worry. She's still basically sound. If we get desperate, we can always put the rats to bailing water—there certainly are enough of them. Besides, you've got the best skipper in the Northern fleet to get you through. I've been in rougher weather in smaller boats. And Benna is turning out to be an able hand. He has a knack with the sailfish that even I don't have."

"I'm happy for him," Nikki said sincerely. "He really seems to have found his place."

"As will you."

"I don't know, I don't know at all."

Two days later, Dreyk insisted that they were approaching the Thousand Isles, but Nikki had seen no islands, no sign of land of any kind, and she was beginning to worry. She pulled out the needle that Kodo had given her for the hundredth time, but she could make no sense of it. It didn't glow, it didn't tell her anything. It lay dead in her hand, making her feel a fool.

The weather hadn't improved. Instead, it was growing stormy. Rain pelted the deck, and the tired boat groaned against the strain of the currents. The sailfish was tired and becoming more difficult to control as she struggled against the rain and wind. Dreyk said that they might have to turn her loose and use the emergency sails instead, but that would slow them down considerably. He didn't want to do it except as a last resort.

When the sun rose on their fifth day at sea, Nikki could barely tell that it was dawn at all. The sky was almost as dark as it had been through the night. The horizon was lost in an approaching squall.

Then Benna called out that he could see land. Nikki was ecstatic. She saw the look on Dreyk's face, and her hopes sank.

"What is it?" she yelled above the noise of the wind.

"We must be farther north than I thought. I don't recognize this island ahead at all."

"You mean we're lost?"

"We'll just have to head southeast until we reach familiar territory, or we can find our bearings on the map."

"We don't have time!" she retorted. "We need to find that isle now!"

Exhausted, she sank to the deck. "This damn thing is less than useless," she growled, tossing Kodo's needle away from her. She sat motionless on the deck, unable to gather the courage to go on. After a while, she realized that the others were staring at her, or rather at a point directly behind her. She turned and had to shield her eyes from the light. The water bucket behind her was lit with a greenish glow. As she gaped, the water in the bucket began to rise, still in the shape of the bucket that had contained it, and then began to rotate.

Nikki looked to Wren who returned her look in bewilderment. If one of them wasn't doing it, then who was?

Then she remembered the needle. As she approached the water, she heard Dreyk say softly: "Be careful."

The needle hung in the center of the water, vibrating gently, but always pointing in the same general direction, as if it were tuned to some point on the horizon.

"I think we have our heading," she laughed. "I should have known that it was activated by water."

"Can we trust this thing?" asked Dreyk.

"Unless you have a better idea, it's all we have to go on," she replied. "What can it hurt to try?"

"Nothing, I guess," he said in a sour voice. "Except maybe get us even more lost than we already are. But you're right, we don't have any other options, and we're running out of time."

They passed the first island, and soon another came into view. It was barely an atoll. She perused the shoreline but saw nothing but ragged windshrub and low growing dune grass. She realized that they might not even know they'd reached the island until they passed it, and the needle changed direction. If it really was pointing toward the Isle of Malgryn, as Kodo had claimed it would.

They sailed almost until dark, and still, the needle led them on. Nikki could see that Dreyk was exhausted from fighting the sailfish and navigating the treacherous shallows around the islands. The only bright spot was the weather, which seemed to improve as they moved into the island chain. At dusk, the sun even showed its face, slanting golden light across their starboard. The wind changed direction, and Dreyk raised the sails to aid the sailfish, then they moved along briskly.

Nikki paced the deck, unwilling to tear her eyes from the horizon.

"Nikki, stop pacing," said Dreyk. "If the needle points true, we'll know soon enough."

Nikki couldn't relax, knowing that so much depended on her. Her palms tingled, anticipating the power that she had missed for so long. So intent was she on the shadowy, silver shape of the next island far ahead that she didn't notice when the needle reversed direction. She turned and saw that it was pointing in the way they had come.

"You're going the wrong way," she accused Dreyk. "When did you change direction?"

"I haven't!" said Dreyk defensively. "The needle must have reversed itself."

"That can't be right. We're nowhere near an island! We'll have to turn around and see if it happens again."

Dreyk turned the wheel, and reluctantly the tired sailfish responded. They headed back the way they'd come. Nikki kept her eyes on the needle.

"There!" she shouted. "It just reversed again." She looked around at the expanse of empty water around them and then at Dreyk. She saw the frustration on his face, but he said nothing. She was glad at least that he didn't say: "I told you so." He didn't have to blame her; she already blamed herself. She sat down heavily on the deck. She'd just wasted another precious day following a useless lead. Now it might be too late, even if they could find the isle tomorrow. The sun was already sinking low, and further sailing this day would be impossible without daylight.

She watched Benna lowering the anchor and felt all her hopes sinking with it.

That night, she stayed up late, watching the mercura shimmers on the calm water. At last, she went down below and fitful sleep came at last.

It seemed only minutes later when Nikki woke to an unusual calm and the sound of someone yelling above her. When she climbed up, Dreyk was already on deck, yelling, "All hands on deck! Benna, get that anchor up, now!"

Nikki scrambled up, confused. Wren and Trey were standing in the stern, apparently working on a transmogrifee that might save them, but the looks of consternation and panic on their faces told Nikki that something was wrong.

"Our transmogrifee isn't working," Wren yelled. "Something is blocking it."

Nikki didn't see Char anywhere and wondered if the huntress had escaped to save herself. She hoped so.

Dreyk was frantically undoing the sailfish harness. She tried to stop him, but he pushed her aside.

"What're you doing?" she screamed. "We need her!"

"Look." He pointed with his eyes. Nikki followed his gaze and wished she'd stayed down below. Above them towered a mountainous wave and it was almost on top of them. She whimpered. In seconds it would swamp them. She could see no escape. She stood numb, unable to think or force her legs to move. Vaguely, she became aware that Dreyk had freed the sailfish and was yelling again.

"Everyone, get to the oars. Our only chance is to turn the boat and face that head-on. We might be able to ride it out."

Nikki almost wanted to laugh. How could this little boat withstand that wave? She tried to tell him it was hopeless, but she wasn't sure she could speak. Still, she had to appreciate his will to survive. Forcing herself out of her stupor, she joined the others at the oars. She barely pulled on her oar, yet it seemed that the boat was turning just a little, but it was too late. The wave was almost upon them.

"Now grab something, and hold on!" she heard someone yell, then she was inhaling bitter saltwater. She lost her hold and felt a sharp jolt of pain as her head hit something unyielding. She struggled, but the water was all around her and she was sinking. She gave up the fight and let her body sink. She thought that darkness would come immediately, but instead, it seemed that she was sinking forever, floating silent and still through an ocean as soft as summer air. Her fear drifted away, and she sighed deeply. Stretching, she opened her eyes.

Above her was a tranquil blue mist that went on forever. *I must be at the bottom of the ocean*, she thought. She turned abruptly and almost fell. All around her she saw only open sky. She grabbed in panic at the pulpy flesh of the forking branch she was lodged in.

"Ouch," said a booming voice. "What a strong grip you have for such a little thing. What kind of fish are you?"

CHAPTER THIRTY-SIX

A Child Named Despair

G ormz peered out through the narrow opening of the cave. No pursuers could yet be seen, but how much time did they have? Would Juachimson just let them go? He thought not. The value of one dageki was enough to warrant a search, and two would surely be a grave loss. Juachimson had not been unkind to them. Gormz wished he could have explained to the benevolent slaver why they had to go, but there had been no time.

Squinting back into the gloom of the cave behind him, he started to pull away, then stopped himself. No need to go back so soon. Why was he here with this intransigent mageki anyway, when his real mission remained unaccomplished? He couldn't return to Dmisi with only one ill-tempered dageki to show for all his time in the north. He told himself again that there had been no choice; he'd had to get her away from the farm. At the time, he'd thought that her resistance would break down once she was away from captivity.

It now seemed that he'd misjudged her. Mavon Mageki Uho-Selnz still refused his seed, which would mean the death of her offspring and probably her own death as well. Though he'd never seen it, he'd read about that kind of death and knew it would be slow and painful. Why were they so hidebound?

"I won't give a dageki life in the presence of aliens," she'd said, but now she claimed that she couldn't accept his seed because the proper ceremonies hadn't been performed. Where would he find a chantsayer, or the herb of commitment, in this wilderness? Then she'd complained about the cave; it was dark, it was damp, it was no fitting place for a birth. He rubbed his snout, spluttering into his hands in frustration. He pulled his hands away and stared at them. They trembled.

He had to convince her. He had to crawl back along the narrow way and face her. Still, he lay, his body flat against the cool dirt, his neck craned to see through the shallow crack. He rubbed the scores on his breastplates absently. They'd been lucky to find this cave, dark and chill as it was. It had only been a matter of chance, at that, a little overhang that they'd crawled under in the dark, exhausted and panicked by the cries of wild grellas in the night. He'd looked back to find the mageki gone, disappeared behind him into the ground. He found that she'd fallen through a slender opening, and he'd scrambled and scraped to get in behind her. He now noted that, in his panic, he'd picked one of the narrowest spots to come through. The long slit in the earth widened to his left, though it was still hidden by tangled brush and vines.

At the first gray morning light, they'd started to explore as far back as the light would follow and found that the cave widened into a chamber of fair size, where they could rest in relative comfort and safety. As the sun rose higher, they could see cracks above, where light found its way down, illuminating a depression in the center of the room. It looked as if it might once have been used as a fire pit, and Gormz had worried that they may have stumbled into some wild creature's lair, but his senses could discern no presence more frightful than fungus and damp and cold of stone that penetrated his thickest plates.

He looked back again with a nervous jerk of his head. Mavon Mageki was back there now, waiting for him to return and convince her to live, to save her child. She had to be. He couldn't believe that she would be so willing to die after everything he'd done to get her away from the farm. Mageki; he didn't claim to understand them. It seemed that the harder he tried, the worse the situation became. Now he didn't know what to do. He couldn't force her to accept his seed. If he did, the humiliation might kill her, as surely as the unborn body of the child would. Besides, it had to be done at just the right time, when the birthing was imminent, and only Mavon Mageki would know that. It was a touchy matter all around, this giving of life, or so he'd read, for this would also be his first birthing.

He pushed himself away from the wall and hurriedly scuttled back down the way he'd come, suddenly anxious about leaving her alone for so long. He knew he'd have to go out later and gather food. If the birthing did take place, newborn dageki could be voracious eaters.

When he reached the cavern, breathing hard from his exertions, he was aghast at how pale her plates were, how ill she looked, kneeling silent and cool in a pool of weak light from above. For one irrational moment, he thought that she might be dead already, and his heart thundered in his chest. Then she spoke, and his fear was replaced with another, deeper fear.

"Kiss me," she said softly. "It is time."

Gormz stared, and she must have thought that he hadn't heard her.

"Kiss me," she said again, louder and stronger this time.

"B...b...bbbut..." stammered Gormz.

She sighed deeply. "You were right, Gormz Si Tageki Ri Jorfa-Kera Ri. It is wrong of me to stand on convention now, denying life to this little one, even when life seems so hopeless." She caressed her stomach with a tender, sad motion. Then she looked at Gormz with glossy eyes. "And I am myself afraid to die. There, I have said it." Mavon Mageki hung her massive head, and her eyes eased shut in shame.

"It's nothing to be ashamed of," soothed Gormz, who was beginning to regain his composure, even though his emotions were still in turmoil. "The dageki must adapt to life as it is, or we will die as a people. We can no longer live in the dark, blindly following our leaders and the dictates of social protocol. It is time we made decisions for ourselves; it is time for change." Gormz knew that he was stalling for time, trying to gather the courage to step closer, to take another breath. She sensed his fear, and it seemed to give her resolve. Her shoulders relaxed, and her eyes cleared.

"Could you save your political heresy for a more appropriate time?" she said in a dry tone. Gormz looked up in chagrin, until he saw the teasing light in her eyes. She was making fun of him.

"You are an amazing dageki, Mavon Mageki Uho-Selnz," he said. "I am honored that you have accepted me."

With these words, he gave the ritual curtsy and stepped forward to kneel before her. His heart pounded in wild fear, and he felt dizzy. What if it didn't work? He'd only read of it in primers. What if he was impotent? What if his seed was incompatible with hers? He had no second here to take his place, if need be, no medical facilities, no water to wash the fledgling if it did appear. He realized that he was trembling badly and forced his quivering front limbs to be still. Craning his neck forward, he opened his mouth wide, and she hers. It was a little daunting to be so close to those rows of teeth, even though Mavon was an exceptionally small mageki. Of course, it hadn't happened in recent times, but the old books chronicled a time when the mageki might kill her mate at this moment.

Carefully, he placed his mouth over hers, not knowing what to do next. Their tongues touched, and without warning, something erupted inside of him. It was either the greatest pleasure or the greatest pain he'd ever felt, or both. Then he felt the fluid flowing from the gland under his tongue and into her mouth. Mavon Mageki swallowed, and Gormz fell back, weak and disoriented.

Gormz stared, too frightened to speak, too exhausted now even for worry. For a moment, he was sure that it hadn't taken, then Mavon Mageki started to heave. Her chest lurched, and her mouth opened wide, but nothing came out, not even sounds. Gormz watched in horror as her jaw articulated, distorting her face into a grotesque mass of stretched skin and separating plates. Her throat opened wide, and Gormz could see the placental sack lodged there. He realized in a panic that if the child didn't come forth soon, Mavon Mageki would suffocate. Gormz knew that he didn't have the willpower to reach into her throat, past those rows of huge teeth, and pull the child out. He'd heard that it sometimes had to be done, but never by a male. There were mageki attendants for this.

Her throat was just too small. Even though she heaved wildly now, there was no more air in her lungs to push with. Her eyes clamped on to Gormz with a look of terror, pleading for his help.

When he could take that look no longer, he reached forward tentatively, ignoring his own fear, and felt the tiny beating heart under his touch. He tugged gently at first and then with increasing force. He knew he had to clear the airway, even if it meant killing the child to do it. He found himself wondering if Mavon Mageki would ever forgive him if he killed her child, but he had no more time to consider it as the placental sack came forward into his hands. It burst, and bloody fluid splashed him. He groped at the wildly squirming form, sitting back hard on the stone floor as he tried to keep a grip on the thrashing being in his lap. He squeaked in pain, as sharp teeth bit into his hand, then the tiny creature darted off, circling around, then scrambling under the legs of Mavon Mageki, where it peered out at him with bright new eyes full of wonder and fear.

Mavon Mageki was gasping, pulling in great hiccups of air as she struggled to regain her breath. She spoke in a shaky, but relieved voice.

"She'll be a fighter, that much is clear." Then her tone turned business-like, as if she did this every day. "You'd best get some water and wash that bite. And we'll need food. We passed through a tygrain field last night. Take the food sack, it's almost empty anyway—and bring more water back with you—as much as the water skin will hold."

Gormz obeyed as if in a trance. He was far from the cave before it hit him, what they'd done, what he'd done. To create a life form was a great responsibility, and more so in this harsh environment. He looked across the grain field to the distant mountains south. He ached for his home, for familiar territory, for anything predictable. He sighed and continued gathering the grain. Life might not be predictable for some time to come, and he would have to be strong. In dageki society, the males had little responsibility for the upbringing of the offspring, but surely this situation was different. He'd fathered and been first to hold the child. By law, this made him both sire and mageki-sister. He chuckled out loud at the humor of this. Would he be the one to take the child to her father's house—also his house—for the seed-life ceremony? How would he hand the child over to himself for the blessing? It was too much to consider just now. The memory of the birth burned in his thoughts, filling him with pride and a strange sense of awe. Sire Gormz Si Tageki Ri Jorfa-Kera Ri. It sounded so pompous. Perhaps he had been away from polite society too long.

When he returned to the cave, he found Mavon Mageki asleep with the child curled up on her chest. The tiny mageki eyed him with suspicion, but didn't stir as he moved about the cave, until he brought out the sack of grain. Watching the tiny creature, he was amazed that such a little being would someday grow into a proud dageki female. He didn't know how Mavon Mageki had known that the child was female, but they said that mothers just knew these things, or perhaps they could somehow choose the gender of their offspring, but if this were true, hardly any males would be born. Females were, of course, preferred.

As he gazed down on the sleeping face of his mate in wonder and pride, Mavon Mageki stirred and woke. The child was already busily crunching at the grain he'd brought, but he hadn't been able to get close enough to wash the creature; he didn't want to risk another bite.

After stretching and drinking long, Mavon Mageki raised the water skin and splashed water on the little mageki's head, while the little dageki squirmed and struggled beneath her gentle touch. As she washed the baby, she said not a word, and Gormz grew uncomfortable.

Without preamble, she said, "She will be Despair."

"What was that?" asked Gormz, totally befuddled.

"Despair. Despair Mageki we will call her, that's all. We have no Kye sticks to toss in the ritual manner. She will have no Kye stick wisdom to guide her. The world is dark, and so it will be for her, without hope, without direction."

"But Despair is a human word, Mavon Mageki. It isn't proper."

"It is entirely proper, Gormz Tageki." Mavon gazed into the darkness of the cave with a blank expression. Gormz thought she looked tired. She was probably exhausted by the birth and surely in pain, though she'd said not a word. In sudden compassion for this strong mageki, Gormz reached forward to touch her shoulder gently.

"We will have our Kye stick reading," he said resolutely. He got up, searched in his pack for a moment, then crawled back out of the cave, even though he too was approaching exhaustion.

It took him time to find the right kind of tree, and he was still worried about being found, although he heard and saw no one, but a wandering sagehorse far off. He carved the sticks with a dull knife he'd stolen from the farm. At the time, he didn't know why he'd even bothered to take it. It was too small for self-defense, and the blade was so worn as to be practically useless. He made the best use of it that he could and managed to get a passable version of Kye sticks, the correct length and diameter, but he realized that he had no paint to mark the sticks as they needed. He walked back towards the cave slowly, unwilling to face Mavon Mageki without the promised Kye sticks. He wandered out of his way until he came upon a slight depression that was choked by vines. Even from a distance, he could make out the bright glow of colorful berries. He realized that he didn't need paint. With the berries, he could stain the sticks with the required patterns. The berries would also make a nice treat for the two mageki, and he might eat a few himself as he worked.

Gormz set to work gathering the berries and, after a time, found that he had been able to color the sticks in at least a readable manner. This set of Kye sticks would never be an heirloom of the house, he thought, but at least it might make the mageki happy. Gormz got up to leave and crawled up the bank with his sticks and a load of berries in the bottom of his pack. In his fatigue, he paid little attention to the terrain above him as he climbed until he came up over the lip of the hill and found his snout not two feet from the whiskers of the largest grella he'd ever seen.

"Moonchaser, is that you?" he asked weakly, knowing instantly that this was a wild grella. Its fur was matted and dull, its ribs protruding from malnutrition.

"Not a good sign," he told himself aloud as if somehow speaking his thoughts might stall the inevitable attack. "I must be hysterical to say this, but I've got to get back to the magekies. They need me, you see, so if you think I'll be an easy meal, you'd better think again."

Gormz stared openly at the grella, and he thought it hesitated. Perhaps the cat was already too weak to attack. He didn't want to test that theory, however. Moving slowly, he pulled a handful of the berries from his pack and set them at the grella's feet, then, without turning his back on the cat, he began to move away with great care. The grella looked at him and then sniffed at the berries. Gormz wasn't sure that grellas ate fruit, and he was sure they would eat dageki if they could, but the cat didn't make a move for him.

Gormz turned and started to walk away. When he looked back, the cat was still bent over the berries. He forced himself not to run. Running would likely make the grella attack, but it was the longest walk he'd ever taken. By the time he reached the cave, he felt ready to collapse from fear and fatigue. A few times, he looked back but could see nothing following him.

When he reached the cave, it took the last of his energy to pile more brush into the opening to block the entrance. He only hoped the cat wouldn't trail him and break through his meager barricade.

Inside, Mavon Mageki looked better, but her plates were still pale. She brightened when he showed her the sticks, however. She noticed that his hands shook and that his plates had more scratches than before.

"Is there danger?" she asked, eyeing him sharply.

He hesitated, not wanting to worry her. "It was nothing, just a lone, starving grella. I managed to escape, and I don't think he followed, but just in case, I concealed the cave entrance completely. Even if he did follow my scent, he'll find that the trail disappears before his nose. We'll be safe, for now, but we're going to have to leave here soon." He looked down at the young mageki, playing on the floor. "We'd never make it all the way to dageki territory with the mageki child, especially with winter approaching. I think we'll have to return to the farm."

"I know," said Mavon. "I don't mind so much now." She fell silent as she arranged the Kye sticks. Saying the necessary chants, she tossed them high in the air. They hit the dirt with a rattle, and the little mageki scuttled away, startled.

Gormz looked down at the pattern, not really believing his eyes. Mavon Mageki beamed in pride.

"Still Water in Balance," she said. "No better reading could we hope for, though it will mean great responsibility, and she may not have the simple happiness of the lesser readings. She will be a great leader of the dageki people, and a power among all the peoples of the world. Despair Mageki Sy Souka-Ta."

"Then you still insist on this human name, Despair?" asked Gormz.

"Why not? Perhaps it is even more relevant now than before. Always it will remind her of her duty, of her past, and it will make her journey even more meaningful."

Gormz looked down at the child, for the first time realizing the full import of the responsibility he'd taken on. Before him, on this plain dirt floor played the future Queen of the Dageki Empire.

Two days later, they were still in the cave. Although he knew they had to return to the farm, Gormz couldn't force himself to take the first step, and Mavon Mageki seemed as hesitant as he did. The thought of returning the magekies into slavery made him feel terribly guilty, as if he were the one selling them. So, they rested and talked, each waiting for the other to say it was time to go.

Gormz stared absently at the little mageki at play on the floor. Suddenly he heard a clattering noise; the brittle noise of something breaking on the stone floor. He forced his eyes to focus on his daughter, who sat poised over the pieces of a sharp, shiny material. She raised a fragment to her mouth.

"No!" he screamed, grabbing the glass from the startled mageki just in time. Mageki Mavon jumped, aroused from her own daydreams.

Gormz gathered up the shards of material, intending to toss them aside, when a pattern caught his eye. Words.

"Where did you get this?" he asked, not really expecting an answer, but the little mageki's gaze led him into the unexplored shadows at the far end of the cave.

"Don't go back there!" he said, then disappeared himself into the gloom. When he returned to the light, his arms were filled with the unassembled crystal pages of a dageki primer. Many of the pages were broken, but some were still readable. The dialect was ancient, but Gormz, a student of language, was immediately intrigued.

He sat down on the stone floor and began to read.

CHAPTER THIRTY-SEVEN

Malgryn's Dream

F irst came the cubes, and she barely noticed them. The devices were cold and empty, surely no use or threat to her, though they contained particles and elements alien to her chosen world, and they tingled with a fuzzy, changeling essence. It became somewhat more interesting with the first arrivals to step from the boxes, but even then, Malgryn was not impressed. The creatures that were unceremoniously dumped onto her world possessed frail, small-mass, one-shape bodies and weak minds untrained in transmogrifee. They were misfits, artists and other losers, culled by a race that obviously valued only reason and technical aptitude. She harrumphed and raised her many limbs to the sky in disgust, taking a season or two to shrug.

Did they really think this motley few could challenge the skilled warriors and shapers that she had honed to a fine, bloody edge for the game? Could they even survive one bitter winter or volcanic eruption?

But they did have something, some small iota of potential. They could create, they strove for more, always more. They molded for themselves impossible stories they called dreams. They possessed a prodigious depth of caring and most usefully, an infinite capacity for hate. Perhaps she could use these interlopers for her own amusement, in the unlikely event they did survive.

Malgryn had been sleeping too long, she knew, but now at last she felt the Bloom coming on. It filled her with unrest. She was bored with the same old avatars, sunturn after sunturn. Perhaps it was time for some new blood to flow, for a new spice to awaken her peculiar tastes. At the thought, she felt the sap rising in her core and her lust for change, caressed her bark like the first trickle of warmth from the spring sun. For the first time in a long time, Malgryn looked forward to the game.

Chapter Thirty-Eight

Imposter

The speaker went on, listing kinds of fish in a droning voice. It seemed to be cataloging every fish known to exist in the seas. Most, Nikki had never heard of, but she wasn't listening very closely. Instead, she was trying to remember where she'd been and what she'd been doing before this strange dream began.

She looked around her again, but saw nothing familiar. The ocean stretched on into the distance, gray and monotonous. Then she remembered the boat and the wave.

"Where is everyone else?" she gasped. "Am I dead? I was drowning."

This seemed to draw the attention of the voice; it paused in mid-sentence.

"Fish don't drown—usually, though they can get caught in the rising. I do regret it, but I've got to come up for air occasionally, you know." The speaker chuckled as if it had made a joke.

"What are you?" asked Nikki, now totally bewildered.

"Well, I guess I'm what I choose to be. And what are you, little creature?" A huge face bent down to her with these words, a face made of bark and streaming seaweed. Nikki was terrified, and she struggled frantically to escape, but the branches tightened around her waist until she was gasping for breath.

"Just a second, little impostor, I would ask a few questions before you swim away."

"I'm not an impostor," she rasped, struggling for breath. "I'm not a fish. I never claimed to be one. You just assumed that. I'm human."

The gruesome face tipped to the side as if it were contemplating what she said. Its grip loosened, then she thought it smiled. She heard a creaking and popping, like branches breaking in a storm.

"Not entirely, I think, but that is what you think you are. I sense no deception. That's good. I don't like liars. They waste my time. I remember creatures like you. One was my friend once. I suppose he's long gone now. Still, I don't suppose it would hurt to ask if you've seen him. His name is Balistondro. He lived on the Skookumchuck River then, but he may have moved on by now."

"What are you?" Nikki asked again. "Where am I?"

"You are an abrupt and impolite species, aren't you? But I suppose that comes with the tiny brain. I am Malgryn, and I am what I choose to be. I live where I choose to live. This is my world, and my island, though you're lucky to catch me on the surface. These days, I spend most of my time underwater. I find that my thoughts just flow better down there." The tree chuckled, and Nikki had to grab at a branch to keep her place. "But I do come up occasionally for the Blooming. Sometimes when I rise, I find these things caught in my branches. Usually, they fall to their deaths. You were lucky. A lucky little creature you are." The tree eyed her quizzically.

Nikki tried to grasp all that she had heard. Could this really be the isle they had been searching for? She looked around her, but the surface of the ocean was still and empty. The boat was gone and with it, her brother and the only true friends she'd ever known. Had this tree's rising caused the wave? She had to face the fact that her companions were dead. At the thought, she was filled with overwhelming despair. She must have sobbed out loud.

"There, there, little one. I'll help you down. I hate crying, just hate it."

With more cracking sounds, Nikki was lowered to the sand. She tried to stand, but her knees gave out. She knelt on the sand, coughing seawater. When she felt strong enough to rise, she stood, looking up at the largest tree she'd ever seen. It stood on a tiny sand island. The trunk was so huge that it obliterated half the sky in front of her. The gnarled branches twisted and swirled into unknown heights and extended far out over the ocean. At the tips of the branches, Nikki could barely make out tiny orbs sparkling in the sun. Could these be the drakyn's eyes?

"Are you the Tree of Malgryn?" Nikki asked in wonder.

"Well, that's not exactly correct, you know. I am Malgryn, but I am not a tree. I am other. This is my planet. I chose it out of many. It seemed a good place to settle down for a bit; It just needed a little remodeling. I think those gardlanders who sent humans here would call me a terraformer. I'm very sorry for the damage my rising has caused. Your companions—"

The tree stopped mid-sentence and the branches seemed to droop. A gentle buzzing emanated from the trunk. Nikki wondered if it was sleeping. But why so suddenly?

Before finding out what the tree was about to say, the sea erupted beside her, spewing out a hideous shape, huge and gray, with a pointed snout and long, naked tail. It rose into the air, transforming as it hovered above her. Nikki cowered down to the ground, but there was no place to hide.

"Almost lost you that time, little trickster," roared the drakyn. "But fortunately, rats are excellent swimmers. You won't escape this time. Thanks for leading me to the eyes of power. You've led me on quite a chase, but I'll pay you back for that later." As he spoke, he started to circle the tree at great speed, until the wind threatened to tear Nikki from the ground, but she clung as best she could as flying sand stung her eyes and skin. She heard popping noises and daring to look up, she saw some of the orbs releasing from the tips of the branches. A howling joined the wind, the drakyn's laughter. The wind stilled, and she looked up. The drakyn was growing as she watched, slowly at first, and then with increasing speed. Soon he was huge, and she could see the power glowing inside of him. Then he noticed her, as if he remembered a small annoyance, and in a flash, he was standing beside her on the sand. This must be his true shape, a male drakyn, but a small one, with blotchy skin and crooked limbs.

"Semli, you're a monster," she said, now beyond fear. "Just a pathetic misfit, who must hurt others to feel whole."

He laughed bitterly. She could see that she'd hit a nerve. Small reward, she thought, since I'll soon be dead.

The drakyn eyed her coolly for a second, then stepped forward. Nikki looked behind her, but there was no place to run. She couldn't even swim. She could feel the power emanating from him. She could smell it, like the residue of lightning; it burned her nostrils. He reached out to her, gently caressing her with one blood-caked claw. Nikki felt sick from the smell. He rushed her, forcing her down and ripping at her clothes. As he did so, he cut a ragged gouge in her breast, and Nikki felt the trickle of blood run down her side. When he entered her, he was the handsome man from the inn, but as he moved, he changed; first a wolf, then a grella, and then something rotten and fetid. She screamed, but it was too late. He was inside her, spreading throughout her body like a fungus, but infinitely faster. He had attached himself to all her nerve endings, and she felt intense pain in every part of her body. The pain seemed to go on forever, and very soon, she wanted to die. She begged him to kill her, but he wouldn't. He was laughing. Then he was torn away from her, and her mind went blank.

The tree was speaking. "Get away, you foul little nuisance. Why did I even allow you to be in the first place?" Semli struggled in the limbs of the tree, which were now holding him tightly. Without warning, the limbs twisted in on themselves, then spewed the drakyn away from the island with incredible force. Another branch raised up one of the shining orbs and threw it at the spinning creature. When the orb collided with the drakyn, they both burst into a million bits of matter, cascading over the water in a kind of messy biological rain. Semli was gone.

"Sorry about that," said Malgryn. "It takes me a while to wake up, you know, and the Bloom really takes it out of me."

The tree droned on, but Nikki heard nothing. She had fainted.

She woke to the touch of gentle waves on her feet as she lay at the shoreline. Her first thought was a wish for water. Her throat was incredibly parched. The caress of the ocean tempted her, but she knew that this water would only increase her thirst. She tried to rise and found that although stiff and burned, she had no major injuries, though her head felt like it might explode. The gash on her chest had stopped bleeding. She used what was left of her clothes to bind the wound.

She looked around, but the ocean was still. The tree was silent again. She wondered if the drakyn had injured it. Torn and broken branches littered the sand.

Then an invisible wind seemed to stir the branches, though Nikki felt only stillness. The branches stood up straight and tall, the damaged parts grew back in a flash of growth that was quicker than she could follow. The tree shook itself.

"There, that's better. Miserable little troublemaker, that one. Glad to be rid of him, to tell the truth. Hated to even waste one orb on him, but there you have it. He's gone for good, now. Where was I?"

Nikki shook herself to remember what the tree had last been saying. It was something very important to her. "My companions!" she cried "You were saying something about my companions."

"Oh. Yes, now I remember." The tree stretched and a limb extended, first, far out over the waves and then straight downward, deep into the ocean. When it pulled back up, a ragged, dripping *Prophesy* lay in its clutches. Malgryn dumped the boat unceremoniously onto the sand. It was empty of life and looked waterlogged.

Nikki stuttered, "But, what about—"

"Patience, please, thou ungrateful afterthought that is humanity. I am not yet finished recalling them."

The tree repeated its actions, coming up with one of her soggy companions at a time until they all lay unmoving on the beach beside her. None appeared to be alive.

"But they're all dead!" Nikki cried in shock.

"Oh, my, but aren't we demanding? All right, then, watch this."

The tree bent a huge limb down toward each of the limp humans. A knot formed like lips and opened in the bark. On each face, Malgryn blew a gentle breath. When the tree was done, all but one sat up, coughing up seawater and looking very confused. The one who didn't rise was Wren. Trey went to her and called her name, but she didn't wake.

"Wren, please wake up," he begged, looking about him in bewilderment.

"Ah, this one called Wren is definitely not a fish," said the tree. "Very determined."

"Can you help her?" asked Nikki, who had had more time to adjust to the existence of Malgryn "She's very ill from using the abacusian. It's a device that—"

"Yes, I know all about that," said Malgryn impatiently. "I watched her closely in my dreams."

Malgryn stretched out and a gentle leaf touched Wren's cheek. One of the shining orbs appeared, cradled in the leaf.

"Wake, little one. I won't let you die so easily."

Wren opened her eyes, and a look of total amazement colored their mercurial depths. Trey helped her sit up.

The tree continued, "Here, take it, Wren. This one is for you, a kind of thank you for watching the store while I slept."

Dreyk mumbled, "Watching the store?"

Wren seemed hesitant to touch the seed that Malgryn offered. Nikki willed her to reach for it. Didn't she see that she had little choice? Without it, she would soon die.

As if following Nikki's thoughts, Wren finally reached forward to take the orb. Trey jerked out a hand as if to stop her, but she lifted a warning finger toward him, and he seemed to understand that this was their only chance. She reached up, as Malgryn bent down. The drakyn's eye fell into her grasp and she inhaled sharply. Something bright and warm filled her eyes, as if a chronic pain had suddenly been removed.

Malgryn continued, "Normally, I don't take an interest in my pawns. Kings and queens are my usual avatars, you see, but you did so well, covering for me when I overslept. For such a small, inconsequential species, you really do have some potential. Grit, I think is what you call it."

Wren said simply, "Thank you."

Trey's face showed warring expressions of confusion and indignation.

"Pawns? When you overslept? What the—"

Wren took his arm. "Trey, no. I'm healed. The tree healed me of the abacusian disease."

"What?"

They all gazed up at the tree, waiting for an explanation.

"Malgryn," asked Nikki, with only a touch of sarcasm, "can you explain to us lesser beings what actually happened?"

"Well, here's the thing, little one." The tree paused as if embarrassed. "I overslept, just a bit, you see. I should have prevented the war eight-hundred years ago. I'm so sorry you had to do it for me, Wren. But I must say, you did rather well with what you had to work with." Was the tree looking at Trey as it spoke?

Trey was now in fully indignant mode. "Overslept? You've got to be kidding. All this time, all the misery she went through, losing our daughter, all because you OVERSLEPT?"

Wren took his hand and he seemed to calm somewhat.

Malgryn continued, "I go into a kind of *hibernation*, I think that's the word for an extended dream time. And I'm no spring chicker anymore, as your kind say. Anyway, as I dream, I grow the seeds, deep in my ocean home. Then I rise and the seeds mature and are released to do their work. I call it the Bloom."

"But what are they, really, these seeds?" asked Benna.

"The seeds—what you call drakyn's eyes—are not seeds or eyes or stones at all. They are the messengers of my transmogrifee, the fingers of my power. They are potential, growth, becoming, even the ultimate destruction, if called upon for such use. But their power wanes over time. The one you had was nothing but a shell after so many centuries. All it could do was lead you to me. But with the fresh seeds, my heir will be able to do so much more. The rest of you can go back to the normal, uneventful lives that your kind seems to prefer. 'As you were.' Isn't that how your gardlanders used to say it?"

Benna asked, "But why do you even need an heir? Aren't you some kind of omnipotent being?"

"Ah, well you see," said the tree reluctantly, "there have been signs: sleeping late, aches and pains in the eventime of a world, forgetfulness.

I'm afraid even a planet-shaper's time is limited. Soon it will be time for me to sleep again, and next time, I may not wake."

"Your heir," sighed Nikki in a tone of resignation. "You mean me, don't you?"

"No, of course not, silly one."

Wren said, "What? It's not Nikki? But she had the drakyn's eye. She looks so much like me—"

"I'm afraid you were misled. It's true, the seed was drawn to her, and she heard it calling. Why do you think you were able to find her, alone and injured in that time-slipping forest? And she does look like you. Just a darker version, perhaps?"

They all looked at Char, who had been staring up into the branches of the tree in a trance. There was a rapt expression on her face, as if she were listening to a symphony that only she could hear.

"Char?" exclaimed Nikki and Wren at once. Wren looked chagrined and Nikki looked relieved.

"I knew it," cried Nikki. "I knew it wasn't me, but no one would listen. Now it makes sense. It was Char all along. I knew there was something special about her. *She* has the power."

Dreyk said under his breath, "Yah, but is she ready for it?"

"But I don't understand," cried Wren in confusion. "There's something about Nikki that is very different. I can feel it."

Malgryn appeared to laugh, and a thousand leaves tinkled and danced.

"Must I show you?" asked Malgryn. "What strange creatures you are. So talented and passionate, yet so blind at times."

Malgryn reached a leaf-covered limb toward Nikki, and everything changed.

"You see," said Malgryn triumphantly. "Now you see your friend as she truly exists."

There was a flash and Nikki was gone. They heard a sharp cry and the air smelled of lightning, and something else.

"What have you done to her?" cried Wren.

"Done to her? Done to her?" laughed Malgryn. "I have merely returned her to herself. That is all."

Nikki felt disoriented. Her skin was too hot, her breaths too large, her heart too slow.

Then suddenly the world disappeared, and a new one took its place. Where the old one had existed on only one level, flat and colored in shades of gray, this one was now filled with brilliant tones that she had never seen before. Shapes took on extra dimensions, thoughts had infinite clarity. The world was fresh and wonderful and complete. She felt newly born, newly awakened. The power consumed her, filling all her empty and needing places, healing her wounds. Her awareness began to swell. She found herself floating in the air above the island. She looked down at the tiny beach as it approached, and death seemed so inconsequential. As she hurtled downward, she remembered, a moment before impact, that there was something she needed to do. In that moment, she took on a new shape. Something of her own creation, she thought, yet it was familiar. It fit. It fit this world, a shape made for survival, and killing.

She laughed as she rose on her new wings, and the sound rocked the waters. The dying tree teetered on its tiny island perch, reminding her of who and what she had been. She would not make the mistake that Semli had made, believing that the eyes granted power. She now knew the bitter truth. The eyes did not always give power; they could consume it, as well. In disgust, she ripped the necklace that Tbrin had given her from her neck and threw it far across the sea. He hadn't given it to her to increase her power, he had done it to limit her strength, to keep her week and human, to never discover her true self. Now she finally knew who and what she was.

"I am a drakyn!" she roared, and the ground shook with the power in her voice.

We are all drakyn, she thought, every Mistran. Hidden all these centuries in human form. Held there by the suppressing power of the eye.

"Semli, you were a fool," she rasped. "You died for nothing, blinded by your greed, when this whole world could have been yours. Now it will be mine."

She looked down at the tree, through it to its core. She sensed in it incredible age and experiences almost as ancient as the universe itself. She wondered if the power of the seeds this tree produced might be of some use to her after all, perhaps to control her enemies. In an impulsive gesture, she chose to leave it rather than kill it, not out of compassion—she was far beyond compassion now—but because she recognized it for what it was, the source of a power she could use, a tool she might one day wield against her enemies.

"Don't thank me for restoring you," boomed the tree. "But I fear you misunderstand the gift I have given you. Why would you want this ultimate power to hurt others or exact revenge, when the only true power is to create?"

"You're wrong. The greatest strength lies in the power to destroy. Look at the universe, old fool, it is destroying itself bit by bit. Faster than the order and beauty we can create, it is spreading and losing energy, until one day very soon, there will be only chaos and ruin. Face it. Revel in it. It's the only way."

Malgryn stretched, creaking and popping as she did so, then she sighed, a wind in the branches. "But that is the easy course," she replied. "The course of weakness and resignation. But you will change in time. There is great strength in you for creation and it will surface again."

Nikki didn't believe what the old fool was saying. The eye at Mistra must have been taken there many centuries ago, when this tree last surfaced to release its fruit. Was Kodo the creator of Mistra, or was he the destroyer of a race of extraordinary beings, the once all-powerful drakyn?

She knew that she had to find the truth. She would be a pawn no longer. Taking wing, she was far above the ocean in moments. She glanced back to see the tree just submerging below the waves. It didn't matter now. She knew she could find Malgryn again if she needed to. Better that she stay hidden from curious eyes. Just to be sure, she wove a transmogrifee to hide the spot where the tree had disappeared to all but herself.

Filled with the exaltation of freedom and flight, she flew even higher. Soon the air started to grow thin. She struggled, breathing hard until she realized that she was not limited as she had been in the shapes that she could take. In the instant of understanding, she transformed her heart into a core of pure energy, needing neither breath for life nor movement to attain position. In a flash, she was far above the world. It looked tiny and fragile as it spun slowly below her. She was surrounded by blackness, utterly cold and airless.

Now she concentrated on the waves of power in the world. They filled all of space, the byproduct of every transmogrifee act. Some were convoluted and wandering, some were tightly woven masses of hair-thin roots, and others were sharp and direct, brittle glass streamers that flashed like splinters in her eyes. She was able to isolate the one she wanted and follow it, a bright, wide beam of power leading back toward Mistra. Someone had been affecting her life. Was it Tbrin, or Jelebron, or even Akriast? Or was it all of them working in concert against her? Whoever it was, had been hiding their true power. Whoever it was, would pay for everything that had happened to her. She would have her revenge.

She returned to her world, pausing at the place where the air began to look down at the planet below, but it didn't look the same as it had when she'd left it just a few short moments ago. She knew it would never look the same again.

Back on the island, Wren looked up at Malgryn in irritation and confusion. "But I don't understand! How could Nikki be a drakyn? The abacusian allows me to see all the drakyn on Drakonia. Why didn't I know?"

Malgryn, with much creaking, bent down over Trey, who leaned away.

"Well, one of you knew. He knew." A limb pointed at Trey. "He hid them from you."

Wren's eyes burned with anger and disbelief. Pointing an accusing finger at Trey she said, "Why would you do that? Didn't you trust me?"

"Of course, I trusted you—"

"Then why—"

Trey sighed. "Because I didn't know what you would do in the end, and I needed to protect the species."

"I don't understand."

"Remember that when I chose to become human and give up being Kodo the drakyn, you had only the prototype abacusian, and we were all uncertain how much control you had over the power it gave you. To be honest, I didn't know that you might not decide to simply destroy all the drakyn on the planet. Despite their faults, I couldn't risk that. Eventually, you got the more powerful abacusian and transformed them into humans instead of destroying them—but of course I couldn't know what you were going to do."

"So, when you were still Kodo, you hid some of your people, the drakyn, from me, at Mistra, and told me nothing of it."

"I'm sorry, truly, but I couldn't tell you."

"That's why Nikki looks so much like me then? You created her like that on purpose? Why?"

Trey smiled apologetically. "As Kodo, I had to leave a part of my soul at Mistra, to guard them. Can you blame me for wanting a little reminder of you in my exile?"

"And the tree? You felt you had to hide the knowledge that it existed from me as well? The one thing that could have saved my life—our lives?" Wren turned away from him.

Trey spoke, now in a pleading tone. "Wren, please listen to me. At the time, the next bloom was still centuries away."

"That doesn't matter. You didn't trust me with knowledge that could have prevented all this."

Trey said, "I did lead the group to Malgryn, didn't I? We still had to arrive when Malgryn was about to rise. I thought many times about letting you in on the secret, but I had to be practical. You were so weak from the abacusian disease. What if you had been captured by Semli or Jelebron? You know that torture is a high art for them. You would have told them everything. They could have reached the tree before us and possibly recalled *all* the drakyn. The war would start all over again. I couldn't risk that. Wren, I'm so sorry."

Wren was silent for a long time. Finally, she turned back to him. "I guess I understand, but these must be the last secrets you *ever* keep from me. Understood?"

"Understood," said Trey with a contrite, but relieved smile.

CHAPTER THIRTY-NINE

Char Wakes

C har stared up into the disquieting limbs of the tree. Each seemed to possess a life of its own, swaying independently of the others, creating a dance that no breeze ever could.

The fruits of the tree—what Nikki had called the drakyn's eyes—sprouted from the tips of every limb, creating a tableau of a thousand lanterns, each with its own lightning bolt enclosed in a burning orb. She reached upward, and a stream of milky colored light leapt down to meet her fingers, as if the seeds were eager to find her palm. As her fingers grew near, the seed separated from the tree with a pop into her waiting grasp.

At its touch, Char's world changed, expanding beyond her capacity to comprehend. Her eyes saw colors that couldn't exist. She saw what had always been there, just beyond purple, ultra-neon magenta and unquenchable cyan, infra-chartreuse and wind tossed, daisy yellow. Her ears cupped the sounds of the world breathing. She felt the heartbeat of a billion tiny breaths, so fragile, yet so enduring, when given time and space to grow.

Back at the cabin, Char had overheard Wren explaining to Nikki how the abacusian worked, but this was something beyond anything she could have imagined. Overwhelmed beyond her ability to cope, her brain went into a focused state, as it tried to absorb infinity.

Eventually, eternal second by eternal second, Char returned to the world. First, she searched for Nikki, but Nikki was gone, embroiled in a tantrum or some existential crises of being. She would come around. Right now, there were more pressing matters to attend to. She saw how limited and limiting the abacusian had been. The tree, not a tree at all, but a creature alien to Drakonia, was the source of all transmogrifee on the planet. Malgryn was a world-shaper and she had chosen this world as her playground. Long before the arrival of humans through the cubes, Malgryn had been playing her games with the inhabitants. The drakyn had been her favorite pawns.

But Malgryn had made a fatal error, giving some of her human avatars an ability that only a world-shaper should possess. It started small, with Wren, who needed the abacusian to work her magic on the world. But while the world-shaper slept her long sleep, the ability to shape matter grew in Wren and Trey's descendants, until the genetrics produced Char.

Now she gazed down at the state of the world-shaper. Malgryn was dying, there was no doubt. Maybe not this moment, but soon, and in the meantime, her extended sleeping periods would wreak havoc on the world, past the point that anything could be saved. But was Char ready to take her place, determining the fate of every creature on the planet? It grated at Char's need for freedom. How could she enjoy her liberty while chaining everyone else to her implacable will? If she let Malgryn die, she would be forced to take her place. Char didn't want to face eternity as nanny to the world, though she realized that, even with Malgryn's help, she was going to have to take on a much greater responsibility than she felt prepared to shoulder.

"Malgryn?" she called in her mind. Char detected the slow response. Malgryn was going into a state of lethargy, just one step before non-being.

"Malgryn, listen to me," Char said firmly. "I don't want your job, at least not all of it, but if I heal you and let you continue to play your games, there will be some conditions."

"Conditions?" chortled the tree. "You little being, are you going to tell *me* what to do?" But the tree tipped forward, her snoring like the grating of branches against each other in a storm, already slipping into sleep.

"No more war games, no more unnecessary conflicts," Char continued, unperturbed.

"Well, that sounds boring, doesn't it," harumphed the world-shaper in her sleep. "What would I do with my time?"

"Well," mused Char. "You'll just have to get used to it. You are moving on in centuries, after all. Maybe a more contemplative game would suit you, eh?"

The world tree sighed, and all her limbs tinkled, like a thousand glass windchimes disturbed by an unexpected breeze.

"A life without violence may not be worth living, but I'll give it a try. Just because you are a part of me, Charisma. You are the best of me, I think. I'll give it a try. That's all I can promise."

"Good," said Char, and turned from the world tree for the last time.

Char awoke in the material world. Her tongue felt numb, and her legs tingled with some other-worldly energy that made her legs jerk with every breath. Finally, her nerves stilled enough that she could realize where she was. She was on the boat with the others as they made their way back to Bay Towne.

The Tree of Malgryn had sunk below the waves to sleep again. Nikki was gone, flying south to exact her revenge, and Char regretted missing her. Perhaps she would have been able to talk her out of this unrealistic angst that drove her to destroy her birthplace. But maybe it was better this way. Some games just had to play themselves out, after all, to their inevitable, ugly end.

Chapter Forty

The Aerie Restored

Nikki flew south, toward Mistra, but something drew her down toward the water, as if she could not yet bear to leave the place where she had lost her friends. She wandered above the ocean for some time until she found a tiny speck on the water, far from the spot where Malgryn had been.

What am I doing? she wondered, but she flew downward with the energy of hope.

As she approached, she realized that she was coming in too fast, and pulled up. To her chagrin, the resultant wave almost swamped the listing boat, which was barely staying afloat. Tiny figures scurried, screaming and falling in their panic. Why were they running? There was nowhere to go. Nikki laughed, but it came out as a gale. The little creatures were thrown to the deck by the force of her breath. The pitiful little boat rocked, and the beings were tossed again. A man called out for the moons to save him, and she recognized that voice. Something tugged at her, a memory, a friend.

"Dreyk?" she cried, but it came out as a roar. She settled gently to the water, remembering that other shape, the one she had held all her life before the awakening.

She stood on the surface of the water as a human, forgetting that humans couldn't do this. She peered tentatively into the boat. It hadn't weathered the wave; it was taking on water and listing badly, but it was still afloat.

"Char?" she called. This time she remembered to sound like herself.

But Char was still lost in her trance. Her sparkling eyes still saw nothing. She sat stiff and silent, as if her mind were engaged elsewhere.

The other humans cowered in the boat, all except for Wren and Trey who stood to face her stiffly. She climbed onto the deck. For the most part, her friends looked unhurt, though Benna wore a bloody bandage around his forehead. When she approached with her arms outstretched, he pulled back, staring at her in blank terror.

"It's me," she pleaded. "Don't you recognize me, Benna? Moonchaser, come here." But the cat backed away from her. Why couldn't he see her?

Dreyk rose on shaking legs to face her defiantly. "You're not Nikki," he said. "Nikki was taken by Malgryn and turned into a beast. She's gone."

"No, I'm still me. Malgryn—"

"Don't play your tricks on us, drakyn. Do you think us total fools? We saw you in the sky. We could all see what you are. Did you think you could hide from a transmogrifer? Wren can see you as you really are. Kill us and get it over with, but don't dishonor her memory by putting your vile soul in the shape of one we loved!"

Turning to Char, she said, "Char, you've got to understand. I've changed. My power has been restored—and more, but I'm still the person you knew, the same person who still cares about you all." Nikki reached out to Char, but Char didn't respond, still staring blankly into a reality that only she could see.

Nikki turned from them, unable to face the rejection in their eyes. She looked to Tbrin, who only shook his head, and she saw it was no use. They could see her for what she was, a drakyn, a transmogrifer of great power, and that was all they would see. Tbrin waved his arms, beginning a transmogrifee, but Nikki put up a finger, and the man gasped, reeling back in pain.

What could she do if they refused to see the truth?

In sudden anger, she rose into the sky, returning to her drakyn shape. What did it matter if they believed her or not? She rushed away, forcing her wings to fight the air until they ached and burned. The pain brought her back to her senses, and she turned around. She had to save their lives now. She owed them that. As she returned to the boat, she increased her size, extended her front limbs, and spreading her claws to encircle the boat. Lifting it, dripping, from the water, she started landward, ignoring the cries of her frightened passengers.

Soon, the continent came into view, and she headed down toward Bay Towne. As she approached the bay, thousands of tiny creatures scrambled, some running, some throwing themselves into the water just to try to escape her. She felt the joy of her power, and at the same time, she felt a great loss. They would never accept her now. She'd lost her humanity, her friends and her life, and what had she gained? Immortality if she wanted it? What was that worth now?

She set the boat down as gently as she could. Extending her awareness into the hills, she felt for the presence of her enemy Jelebron until she found it. Weak and faint, the power of the drakyn still glowed. Jelebron must be holed up in some cave in the hills, nursing her wounds and trying to regain her strength. But Jelebron would never be a threat to her now. At most, she could be only a petty annoyance. Nikki had more important things to deal with. Maybe later, she would return to kill the drakyn, at her own leisure. But it didn't matter now. Jelebron was nothing. The one who had been directing her life every step of the way; that was the one she wanted now.

Turning sharply, she rose on powerful wings, not looking behind her. She started flying south with a new sense of purpose. There was one more task, one more battle to fight.

She flew without rest, the power in her wings born of anger and loss. She felt invincible, because she no longer cared if she lived or died, but she also felt that someone would die at her hands this day. As she flew, she planned her attack. It probably wouldn't be easy, even though she had learned an important skill that her enemy wouldn't suspect her capable of. She could be without compassion. Only by being totally ruthless could she win this battle.

Nikki walked the familiar halls without emotion, as the confused Mistrans made way for her in fear. Some of them she recognized, but it wasn't easy. Most of them were now half-human monstrosities writhing in pain. The dead were everywhere, the oldest victims rotting where they lay. There were drakyn heads on human bodies, human faces distorted by rows of carnivorous teeth that sprouted from faces too small to accommodate them. Some looked as if they had died in battle, but most wore the expressions of those who had died in horrible pain, as their bodies were unable to weather the ghastly changes overtaking them.

Nikki walked with anger growing hard in her like cold steel. Who'd done this? Jelebron, or Akriast? The once beautiful aerie was in a shambles. The Mistrans who remained were living in their own filth. Nikki knew that she had to restore what was left of the aerie to its former beauty, but knowing as she did it that she would never return here. Even as she restored it, the knowledge of all she had seen would haunt her. In Mistra, the memories would always be near, to remind her of the life she'd lost.

It took all her energy and transmograffic talent to restore the beautiful palace to the state she remembered, but the residents were the greatest challenge. Should she return their humanity, or let them fully transform into the drakyn, deadly and unpredictable? In the end, she reluctantly chose human over drakyn, knowing it was the best way for her people to survive.

Nikki took her time, as she walked toward Akriast's quarters. Though the lines of power had led her here, she couldn't locate their source, as if the power was a part of the mountain itself. Puzzled, she realized that the great power here wasn't Akriast. From what she could gain from the Mistrans she questioned, Akriast had tried to counter the changes that were destroying them, but in the end, she'd failed. Exhausted, she had retreated to her quarters to die.

Nikki knew that the old woman could do nothing to hurt her now, but she wasn't sure that she wanted to kill Akriast outright. Perhaps another punishment would be more appropriate and definitely more enjoyable.

She came to Akriast's door, easily breaking the transmogrifee that protected it. Inside she felt sudden abhorrence and disgust; Akriast lay half on the floor, half on her cot. Spittle dripped from her mouth, and the half-clothed old woman looked as if she hadn't eaten or bathed in days. Nikki thought that perhaps she was too late, but a light came to the old transmogrifer's eyes when she saw Nikki.

"You're too late, little one," she coughed. "I'm afraid I'll have to deny you the pleasure of killing me. Time is going to do it for you. I haven't even the strength to transfer now, even if a viable birth were imminent."

Nikki looked for some trick, some illusion, but she could find none. The old woman really was dying.

"You had a great talent," said Nikki in a tired voice. "Why did you waste it, deserting your own kind. You've caused much grief, Akriast, and for what?"

Akriast snorted, a weak gurgle. "You're as much a hypocrite as the others, Nikki," she wheezed. "Tell me you wouldn't have given anything to regain your talent once you'd lost it; betrayed your friends, murdered your master..."

"Don't play your guilt games on me, Akriast, I am no longer a child that you can manipulate."

"Deny it if you like, but we both know, don't we? We know what makes a true artist. We must be selfish—totally narcissistic—to be any good at what we do."

"If that's true, that explains a lot about how very adept you were at creating the horrors you conjured from the past."

"Ah, it is so easy for your kind to take the upper ground, isn't it? You can change your shape, but not your soul. You are drakyn, and in my heart, so was I."

Nikki looked down at Akriast in wonder. How did she still have the strength to lie? "No, Akriast. In your heart, you are a beast, a scheming, bloodthirsty murderer, but you were never drakyn. Just a human wretch with an overpowering need to be recognized by your betters. You are the real monster here."

Akriast looked thoughtful, then smiled, a slow creeping grin that made Nikki's skin twitch.

"Thank you for the compliment," cackled Akriast. "In the drakyn tongue, bloodthirsty means healthy. Too bad it's not true in my case. I've overextended myself." The woman paused for a gasping breath, and Nikki could see the gray patterns playing beneath her skin.

"My life may be over," continued Akriast. "But my malice has just begun."

"Did it rankle you so, to be human?" asked Nikki.

"Ah, maybe I just wanted to be on the side of the winners," cackled the old woman. "I never thought they would lose. I still won't admit it. They'll be back, and they'll make you pay for your treachery. Like Kodo, you just couldn't leave well enough alone, playing games with their lives. But I'll be vindicated. If I can't live to fly again, then none of these half-human abominations will survive either."

"What are you saying, Akriast? I've restored the aerie. There's nothing you can do now."

The old woman cackled, coughing up blood as she did. "It's already done. I set the transmogrifee in motion centuries ago, and it's grown in strength as my strength has waned. When I die, all will die with me."

Nikki could take no more. The woman was obviously mad and far past any pain that Nikki could cause her. She left the room and started down the hall, trying to decide what she should do next.

When it happened, she felt it, a sudden void, as the old woman's spirit faded, but in its place, she felt something else growing, something far more powerful than Akriast had ever been. Could the old crone have set something in motion with her death? The mountain started to rumble, and Nikki changed shape to fly swiftly from the aerie. She flew out a distance, then looked back, expecting to see the mountain shaking with a temblor, but it wasn't crumbling at all, but changing shape. To her horror, the whole mountain was taking on a life of its own. Inside, Mistrans were screaming and running, but there was no place for them to go.

As she watched, the mountain unfolded, pulling its feet out of the earth and stretching upward, opening great wings of solid stone. Then the head came into view, a huge parody of a drakyn, distorted and twisted in a grimace of terrible rage. Nikki had no idea what she could do. How could she fight a living mountain?

As she gaped in terror, the beast began to compress. Its face strained as the caverns and halls collapsed on the people inside. Nikki could hear their screams, but she didn't know what to do. She worked frantically at a transmogrifee to bind, but she feared that nothing she could do would stop this beast now. As she watched in terror, the chambers began to close, and she feared that all inside must soon be dead. Then the beast screamed, the roar of another earthquake. Huge arms of rock came around to grasp at its abdomen, but something was coming through. It burst out through the hands of the beast, belching stones that cracked and smoked, spreading flowers of dust and splintering pebbles that exploded as they impacted far below.

At first, Nikki thought that it must be another drakyn, but it was bright, much too light in color. Then she recognized it, and she couldn't believe her eyes. It was the crystal drakyn. The sculpture was now living, breathing. Nikki searched the lines of power. Somewhere there had to be another transmogrifer with great strength and talent to work such a transmogrifee, but all the power she sensed was in the crystal drakyn itself. Even now, she had to appreciate its beauty. To see it flying brought a tingle to her spine. It glowed with power and clarity of purpose. It lived as she had always dreamed of living, like a hawk, clean of heart, and free of desire. To see it set her hopes free. For the first time in a long time, she felt the joy of life.

As the beast clutched at the rent in its abdomen, the drakyn flew out toward Nikki, then turned to face the mountain. As it did, light erupted from its eyes, a more powerful transmogrifee than Nikki had ever imagined, and the mountain ceased its movement. As Nikki watched, the mountain slowly reverted to its former shape. The caverns opened to the sky again, and Nikki could see the Mistrans inside, running to the edge to see the crystal drakyn as it hovered before them.

Too late, she realized that the transmogrifee had affected her as well. She couldn't move her wings. She started to fall, and somehow it didn't matter to her. She'd lived to see something more beautiful than life itself. She let go of her consciousness and felt what she thought was her last thought. She opened her eyes with a jolt as the drakyn grabbed her in its claws. She looked up, but the light was blinding. She relaxed, letting him take her.

He set her down in the moss beside the dreaming pool and stood over her while she struggled to rise. His hands moved, though his lips did not, and somehow Nikki understood him.

Be calm. You will recover in a moment, came the thought to her. *I didn't mean to let you get caught in the transmogrifee. Please forgive me.*

"Forgive you!" she blurted. "You just saved the lives of everyone in Mistra."

Actually, I'm quite glad it's over, he thought to her. *I was never very good at waiting.*

"Who are you?" she dared to ask.

The drakyn looked puzzled for a moment, as if he were struggling to recall distant events. He lifted one clear claw to scratch his chin. Light glinted from his eyes, and Nikki lost all thought. He was so beautiful.

Well, he began hesitantly, as if he were just now remembering. *Perhaps it is not 'who', but 'what' I am. I was born Kodo to the queen of the drakyn, or at least part of me was—*

"You're really not making much sense."

The crystal drakyn laughed in her mind, and to Nikki, it was like the sound of a high mountain creek being teased by the summer breeze. It sparkled.

His expression grew stern. *You know me as Kodo, the crystal drakyn. Before I met Wren, I was a living drakyn. I fought with bitter pride and no mercy. I killed thousands of humans. I meant to kill her as well, but instead, I came to love her. Humans really aren't such a bad species, you know, once you get past their odd habits.* He laughed again.

"Then you are the one she spoke of," mused Nikki. "She said you gave up being a drakyn to become human, to be with her. In our reality, you're Trey."

He smiled, almost apologetically.

That's true. When I became human permanently, I saved a bit of Kodo, a little of my consciousness in the crystal drakyn, to watch over my Mistrans. You see, the tree only produces its fruit every thousand years or so. The power of our eye was waning, and we needed to get another. It augments the binding of Mistrans to human form. Without it, the binding will be weakened. You saw the effects as the Mistrans started to revert to their true shapes. But with the transmogrifee still in effect, they couldn't revert completely. I'm sorry I had to use you as I did, but this transmogrifee is limited, it only preserves my awareness to protect this place and the people of the keep. As I exist, I can never leave here.

"But what transmogrifee to bind? What true shapes?" blurted Nikki, not wanting to hear the answer.

You know this already, I think.

Nikki paused, suddenly remembering words that Akriast had spoken before she died: *You can change your shape, but not your soul; you are drakyn.*

"But how can we have been drakyn all along and not known? It's just impossible!"

The crystal drakyn looked down at her patiently, as if she were a child trying to grasp a rudimentary truth.

He sighed. *In your heart, you know it's true. But does it matter? What is a shape, but a shell for awareness? Does it matter what coat you wear? My aim was to change the soul of my people. We were dying, living for our hatred and obsession with humans until that hatred began to eat us alive. And the transmogrifee had gone too far. You saw Semli. He was born that way, stunted and crippled, as many were. Soon there would have been no more drakyn. I have managed to preserve the best*

*we had, our strengths and lust for life and combine it with human traits
that I admired so in Wren and the others. Here I created a new people
who lived for beauty and art, the Mistrans.*

"Mistrans are not the saints you make them out to be. They tried
to kill us."

He smiled, apologetically. *It's a process, I fear. It may take some time
yet for Mistrans to evolve into their higher selves. We need to give them
time.*

"But they've had eight hundred years." Nikki looked at her hands.
"It will never be the same for me, knowing what I know. I can't live
with humans, and there are no more drakyn. I'm not even sure what
the Mistrans are now."

*Like you, they're no longer drakyn or human. You've grown, as Wren
helped me overcome drakyn tendencies that were killing our people, and
hers. You are the ultimate result of my grand experiment to create a race
with great power and great compassion. You did not become a monster
when the eyes disappeared. You did not go on a killing spree as Semli did.
You went back to save your friends. You have proven to me that we are
worth saving.*

"But how do you know all this? I haven't told anyone about what
happened yet."

*The necklace that Thrin gave you was more than a piece of the eye.
With it, I could know where you were at all times and see your movements.*

"But I threw it away—"

*When you came into your full power, I didn't need it anymore. You
broadcast like a star that fills the sky. But don't worry, you will find your
place in our history, in our future. We are more than both races now, and
you'll see this in time, as I did. If you wish to see yourself as you truly are,
look in the mirror of your companions. Do they see a beast?*

Nikki looked up at him in horror, remembering how her companions had reacted to her on the boat. They *had* seen her as a beast. What had she become, if only for a moment? She shuddered to think how close she'd come to moral oblivion.

The crystal drakyn turned, and Nikki thought he might leave her. The thought filled her with loss.

"Are you—alive?" she asked suddenly.

No, and yes. I am made of thought and memory. While my body lived on in human form, I chose to put a part of my awareness into the statue, waiting for the time that I would be needed. Does that give me being? What you see is an illusion, but in some ways, I'm more alive than those who waste their lives on anger and despair. Don't be one of those.

"I won't," she said, then wondered if she could keep her promise.

She looked down on the aerie of Mistra.

"But Akriast, what did she do?" she asked.

She was determined to undermine the transmogrifee that binds our people. Sometimes I can't believe that she was human; her hunger for power was so like a drakyn. She worked on that transmogrifee for centuries, keeping herself alive, trying to restore the drakyn. She succeeded by recalling a long dead drakyn in human form. She assumed correctly that Jelebron would be able to revert to her true drakyn shape eventually. But Jelebron grew weary of Akriast's schemes for power. She decided that she didn't need the Mistrans to set herself up as queen. She had the rudiments of the transmogrifee that Akriast had used to recall her, but she lacked the talent that Akriast had. Her arrogance, that was her downfall. Alone she was no match for Thrin and Wren. She still lives, however, and may cause you more trouble still.

Meanwhile, Akriast continued her attempt to transform the Mistrans, but the transmogrifee that bound them to human form was too strong, even as the power of the eye waned. The result was the half-human monsters that you saw when you first arrived. When she had no more strength and knew that she had failed at last, she decided that no one would live, and she loosed the transmogrifee on the mountain. But I had some awareness of future events and awakened to prevent her from carrying out her plan. Had I not been prepared, she might have succeeded in killing the Mistrans.

"Then, the drakyn really are trapped in human form?"

As long as the binding lasts, and Wren and I wove it well. But don't you think it's for the best? If we'd continued, we would not only have killed ourselves, but eliminated another entire species that did nothing to deserve such genocide. It was the only way. I did it for Wren and all her kind, but in the end, I did it for the drakyn as well. When I transformed myself into the crystal drakyn, I was alone. I will be alone for eternity, but it's the price I must pay.

"Why did you send me to find the eye?"

Because the eye maintains the transmogrifee that binds us, but also because of what you would become along the way.

"I'm not sure yet what I really am."

But you do know. It's not so much that you've grown, but that you've been tested so and survived with your soul intact. That's more than most could manage. It was traditional in drakyn society, that when a warrior achieved great success in battle, they were given a war name. You have earned yours now. I name you DrakynHeart, savior of our people.

Nikki snorted. "That's very generous of you, not that it matters a whole load of fletshit to me that—"

Ingratitude does not become you, Drakynheart.

"I'm sorry. It's just a lot to handle, that's all."

You will adjust. Now, I must return to my self-imposed prison. I only wish I could have spent time with Wren, as you have. The one thing I didn't plan for when I splintered my soul was that even a small part of me would still love her and miss her with my whole heart.

Nikki wondered if there was anything she could do for Kodo. It was so sad to think of him suffering through time, missing his lover so much. There had to be something she could do, but right now, she had no ideas. She knew that the fear of failure could cause her to fail if she didn't control her emotions. Lost in her thoughts, she realized that she was facing the empty sky. He was gone.

Hours later, when the aerie had settled down and she had placed the new drakyn's eye in its pedestal in the meeting chamber, she returned to the hall of the crystal sculpture. Kodo stood again unmoving, in the same spot he had always occupied. Gathering her courage, she stepped toward him.

"I have no choice but to try," she whispered, more to herself than to Kodo. She raised her arms and began a transmogrifee. She wove into it the vision she had of Kodo, his bright spirit flying free and proud, and melded it with the obvious love that Wren and Trey had for each other.

There was a flash and the sculpture disappeared. Where Kodo had stood, soot stained the floor and gray smoke curled upward.

I've killed him, she thought. *He's gone forever.* Nikki left the room, now totally dejected. She wandered the halls in a daze, unsure where she was, until she realized that someone was looking at her. Somehow, she'd returned to the hall of the crystal drakyn.

He was there again, cold, motionless stone looking down on her with that mocking gaze. Nikki turned away, then realized that there was something different about the sculpture. She turned back, and to her amazement, the sculpture had changed. Where there had been only one figure, now there were two. Beside the crystal drakyn was another, smaller form, with hints of croma shining metallic in the glass. A sculpture of a lovely woman with long silver hair stood beside him proudly, looking up at Kodo with the gentle glow of love in her eyes.

CHAPTER FORTY-ONE

The Dageki Prophet

Nikki flew over the farm, descending into a copse of trees near the southern fields. Here, she took on human form. If she'd learned anything, it was that it wasn't wise to reveal her identity to anyone, especially if she wanted to have a reasonable discussion.

She found Gormz in the fields, at work harvesting grain. Strangely, she thought he looked happy. Beside him worked a smaller female dageki, who carried a squirming, baby dageki in a pack on her back. As she approached, Gormz looked up, but he didn't seem overly surprised to see her.

"Gormz," she began, "I said I would return for you. You don't have to stay here any longer."

Gormz looked at her quietly, almost sadly.

"I have a family now. I can't leave them."

"I'm very happy for you, but you can take them with you. I can take you all anywhere you want to go—back to Dmisi, or—"

"We can't go, any of us."

"I don't understand."

The dageki pulled one of his clear stone primers from a bag at his feet.

"It was the primer that started it. We found it in a cave. He must have left it there, or died before he could finish it. His name was Groosjk Ru Tageki Si-Yso, and he was a slaver."

"What? A dageki who kept slaves?" asked Nikki.

"You didn't know, did you? No one knew. Even the dageki must have buried the memory and the shame. Eight-hundred years ago, the dageki did not just capitulate to the drakyn. We became their cohorts in genocide. Dageki ran the farms where humans were slaughtered for their blood. Groosjk was one of the guards, until he could take the horrors of it no longer. By his will alone, he broke the spell that the drakyn used to hold the dageki in thrall. He fled to the north, to a cave where he wrote his diary. We found it there. It is a great work."

"I still don't understand why you can't leave."

"Don't you see? In a way, we're paying the price for our collusion, all those years ago. Maybe this is the penance that we must pay."

"But Gormz, that's not your responsibility. It was centuries ago."

"If we just return to our old ways, nothing will be gained. Here, I have a chance to make real change, to lead the dageki in a new direction. Already we've started an underground, of sorts, not to aid the dageki in escape, but to educate them. The ideas of Groosjk have given the dageki new hope. The awakening has begun."

Nikki looked at him in amazement. Of all the things she thought he might become, prophet had never entered her mind, but she couldn't deny it; there was a strength in him now, a peace that she envied.

Later, she said her good-byes and left them, but long after, she would remember his face and the look of contentment she saw there.

She almost didn't stop at Hyla's cabin, but in the end, she just couldn't stay away. As she approached, she saw someone on the porch, lazily carving at a stick. She recognized Dreyk, and she almost turned away. So, he was here. At the bay, they'd said that Benna had shipped out with the winter fleet, headed north, but that Dreyk had decided to spend more time with his new family. She wondered at this. She couldn't imagine him staying away from the sea that he loved for very long. Then she saw Chendri and the baby playing on the porch behind him. He was carving a little striped zoobilet for his girl.

Not wanting to alarm him, she took another form, landing on the open windowsill as a small brown wren. Inside, someone was bent over the hearth, stirring the coals.

"I knew you would come," said the stooped form.

Beside the fire, Moonchaser dozed but raised his head sharply at her words.

The figure straightened and Nikki recognized Wren.

"It seems I'm not the only one who can change faces at need," said Wren.

Nikki stepped into the room, taking her familiar human shape. Moonchaser leapt to her, nuzzling her hand.

"Good to see you, little beast." She ruffled his fur. It seemed that Moonchaser at least had forgiven her. Nikki turned to the transmogrifer.

"I'm surprised you're still here," said Nikki. "I knew that you and Trey were anxious to go home to your own time."

"Yes, we are, but we decided to spend a little more time with Char, just to teach her what we could about the abacusian before we leave. Fortunately, she's a fast learner. We'll be going home soon."

"Is she around?" asked Nikki hesitantly.

"She's out hunting right now, but I'm sure she'd be glad to see you. She's just been so busy learning to control her new powers."

Nikki wondered if that was the only reason she hadn't seen Char since the whole episode with the Tree of Malgryn. She couldn't blame Char if she didn't want to be around the beast that Nikki had become.

Wren reached forward and took Nikki's hands in hers. "Nikki, I'm so sorry we reacted to you the way we did on the boat, but you must admit, arriving as a drakyn was not the best way to ease our fears. We had no idea who you really were."

"Because I didn't know myself," replied Nikki sadly. "But I've learned a little since then."

The transmogrifer gave Nikki a long considering look, then her expression softened. She said, "Come sit by a warm fire, and tell me a story that I will tell my grandchildren one day in the past."

Nikki looked back towards the porch. "And Dreyk?"

Wren looked at her apologetically. "I fear that he's not quite ready to face you. I wouldn't push it, just yet, but he'll come around."

Nikki knew from her tone that Wren was not entirely telling the truth. Perhaps she too feared that Dreyk would never forgive her for what she had become. She left the cabin later, believing that she would never return.

CHAPTER FORTY-TWO

Palace for One

For the most part, Nikki stayed in human form, until the autumn winds arrived, bringing with them warm and disturbing memories. Then she took a winged drakyn shape, flying wild in the trees while the falling leaves danced about her. Under branches and between the boughs she flew, curling around trunks of trees in a yawning forest that would soon turn to sleep.

And when she returned to human form, exhausted, her heart would still ache for the life she had lost. It was a burning sorrow that left her numb outside, but a ragged wound inside. At times, all hope would leave her, and she would be unable to see color in anything; the world swirled around her, a mass of gray and flat shadows.

She thought of returning to Bay Towne. She often took wing and headed in that direction, but at the crest of the mountains she would always turn back, unable to face her friends, and their inevitable rejection, again. So, she went home to the palace of the ancient queens and tried to forget.

Life continued. She hunted and gathered berries and shrooms. She harvested grain from seeds the dageki had given her, setting aside a portion of the harvest so she could grow grain again when spring came. Food was plentiful, and the world was at peace. Life was good, she told herself, yet in truth, life was empty.

One day as winter was deepening, she went out to the pool. The nights had been cool, and now the water was too cold to swim in, even for a drakyn. Still, she loved just to stand here, letting the smooth water calm her thoughts.

Suddenly, she was aware that someone watched her from across the pool. She started, then her heart pounded ferociously.

"You," she gasped. "How did you get here?"

Char laughed, covering the distance between them in a heartbeat.

"Why is it with you that I am always the one answering the questions?" she asked in a teasing tone. As Char approached her, she hesitated. Nikki knew that she couldn't possibly be here for the reason she hoped.

"Over there." Char pointing to a sleek crenda at the far side of the pool. From the deck, someone waved.

"The others are here? Dreyk too?" Nikki asked, incredulous. "How did that thing get in here? This pool isn't accessible to the sea."

Char only laughed. "I'm a transmogrifer, remember? And who do you think piloted that thing here from Bay Towne if not for Dreyk? The others volunteered to spend the night on the boat." Char grinned mischievously but Nikki returned her look with doubt.

"I thought we could talk." Char hesitated.

Nikki looked at her feet. "You know what I am. I can't change that."

"I know what you are," Char said firmly. "A beautiful, intelligent and caring woman. Besides, I've had stranger relationships—"

"I very much doubt that." Nikki tried to sound stern, but then she had to laugh.

"I've spent a lot of time with Wren," Char continued. "Learning how to control this new power I have and coming to grips with the responsibilities I've inherited. I know what you did at Mistra. In the end we're not so much the way we appear as the way we think and act."

Nikki stared at her blankly.

"What I'm trying to tell you is that I like the way you think."

Nikki laughed, hugging her friend close. "I've missed you so."

Char pulled away from her.

"What is it?" Nikki asked nervously.

"There's just one more thing I need to tell you," Char said in a foreboding tone.

"What's that?" asked Nikki, suddenly worried again.

Char put on her serious face. "I can be a real beast at times, too," she confessed.

"That's not funny. That's not funny at all!" Nikki chided, but then she started to laugh.

At dinner the next evening, the mood was subdued. Nikki could feel the silence growing until she couldn't take it any longer. "Will someone please say something!" she burst out. Dreyk looked at her with a guilty expression.

"Nikki, we just didn't want to spoil the evening. It's been so long since we've all been together—too long. But the truth is that we have some bad news."

"What is it, Dreyk? Is it your family? Is everyone alright?"

"No, no. They're doing great. It's that beast, Jelebron."

"What? She has very little power left. What trouble could she cause now?"

"A great deal, I'm afraid," interjected Tbrin. "She's been making forays into the city. At first, there were only scattered reports, odd thefts and tales of a woman who was said to change shape. At first, we thought it was just local hysteria, after that scene you made in the bay, but the reports are growing increasingly worse. She's becoming braver, taking more chances."

Wren continued for him, "We tried to track her down, but she's become a shadow, creeping into town and back out again before we can catch her. My greatest fear is that she will gather the ingredients she needs to complete the transmogrifee that Akriast invented and recall other drakyn after we're gone. I know she doesn't have the talent that Akriast had, but with enough time, she might be capable of it.

"We need your help. Trey and I need to return to our own time soon, and we don't want to leave a loose end like her to plague the world."

"What can I do? You and Tbrin are both powerful transmogrifers in your own right."

"As a drakyn, we felt that you should be the one to decide how to deal with her," said Tbrin. "With your power, you could track her down and eliminate her once and for all. It needs to be done, Nikki. Besides, you can't spend your life up here in the mountains. You have friends who miss you."

Nikki looked around the room, at the faces of her friends as they patiently awaited her answer. She saw no beast reflected in their eyes now. She was to them just a friend whose company they missed. How could she refuse them? She realized that she missed them more than she had ever admitted to herself. But the thought of more killing filled her with horror. She had changed a great deal in her time alone. She felt that she'd finally come to understand the awesome power and threat of her drakyn heritage. She thought she could control it now. But would she slide back into that state of rage and uncontrollable violence, if she had to wield her power again to kill?

They must have seen the hesitation in her face. Gormz said quietly, "Nikki, I have been reading the diary of Groosjk as it concerns the drakyn. He was a great scientist. He believed that the dageki would pay a great price for our collusion with the drakyn, but we would be saved from enslavement by helping the humans overcome them in a non-violent way. We can make his prophecy come true. The book is quite detailed, with formulae for specific, very esoteric transmogrifee. I believe I have found a way to eliminate Jelebron forever without killing her, exactly. Will you consider my proposal?"

Nikki looked at Gormz in wonder. Had he been reading her thoughts? Sudden warmth filled her as her sense of foreboding was replaced by a rush of tentative hope.

CHAPTER FORTY-THREE

Greshna, Greshna

Nikki watched the horizon in growing concern. Char stood beside her, and her mere presence gave her courage, even though she still had doubts. Would this work? And if it didn't, who would pay the price? And if it *did*, who would pay the price? She could feel the presence of Tbrin and Wren, behind them. She had insisted that they stay far out of harm's way. It was all in her hands now. Gormz had told her it was possible. She had read it herself in his translation. But how could Groosjk have found this formula? He must have known Kodo himself, to have gotten the instructions to this transmogrifee. Nikki fidgeted nervously, feeling the bags at her waist and going over the required ingredients for the hundredth time. The smells of bergamot and wandermint in one of her pouches reached her nose, clearing her thoughts. There was nothing left now but to go through with it.

She knelt on the cold ground and began pulling things from her pouches. As she worked, she concentrated on clearing her mind. She must be empty of all emotions if this was going to work. When she knew it was ready, she raised her arms to begin the strange dance of a great transmogrifee. The air between her palms pulsed with a variegated glow as her thoughts aligned with the effect she desired. The rainbow light steadied into a brightness that grew until Nikki had to shield her own eyes from it. With a burst, an explosion turned the world into a shadowland of black and white. When Nikki was able to look up, her vision was clouded by the shadow of a stooped and crippled drakyn, her skin so mottled that even in shadow, it worked as camouflage, blending her figure into the hills behind her.

"Jelebron, you sad creature," she whispered, almost to herself.

The drakyn half-turned, hiding her surprise. "Why do you disturb my labors, little beast? Haven't you done enough to destroy your race already?"

"You and I are not of the same race, Jelebron, even though we may occasionally share the same skin. What you are must end here."

The drakyn laughed, but the sound was brittle, untrue. She feared for her existence, for her legacy.

"I am not here to kill you, Jelebron. At least, it's not my intention to take a life, but to substitute one who should never have died for one who should never have lived. Once you were a proud drakyn. No more. What you are now must end. The drakyn must end and they must be forgotten."

"What kind of nonsense is this, little whelp? Do you think I don't know what lies that old man has been telling you? Such a transmogrifee is impossible."

Nikki looked at Jelebron in sudden confusion. How could she have known? "It was not Tbrin who told me, but Groosjk."

At these words, the drakyn's mottled skin turned a paler shade of gray. Nikki knew that she must act now, before Jelebron regained her composure. With a flash of her hand, she willed the transmogrifee into action. Beneath her, the ground began to smoke. Jelebron backed away, opening her decrepit wings as if to fly. For an instant, Nikki feared that she would escape, but the old drakyn no longer had the speed. With a flash, Jelebron vanished.

When Nikki recovered, she looked around. Of Jelebron, there was no sign. The plain was empty. Sighing, Nikki turned away, resigning herself to the fact that this strange transmogrifee hadn't worked, that she might have to hunt the drakyn down after all and kill her. Nikki hesitated, not wanting to face the inevitable. She walked away slowly, until Tbrin and Wren ran out in front of her.

"I thought we agreed that you would stay back!" she began, then she saw the strange expression on Tbrin's face. He was staring at something behind her. Nikki turned, just in time to see a woman rushing past her, into Tbrin's arms.

"Greshna, Greshna!" he murmured repeatedly. It was a long time before they were able to get any other words out of him.

CHAPTER FORTY-FOUR

Lost and Found

That evening, the friends dined together at a small house in Bay Towne. It was so close to the ocean, that Nikki could hear the gulls crying and the distant crash of the waves on the jetty. She liked it, but it had an empty feeling to it, as if something had been lost here. She told Dreyk what she felt, and he gave her a quizzical, thoughtful look.

"This was my father's house. I guess it's mine now, and something *was* lost here. There was a family here long ago, including a pale, skinny kid with dreams of going to sea and escaping this crazy world. He's long gone, I guess. Lost. Is that what you feel?"

Nikki smiled at him. "Not as lost as you think. He's still here. He was a smart, loyal kid with a sense of humor and the strength to go on when the day is dark. He's you now, all grown up."

He looked out the kitchen window, and his expression was distant but soft. "Maybe this house will be a home again, with Chendri and our daughter."

Nikki was happy for him. She had a feeling it was going to work out for him and his new family. She said, "Well, if we don't get this food on the table soon, you'll never have dinner guests again, I can guarantee you that."

At the table, spirits were high. Everyone knew that something was gone—a threat that no one could exactly explain, had disappeared forever. Nikki felt guilty for having to play this game with her friends, but she had done it for their own safety—for the safety of the entire world. When she'd employed the transmogrifee to transform Jelebron into Greshna, she had ensured that no one would remember that Jelebron, or any of the drakyn, had ever existed. It was the only way Nikki knew to ensure that the drakyn could never again be recalled.

Nikki looked again at Tbrin and Greshna. She had spoken to Tbrin earlier about Mistra, asking him to return to be its Master Artisan. She thought it was where Tbrin and Greshna belonged and could do the most good.

Tbrin had been silent for a long time before replying.

"I'll do it, Nikki, on one condition. The position of Master Artisan is yours if you ever decide to return."

Nikki knew she'd never return to Mistra, but she'd agreed, just to appease him.

She looked around at her friends now. Gormz was busy talking dageki politics to Dreyk, who was doing his best to appear interested. Nikki had offered to help Gormz educate and eventually free his people from captivity. She knew it was no small task, but she wanted to make a better life for these amazing creatures.

Char was characteristically sitting alone, but her expression was contented as she watched the others. Moonchaser was sound asleep beside the fire, where Wren was chatting with Benna, who stirred the coals absentmindedly. Tbrin's face glowed with joy as he quietly watched his beloved Greshna. From the little time she had been able to tear Tbrin from her side to talk to her, Nikki had found Greshna to be an amazing woman, gentle and wise, yet with a strength that required no demonstration.

Nikki lifted a finger to get Wren's attention, and the woman instantly understood, leaving Benna to join her at the empty kitchen table, where they could converse in relative privacy. To be entirely safe, Nikki transmogered a subtle shield around them.

"Do you think it worked?" asked Nikki hesitantly.

"I'm sure it has. Except for the four of us—you, Char, Trey and me—the drakyn are forgotten."

"Sometimes, I can't believe what we did. The drakyn ruled this world at one time. How can I assume to know what's best for an entire planet?"

"I too doubted myself when I decided to bind the drakyn to human form, but you saw what the early ones were like, Jelebron and Semli. To allow them to return would lead this era down the same path to destruction, eventually. Perhaps Kodo's experiment, your people in Mistra, will eventually bring them to a state of social maturity, when the drakyn can return in their natural forms. That will be up to you."

"That's not a decision I want to make."

"Perhaps not now, but the time may come. At least there will be peace. Trey and I can go home, knowing we've left the future in good hands."

"We'll miss you, but you've more than done your part. Will you return to the age when your daughter lived?"

Wren's eyes glowed. "Yes, we had to leave her to be adopted before we left. We'll go back to the time just before we gave her up and start over. To tell you the truth, I can't wait to get home."

"I'm happy for you."

The two women hugged, Nikki sadly believed, for the last time.

Nikki left the room quietly, wishing to be alone with her thoughts. Outside, the sun was setting with a rich show of crimson and chroma. Nikki lost herself in the colors and sounds of the nearby shore, until the light and warmth began to fade. She turned back toward the house, stopping at the window to peer inside. The window framed her friends in animated conversation, like a portrait painted with moving subjects. Although she couldn't hear their words, she could see that they were laughing, enjoying a joke as only close friends can. Suddenly she wondered if it would ever be the same with her, or if she would always feel the outsider, the alien intruding on a close circle of friends. Even though the drakyn were forgotten, she couldn't forget who and what she was.

Behind her, a voice said, "They don't see a monster, they see you."

She looked back at Char, seeing her beauty, her strength and intelligence, her integrity and loyalty—her love.

Char mirrored her look and Nikki finally understood. Like Malgryn, she could be whoever she wanted to be and she chose this; a lover, a fighter, someone living every moment as if it were her last.

With a fledgling, but dauntless joy in her heart, she turned from the window, taking Char's hand in her own.

"Let's go home," she whispered, and they did.

CHAPTER FORTY-FIVE

Epilogue: The Prince of Time

M atter is coalescing in the northern ocean among the Thousand Isles. After many years, a greasy, organic film bubbles to the surface. Endowed with the powerful essence of a drakyn's eye, it begins to coalesce. The water sparks and boils with unfocused transmograffic energy. At last, an amorphous shape surfaces, bobbing gently on the current as it drifts shoreward to a mostly uninhabited spit of sand called the Lonely Isle.

Telgar doesn't see so well, and he has a limp and a stunted hand. Along with an ornery attitude, these qualities make him useless for most tasks, or at least so Auntie says. That's why he doesn't go to sea with his papa. He stays home to help Auntie tend the livestock and do chores, except on days like today, when the possibilities of the seashore call to him, and he is inexorably drawn to the water's edge.

The boy limps along the shore, trailing a ragged stick behind him. He's supposed to be milking the goat. He will undoubtedly receive a sound thrashing when he gets home, except that he won't. Instead, he'll have plenty of time to finish his chores. Telgar makes time.

He revels in the warmth of the sand beneath his bare feet. He cherishes the little treasures he finds along the shore. Stuffed into his frayed pants pockets with dirty fingers are a rock with an interesting texture, a stick that takes the elegant shape of a flet's neck and a course pebble of no obvious value. Once, he even found a small fishing float.

The attached line, rotted almost beyond any usefulness as a rope, still allowed him to drag his find to his pirate's lair, the little cave on the water's edge where no adults would venture. It's there he hides his precious tidewrack. It's where he's headed today.

He revels in the touch of sea mist on his golden skin. The distant thunder of the waves on the rocks makes his chest thrum. The tide, higher than usual and just now receding, promises to reveal new pretties today.

As he walks, Telgar scans the sand at his feet, occasionally gazing down the beach to see a blurry image of what awaits. The breeze teases his ragged, sandy hair to reveal, then hide his unfocused hazel eyes, eyes that his father and aunt find disturbing.

He spies a curious blob far ahead in the wrack line, but he is unconcerned. At this distance, everything's a blob to Telgar. As he approaches the mass, it stirs, and Telgar jumps back in alarm. The shape turns toward him, in its slow, stuttering way. Though it lacks five senses, it has a sixth, with which it assesses him.

Telgar has little fear. He's not wise enough in the ways of the world to perceive danger. His curiosity takes over. He plops down carelessly amid the motley captives of the wrack line; bedraggled, sodden feathers, globs of rotting eel grass, crab carcass tidbits, miscellaneous fishing gear, kelp mush, and sharp bits of broken mother o' pearl.

He pulls the blob into his lap, dexterously feeling for life with his good hand.

Telgar doesn't understand that he has a great talent, only that things obey him without the need for words. His toys are the infinitesimal particles whirling in his mind like pollen in the warm spring air. When his fingers tingle, the broken things he touches become whole again. Still, it's a long time before he finishes—years, in fact—but this doesn't matter to Telgar. He makes time.

Now he finishes, but he's unsure exactly what he has revealed.

"What is you, a man?" the boy asks, his pubescent voice cracking. The thing rolls over, and to Telgar's surprise, answers through a mouthful of gel.

"Yeth, I'm a-a m–man, I am." The pale creature's translucent head bobs jerkily. Feeble and confused, it has no eyes, nose or ears.

Telgar looks closer, until he can make out features; a strong nose, ebony hair and bright, liquid eyes filled with voracious need. Telgar is used to this happening. Things often take on the aspect he envisions, after he looks at them for a while.

After another spell of time, this living object of his artistry sits up. The man is naked and still imperfect, but Telgar can see that he is of regal bearing, or at least as Telgar imagines regal bearing.

Perhaps an orphaned prince, he thinks, *who was kidnapped before he can take the throne and sent to sea by his evil uncle, until his ship is destroyed in a storm and—*

"What's your name, boy?" the man demands imperiously.

"T-T-Telgar," he stammers. "Be you a lord? Or a prince maybe? What is *your* name, sir, if I may so humbly ask?"

The man's eyes caress the rolling waves for a long time. Finally, he examines Telgar critically and states, in an assertive voice, "Semli. That's it. My name is Semli, Jelebron's son, and yes, I am a prince. Well-spotted, young transmogrifer."

"T-tran-smoger-what?"

"You have an amazing talent, Telgar. Would you like to join me on an adventure, where you can learn to use this talent?"

"Oi, yes sir, I would very much like an adventure, sir, but I gotta milk the goat first or I be gettin' a thrashin' from Auntie. It won't take any time at all. I can be here bright 'n early yesterday morning an' ready t' go."

"Ah, it's amazing that you can do that, boy. You know, I think we're going to be fast friends." Then the man speaks, more to himself than the boy, "We'll go back to when this whole fruckin' disaster started and fix it. We'll make it so that interfering witch and her friends never get a chance to do this to me again."

Telgar's boyish, innocent face glows with the desire to please his new lord. He envisions a life filled with the tributes and bounty he deserves, maybe creating and destroying empires, even worlds.

Normally, it would take a lifetime, or many, to achieve such creative and ambitious goals, but for Telgar and his prince, it's only a matter of time.

THE END

Read the Whole Series

If you enjoyed this novel please leave a review on Amazon.

Find all three of the Drakonia novels on Amazon.
Book One: **Chronicles of the Drakyn War**
Book Two: **Born of the Lesser Moon**
Book Three: **Thief of Destiny**

https://www.amazon.com/dp/B0BKXBDW1G

About the Author

Dap Dahlstrom is an American author and artist who is part hobbit with a sprinkling of dark elf. Her greatest hope is that she will never be forced to live in the real world.

Before starting her writing career, Dap was a successful copywriter and graphic designer, earning numerous national and international awards. Her passions include big game hunting, ocean fishing, martial arts, German shepherds, and reading, reading, reading!

Intricate world building, logical magic systems, and relatable characters who shine with humor and wit combine to make her books the complete package for fantasy fans everywhere.

Please leave a review on Amazon. Available in paperback and ebook formats. For bonus material, visit her website at

dapdahlstrom.com

If you'd like to be put on the mailing list to receive an alert for updates on future publications, contact

dapdahlstrom.com/contact

www.ingramcontent.com/pod-product-compliance
Lightning Source LLC
Chambersburg PA
CBHW071305200626
46813CB00015B/50